MARVEL

THANOS

TITAN CONSUMED

Cover design by Ching N. Chan. Cover illustration by Stephan Martiniere.

Little, Brown and Company
Hachette Book Group
1290 Avenue of the Americas, New York, NY 10104
Visit us at LBYR.com

First Edition: November 2018

Little, Brown and Company is a division of Hachette Book Group, Inc. The Little, Brown name and logo are trademarks of Hachette Book Group, Inc.

Library of Congress Control Number 2018949558

ISBNs: 978-0-316-48251-6 (hardcover), 978-0-316-48258-5 (ebook)

Printed in the United States of America

LSC-C

10 9 8 7 6 5 4 3 2 1

MARVEL

THANOS

TITAN CONSUMED

by Barry Lyga

Little, Brown and Company
New York Boston

TO THE FOLKS AT THE COMIC SHOP.

There are as many tales of the origins of the Mad Titan, THANOS, as there are stars remaining in the sky. This is but one of them.

It is also the truth.

TIME

We live in a prism, not a line.

CHAPTER 1

~·--·~○~·--·~

I'VE SNAPPED MY FINGERS.

And—

I am adrift in myself, alone with my past, my present. The sheer existence of *me* is at once a weighty and a weightless thing. Time is not an arrow or a line or any other convenient metaphor; Time is not an abstract notion.

Time is a Stone.

With the Stone, all history is open to me. I am *in* history. I *am* history. I witness it and relive it and experience it in the same quantum instant.

For the first time in years, I behold the orange-swaddled orb that is Titan. From a distance of thousands of kilometers, the planet looks the same as when I left, with no indication as to the havoc that lurks beneath the haze.

And then it's years later, and my forces wage combat against Her Majesty Cath'Ar's troops aboard the Executrix. *Bodies spill into space as the Leviathans mass for a second attack run.*

And now Korath tells Ronan:

1

"Thanos is the most powerful being in the universe!"
And Ronan, the fool, responds:
"Not anymore."

Unmoored from the present, observing without interfering, I watch my life and my certainty as they play out. I am the foregone conclusion to my own prophecy. Korath's warning has come true, and now I truly am the most powerful being in the universe, perceiving all reality from the vantage point of ultimate power.

Not much more than a boy, I tilt the glass to my lips. The liquid within is green, bubbly, and too sweet, tasting of melon and elderberries and ethyl alcohol.

I am a child and my father tells me, "Your mother went mad the moment she laid eyes on you." There is a softness to his voice noticed only in retrospect, with adult eyes laid upon the childish past.

This changes nothing. Everything is done. Everything will be done.

Years later, my ship launches from the surface of Titan, bearing me into the unknown. I tell myself that everything I know lurks beneath that haze, and then I tell myself that it doesn't matter.

Swaddled in the verdant energies of the Time Stone, my mind traverses decades at the speed of thought, spinning the jewel of my life from facet to facet.

"You'll die there, Titan," says Vathlauss, choking on his own blood and Kebbi's poison. "You'll die in the glory that is Asgard."

I watch, paralyzed and helpless, as Gamora swings her battle-staff...

...and Daakon Ro postures and threatens on my viewscreen...

...and the Other speaks to me in the wreckage of the Chitauri staging base:

"Humans... They are not the cowering wretches we were promised. They stand. They are unruly and therefore cannot be ruled. To challenge them is to court death."

I am striding through the bodies of Asgardians, the dead remnants of that once proud civilization, as Ebony Maw proselytizes to the few who still live.

I am beating the Hulk nearly to death...

...and hurling Gamora from the cliff on Vormir...

...and then—years previous—a voice, the voice of my only friend:

"You're a coward, Thanos! A coward! You hide behind this ship, behind the Other and the Chitauri, and now behind those girls!"

Years leapfrog one another, spurting ahead in an instant, and I am aboard Sanctuary. *The protective doors to my vault slide open, and the Gauntlet glimmers there in half-light, not quite gold.*

I have seen this moment before. I have lived it. It is happening for the first time, the second time, the millionth time.

I reach for it.

"Fine," I say. "I'll—"

REALITY

Truth is a mistress harsher than death.

CHAPTER II

THE PROBLEM WITH TITAN WAS THAT IT WAS PERFECT. AND even as a child, Thanos knew nothing was truly perfect. Every diamond had its flaw, and every saintly soul had its black spot of guilt, shame, or restless abnegation. Titan, too, suffered from an imperfection.

That imperfection, as best he could tell, was Thanos himself.

Son of A'Lars—the High Mentor of Titan, architect of the Eternal City—and Sui-San, his absent mother, Thanos was, at birth, a shock to his people. His appearance was a jolt of adrenaline to a body at rest. Distinguished from Titan's populace by dint of his deformation and purplish hue, he was prominent in ways and for reasons beyond his control yet fixed permanently in his very physical being. On Titan, the people's flesh reflected a range of splendid colors. But none was purple, the color of death, the color of ill omen.

Save Thanos.

From the Vast Salt Sea on the other side of the planet to the glimmering bronze range of cryovolcanoes just outside the Eternal City, Titan was a united world, more than the sum of its parts, a resplendent and cohesive whole. The Eternal City was a perfect blend of architecture and engineering, its soaring spires and towers nestled together in a collection of utmost harmony. A world absolutely in tune with itself.

Except.

For.

Thanos.

His skin color, along with a series of vertical ridges—furrows that made his flesh look as though it had been raked—widened his expansive jaw. These traits marked him a deviant, a mutated *thing*. Had his father been anyone but A'Lars, his mother anyone but Sui-San, he most likely would have been consigned to a medical facility somewhere. Poked and prodded his whole life, quarantined from polite society.

Instead, he was left in A'Lars's care. Sui-San disappeared shortly after his birth.

He walked at six months. Not the drunken toddle of a baby, but the confident stride of a man. He could already hold himself erect, control the movement of his head and neck. He had complete coordination of his limbs, and his bearing was that of an adult.

Two days shy of his first birthday, he spoke. Not a word, but rather a full sentence: "Father, will there be a birth celebration for me, and will Mother attend?"

He'd been capable of speech for weeks but had waited until he'd fully parsed the nuances of sentence structure to issue his first words.

Before either of those milestones, he knew he was different in a world that prized conformity and unanimity above all else.

"Mother will not attend," A'Lars had said. If his father was surprised by Thanos's speech and his diction, he did not show it. "I will arrange for friends."

I will arrange for... Those words preceded most of A'Lars's statements. Thanos's father rarely touched his son, rarely even looked at him. In regard to Thanos's needs, he only ever said *I will arrange for...* and then did just that, with efficiency and aplomb.

Thanos wanted for nothing. Needed nothing.

Except to belong.

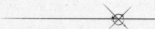

As good as his word, A'Lars arranged for friends: a collection of androids designed to look and act like toddlers. They were programmed to distract Thanos and keep him dumbly happy and content.

In time, he'd figured out their programming and rewrote their algorithms. He now had a coterie of robotic servants that amused him but accomplished little else. His restless mind craved more.

"Very well," A'Lars relented. "School."

Generations ago, it had been the common practice to install children in thought-cribs and educate them through direct cerebral interface. That practice had long fallen out of favor by the time of Thanos's birth. It was now fashionable to add an interactive social element to education, placing a group of children together in a school, where they could theoretically enhance one another's learning and also facilitate socialization.

Thanos was excited by the prospect of school. Other than the reprogrammed androids, he'd had no companionship, and he looked forward to meeting other children his age.

"Be polite," A'Lars told him on their way to the education complex in their floater. "Speak only when directed to."

"Yes, Father." Thanos bobbed his head in agreement. Through the clear shell over the floater, he could see other floaters, the tops of buildings, and the distant mountain ranges of Titan. His world was beautiful and at peace, and he longed to explore every part of it.

"The teachers have been warned about your appearance," A'Lars reminded him. "Try not to do or say anything upsetting or untoward."

His appearance. Almost unconsciously, he ran one finger along his jawline.

At some point in Titan's distant past, for reasons no one could any longer remember, the color purple had become associated with death, a connection that persisted to the present. When Titans died, their bodies were covered with purple shrouds. The lights in their residences were tuned to the violet portion of the spectrum for the grieving period.

He'd first encountered this association when his father received a visitor in their home. Thanos was four years old, and the visitor was an elderly woman, a friend of A'Lars's parents, seeking advice from the High Mentor of Titan. She wore shades of purple from head to toe, including a veil covering her face, a veil that was the precise color of Thanos's own skin.

The coincidence of her clothing and his own skin color thrilled Thanos, as coincidences often do to children. When she left, he babbled to his father about the color of her clothes, about the way the veil so perfectly matched his own flesh.

And A'Lars had explained, in blunt language, that she wore that color because she was in mourning. She was a widow, and so she wore the color of death.

Thanos's excitement had curdled. Of all the hues his maladapted genes could have chosen to express, why did it have to be purple?

Now, at the education complex, A'Lars led him down a corridor, peering around and occasionally sniffing in barely disguised annoyance. "Uninspired design and workmanship," he commented. "Do not allow your surroundings to infect your breeding, Thanos."

"I will not, Father," Thanos promised, fighting to match his father's disinterested deportment. Inside, he was ecstatic to be among his peers; he knew his father disapproved of expression of emotion, so he suppressed his excitement.

At a doorway, father and son paused. Thanos waited as his father thumbed open the door.

This would be the first time in his awareness that Thanos

would be separated from his father for more than an hour or so. He opened his mouth to say something, but A'Lars nodded curtly at him and said, "Don't be late," followed by, "Learn well," before turning and striding back down the corridor they'd walked together.

Thanos nodded to himself, then stepped into the education chamber.

It was a smallish room with a series of twelve personal interface pods that could be arranged in any formation. At that moment, they were lined up in two ranks of six each, all facing the front of the chamber, where stood an adult in a gray tunic and slacks, his hands clasped behind his back. He had thick black hair pomaded to his skull like a helmet, and skin the color of a pale morning sky.

The teacher smiled and—to his credit—did an admirable job concealing his startled reflex at the sight of Thanos.

But Thanos noted it. The school had been advised he was coming. They knew who and what he was. And yet still, his appearance shocked.

"And you must be Thanos," the teacher said. Thanos thought it an absurd thing to say—who else could he be?—but the teacher's smile was pleasant, and Thanos bore in mind his father's admonitions. So he simply nodded and said, "Yes."

"Class, welcome a new friend and fellow learner: Thanos."

Eleven of the pods rotated enough that the children within could get an unobstructed view of the newcomer. Thanos felt a frisson of panic at twenty-two eyes boring into him, then forced the panic away. They were children. Like him.

"Take the empty pod, please," said the teacher. "Today we'll be studying color and patterns."

He scrambled into the pod. Its padded interior shifted into a cocoon as he settled into place. Now, here, he was comfortable. In his element. The interface pod was an older model than the one he had at home, but it was serviceable. He ran a few updates on its firmware, then connected it to the pod at home.

Colors and patterns. As the teacher spoke and the pod conjured images for him to absorb, he realized how incredibly bored he was already. He'd already learned about color from his father, from the nature of light to the manipulation of pigments. Patterns—from plaids to stripes, dots, and organics—were similarly old news to him. Was this really the best way for him to learn?

He tamped down his impatience. He had *wanted* this, after all; he couldn't give up on it after a few minutes.

With a sigh, he switched his pod to accelerated mode and flashed through the lesson at twice the speed.

If the learning portion of school was dull, then at least there was the social aspect to look forward to. There was a break at noon for food and physical recreation. Thanos was no fool— he understood that the physical component was designed to tire out the students and make them more manageable. He felt he was already incredibly polite and deferential (having not pointed out two or three errors his teacher had made earlier), so he forsook the running around and wild play of his classmates and instead sat quietly in a corner, studying a rudimentary hologram of a synthetic neural pathway. If improved, it would make synths much more lifelike.

A cluster of children gathered not far from him. They spoke in hushes and murmurs, occasionally pointing in his direction. He did his best to ignore them, while at the same time wondering how he could engage them.

Maybe this had been a mistake, this schooling. Maybe he should have stayed at home. He had not imagined himself the center of attention, a thing to be spoken of and not to.

But just then, a girl named Gwinth approached him. "We have a question for you," she said. And before he could say anything, she went ahead and asked it: "Why are you purple?"

Thanos blinked with something like confusion. No one had ever asked that simple question before. She seemed more curious than frightened or disgusted. Perhaps his father had overestimated people's reaction to his appearance.

"I'm not entirely sure," he admitted. "It's a mutation."

"A what?"

As they spoke, the other children gathered around them. Thanos tried to figure out the best way to explain it, but the truth was that he only partly understood it himself. There were things called *genes* that made people who and what they were. Something had gone wrong with one of his.

"Where are the genes?" Gwinth asked, and ran her hands randomly over her body, feeling for them. Others followed suit.

Thanos shook his head. "They're tiny. Microscopic." A thought occurred to him and a light blossomed within— here and now, he'd been presented with a great opportunity. He had the attention of his fellows. They didn't seem afraid of him or disgusted, just curious. If he could explain some part of himself to them…

The previous night, he'd memorized the layout of the school so that he would not get lost. Now he led the group— about ten of them—back down the hallways, to a bio lab for the older students. It was unused at the moment and it had everything Thanos needed.

He arranged his retinue around a workbench with a microscope filter, then rummaged around until he found a needle, typically used for pinning down samples. He had a different use for it.

As the clutch of children watched, their breaths held in unison, Thanos pricked the tip of his thumb with the needle. A gasp went up as the red bubble formed.

He squeezed a drop of blood onto the microscope filter and a light filled the room. A holographic image of his own blood, now projected into the air. A chorus of *ooh*s and *aah*s rose up from the other children.

Pleased, Thanos fiddled with the controls to sharpen and

clarify the image. Globules pulsed and danced across the room. The other children pointed and laughed with delight at the show.

"This is my blood," Thanos explained. "And for comparison..."

He took the hand of a boy near him and poked at his thumb with the needle. A spot of blood welled up there and the boy shrieked as though gutted.

No one was pointing and laughing now. There was a moment of group silence, counterbalanced by the boy's ongoing cry of pain and shock, and then the rest of the children howled as though they, too, had been jabbed.

And there, now, was the fear his father had promised. It washed around Thanos. It enveloped him.

Thanos dropped the boy's hand and stood in stunned silence as the screams grew higher and higher around him.

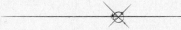

Later, he waited in the office of the school's proctor, alone. A sound caught his attention and he looked up.

A'Lars stood in the doorway.

"This experiment is a failure," his father announced. "Come home."

That night, Thanos stole out of bed and listened at the door to his father's cogitarium, the study where A'Lars spent most of his hours in deep thought. A voice not his father's came to him through the door.

"You know I revere you, A'Lars. We *all* do—"

"Then speak plainly," A'Lars demanded.

"Your child. He is...different."

"Indeed. You've noticed. I salute your perceptions."

A'Lars's sarcasm silenced the other for a moment. Then: "Perhaps there is something more suitable for the child of the esteemed A'Lars than a pedestrian school."

"Without doubt," A'Lars said smoothly. "Thank you for your time, your consideration, and your counsel."

A'Lars switched off the comms, and Thanos, straining, heard his father mutter, "Dolts."

It was irregular, to say the least, for a child to be withdrawn from school and taught by a parent. But A'Lars's shadow was long, his fame all-encompassing.

And besides...everyone knew it was for the best.

While his father's specialty was synthetic intelligence, he was something of a polymath and also dabbled in materials science and architecture, which had led to his prominence on Titan. There was only so much livable terrain on the planet, and A'Lars had figured out how best to use that space and, furthermore, how to protect it from the vicissitudes of nature.

His skills translated into considerable fame and political power, making the absence of his wife and the grotesqueness of his son all the more shameful.

He was an indifferent father, but a challenging and unfathomably brilliant teacher. While Thanos resented the loss of the opportunity for companionship and friends, he had to admit—begrudgingly—that A'Lars was a more fitting teacher for him.

Praise was rare. His father would sometimes comment on Thanos's intelligence as though it were a fait accompli, as though its very existence made Thanos's enormous mental capacity exceptional and unexceptional at the same time. Lessons were quick and expected to be passed with one hundred percent understanding.

"Your intellect is your primary and best tool," his father said once in a scarce shared moment. "Someday, if your achievements merit, you may have the honor of being called Tha-nos. Or perhaps even T'Hanos, though I'd advise you not to set your sights so high," A'Lars cautioned.

"I am still lonely," Thanos said, struggling to keep a note of whining out of his voice. He knew his father loathed such childish things.

A'Lars sighed in defeat. "I will arrange…" he began.

A'Lars was as good as his word and did indeed arrange something. He brought Thanos an actual, living boy. Several of them, actually. To vie for the role of friend. Only one passed muster.

Sintaa was, by definition, Thanos's best friend, since he was Thanos's only friend. Lean where Thanos was broad, Sintaa had an enviably smooth, normal-size chin and skin the acceptable color of raw peaches. He was possessed of a sunny disposition, in contrast to Thanos's taciturn, withdrawn nature.

As the years passed, Thanos suspected that A'Lars had paid, blackmailed, or threatened Sintaa's parents into having their child become his son's friend. His father would never admit to such a quotidian and desperate tactic, but by the age of ten, Thanos could prize out certain words and phrases that led him confidently to this conclusion. Cruelly, fate and genetics had cursed him with a phenomenal mind, one that made him all the more keenly aware of his deformation and of the singular nature of his ostracism. From what he gleaned by watching news and entertainment holos, he realized the depth of his isolation, but was powerless to rectify it.

And yet Sintaa himself—regardless of what pressures had been brought to bear on his parents—seemed genuinely to enjoy Thanos's company. Of all the children who had been paraded before him to audition for the role of "friend," only Sintaa possessed an easy smile, a laconic and relaxed mien, and the glint of trouble in his eyes. Thanos attempted to resist liking him, and failed.

"You are the first thing my father has brought to me that I actually enjoy," Thanos said at one point early in their friendship.

Sintaa grinned. He was too intelligent for his age, too, though not nearly as brilliant as Thanos. "I'm not a thing," he reminded Thanos. "I'm a person."

Thanos grunted in assent. "Of course."

They played together in the chambers Thanos shared with his father, never in public, never at Sintaa's house. Thanos had figured out a way to paint with light, devising a series of databrushes that collected photons and froze them temporarily in place, and they spent hours painting the air, watching the holograms glimmer and shine before they eventually corroded and bled off like slow fireworks.

"Can I ask you a question?" Thanos said.

Sintaa seemed surprised. He paused in mid-brushstroke. "You *never* ask questions. You know everything already."

"I wish that were true," Thanos admitted. "There's much I do not know. Especially with regard to one thing."

Sintaa sat back. The holograms danced and sparkled around him, flickering dreams caught and dragged into the waking world. "Ask."

Thanos hesitated. For the first time in his life, he understood the idea of *being nervous*.

"What is it like," he managed eventually, "to have a mother?"

Sintaa laughed. "Everyone has a mother, Thanos."

Had Thanos been capable of blushing, he would have done so at that moment. "Biologically speaking, yes. But what is it like to *have* one, not merely to come from one?"

Sintaa's eyes softened. He opened his mouth to speak, then closed it. Opened it again. Closed it. It took many such cycles before he found his voice.

"I don't know how to describe it to you," he confessed. "It's all I've ever known."

It's all I've ever known. Those words struck Thanos with a sharp pain he'd never experienced. More than the words, though, was the tone of Sintaa's voice as he said them. There was a warmth and comfort there, and Thanos knew that this was what he was missing—the succor of his mother. As far as he could tell, every living thing on Titan had the love of its mother except for him.

"I don't even know where she is," Thanos said. "One of the few secrets A'Lars has succeeded in keeping from me."

After a moment's hesitation, Sintaa said, "*I* know where she is."

By this point in his life, Thanos had the shape and height of an older child. His growth spurts were frequent and painful. At almost one and two-thirds meters tall, he had the appearance of an early adolescent, masking the mind of a genius. His skin had lightened somewhat since birth, but was still the hated and feared purple. He seldom ventured forth from his father's house—A'Lars had told him many times that it was best not to upset people.

So today Thanos wore a cloak with a hood that covered his head and hid his face in shadow. Dragging the tail of the cloak along the ground, he approached a specific building not with fear, but rather trepidation.

Behind him, Sintaa nodded, encouraging him forward.

The building was nondescript and squat, a rare low structure in a city dominated by towering skyscrapers and floating edifices buoyed aloft by antigravity technology.

Sintaa had heard of it from his parents. They referred to it as a kind of *hospital*. Thanos knew what a hospital was, of course—a place where ailments were cured, injuries given balm.

Was his mother ill? Is that why no one would let him see her? But in that case, why not just *tell* him? Why the secrecy and the shame?

It didn't matter: His mother was in there. That was all he cared about.

He hesitated just a moment at the door. He was a boy of ten, a child, and despite his intellect—or maybe because of it—he knew that the combination of his age and his appearance would not stand him in good stead here. He knew rejection lurked in his immediate future.

He opened the door anyway. He went inside.

Within, the air smelled of ozone and antiseptic. The walls and floors were dim and soft, the ceiling a series of lighted panels. He walked down the entry hall until he found another door. Opened it. Went inside.

A man stood there, his furrowed brow the color of faded grass on an autumn day. He wore the black tunic and red epaulets of a doctor, but his expression was anything but comforting.

"Thanos," he said in a disapproving tone. "I was told you were coming."

Thanos and Sintaa had told no one of their decision to come here. For the first time in his life, Thanos realized that he was being watched. All the time.

"I would like to see Sui-San," Thanos said with as much dignity and intensity as he could muster. "My mother," he added.

The doctor's eyes narrowed, and something like pity flickered there. Thanos suppressed the rage that rippled through him. He had no use for pity.

"I'm truly sorry," the doctor said. "I can't allow that."

"I didn't ask if you could allow it," Thanos said, marshaling all his outrage. "Let me see my mother."

"You'll need to speak to your father about that," the doctor said, gesturing mysteriously. "If you don't leave, I'll have to have you removed, and I don't want to do that to you."

Speak to your father.... He had. Since his very first words—*Will Mother attend?*—he had asked after his mother, had all but begged A'Lars to let him see her, but he had been stonewalled at every opportunity, denied, told by word and deed and inaction that he would never see Sui-San.

"Do not deny me," Thanos said, and balled his hands into fists.

The doctor did not laugh at this sight. He cleared his throat and said, "I will summon a security—"

And Thanos felt more than saw a red scrim of rage unfurl between him and the rest of the world. Without conscious thought, he flung himself at the doctor.

He was ten years old and he was angry and he was strong and he had the advantage of youth, which does not know how to conserve its energies. The doctor howled and dropped back as Thanos attacked, leaping up to collide with the man's chest, knocking him to the ground, where Thanos's smaller stature was no disadvantage.

In the instant it took for them to crash to the floor together, a light burst in Thanos's chest, and something heavy and sodden in him vanished. He felt lighter and happier than he'd ever felt. As though the world suddenly made absolute *sense*.

That was only an instant, a click of a dial between ticks. His mind went blank with the impact on the floor and he lashed out with both fists, pummeling the man's face, and soon Thanos's purple fists were smeared red with blood, and then strong hands grappled him from behind and dragged him away, screaming nonsense syllables, all his intelligence reduced to the raw meat of need and denial, the veneer of culture ripped away, leaving behind only an animal, an animal hauled away as its screams and bellows were swallowed by the soft, sound-dampening walls.

Later, A'Lars came to him in his room. Thanos sat on the floor in a corner, swaddled in darkness, staring at his hands, which he held interlinked in his lap.

"Will the doctor recover?" Thanos asked, a note of urgency in his voice. "The one I hurt?"

A'Lars clucked his tongue. "The 'doctor' is a new synthetic life-form I bred specifically to care for your mother. Designed with enhanced empathy and compassion. Congratulations, Thanos—you bludgeoned to death something that was not truly alive...and something that was designed from the start not to know how to fight back."

Thanos twisted his hands together. They blurred as his eyes lost focus.

"That facility," A'Lars went on, "is off-limits to you, Thanos. You were never told that, so I will not punish you for going there, or for the damage you caused to my creation." His father glared sternly. "Go again and the punishment will be severe."

Punishment...Thanos knew what that meant. The Isolation Room. A tiny chamber just off A'Lars's cogitarium. Thanos would be placed within. Lights and noise bombarded him constantly so he could not think. It was the worst thing he could imagine, the worst thing he'd ever suffered.

But…

"Mother is there," Thanos said without looking up. "How can you hide her from me?"

"You are a bright boy. You can find other things to occupy your mind than searching for your mother. She is irrelevant to you."

"Irrelevant?" Thanos shouted, rising. "She is my mother!"

A'Lars did not so much as flinch. "She bore you. Nothing more. She has not seen you since the moment of your birth. She means nothing to you, and you mean nothing to her. Forget her, Thanos." He gestured to Thanos's desk and the holographic interface floating above and around it. "Return to your studies. You have a prodigious intellect, one that should not be distracted by such emotional concerns."

Yes, he had a prodigious intellect. He had words that could counter his father's argument, but in that moment, he was still just a boy. A boy who had come close to his mother, but not close enough. And in that moment, he could not combine those words into anything suitable or sensible. So he simply returned his gaze to his hands, staring at them until A'Lars gave up and left.

It didn't take long. A'Lars always had something more important to do.

CHAPTER III

As time passed, Thanos and Sintaa grew inseparable. One day they ventured out beyond the boundaries of the Eternal City and climbed into the foothills surrounding the range of cryovolcanoes that studded the land around the City. From this vantage point, they could see the entirety of the Eternal City beneath them—the drifting antigrav buildings, the towering edifice needles that blossomed into metal-and-glass flowers at their apexes, the slick black of the streets, so congested with solar traffic, and in the center of it all...

The MentorPlex! Rising over five hundred stories above the ground, it began as a slender pin, its shape warping like a sine wave turned on its side as it rose higher and higher, eventually unfolding into a perfect disk at its zenith. It would provide housing for tens of thousands of Titans. It had been designed by A'Lars as the paradigm for all new construction in the Eternal City, growing up, up, ever up, as more and more people required homes. A'Lars was personally overseeing its construction, and he was obsessed with making it absolutely perfect.

"The MentorPlex is the future of Titan," he told Thanos in a rare moment of sharing and excitement. He stroked the air, rotating a hologram of the building. "With many such buildings, we will change the landscape and the future of Titan even as we change the skyline of the Eternal City."

The building generated vast heat as a result of its energy requirements, but A'Lars had—brilliantly, Thanos admitted—mitigated this problem by redirecting the native, subterranean nearly frozen ammonia from beneath the nearby cryovolcanoes to act as a natural coolant.

Now, gazing into the valley, at the city that was the only home he knew, Thanos felt a disturbance at his core. He couldn't identify it. He only knew that something was off. Something was askew in some way that he did not yet understand.

There is something wrong with Titan, he thought.

"What did you say?" Sintaa asked, and Thanos realized that he'd spoken aloud, much to his surprise.

Lying never even occurred to him. Sintaa was his friend, and friends spoke truth. "There is something wrong with Titan," Thanos told him. "Can't you feel it?"

Sintaa shrugged. "All I feel is a breeze coming off the cryovolcanoes. Are you sure they're dormant?"

"Most are," Thanos said airily. "But truly, Sintaa—there is a rot in Titan. I've often thought it was *me*."

"Thanos…"

He waved off his friend's concern. "I see now that it's something else." He stood and gazed down on the Eternal City. Lit by millions of quantum-powered diodes, the City was a sketch made of light, a pulsating circuit board laid out in exacting lines and meticulously mapped plots of land. There was no name for it, merely the identifier, the truth: the Eternal City.

Sintaa rose as well and slung an arm around Thanos's shoulders. "We have everything here. There's nothing wrong. You're just..."

"Mordant?" Thanos suggested.

"I don't know that word," Sintaa admitted, "but it sounds about right."

Thanos brooded, staring straight ahead. Something was wrong. Something he could not identify. And for the first time in his life, the wrongness wasn't him.

On their way back from the edge of the Eternal City, they encountered a cluttered moving walkway, jammed with pedestrians. Mornings and twilight were congested like this, as the Eternal City's work shifts swapped places. Thanos and Sintaa threaded their way carefully through the throngs, making slow but steady progress against the wave of commuters. There was little room to maneuver, and without realizing it, Thanos was soon rammed into by a man walking hurriedly in the opposite direction.

Thanos was a child, but he was big and solid; the man stumbled, slewed to one side, and tried to replant his foot to stay upright. Unfortunately, his foot slipped into the groove where the moving walkway met the berm, shifting his center of gravity. Thanos understood too well the physics of it as he watched the man lurch to one side, almost catch himself, then continue down.

He also understood what the loud *crack* meant, even before the man—now prone—grabbed at his ankle and screamed in pain.

The crowd noticed only insofar as it rerouted itself around the clot in the commutation stream. Thanos grabbed Sintaa by the wrist. "We should help him," he insisted, dragging Sintaa off the walkway and to the man's side. The man was still stuck in the groove, his leg twisted at an unnatural and painful angle. Thanos crouched down, surveying the area.

"I need you to stand up," Thanos told the man. "We'll help support you."

"You did this to me!" the man whined through clenched teeth. His eyes were shut against the pain. "You knocked me over!"

Sintaa fumed. "*You* walked into *him*."

Thanos shushed his friend with a glance and gestured for him to help, but Sintaa obstinately refused, shaking his head and folding his arms over his chest. So Thanos slipped his hands under the man's leg and levered it up, trying to straighten it enough to get his foot out of the groove.

The man howled in new pain.

"Stop fighting me," Thanos said, struggling with the

writing limb. "It will only hurt for a moment, and then you'll be free."

The man's eyes flew open and fear overrode the pain. "What are you doing to me?" he demanded. "Help! Help!"

"I *am* helping!" Thanos told him. Another centimeter, maybe two, and he'd be able to slip the man's foot out of the groove.

"Help me!" the man cried out, a new urgency and terror in his voice.

"Stay still or try to stand," Thanos insisted. "I can get you free—"

"Stop him!" the man howled. "Someone stop him!"

"Um, Thanos…?"

Thanos looked up at Sintaa, then over to the crowd. The man's fear seemed to reach out and plunge into the crowd. People stopped, turned. They stared at Thanos, who was trying to pull the man free from the walkway groove, which would be an easier task if that leg would stop jittering and moving around.

"You," Thanos commanded, pointing to a man in the crowd. "Get on the other side. Stabilize his leg."

The man did nothing.

"Did you not hear me?" Thanos demanded. "He's in pain!"

When the man still demurred, Thanos barked his order at someone else, a woman standing nearby. She, too, shrank away.

"Get help!" the injured man cried. "He pushed me down! He's trying to rip my foot off!"

"What?" Thanos turned away from the crowd. "I did no such thing!"

"He didn't," Sintaa offered, but Thanos could tell from the man's expression that he would continue to cling stubbornly to his blinkered version of events.

And now Thanos heard muttering from the crowd. Heard his own name, his father's. He was known. Of course. He wore an indelible form of identification.

The man lying next to him moaned as the pain overcame him. Thanos saw a bit of bone breaking through the surface of the ankle, along with fresh blood. If the man had stopped thrashing...If he'd just let Thanos help...

"You would rather suffer than—"

"Thanos," Sintaa interrupted, putting a hand on his shoulder. "We should go."

Thanos didn't want to go—he had a case to make, and it was persuasive. But a tremble in his friend's voice made him reassess the situation. The crowd's fear was quickly corroding into anger and outrage. They were many and he was one.

He let Sintaa help him to his feet, and then they pushed their way through the crowd—it parted, almost reluctantly—and raced away.

"That could have gotten ugly," Sintaa said.

Thanos marveled at his friend's comment. It *had* gotten ugly. For all the wrong reasons. Random chance and brute serendipity had met up with prejudice, and the result was anything but pretty.

When he returned home, his mien was so despondent and his affect so maudlin that even his father could not help but to notice. With a resigned sigh, A'Lars grudgingly asked what was wrong.

When Thanos related the events on the walkway to his father, A'Lars merely shook his head. "You should have known better," he said, and returned to his work.

Thanos decided then and there: He would venture outside only when absolutely necessary. There was no point to doing otherwise.

Years later, Thanos stood atop the MentorPlex, gazing out onto the sprawl of the Eternal City beneath him, out to the rolling foothills where, a decade past, he and Sintaa had sat and watched the hovering robots build the very edifice in which he now lived with his father. A'Lars had reserved the top of the MentorPlex for himself.

Of course.

Of course his father would want to look down on the rest of Titan, the way he looked down on his only son.

Thanos imagined he could espy the exact spot where he'd sat on that day, even though he knew that was a foolish conceit. Ten years had passed in the blink of an eye, and he had spent that time doing his level best to forget the childish ways of his past and move into his future.

He'd applied himself to his studies with a diligence and an intensity that even his father noted. He understood the complexities of physics and biology, astronomy and chemistry. He could identify stars and planets with a glance at the night sky, could manipulate energies to create astonishingly lifelike images that spoke and moved, their fidelity far beyond the crude holograms of Titan's technology. He could scrutinize living tissue on the subcellular level, tweaking mitochondria and lysosomes to engender new life.

And he had done his best to forget Sui-San. His mind, when pressed into service, was capable of many things, and so he commanded himself to forget her.

But it was impossible. He could push her aside for weeks or months at a time, yet she always returned to him. He dreamed her face, enormous and pained and weeping. It was her face at the moment of his birth, he imagined. No one could remember the moment of birth, he knew, and yet with frightful regularity, he dreamed of it anyway, and was convinced it was a memory, not an invention of his subconscious.

Two years ago, he had finally uncovered proof positive that A'Lars had bribed Sintaa's family into providing friendship for Thanos—living quarters in the much-sought-after MentorPlex upon its completion. A'Lars had said not a word when presented with the proof, but since then Thanos had not seen Sintaa, had spent most of his time at home, pursuing his endless studies.

His subsequent loneliness eventually overcame his reticence, and in those two years, he'd tried going out, being among his people. But he could not bear the expressions on people's faces, the barely suppressed horror, the outright revulsion. His parents' reaction to him had set the precedent. His decision from years ago was the right one.

But was he really so monstrous? he wondered. Was he truly such a vile creature? Or was it just the perception of others?

A look in a mirror—reluctantly—confirmed it. Yes. Yes, he was.

And yet he wondered: Could it really be something as simple, as superficial, as the color of his skin and the raked-sand slant of his broad chin that cast such fear into them? Were the people of Titan—*his* people!—such cowards that they could be terrified by something literally skin-deep?

Titans were more sophisticated than to cleave to ancient superstitions, but they still associated purple with death, with misfortune, as though the photorefractive properties of a substance had anything at all to do with…

He sighed. It exhausted him just thinking about it.

He couldn't believe it to be true. It had to be something else.

He knew he was…unusual. Appearance aside, his intellect cast him apart from others. With each day, he grew smarter and more cunning. He understood more and more, though he could not understand the fear of the others.

The disgust he sensed in A'Lars? Yes, he understood that. He was a wretched creature, he knew, and as he grew, he became only more threatening. His shoulders broadened. His muscles swelled. He was a brute, a genius intellect trapped in the overmuscled body of a laborer. He did not glide; he stomped. Even at his most cautious, he elbowed and shouldered people out of his way.

He'd long ago given up apologizing. No one was listening.

He was getting older. Soon he would need to make his way in the world, not above it. He would have to go out into the City as a citizen, as his own person. How could he do that when he was rejected at every turn?

In a rare moment of utter desperation, he confronted A'Lars with that very question, seeking an explanation, looking for some kernel of wisdom that had eluded him thus far, something he could exploit to change the hearts and minds of Titan. It came on a night when A'Lars approached Thanos in his room. It was late, and Thanos was exhausted, his eyes burning from long hours spent studying his own DNA, the double-helix holograms twisting and turning at his direction, offering no answers as to how he'd become such a creature.

Perhaps with a DNA sample from his mother...

Sitting at his desk, he slumped in his chair, then rested his weary forehead on the palm of one too-large hand. If his genius could not decode his own deviance, it was useless.

A'Lars, as always, entered without knocking or asking the home's intelligence to announce him. His voice startled Thanos, who resisted the impulse to jump in surprise.

"I just wanted to remind you that I'll be leaving for the Rakdor Crater in the morning," A'Lars told him. "My geographical survey will have me away for three nights. Remember to—"

"Stay in the house," Thanos grumbled. "Yes. I know. Stay inside as much as possible, lest the mere sight of me send a fatal shockwave through Titanian society. I've absorbed that lesson."

"Your sarcasm is noted. And unappreciated."

Thanos spun around in his chair. "They *hate* me, Father! They fear me! For nothing I've done! Nothing at all!"

As ever, A'Lars's empathy was nonexistent. "Yes. And there is nothing you can do about that."

Thanos groaned and stood, swinging his arms about aimlessly. "Why? What have I done?"

A'Lars crossed his arms over his chest and regarded his son coolly. "As you've already said: nothing. Every species in the universe has an instinctive fear of its predator."

"Predator?" Thanos groaned again, in discontent, in anguish. "Whom have I preyed upon?" For a moment, the memory of his time at the hospital flickered. It was actually, he later learned, called a *psychosylum*, and it was not a place to heal injuries or wounds. His memory of it was as real and as alive as it had been in those instants. The synthetic blood, so slick and so real on his fists...

But A'Lars owned the psychosylum and the synthetics within who ran it. He'd covered up Thanos's moment of childish violence. No one knew.

"You are intelligent," his father said. "And your intelligence brings with it a remove, a distance from others. At an unconscious level, others pick up on this. They interpret it as ruthlessness. As a threat. Combined with your ... appearance, they feel fear. And, inevitably, what they fear, they hate."

His father said it all so matter-of-factly, so coldly, that for a moment Thanos thought that perhaps this was not so bad. But then the meaning of the words sank in, and his shoulders slumped as he realized exactly what his father was saying.

"Then there's nothing I can do," he said. "They hate me for no reason, so there is no logic I can apply, no rationale I can expound, that will change their minds."

"No," A'Lars said with firm finality. "Put it out of your mind. You are as you are, and the world is as the world is. You can change neither."

"Then what am I to do with my life?" Thanos cried. "How am I to find my way if I am hated and feared at every turn?"

A'Lars stood silent and still for so long that Thanos wondered if he had at last stumped the great man. A savage satisfaction coursed through him, and his lips quirked into a grin.

But then A'Lars merely shrugged. "Every creature finds its way. Even dung has its purpose, Thanos. You will find yours."

Before Thanos could respond, his father left, the door whispering shut behind, leaving Thanos alone with a useless, crooked smile and the certainty that his own father thought he was dung.

CHAPTER IV

So HE STOOD ALONE ATOP THE MENTORPLEX, ATOP THE world. In the distance, robots glided and drifted, hauling titanium and aluminum sheets, grafting them to the central spine of what would be MentorPlex II, built in the remains of the Rakdor Crater. More living space for more people.

A tone sounded, and Thanos turned to the door in surprise. His father was gone, and everyone knew it; there was no reason for visitors.

The door camera showed Sintaa, shifting impatiently from foot to foot as he waited. His friend had grown more than fifteen centis. His hair was now long and sleek, spiked in front and on top, then falling to his shoulders in the back. He had an effortless ease about him, a sense of relaxation that Thanos envied.

"What are you doing here?" Thanos asked, thumbing the control that allowed him to speak to the outer corridor.

Sintaa glanced around until he found the camera, then looked straight into it. "What a ridiculous question. Especially for a genius. I'm here to see you."

Thanos pursed his lips. "Go away," he said, and thumbed off the camera.

A moment later, the door vibrated with impact and a rhythmic thumping. Sintaa, the barbarian, was actually striking the door with his fist. Thanos re-engaged the camera and watched in amazement.

"Let me in!" Sintaa shouted, barely audible through the door. "I won't leave until you let me in, Thanos!"

Sintaa's abrupt irrationality caused annoyance to war with concern within Thanos. After a few moments of the insistent pounding, Thanos relented and opened the door.

Standing in the doorframe, winded, his hair in disarray from his exertions, Sintaa managed a lopsided grin. "There!" he panted. "Was that so hard?" And when Thanos said nothing: "Now is the part where you invite me in."

"Come in...?" It was more a question than an invitation, but Sintaa took it as a welcome and strode inside, smoothing back his hair along the nape of his neck as he did so.

"Thanks."

The anteroom was large and spare, in the Titan style. Its walls curved gently from floor to ceiling, giving the sense of being enclosed in a large, comfortable egg. A massive picture window formed one wall, its glass curved and fitted with perfect precision. The furniture floated.

Sintaa picked a floating chair with a good view of the Eternal City and dropped into it. As programmed, a floating table glided into place before him.

Thanos knew that there were rituals when one received a guest in one's home. He'd never performed those rituals, nor had he been on the receiving end, but he had read about them. And so he sent one of his enhanced toddler-androids—now programmed to act as a servant—to the larder to fetch cakes and honeywater while Thanos stood, hands clasped behind his back, in silence. For his part, Sintaa sat comfortably, scrutinizing Thanos with an inscrutable grin.

"I thought—" he began, but Thanos stopped him with a raised hand.

"Custom dictates we wait for refreshment."

Sintaa shrugged. A moment later, the android returned, bearing a tray of food and drink. Taking the tray, Thanos paused in the presence of his former friend. "Why have you come here, Sintaa? My father's obligation to your family is complete."

Sintaa's expression soured. "Ever since you told him you knew about his deal with my parents, your father hasn't let me see you. I tried a few times, but he always blocked me. He was either here or nearby or by the time I knew he wasn't around, it was too late. So when I heard he would be gone for a few days, I came right away."

Thanos placed the tray on the table and then sat opposite Sintaa. "Why?"

Sintaa chuckled and shook his head. "Because, you ugly purple cuss, I actually like you. You're my friend. And it's long past time for you to have more than one friend of your own. You live up here in isolation, trapped in your father's titanium palace, and you don't even know how to interact with people. So I'm going to lend you some of my friends, all right?"

"I don't believe that is part of the deal with A'Lars."

"To hell with A'Lars," Sintaa said with pleasant satisfaction, as though he'd been waiting years to say exactly that and had just figured out how. "He never had a deal with me, do you understand? He had a deal with my parents. Everything here"—at this point, he gestured back and forth between them—"was real."

Real. The reality of his friendship with Sintaa had always seemed fraught and fragile. Thanos steepled his fingers before him and leaned in, thinking. He couldn't imagine a scenario in which it would profit Sintaa to lie to him. Not about this. He applied his mighty brain to the task and realized, in a stunning blast of epiphany, that he did not *need* to apply his brain to this. This was not the matter of the flavor of quarks or the spin of electrons or the reactions of enzymes or the cleavage planes of crystals. This was a matter of emotion. Logic could not apply. It *did* not apply.

"You're my friend," he said very slowly.

Sintaa applauded and even pursed his lips for a loud, piercing whistle. "He got it! Ladies and gentlemen, the boy genius of Titan figured it out!"

His skin could not betray a blush, but Thanos felt the blood rush to his cheeks nonetheless. He turned his head away. "You dolt."

"A dolt who has an evening planned." Sintaa bolted out of his chair and grabbed Thanos by the arm. "Come on."

The sky never truly darkened over the Eternal City. The City itself seemed made of light, its bright surfaces limned with light-emitting piping that brightened even as the daylight dimmed.

They walked from the MentorPlex. The sky was cluttered with aerorafts and floaters, thick with artificial congestion.

The land-bound walkways were no better. Thanos, too tall and too broad, was aware of how disconcerting his presence was. The population of the cluttered, jammed walkways tried to give him a wide berth, stepping aside as he passed, stepping into and onto one another. Still, he found his elbows and his shoulders knocking people aside, his feet stepping on others' feet.

He tried to ignore it. Focused on something else. He wondered what would happen if there were suddenly an emergency. If all of these people had to *run*. It would be madness.

"It's so crowded. Worse than it used to be," Thanos complained. "I don't usually get to venture out this far. I didn't realize. From above, it's hard to tell."

"And this is why you should come outside every now and again," Sintaa joked at his side, shoving his way through a clutch of people headed the other way.

"I thought it was bad when we were kids, but this…"

"It will get better when MentorPlex II and III are built," Sintaa said. "What your father lacks in parenting skills, he makes up for in city planning, I have to admit. The overflow will be directed up, as always."

Thanos grunted something affirmative. His father had designed the Eternal City, had overseen the terraforming of Titan into a livable place. As distant and as unforgiving as his father could be, Thanos had to remind himself that the man had responsibilities that would crush lesser men to paste. A'Lars could be forgiven his endless distractions and neglects.

Thanos found himself smiling, much to his surprise. Fifteen minutes in Sintaa's presence and he was already much happier.

In the entertainment district, Sintaa guided them through a crowd to a club, where light and shadow pulsed in time to bass-heavy music. Thanos paused, much to the anger and frustration of the throngs trying to make their way along the walkway.

"A club?" Thanos rumbled. "What do you think I am, Sintaa?"

"I think you're a deadly dull killjoy who's never had a moment that wasn't devoted to figuring something out," Sintaa said. "I think you need some time to be with other people and to stop thinking so much. Maybe even do something crazy and radical, like kiss someone."

Thanos barked with horrified laughter. "Kiss someone? Have you lost your mind? Look at me. Look at them." He gestured at the Titans who flowed around him, doing their best not to look too long or too closely at the mutated *thing* in their midst.

Sintaa waved away his concern like a bad smell. "One kiss and you'll forget all about these provincial idiots and their base prejudices. You've spent your life letting your father convince you that you're worthless. That your size and your appearance make you a monster. And because he's a big deal and because he's important, if he believes it, everyone else does, too."

Thanos opened his mouth to speak, but Sintaa silenced him with a gesture. "None of that's your fault; it's his. But trust me—when you kiss someone, you feel it. The connection. The intertwined nature of it all. You're part of Titan, Thanos, and I'm going to prove it to you. Tonight."

Thanos allowed himself to be ushered inside. People stared as he squeezed through the door, which was too low for him and narrowed by a cluster of loiterers.

Inside, the air was thick and close, and the club had gone dead quiet. The music was only outside; the inside was soundproofed. It felt as though walking through the door immediately submerged him in a vacuum, cutting off all sound. He put his hands over his ears for a moment, heard the reliable thud of his own heartbeat, and relaxed a bit. The claustrophobia of it took a moment's adjustment.

It was a so-called silencurium, a "quiet club," where sound was forbidden, eliminated through the use of acoustically null flooring. On the central dance floor, a pulsating globe of multicolored light flashed and throbbed as bodies gyrated and ground against one another in a languorous, indecorous pantomime. The silence was so loud as to be deafening—utter quiet, utter lack of sound.

It was a wholly impressionistic place. With no music to guide them, the dancers moved as their bodies dictated, and their motions were interpreted freely by the onlookers. There were as many shows going on as there were people in attendance.

Sintaa led him to a table, where two young women waited. One—a green-haired beauty with flickering holotattoos at the corners of her eyes—lit up at the sight of Sintaa, gaped her mouth in a silent squeal, and threw her arms around him. Clearly, he was mated—at least temporarily—with the green-haired girl.

Sintaa gestured for Thanos to join them at the table. The other girl wore her hair close-cropped and red like a ripe cherry, her skin pale yellow and speckled with green dots. She offered him a shy smile and moved enough that he was able to sit between her and Sintaa.

He longed to speak, but the rules and science of the silencurium forbade it. So he sat in silence, hands clasped in his lap, and watched the whirling and twisting of the revelers. Even the dance floor seemed too crowded, bodies colliding in tranquility.

Sintaa and the two girls wore polychromatic jumpsuits with holographic piping down the legs that shifted colors and transparent epaulets filled with a viscous fluid that languidly copied their shoulder movements. It was the fashion, and most of the dancers wore similar outfits: skintight leggings that shifted color and brightness, neon-bright elbow patches, knee-high boots with flickering holo detailing.

Wearing prosaic, staid pants and a tunic in deep blue, Thanos felt even more out of place. But as time passed and as everyone's attention remained on the dancers, his unease abated, and his shoulders lost their rigidity. Compared with the bustle and noise of the world outside, the silencurium was a haven. He'd heard of sensory-deprivation experiences before, but this place merged deprivation with sensory immersion, turning off the sound so the other senses came more alive.

He turned to the girl next to him, and she offered him another smile. He tried out his own, cognizant as always of the way his misshapen chin distorted his expression.

A robot drifted by, a platter hovering before it on which stood several glasses. The girl held out a hand to stop the robot, then grabbed two drinks and fingerprinted a transaction. She offered one of the drinks to Thanos with a questioning mien.

He took it. Studied it. Sipped. It was green, bubbly, and too sweet, tasting of melon and elderberries and ethyl alcohol. Still, she drank, so he did, too.

They watched the dance floor for a time, the bodies moving as though triggered by hidden signals, contorting and twisting in time to the pulse of the light globe. Shadows leaped and shivered on the walls and ceiling and floor, reconfiguring as the dancers shifted, paused, shifted again. Thanos was lost in it, in the sheer artistry of it, in the impeccable timing and press of it. Outside, the bodies crushed together were inconvenient and hassled. Within, they were art.

He lost track of time, sinking into individual moments. And then there was a touch on the back of his hand, a light skim of sensation. It was his companion, who regarded him quizzically.

Outside? she mouthed.

He looked over at Sintaa, who raised an eyebrow and nodded. Thanos rose. To his surprise, she took his hand and led him through the crowd to the door.

Outside, the sudden noise assaulted him as though it were a physical thing. He winced in pain—footsteps, music, throats cleared, voices raised. A mélange of sounds, all blending into a sonic battering ram attacking his senses.

She stood with him, holding his hand as he readjusted to the world of noise again. "It's hard the first time," she said when he finally cleared his mind and looked over at her. "The adjustment," she clarified.

It was the first time he'd heard her voice. There was, he admitted, nothing special about it, and yet he wanted to hear more of it.

"Speak more," he told her.

She laughed. "The genius has never heard of small talk."

"No. But I enjoy the sound of your voice. Am I supposed to offer a subject for discussion?"

She shook her head. "It's all right. My mother tells me I never shut up, so it's nice to have someone who actually wants to listen." She paused. "So. The famous Thanos. Son of A'Lars."

"Son of Sui-San," he told her. "How could you tell?"

It was an attempt at levity, and it worked. Her eyes danced with merriment. "You just look like a Thanos, I guess. Not a Jerha or a Dione or a—"

"Sintaa?" he asked, looking over his shoulder for a moment. Sintaa was still inside the silencurium.

"Definitely a Thanos," she said. She cocked her head. "In this light, your skin doesn't even look purple."

He didn't know how to respond. The mutation of multiples of his solute carrier genes that had resulted in his purple phenotype was no fault of his own. And yet he had been ashamed and embarrassed by it his whole conscious life.

"Then I suppose I like the light here," he told her.

She shrugged. "I like purple. It's my favorite color."

He blinked, then blinked again. Was this why Sintaa had chosen her to sit with him tonight? Because his skin color wasn't abhorrent to her? To say purple was her favorite color...On Titan that was akin to saying that death was her favorite part of life.

As he pondered this, she regarded him with something like amusement. Finally, as though she had been holding her breath, she exclaimed, "Do you really not remember me?"

He froze. "Remember you?" He'd met precious few people in his life, as isolated as he was. How could it be possible that he wouldn't remember one of them?

"I'm Gwinth," she told him. "Gwinth Falar. From your infamous four hours of formal schooling."

The memory rushed at him. The projection of his blood. The pinprick that set off screams. And the girl who had so innocently and without recrimination asked about his purple skin.

"You look so different," he said. Somewhat lamely, he realized too late.

She laughed almost musically. "That happens. You look the same. Just bigger. I can't believe it's really you. It's so amazing to see you again."

He shook her hand, taking great care not to squeeze too hard. "I am pleased to meet you, Gwinth Falar. Again."

"Sintaa says you're a genius."

"Sintaa says many things."

"So you're not?"

He found himself enjoying this...this...thing. It was called *banter*, wasn't it? The pleasing wordplay between two people. He'd heard of it but had only become used to using words to argue with his father or to issue commands to androids.

"I didn't say that. I just said Sintaa says many things."

Her mouth quirked up on one side, and she seemed to chuckle. They moved into the crowd and walked together, still holding hands. The masses parted for them; the looks of shock and disgust were unavoidable, and Thanos felt obliged to apologize to her for the ugly glares in her direction.

She merely shrugged. "When Sintaa told us he was friends with you," she said, "none of us believed him."

"Could you not believe that I was capable of having a friend, or was it that you didn't think I could tolerate him?"

She laughed. "You're funny. And you're not trying to be, which makes it even funnier. We just didn't believe him, is all. Everyone knew about you. You went away, but you were still famous."

"Notorious, more likely," he told her.

She chuckled the notion away. "Our parents talked all the time, especially when they knew you would be at our school, and then after you left. About how A'Lars and Sui-San gave birth to a..." Gwinth trailed off.

"I have heard all the words before," he assured her. "Monstrosity, perhaps? Grotesquerie? Deviant?"

"We're not our parents," she whispered, eyes downcast. "We don't hate and fear just because something is different." She scowled at a passerby who stared, openmouthed, at them. "Not like *these* imbeciles, who can't let things go. Who are afraid because it's easier than thinking."

"Their fear is understandable," he said, surprised to find himself taking their side against him, "and even logical. From an evolutionary standpoint. Tribal safety relies on keeping outside elements at a remove. Fear and hatred of 'the different' or 'the distinct' makes sense."

"Maybe thousands of years ago, when we lived shorter lives and had no medicine," she argued. "But now? It's a vestige of our past. It's prejudice without a point."

He stopped walking for a moment and looked down at her. She smiled sardonically. "I'm no genius, but I'm not an idiot, either. Stop defending the people who hate you."

Thanos pulled her through the crowd and found a platform that jutted out above the walkway. It was a landing pad for cleaning bots, but currently empty.

With his big hands around her waist, he lifted her to the platform, then clambered up himself. Below them, the crowd filled in the space that they had taken up, swallowing it whole, making it seem as though they'd never even been there.

"I can't find it in me to hate them back," he told her. "Until I met you, I thought only Sintaa did not hate and fear me."

Sadness clouded her eyes. "Really? Only Sintaa? What about your father?"

Thanos shook his head. "A'Lars does not fear me. And, truthfully, I do not believe he hates me. But he is disgusted by me."

"What a hypocrite," she said with heat. "He's your *father*. You're *from* him."

Thanos considered. "That is probably why he feels so much disgust." He pointed into the distance, to the Mentor-Plex. "See his works. See them all around you. This city is his true child, the child he always dreamed of. Beautiful and perfect and meticulous and obedient."

"And overcrowded," Gwinth said drily.

With a chuckle, Thanos gestured to the skeletal sketch that was the beginning of MentorPlex II. "He will fix that, too."

And then, a sensation he'd never experienced before—a touch on his face. His furrowed chin, to be exact. Her hand, tiny and delicate against the heft of his jaw, felt soft and smooth. Thanos tilted his head just slightly, leaning into her cupping palm.

"Do you kiss?" she asked.

Answers warred along his tongue, fighting to escape his lips: bravado, machismo, deflection, agreement.

He settled on honesty.

"I would like to."

She said nothing, merely leaned up to him, then pressed her lips to his.

When you kiss someone, you feel it. The connection. The intertwined nature of it all. Sintaa's promise rang through his mind, over and over.

Kissing Gwinth, Thanos felt…the moist, yielding pressure of her lips. Her breath, warm against his cheek.

And he felt...

Joy.

He named the emotion before he could be sure, then confirmed it. Joy. In those seconds that their lips pressed together, he experienced the first true happiness of his life. It was as though the combination of the two of them made something new, something unknowable until that very instant.

His heart was just an organ, just a sophisticated biological pump evolved from the primitive coelom of early multicellular organisms. And yet... And yet, it seemed to *sing*.

From just that kiss.

"What are you thinking?" she asked him, eyes sparkling as they pulled apart.

"I'm not," he said, as though stunned. "For the first time in my life, I'm not thinking at all." He pondered. "And you? After kissing the infamous Thanos?"

"It's like kissing anyone else," she marveled, as though uncovering a miracle.

He laughed with her. His mood, his spirit—both lightened. And then he realized something. Something old and new at the same time. A blunt wedge of knowledge came between them.

"I have to go," he told her. "I apologize, but there's something that I have to do."

"Now?" She goggled at him.

He did not give her time to protest further. He helped her down from the platform and then left her there in the crowd, pushing his way through, grateful for the first time in his life for the way people recoiled and moved away from him.

"Thanos!" she shouted, lost behind him. "Thanos!"

He ignored her. He had no choice. A puzzle piece lost for his life-span now turned up, and when slipped into place revealed...

Possibilities. At last.

CHAPTER V

THE PSYCHOSYLUM HAD NOT CHANGED IN THE YEARS since Thanos had set foot within it, but his understanding of it had changed. As a child, he'd thought it was a place for those who—like his mother—had illnesses of the mind that could not be cured. A place built and tended to by A'Lars out of compassion for the less fortunate of Titan.

But in the days after his last visit here, he'd learned the truth: The psychosylum existed because of and exclusively for Sui-San. She was its sole patient, its only ward. A'Lars had built it and maintained it not out of generosity of spirit but out of disgust and evasion. He'd shoved Sui-San in there and left her.

And now. Here. An entire building devoted to the care of one person. Sui-San. The runaway mother. The Mad Titan.

How long, Thanos wondered, had A'Lars considered a similar fate for his grotesquerie of a son? How had Thanos avoided a cell alongside his poor mother? Sheer luck? Surely not a father's mercy—A'Lars had none.

My brain, Thanos thought. A'Lars had recognized his offspring's intelligence and thought it might be useful. That was the only logical reason to keep Thanos around.

In the years since his birth, Thanos had yet to prove

himself worthy of that leniency to his father's satisfaction. How much longer would A'Lars suffer his presence?

The kiss with Gwinth had awakened him to the possibility of belonging, of family, of love. Thanos feared the Isolation Room more than he feared losing his own life, and so until now, he'd never returned. But there was the kiss. The kiss that made him realize that he *could* fit in; he *could* belong. He *deserved* to belong.

Sintaa had once told him that all living things had mothers. Thanos knew there was a hollow spot at his core, the place that was supposed to be filled with his mother and her love. He hadn't thought he'd deserved those things, but Gwinth, with her kindness and her kiss, had proved him wrong. He had to see Sui-San and seek that connection and at least *try*.

If nothing else, he would get a DNA sample from his mother. She might not tell him what he wanted to hear or know; she might not even speak to him. But at the very least, he would get that DNA. Figure out what had happened to him within her womb. And maybe—just maybe—fix himself.

Licking his lips, Thanos entered the hospital. A wave of memory struck him, dripped from him, puddled at his feet. What had seemed large and bright when he was a child now seemed cramped and dim. The sound-swallowing walls were to keep Sui-San's screams from leaving the building, he now understood. Fingers splayed, he pressed one hand against the yielding wall, feeling it give against him. How many cries for help had these walls ingested?

A flame of hatred burst in his chest. This could not pass. His position in society to the contrary, A'Lars could not get away with treating his spouse this way.

Thanos made his way to the welcome room he'd entered as a child. Then he'd had a child's understanding, a child's tenuous grasp on his temper and emotions. Now he was nearly a man.

A synthetic biped stood before him, garbed in the same black tunic as the "doctor" he'd beaten years ago. It seemed identical. The same one, or merely the latest version of that model? His hands suddenly felt clammy. Sweat, not the biofuel he'd mistaken for blood all those years ago. Still, the memory was tangible and potent.

"Thanos," the synth said in a disapproving tone. "I was told you were coming."

He parsed the sentence: *Security sensors detected your presence and transmitted it to my synthetic cortex, which then ran a preprogrammed subroutine. Because your father thought of everything, including your trying this again.*

Stifling his anger at A'Lars, Thanos instead forced himself to recall his father's words from ages ago:

The "doctor" is a new synthetic life-form I bred specifically to care for your mother. Designed with enhanced empathy and compassion. Congratulations, Thanos—you bludgeoned to death something that was not truly alive . . . and something that was designed from the start not to know how to fight back.

Enhanced empathy and compassion...

Spreading his arms wide in a gesture of peace and humility, Thanos said, "I'm so sorry for intruding. I mean no harm or disrespect."

It was just a moment, but the synth's hesitation told Thanos that it was switching its response parameters. Now that he knew he was dealing with something artificial, something programmed, he could manipulate it as if he were executing code.

"You haven't hurt anyone," the synth said gently.

"I need your help." Thanos spoke with as pitiful and needy a tone of voice as he could muster without descending into outright whining. *Enhanced empathy and compassion.* He was deliberately triggering the synth's help-and-aid protocols by appearing weak, defenseless, and in need of assistance. "Please," he said. "Please help me. I need your help."

The synth tilted its head to one side. "My directives are to ask you to leave."

"I want to leave," Thanos lied smoothly, "but I can't. I need your help in order to go."

The synth offered its version of a smile. "I would be happy to help you in that endeavor, Thanos."

Thanos nodded gravely. "I want to leave, but I can't. Not until I've spoken with Sui-San. Won't you please help me?"

The synth shook its head, but Thanos detected microspasms in its eyes as its bioware attempted to reconcile its now-conflicting missions. Help people. Don't let Thanos in. They were incompatible directives.

"Please," Thanos said, and considered dropping to his knees. Such theatricality, though, would have been anticipated by A'Lars, who had no doubt programmed against it. Thanos would need something beyond empty and easily recognizable gestures. "I need your help if I am to be whole again," he said. The words tumbled out of him without forethought, and they were so damned *true* for the lack of guile. "I've never known my mother. Never even seen her except in dreams. I want to know her, to know myself, to understand. Please," he said again, "please let me see her. Let me speak to her. She's the only one who can tell me who and what I am. The only one who cares."

The synth's eyes vibrated back and forth, then jittered up and down. Its expression went from neutral to soothing to stern and then, just when Thanos had given up, its mouth wrung itself into a simulation of a smile.

"Of course, Thanos. Let me escort you."

It took little time, the hospital being a smallish affair designed for a single occupant. The synth led Thanos down a corridor and around a bend. Along the way, he saw other synths, dressed similarly, all of whom nodded pleasantly and vacantly to him.

"Here," said the synth, and gestured to a door. Thanos thumbed the control, but nothing happened.

The synth happily thumbed the pad for him, and the door slid up. Thanos hesitated.

"This is her room," the synth said with bright confidence.

He knew. He knew that this was her room, and yet suddenly his feet would not move.

"Are you ill?" the synth asked. "I can procure medication if necessary. Describe your symptoms."

The synth's solicitous tone had grated on his last nerve. That, more than anything else, unglued his feet and propelled him into the room before the door shut.

It was small and well lit. The walls were soft, and that datum alone told him volumes about his mother's condition. Soft walls meant that she tended to fling herself at them.

There was a bed floating against one wall, but no other furniture. No personal belongings that he could identify. A wave of rage toward A'Lars swelled in his breast. His mother was not being *treated*. She was being *warehoused*. Like old furniture.

Warehoused here. Right in front of him. For the first time ever, he beheld her.

His first thought was, *She's beautiful.*

Maybe children were predisposed to find their parents pleasing to look at. He didn't think so; he found A'Lars entirely average in appearance. His mother, though, was exceptional.

Even in this constrained, antiseptic setting, her beauty shone. Her skin glowed, and her hair seemed fluid, a spill of black ink cascading over her shoulders. Looking at her, he found himself thinking what no doubt everyone in the world thought:

How could something so beautiful have given birth to me?

She sat on the floor, legs crossed, hands resting on her knees. Her eyes were closed and her breathing was even. He immediately reconsidered his rage at A'Lars. She seemed in good health, at peace, relaxed. Perhaps this denuded environment suited her. Low sensory stimulation. Nothing to upset her.

As he watched, her head tilted gently side to side and up and down, tracing a relaxed infinity symbol. She was humming ever so slightly.

He took a step toward her and cleared his throat. Her eyes opened slowly, dreamily.

"Mother. It's me. Your child. Thanos."

Her head continued its lazy sideways figure eight, her eyes focused on absolutely nothing. He came closer and, with tenderness and a gentle touch, took her chin between his thumb and forefinger, guiding her attention to his face.

"Mother," he said again. Her eyes still had not focused. The pupils were pinpricks. "Mother, I'm here. Here to help you."

And her eyes snapped into focus on him. They widened as she drew in a horrified breath. In an instant, she slapped his hand away from her and scrabbled backward, scuttling away like a crab, her indrawn breath now exploding out in a shriek of terror.

Thanos checked over his shoulder but remembered the pliant, sound-absorbing walls. No one would hear.

"Mother," he said again, holding out both hands to show he meant no harm. "Mother, it's your son. Your child."

"You!" she gasped, coming up short against a wall. "You! I saw you! I've seen your face!"

"Yes. When I was born. You held me, didn't you?" Tears glimmered in his eyes as he crept closer to her, moving slowly so as not to frighten her further.

She drew in another breath, squeezing herself into a corner. "You're a demon!" she cried. "You're death! I saw it in your eyes! It crawled out of your ears and bled on my bare bosom when you were born! You are death! You are death!"

One hand outstretched to smooth her hair back from her brow, Thanos froze at her words. "Mother." He wiped the incipient tears from his eyes. "Mother, no. I'm just your son."

"Death!" she screamed, curling into a tight ball, knees clutched to her chest, face buried. "Death! Death! Death! You breathe it! You eat it and sweat it out! You! Are! Death! Death! Death!"

She said it over and over, until the words blurred and merged into a single, repeated nonsense syllable, her teeth clacking together on the *D* so violently that he was astonished they did not break out of her mouth. Every time he tried to approach her, to comfort her, she threw back her head and howled, a high keening sound that drilled through his ears and into his soul. Backing away, he froze in the center of the room. He could not help her, but he could not leave her in such a state, could he?

Eventually, feeling behind him, he slid the door open and stumbled out into the corridor, where the synth waited for him patiently.

"She needs your help," he managed to say, and the synth immediately rushed into the room, followed by two identical ones. They crouched by Sui-San and administered a dose of a bright-blue medication. Thanos watched until the door automatically slid shut, cutting off sight and sound.

Outside, Thanos nearly collapsed, catching himself with one hand on the outer wall of the psychosylum.

His mother.

His own mother.

He hadn't even obtained a DNA sample. He had been so anguished, so cowardly. Such a puling little boy, fleeing at the first sign of trouble...He gnashed his teeth and struck the wall with one large fist; it was a thermic wall reinforced with an exotic, rigid steel alloy, and it yielded not in the slightest. He punched it again, then did it again and again and again, until the waves of pain reached his elbow, and his fingers went numb.

Tilting his head up, he caught a glimpse of the panoply of stars in the arcs of space that framed Hyperion, Titan's dwarfish, deformed sibling, a wart on the night sky.

Sinking to his knees, he braced himself against the wall. A great darkness overcame him, followed by a great weakness.

The world swam and blurred, the colors blending together. When he found the strength to look up, the sky had gone awash in puddles of color, reflections from the City's lights melding with the black of space, the white speckles of stars, the bluish hue of Hyperion.

They were no longer separate and distinct things. They had merged. They were of a piece. They connected and they belonged.

He thought of earlier that night, of the touch of Gwinth's lips.

Damn it all, *he* was connected, too. He was *not* an outcast. He was a part of Titan, whether Titan wanted it so or not.

He loved Titan, even if Titan hated him.

It would be easy to meet hate with hate and fear with fear. Flexing feeling back into his fingers, balling his fists, he knew that he could be more than Hyperion to Titan. He could contribute.

For now, there was nothing he could do for Sui-San. Her madness was beyond his knowledge and his abilities. For now.

He would meet fear with love. His father had told him there was nothing he could do to change the way Titan saw him, so he realized that instead *he* must change. Perhaps there would be reciprocity. Perhaps not. But it was better than nothing. At the worst, he would help people and never be appreciated for it. But they would still have his help, even if they learned only how to conceal their hate and fear behind a curtain of benign and anodyne neglect.

He would channel the love of his missing, demented mother. He would love Titan and everyone on it. For no other reason than because he could.

Thanos returned home.

He had work to do.

CHAPTER VI

IT TOOK HIM MORE THAN AN HOUR TO TRAVEL THE SIXTEEN blocks home on the crowded streets and walkways. The skyways were clogged, too, so thick with vehicles as to create a canopy that blotted out the sky in great moving patches. Eventually, these people would have their new homes in MentorPlex II and III, he thought.

The overflow will be directed up, Sintaa had said.

Thanos stopped dead in his tracks at the entrance to MentorPlex.

The overflow will be directed up.

He stood there, immovable. Titans pressed around him, desperately avoiding even a mere brush against him.

His whole life, he'd known there was something wrong with Titan, but he'd never truly tried to figure out what it was. Now he could rectify that oversight, he decided.

The overflow will be directed up.

The fatal flaw at Titan's core...He understood it now. And if he could wrench Titan's rotten tumor from itself and leave behind the healthy tissue, then maybe attitudes like Gwinth's would flourish. They would see him as an equal, not a predator.

The elevator systems in MentorPlex were artificially

intelligent. They balanced their own traffic and could deposit a resident at the appropriate floor among five hundred in less than thirty seconds.

That was thirty seconds too long. Thanos burst from the elevator and exploded into his apartment. In the distance, the cryovolcanoes simmered and brooded, but Thanos had no time for their beauty. He flung himself into the chair at his desk and began to work.

The overflow will be directed up.

The overflow will be directed up.

Not if I can help it, he thought.

A'Lars returned from his trip in a fury. The domicile's artificial intelligence alerted Thanos to his father's presence as soon as A'Lars crossed the threshold, but Thanos ignored it. He had risen from his desk only four times in the last two days. He had not eaten in more than a day, and he still wore the same clothing he'd worn to the silencurium days ago, adding only a dataglove for easier and more precise hologram manipulation.

He was haggard and he stank, but he was focused, as though a lack of food had honed rather than starved his mind. He was staring at a holochart of data when his father thumbed open his bedroom door and stood in the doorway, enraged.

"You've been to see your mother," A'Lars began, his voice

deep with wounded fury. "Did you think I was so foolish as to not monitor the facility?"

"I have no time for this," Thanos said without even turning to glance at his father. The holochart swiveled to the left; numbers climbed. Thanos groaned. It was as he had suspected. It was all true.

"You have...?" A'Lars strode into the room. "You will rise and speak to me *now*, Thanos!"

Thanos wrenched his attention away from the holograms. His father stood over him, cheeks flushed, eyes flashing. The chair floated back slightly, and Thanos stood, facing his father.

"I have something to tell you," he told A'Lars. "It's very important."

"I no longer trust your perception of importance, if I ever did," A'Lars said through clenched teeth. "You were specifically instructed not to seek out your mother, yet as soon as my back was turned—"

"You took her from me!" Thanos shouted. He hadn't planned on allowing himself to be drawn into a conversation about his mother—there truly *was* something vastly more important to discuss—but his father's hypocrisy and sanctimony chafed at him. "You spirited her off and locked her away from me and from the world. Why should I trust your orders, Father? Why should I trust you at all?"

The words spilled out of him in a single breath, and he stood there, laboring to breathe as his father took a small step back. For the first time in his life, Thanos thought his father was reconsidering. Reconsidering *what*, he couldn't tell, but for A'Lars to reconsider at all was a monumental achievement.

"Your mother went mad the moment she laid eyes on you," A'Lars said quietly. "I took her away to protect you from her. From her madness. It was a kindness to you, my son."

"A kindness?" Thanos ground his teeth together. "Kindness would have been to allow me to see her, at the very least. To speak her name. To tell me about her. To let her live in my mind, if not in my presence!"

A'Lars clucked his tongue. "I can't expect you to understand. Your mind is exceptional, my son, but you are still a child, and you understand as do children. This is a matter for adults, and you have violated the rule I established for you."

"You gave me no choice—"

"I gave you every choice!" A'Lars thundered. The tattered remnants of his compassion, shredded by anger, blew away. "I gave you the choice to obey my commands and leave your mother alone! Do you have any idea how much harm she would have done to herself had not the synths intervened when they did? As it is, she seriously damaged one of them, and now I will have to spend at least a day salvaging it."

"I weep for your pain," Thanos said with great sarcasm. He touched his eyes for a moment; his fingers came away dry. "Ah. Apparently not."

A'Lars fumed. "Your punishment will be greater than you—"

Thanos shook his head wildly. "Father, there's no time for you to discipline me for such a small infraction—"

"Small? You were explicitly told—"

"—not when there are more urgent and existential matters to consider." Thanos turned to the desk and the multitude of holograms that floated there. Where to begin?

A hand clapped onto his shoulder and spun him around. A'Lars seethed. "I am not accustomed to my *child* dismissing me so. And I will not *become* accustomed, do you understand me, boy?"

For the first time, Thanos noticed that he was taller than his father. Broader, too. A'Lars was a mere two meters tall and slender, whereas Thanos was at least a deci taller and disproportionately broader. It had happened more than a year ago, he realized, but he'd never felt it so viscerally before. Now, in this moment, he knew that he could end the argument in no uncertain terms with the simple expedient of a strong slap across his father's face.

The idea—the image—raced through him, shuddering as it went. He repressed it with brute willpower.

"Father, there is no time for us to argue. Our world is imperiled, and I need your wisdom to save it."

A'Lars opened his mouth to speak, then closed it. He shook his head and took a step back, as though he knew on some deeper, more instinctive level that Thanos had considered striking him.

"Imperiled? Thanos, your mother's madness has infected you."

The mention of Sui-San again enraged Thanos. How *dare* A'Lars, the man who'd imprisoned her, speak so flippantly of her? Fists clenched, Thanos once again exercised enormous restraint. After long moments, he relaxed and unclenched his fists.

"Father, I need your help."

It had worked with the synths, and now it paused the anger of their creator. A'Lars sighed. "You are... of a certain age. Certain urges and desires are understood, and are now being sublimated into this antirational foolishness. I will arrange for—"

"Damn your arrangements, Father!" Thanos thundered. "I am not a sex-starved adolescent yearning for consummation! I am your son; I am your equal in intellect, and I am telling you that our people are doomed!"

Silence fell in the room, a silence as swallowed and whole as in the confines of the silencurium.

"Doomed, you say?" When A'Lars finally spoke, it was with a haughty, sly humor. "Doomed."

Thanos had expected a different reaction from his father. Fear, perhaps. Or, more likely, a knowing nod of the head, a flash of paternal pride, an acknowledgment that his offspring had achieved something enormous. Some part of him had suspected that perhaps A'Lars already knew what he himself had discovered in the past few days.

Instead, A'Lars regarded him with scorn.

"Doomed, Father," Thanos pressed on. "The numbers add up. I've done the math. We are massively overpopulated...."

A'Lars barked a laugh and waved his hand dismissively, but Thanos continued:

"*Massively* overpopulated. Yes, you've mitigated the crowding somewhat with the MentorPlexes, staving off the worst of the impact, but that can't last forever. We're going to run out of room. And matériel. The resultant environmental catastrophe will—"

A'Lars shook his head slowly and sadly. Thanos gritted his teeth and changed tactics.

"Such overcrowding also impacts hygiene and germ breeding. Even if you're able to hold off the environmental impact of building more MentorPlexes and feeding the people within them, my models project multiple and eventually *constant* plague-level pathogens. Global pandemics that will devastate the population over and over. Because nature always seeks balance, and nature has no sympathy or compassion."

Like you, he thought, but did not say.

A'Lars said nothing for a long time. So long that Thanos had time to replay everything he'd said. Had he left anything out? He didn't think so. It had been two score sleepless hours since the realization hit him, since Sintaa's offhand comment about *the overflow* being *directed up* had made him think of the cryomagma beneath the Eternal City and its environs, made him think of what would happen if the cryovolcanoes erupted, spewing ammonia and methane into the atmosphere. From there, he'd begun thinking of how to protect Titan from an environmental disaster, and while developing evacuation plans, he'd realized just *how many people* lived in the Eternal City. How many were crammed into this space. How many more were born every minute of every day. Titans were healthy, long-lived people; they died infrequently and yet they kept breeding, and the result was a world rapidly draining itself dry.

With science and with technology, they had forestalled the inevitable. But it *was* inevitable. The very same technology that delayed their doom merely changed probabilities and created *new* inevitabilities. When the reckoning came, it would be catastrophic.

The problem with Titan was not Titan itself, was not the cryovolcanoes and the threat of their freezing ammonia and methane.

The flaw in Titan was too damned many people.

I should have said that. I should tell him that—with exactly those words.

He opened his mouth to speak, but A'Lars cut him off.

"I don't know what failure of mine led you to this pass," his father said, his voice bitter and harsh, "but rest assured I will not allow you to infect our world with your fantasies of blight and rescue. No doubt you imagine that your 'discovery' will change people's perceptions of you. You see yourself as a hero, yes?"

Thanos looked down at the floor. A part of him, yes, imagined the relief and gratitude that would be his reward for his discovery. But that mattered little compared to the discovery itself.

"Father," he protested, "my math is impeccable. Data do not lie. Here." He picked up a ChIP, on which he'd encoded all his research and data. "Take this. Examine it yourself. You'll see that I am..."

To his shock, A'Lars slapped the ChIP from Thanos's hand. "Your bravado," he scoffed, "is outstripped only by your hubris, Thanos. To think that you could perceive what I have not? What the others who run our world have not?" A brief, fragile laugh spurted from between A'Lars's lips. "Speak of this to no one, and count yourself fortunate that you've embarrassed yourself before only me, not the public."

"You would rather die than face the truth?" Thanos was incredulous.

"That's a false dichotomy. I don't have to choose between the two. Truth is objective and eternal, Thanos. It lives on independent of us."

"Cold comfort from a grave."

With a noncommittal grunt, A'Lars turned to leave, pausing for a moment at the door to look back. "And rest assured that we will still have a conversation about the appropriate punishment for your visit to your mother."

Thanos stood perfectly still and expressionless until the door slid shut on his father, leaving him alone again.

And then he cried out with pain and frustration and embarrassment, lifted his desk with his bare hands, and hurled it against the wall. It crashed with a resounding thud and a tinkle of glass, split almost down the middle but still intact. So he hefted it and swung it against the wall, this time satisfied as the desk splintered into pieces, crumbling in his hands.

He turned his ire on the rest of the furniture in the room, and by the time he was done, there was not an intact item left. His room had become a junkyard of bent, broken, and crushed metal, glass, and plastic. Every step brought the satisfying crackle of something breaking even further under his foot.

His back to a wall, Thanos sank to a sitting position, staring straight ahead. From above, the lights—damaged during his rampage—flickered, raising and killing shadows all around him. He did not move, but the random bursts of light made the room itself seem to shift and jitter in his orbit. He was at the center, the fulcrum, the focus, as light and dark played and warred. Steeped in darkness, exposed in light, he was the same. Resolute.

And he was right.

He was *right*. He knew it to be true. He could see the end of Titan, the death of everything that lived in his world, and even his own father was too blind to see it.

A pile of wires and scraps of metal rested next to him. Absently, he brushed it aside with one sweep of his hand.

Beneath, a ChIP glimmered at him in the failing light. Thanos plucked it from the debris surrounding it and slid it into the port on his wrist. Data streamed to his headgear. It was the ChIP he'd meant for A'Lars, a copy of all his data.

Our world is dying. So slowly that no one can see it.

He sat there for hours, triple-checking his math, then quadruple-checking it. A part of him yearned to be proven wrong, to find a mistake, even a simple one, one that a child would see. Anything at all. He wanted so desperately to be wrong, to submit to self-mockery, to have to debase himself by going to A'Lars and saying those dreaded words: *Father, I was wrong, and you were right.*

But no matter how much he looked and calculated and recalculated, he could not find a flaw in his thinking or his conclusions.

Titan was doomed.

The fall of his race was inevitable.

He ejected the ChIP and sighed heavily. Inevitable. Nature would take its course. The people of Titan could stave it off as long as possible with their technology, but in the end, death would ride through the Eternal City and dim its lights to utter blackness.

Inevitable.

He drifted off to sleep, thinking that word. It echoed in his mind, a sickening lullaby.

As he awoke unknowable hours later, his head jerking up from his chest, he thought, *Inevitable . . . but not unstoppable.*

There was a way. The inevitability was a predicted outcome that relied on no one doing anything. On the present course of Titan remaining unchanged.

But there was a principle of physics that decreed that the more accurate the determination of a particle's direction, the less accurate the determination of its momentum, and vice versa. That the very process of observing, of sending photons to ricochet off the particle in the first place, inevitably—*inevitably*—changed either the direction or the momentum, making it impossible to ascertain both to the same degree of accuracy.

He was the photon, he realized. Titan's fate *could* change. Because he was observing it. Which meant that he could do something to change it.

He would do more than identify the problem; he would *solve* it. And when he brought a solution to A'Lars, then—finally—his father would listen.

He summoned a brace of androids from the storage room. "Clean this up," he told them, "and install a new interface desk."

They beeped and chirped happily as they set about their tasks. Thanos watched them work; unless he succeeded, when the end came, they would be all that would survive.

CHAPTER VII

A DAY LATER, HE FOUND HIMSELF IN A CORRIDOR OUTSIDE Gwinth Falar's residence. She shared quarters with her family—two parents, four siblings, two married relations, a niece, and two nephews. The corridor was crowded with commuters leaving their own domiciles for the day; Thanos was an unwelcome intrusion into their routine. Snarls and complaints thickened the air in his wake.

"I apologize for abandoning you the other night," he told Gwinth when she commed him from the security camera. "You inspired me to do something I had been putting off for many years." He paused, considering for a moment not telling her what he'd done, but then discarded the idea. She needed to know. "I saw my mother for the first time since my birth. You gave me the courage to do that. You inspired it."

The door slid up an instant later, as though she'd been waiting just beyond it for exactly those words. Her expression mingled shock and sorrow and something else that it took him a moment to identify, so unfamiliar was it to him:

Compassion.

"You saw your mother?" Like everyone on Titan, she knew that Sui-San had been locked away.

"After a fashion," he conceded, stretching out his hand to

her. "I meant to come back to you right away, but ... something intervened. Something enormous. Will you walk with me?"

Her hesitation did not offend him. It was only sensible, and in any event, it wasn't long. She took his hand. "Of course."

He led her to the outskirts of the Eternal City, close to the edge of the safe terraformed zone. The foothills of the cryovolcanoes were smooth and peaceful. Deep beneath, cryomagma burbled and crackled with cold.

"We're all going to die?" she said when he finished explaining his epiphany to her.

"All that lives, dies," he told her. "The catastrophe my model predicts relies on a broad array of variables, but it *will* occur. It could be next month. Or it could be as long as ten generations from now."

"Ten generations..." Gwinth murmured.

"By which point you and I will have been long dead anyway. But, yes, everything we see here"—he gestured to the sweeping skyline of the Eternal City—"will be gone, and everyone within no more than dust. Unless we act."

Her eyes searched his features as though they held the answer. "You can save us?" she asked at last.

"I believe I can. The question is, should I? The cataclysm is enormous; the price to be paid to stop it cannot be small."

"We're talking about the survival of our entire species, our way of life," Gwinth told him. "You have to do it. You have to do whatever it takes, Thanos. Save Titan."

He paused, then bent to her and kissed her. The connection was still there. It wasn't a fluke or a side effect of his first kiss. It was real and it was pounding in his heart like blood.

Yes. Yes, *this* was worth the price, any price, to save.

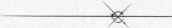

Thanos approached his father not with fear or dread but rather with certainty. Certainty that A'Lars would reject him once again. He knew that his father had no love for him and little respect, yet some intractable filial impulse compelled him to give his father one more chance to be a part of the solution that Thanos knew could save the world.

"Father, I would like to speak with you," he said, standing at the door to A'Lars's cogitarium. "It is a matter of some urgency."

After several seconds, the response came through the comm mounted next to the door. "Is the world about to end?" A'Lars said with some asperity.

Thanos chose to treat the question as genuine, not rhetorically sardonic. "Eventually, yes. Not in the near term, I believe."

There was no rejoinder. No scoffing. No scorn. A'Lars simply said nothing more.

Thanos waited at the door for close to an hour, but his father did not speak, nor did he emerge.

And so Thanos took matters into his own hands.

Holograms were simple manipulations of photons. And sound was merely the vibration of air molecules. Transmitting a fully audible hologram had been perfected long ago. It was science so simple that few people even thought of it as science any longer. It was just part of life.

Thanos needed something a little more robust than the typical hologram, though. He needed to broadcast to every person who lived on Titan, in a way that could not be ignored.

If A'Lars would not take him seriously, then he would put his ideas into the hands of the entire population. Let them take action while his father sat safely ensconced behind the doors of his study, planning the next MentorPlex that would only stave off the catastrophe he didn't even believe in, and doing nothing to stop it.

Thanos developed a hologram of himself that was a hundred meters tall, with a series of photonic refractor particles that would make the hologram appear to be facing whoever was looking at it. His appeal would be personally directed to every individual in the Eternal City. He considered using a different image, perhaps even that of his father. But that would be a fraud. He was about to communicate a great and horrible truth to his people; he could not open with a lie.

He had data that indicated precisely when the greatest number of people were outdoors. He generated the hologram at that time, projecting it via a series of gliding androids such that it loomed over the City. At first it did nothing, merely "stood" in midair. It didn't take long for people to notice, for skycars to drift through it and pause, causing worse traffic congestion than was usual in the skyways.

From buildings and from the street, from vehicles and from rooftops, the people of the Eternal City looked up, and when Thanos was certain he had the attention of as many Titans as possible, he allowed his hologram to speak its message.

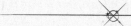

"I am Thanos, son of A'Lars and Sui-San. My people, my fellow Titans, I greet you with great love and with greater fear. Our world is imperiled, and we must act boldly to save it.

"We are—by every measure that matters—a great people. We have conquered the wilderness of Titan and bent it to our will. We have raised mighty structures, tamed the cryovolcanoes, built monuments of art and science and achievement.

"And it will all be for naught. For we are doomed."

He proceeded to recite a series of statistics about arable land, recyclable water volumes, death rates, and birth rates. He spoke briefly about pathogens and disease. With a collection of holographic charts and graphs, he explicated the rapid diminution of the metal ore that would be needed to continue to construct enough MentorPlexes to house the burgeoning population.

"MentorPlexes II and III," he pointed out, *"will be at capacity on the day they open. And still an estimated six hundred thousand Titans will live in constrained quarters. We literally cannot build fast enough to house everyone, and even if we could, we would run out of necessary materials and food before we finished.*

"Everything we do to stave off the threat only contributes to the weakening of our environment and increases the chances that the variables will line up sooner rather than later. We are shoveling dirt out of a hole, not aware that every shovelful rains back down on us and threatens to bury us. We live in a graveyard. We just haven't interred ourselves yet.

"I don't want this to be true. I don't want any of it to be true, but I am a slave to fact and truth and science.

"The conclusion is inescapable, my friends. We face darkness and apocalyptic disaster if we do nothing. However, there is a way out.

"My proposition is simple, so I will be brief: I submit that in order to stave off this inevitable catastrophe, we voluntarily euthanize roughly fifty percent of our current population. This population reset will ensure that our species has the time and motivation to adjust our way of life—it is too late to prevent this catastrophe without drastic measures, but it will not be too late to prevent the next one.

"In the interests of objective fairness, I have developed a

perfectly random selection algorithm that will choose our proud martyrs without bias as to class, age, deportment, or creed.

"Furthermore, in a show of absolute faith in the rightness of my conclusions, I have hard-coded a single Titan into the algorithm, one who will be auto-selected to be put to death. That person is, of course, me. I am happy to die for the greater good, for the sanctity and salvation of our future generations. If nothing else does, let this be proof of my urgency and sincerity.

"I have devised an exceedingly humane method of painless euthanasia," he went on. *"No one need suffer. We are not monsters.*

"According to my math, this solution will guarantee a safe and prosperous Titan for a thousand more generations. Consider the lives that will come into being, secure in the knowledge that the sacrifice of their ancestors—us—has guaranteed them safety, stability, and well-being into the foreseeable future."

The hologram paused here, long enough for the message to sink in.

"A small price to pay," Thanos said to his world. *"A small, sensible price to pay to warrant our future."*

CHAPTER VIII

ODDLY, GWINTH DID NOT RESPOND WHEN HE TRIED TO CALL her. According to her personal beacon, she was online and available, but she did not answer his hail. She was the first person he thought to contact after his message was delivered.

(It was technically still being delivered—he'd set the hologram to repeat itself every half hour for four hours, just to be sure the message sank in.)

Sitting in his room, controlling the broadcast from his interface desk, Thanos had no idea of the reception to his announcement in the Eternal City. When he called Sintaa, his friend only said, anguished, "What have you done? What have you *done?*" and then signed off, leaving Thanos with the echo of Sintaa's terror and the afterimage of the haunted expression on his face.

Thanos emerged from the MentorPlex into a quieter world than he'd ever known. The usually crowded streets were now empty of passersby. Had everyone retreated to their houses to discuss his plan? That would make sense.

Overhead, his hologram recited its dirge. He was pleased and slightly unnerved to find that his photon-refraction technique had worked—the hologram seemed to be addressing him directly. His own visage, several stories tall, stared at him. So strange.

He proceeded to Gwinth's home. He rang and rang, and eventually she opened the door. Tears streamed down her face, blurring the pristine, painstakingly placed green-dotted pattern makeup she wore.

"How *could* you?" she whispered before he could say anything.

"How could I?" he asked. "What do you mean?"

Her eyes widened. "Thanos! Thanos, have you lost your mind?"

He gave the matter a moment's consideration. "Not at all. I'm fine." He took her hands in his. They were limp and lifeless. "Is something wrong?"

Jerking her hands out of his grasp, she took a step back. "Is something wrong? Is something *wrong*? You *have* lost your mind! How could you *do* that?" She flung a hand out behind her, where he could see—through a window in the apartment—his hologram.

"I…" He paused, licked his lips, thought carefully. "I'm doing exactly what you told me to do, Gwinth."

With a glare, she raked her fingers through her close-cropped hair. "What *I* told you to do?"

" 'We're talking about the survival of our entire species,' " he quoted her, " 'our way of life. You have to do it. You have to do whatever it takes, Thanos. Save Titan.' "

Horrified, she took another step back. "Not *this*. Not *this*!"

"Whatever it takes," he told her. "It's the only way. Don't you think I considered all possibilities? Don't you think I would have exhausted every possible methodology before suggesting something so radical? We can't leave the planet—the effort required to construct the necessary fleet would exhaust resources even more quickly and just hasten the—"

"Listen to you!" she shouted. "This is all just *science* to you! But it's people's lives!"

He blinked rapidly. Hadn't she been listening to him? "Yes. Lives I'm going to save. Well, half of them."

She covered her mouth with her hands, tears flowing afresh, and stepped fully inside, letting the door slide shut between them.

No matter how much he thumbed the entry button, and even when he mimicked Sintaa and banged at the door with his fists, she did not answer.

He tried Sintaa next.

"You have to take it back," his best friend said in a slow, careful tone. "You have to recant. Immediately."

They sat in the antechamber of Sintaa's house, the small receiving room just adjacent to the living quarters. Out of deference to Sintaa's family, they kept their voices low, though even the soft volume of his friend's voice could not belie the urgency of his words.

"Recant? I said nothing false. Everything I said is empirically true."

Sintaa groaned and leaned back, hands on knees. "Thanos, no one cares about your empirical truth. Have you seen the reports? After your broadcast, there were *riots* in the Eternal City! Panic-driven. People fled to their homes. Accident rates quadrupled. There are reports of suicides. *Suicides*. Do you know the last time there was one suicide in the Eternal City, to say nothing of multiples?"

Thanos actually did know, and he opened his mouth to tell Sintaa, but his friend cut him off with a gesture. "You have to recant. Say it was a really bad practical joke. Or say you've rechecked your math and you were wrong."

"I will do no such thing. I will not lie."

Sintaa shook his head. "Then at least rescind this euthanasia plan of yours. Tell people you'll come up with a better way."

"There is no better way. I've expended considerable time and thought on this, and my plan is the only one guaranteed to work."

"Then do something that's *not* damned guaranteed!" Sintaa exploded, rising up, the cords of his neck rippling as he screamed. "You can't just say you're going to kill half the planet!"

Thanos considered this. "But I did."

Sintaa swallowed with difficulty, as though his throat had to choke down words. "I think you should leave, Thanos."

"But—"

"There's nothing else for me to say to you."

"I thought we were friends."

Nodding slowly, Sintaa pursed his lips. He looked down at his feet and took a great deal of time before he finally spoke:

"Would you kill me if your algorithm dictated?"

Thanos tilted his head to one side. It was an odd, almost childish question. He turned it over in his mind for a moment, in case he had missed some sort of subtle nuance. But there was none.

"Of course," he told his friend. "I'm going to kill myself, too, Sintaa."

Sintaa nodded again, this time with his jaw clenched. He looked up at Thanos, his eyes glimmering and burning at the same time. "Go home, Thanos. There's nothing more to say."

On the way home, news spikes came through his personal receiver. Twelve hundred had died in the riots and five times that number were injured in the wake of Thanos's broadcast. At home, he sat in darkness for a full six hours, thinking.

He had lived with the knowledge of Titan's impending destruction for many days. He had steeped himself in the data. As a result, he was somewhat immune to its impact. He hadn't calculated the possibility that the mere knowledge of the catastrophe to come would have repercussions of its own.

"Twelve hundred dead." A'Lars had appeared in Thanos's

doorway and was not bothering to conceal his abject fury. Thanos had never seen his father struggle so with emotion. A'Lars almost always was able to control himself, to keep his feelings bottled up, letting slip only the disgust and annoyance engendered by his son. Now, though, his full rage was on display, his complexion mottled, his face twisted into a rictus of ferocity.

"Twelve hundred! You claim to love this world, Thanos, and you just killed twelve hundred of your fellows! What do you have to say to that?"

Thanos thought for a moment. He thought about the future generations that would never draw breath, of the children yet unconceived who would never be born, of the end of Titan.

It was all too easy to imagine. He could see it in his mind's eye, hear the cries of the dying, the mourning of those left behind just long enough to feel regret.

"Twelve hundred," he said. "Twelve hundred souls. Statistically insignificant. Not nearly enough to have the ripple effect of my plan to save Titan. We'll still need to eliminate half the population."

A'Lars uttered a wordless cry.

"I have larger concerns than a mere twelve hundred lives," Thanos said equably. "I am trying to save millions and, going forward, billions. I cannot be held responsible for what happened. I explained myself in simple terms. No one listening should have panicked."

"Listening?" A'Lars fumed. "*Listening?* You intruded on people's lives. You projected a…They saw a great monster bestride the City, promising to murder half of them. What result did you expect?"

"I suppose I expected them to react with reason and compassion, not base animal instinct."

His father took a step back, the anger on his face rewritten into a sort of quiet horror.

"We thought your mother was the Mad Titan," A'Lars said in a voice barely above a whisper. "But I see now that this was false. *You* are, Thanos. Your mind is as warped as your appearance. Your thoughts are as deviant as your flesh."

Thanos cleared his throat and stood, pulling himself to his full height. He clasped his hands behind his back and leaned in, towering over A'Lars.

"And what, Father, do you plan to do about it?"

To his credit, A'Lars did not flinch when he answered.

CHAPTER IX

---◦---

CRIME ON TITAN WAS NEARLY NONEXISTENT. THERE WAS NO such thing as capital punishment and no facility that could hold someone of Thanos's strength and intelligence.

So the people of Titan decided on the most direct solution: exile.

Not exile from the Eternal City. No.

Exile from the *planet*.

And so at the age at which Titans usually ventured out into their great society to discover themselves and their individual destinies, Thanos was cast not into the world but rather *from* it.

SPACE

The universe is not infinite. It merely pretends to be so.

CHAPTER X

THE SHIP WAS NAMED *Exile I* BY THOSE WHO'D PUT HIM in it.

Thanos rechristened it *Sanctuary*.

CHAPTER XI

HE ALLOWED HIMSELF A SINGLE LOOK BACK ON HIS HOME-world as the ship breached the outer atmosphere and exploded into the star-pocked black of space. Titan's atmosphere, a thick, unyielding organonitrogen fog, appeared orange from space. The Eternal City, swallowed by the haze, was invisible to the naked orbiting eye. Thanos told himself that everything he knew lurked beneath that haze, and then he told himself that it didn't matter.

The ship's autopilot had been set to send him into the inner solar system, to worlds considered habitable places for one such as he. That was the safe course, the reliable choice. But he had no desire to be safe or reliable.

They could banish him from Titan, but beyond that they could not claim his destiny. For the first time in his life, Thanos was free. Trapped in a tiny spaceship with few resources, yes, but free of second-guessing, free of hatred, free of fear and disgust.

Free of love. Of the need for it.

There was no one to love in *Sanctuary* except himself, and Thanos had better things to do with his time.

The ship was tiny, essentially an oversize coffin grafted onto a sublight engine. Aimed into the inner orbits of the solar system, it had just enough speed and power to get him to one of the allegedly habitable worlds closer to the local star.

He hacked the autopilot immediately.

Every last atom in his being yearned to turn the ship around and head back to Titan, but that would only delay his exile, not end it. They would just fire him off into space again.

If he headed inward, he would land somewhere within the solar system, somewhere primitive and raw and lacking the technology needed to eventually return and save Titan. He would be stuck.

But if he headed *out* of the solar system, away from the sun, there was an entire universe of possibilities. A panoply of worlds. A menagerie of races and species. Somewhere out there, he would find the help he needed. He would find a way to return to Titan and save his people despite themselves.

Sanctuary was not designed for interstellar travel. Built to carry him a few light-minutes away, it had limited fuel and only enough food and water for a month.

He told the autopilot to plot a course to the Kree home-world, Hala, the closest civilization he could identify. Proud, militaristic, the Kree possessed the technology and the know-how he needed. Titans were brilliant, but isolated. Conflict accelerated science, and the Kree had years of experience at war. They had armies and fleets of ships. Everything Titan lacked. He would return to Titan with an army at his back, if necessary. Whatever it took to convince his people to listen.

When the time came, he would figure out how to persuade the Kree to help him. For now, it would suffice to get there.

There was not enough power in the engines to make it to Hala, so he rerouted power from all other systems, including life support. The temperature in *Sanctuary* quickly dropped to below freezing. Thanos fought off the urge to shiver, and instead he closed his eyes and meditated himself into a trance state.

Dimly, as though from a far-off distance (although it was from a speaker ten centis from him), he heard the synthetic voice of the autopilot counting down to the maximum fuel burn he'd programmed. The course was plotted. The ship would do the rest.

By the time the engines flared and *Sanctuary* lurched to life, blasting its way out of the solar system, Thanos had already meditated himself into a coma. He never saw the beauty of the stars blurring by as *Sanctuary* ferried him out of the solar system and into the galaxy beyond.

And he dreamed.

He dreamed of *her*. She came to him. She touched him. She told him what to do.

Remember when you wake, she told him. *Remember what I have told you.*

I will, he promised, but even in the dream, he knew that

he would not. He knew that he would awaken and forget, that he would fail at so rudimentary a chore.

And yet he promised anyway. In the dream, he imagined the memory was a physical thing, and he clung to it, holding it tight, swearing never to let it go.

CHAPTER XII

"'E'S A BIG 'UN, HE IS!"

A voice swam into the darkness and the silence. Thanos tried to turn his head toward it but couldn't move.

"Truth, not lie!" said another voice. "Not lie! Truth!"

"Aye, an' sure!" said the first.

Hands on him. At his neck. Something solid and heavy clicked into place there. Thanos struggled up, kicking against the tide of his self-induced coma. He tried to open his eyes, but they wouldn't cooperate.

"Big an' alive," said the first voice.

"Alive and big!" agreed the second.

Thanos lost his fight against the dark. It swallowed him whole.

When he at last opened his eyes, he thought first of his dream. He remembered *her*, remembered her whisper in his ear, her admonition to *remember*. And he recalled with perfect clarity his own certainty that he would not remember, that his memory would fail him.

It had. He could not remember what she had told him.

This all occurred to him in the instants between opening his eyes and his vision clearing from the blur of his long sleep. He lay on a bed, an old-fashioned affair that actually rested on a floor. Blankets—blankets!—swaddled him, rather than the comfort of a heat field.

This was not the Kree homeworld, he realized immediately. The Kree possessed far better technology and comfort than this.

Sitting up, a wave of nausea and vertigo overcame him, sending his head spinning and then crashing back down onto the pillow.

Remember, she had told him. *Remember*.

But he couldn't. He remembered setting the autopilot, inducing his own coma so he could survive on limited life support. He remembered the dream in exquisite detail except for that one damned part!

He clenched a fist. In his weakened state, it drained him but felt good nonetheless.

"'e's awake!" said a now-familiar voice. "Big 'un's awake!"

"Awake and big, now! Big and awake!"

And then a third voice: "So he is. On both counts."

Thanos lifted his head from the pillow again, this time slowly. The world spun, blurred, then resolved itself.

The chamber in which he found himself was dirty. The walls, made of metal, were pocked with patches of dull red rust. Light came from a single glowing orb overhead that occasionally pulsed dark just long enough to cause his eyes to adjust, then readjust to the return of brightness.

A wheeled cart, one leg bent such that the whole thing appeared ready to kneel, stood off to one side, and by it stood a tall, slender biped with orange skin and pointed ears. His face was fleshy, the mouth wide and generous, and his eyes were round and yellow. He was bare-chested; he wore only a belted green kilt and boots and a collar no doubt similar to the one Thanos had felt snapped around his own neck. He had an easy grin, which was both comforting and terrifying at the same time; Thanos wasn't accustomed to anyone being happy to see him.

Standing by a door was another biped, this one with green-pocked white skin, sunken cheeks, and a thatch of patchy brown hair. Thin to the point of emaciation, he wore rags for clothes, along with a metal collar. On his shoulder perched a creature that resembled nothing so much as a gray blob of protoplasm merged with the top half of a hawk. Its wings and body melted into gray sludge on the man's shoulder, clinging there like stubborn snot.

"I'm Cha Rhaigor," the orange one said in a pleasant voice. "How do you feel? Other than almost dying from asphyxiation, explosive decompression, starvation, hypothermia, and thirst, that is?"

Thanos groaned as he sat up in bed. "You are a doctor?"

Cha Rhaigor chuckled. "No. But I have some medical experience, which qualifies me on this ship."

"Ship?" He'd set *Sanctuary* to go into orbit and broadcast a distress call once it arrived at the Kree homeworld. "I'm on a ship? What ship? How did I get here?"

"You got lucky, 's how," chimed in the bedraggled one. His pet immediately responded, "Truth! So truth! Lucky! Lucky!"

Cha Rhaigor glanced back at them and shrugged. "They're not wrong. Your ship was on a collision course with ours. We almost disintegrated it, but His Lordship didn't want to spare the blaster power. So instead we sent out an EVA crew to knock it off course. They picked up your life signs aboard and brought you in."

"And where is my ship now?"

Cha looked back at the others. "Demla?"

Demla's eyes lit up. "Prolly 'bout twelve light-months thataway," he said, hooking a thumb over his shoulder.

"Twelve! Thataway! Maybe thirteen!" the odd bird-thing croaked.

Thanos decided that his first act upon standing erect again would be to throttle the annoying bird-thing.

His second act would be to use this ship to arrive at his destination. It was owed to him, given that they'd left *Sanctuary* adrift in space.

"How far am I into Kree space? How far from their homeworld?"

Cha laughed. "Kree space? Is *that* where you thought you were going? You missed by quite a bit."

Thanos did not readily sulk, but he brooded quite well. He sat alone in the medical bay after Cha and Demla and the bird-thing left, mulling over what he'd been told.

He was hundreds of parsecs from the Kree homeworld, nearly starved and wearing around his neck the same tight gray collar he'd seen on Demla and Cha. It resembled images he'd seen of ancient shock collars. No doubt it was designed to harm or kill him if he attempted to remove it. He knew almost nothing about the ship on which he was recuperating, except its name: the *Golden Berth*. Judging by the medical bay, it was an aspirational name that had fallen well short of its goal.

He'd missed Kree space entirely. "There's a new black hole out by the Arthrosian Cluster," Cha had explained. "Maybe it wasn't on your nav charts? Your autopilot wouldn't have compensated for the gravity well, so it dragged you off course."

Thanos had considered this for a moment, and then Cha had put a hand on his shoulder and said, "Sleep, my friend. All things move us forward, even our mistakes."

My friend, Cha had said. No doubt it was meant to be comforting, but the familiarity had only surprised and bemused Thanos. He was not used to being considered a friend so readily.

Nevertheless, he took the advice and slept. He had lain

near death for too long; his body was depleted; his mind buzzed and made concentration difficult.

After a few days' rest, though, his body felt more robust, and his thoughts came more easily. Cha gave him permission to leave his sickbed, and Demla came to show him around the ship. The bird-thing (it was named Bluko, and it was technically a shift-blot, a semi-sentient creature occasionally found in Rigellian territories, not a bird at all) went with them, of course, parroting Demla. Thanos didn't know which was more vexing—Bluko's echo or Demla's recursive, oblique speech pattern. One of them gave him a headache almost immediately.

He was issued a large gray tunic to wear, along with a pair of boots. The tunic had been white once upon a time—its original color still showed in a few patches at the seams. The boots' soles were worn through; he could feel the floor, cold against his feet, when he walked.

The *Golden Berth* was a wheelship, a curved tube rotating around a central axis, with sixteen spokes that led into and out of the hub. From the look of the corridor Demla led him through, the medical bay was a good indicator of the condition of the ship as a whole. Curved reinforced pulsoglass portholes offered a view outside, but at least a third of them were patched over with a viscous paste to cover cracks that would otherwise suck out the ship's atmosphere into the vacuum. Thanos felt as though every step he took could be the one that rattled something crucial loose and killed everyone on board, including himself.

"She spins sumpin' sumpin' number of times a day," Demla was saying, "usin' central force—"

"Centripetal force," Thanos corrected under his breath.

"—to mimic whatchacall, *gravity*."

"Gravity!" Bluko added. "Weighs us down!"

"Don't rightly understand it all," Demla admitted, "but I ain't bangin' into the ceiling, so I guess it works."

"Sure does!" Bluko burbled.

"Who is *His Lordship*?" Thanos asked. "Cha Rhaigor mentioned such a person. He owns the ship, I assume?"

Demla shrugged. "You'll meet soon enough, s'pose."

"Meet His Lordship! On your knees!" Bluko spat.

Thanos ground his teeth together and essayed a pleasant smile. "Could we make it sooner than 'soon *enough*'?" He had already been delayed too long from his plan to raise help on Hala. Formality and niceties were luxuries he couldn't afford.

Demla shrugged again. "Ain't no harm, I guess."

"On your knees!" Bluko repeated.

They made their way through one of the spokes, passing many other aliens on their way. None of them made eye contact for more than a few moments (those with eyes, at least), and most seemed not to bother evincing any sort of interest in Thanos. Even in the tight, cramped confines of the ship, where his size was, if anything, more a liability than in the Eternal City, Thanos felt...

Comfortable.

Here, in this motley crew of aliens, he finally blended in. Each of them wore a collar like the one around Thanos's neck.

At the wheelship's hub was His Lordship's collection of chambers. Demla led him into a large, open room that served as a sort of throne room, apparently. It was dimly lit and in the same state of disrepair as the rest of the ship, which told Thanos that whatever His Lordship might be, *wealthy* did not apply.

His Lordship sat, appropriately enough, upon a throne made of junk. Thanos recognized a chair leg jutting out from one side, a lightspeed drive's inertial dampener (burned out) as part of the seat, and more broken pieces of debris welded together to form the ugliest, rustiest throne imaginable. The man was a study in contrasts, draped in a luxurious red velvet cloak that covered an old set of overalls and a dirty smock. He was tall and gaunt, with spare flesh hanging from his jaw and neck, as though he'd gone on an unexpected starvation diet. One eye was blue, the other brown.

He was surrounded by a cluster of armed creatures, some of which were humanoid, a few with too many limbs or not enough.

"Ya kneel," Demla muttered from his position on his own knees.

"Kneel!" Bluko chirped loudly.

"The pet's right," said His Lordship in a bored yet pleasant voice. "On your knees," he said, as though tired of the pageantry but resigned to it.

Thanos sized up the situation quickly. He was stronger than anyone in the room, he knew, but there was the matter of their weapons…and of the collar around his neck. Still, it was best to test His Lordship first, he reasoned. Thanos would never again have the element of surprise on his side. He could not overcome His Lordship, but he could show that he would not quietly acquiesce.

Be careful, he told himself. *Don't capitulate, but don't antagonize, either.* "I am unaccustomed to kneeling," he said neutrally.

His Lordship's eyes widened. The blue one turned red and the brown one shimmered a bright white for a moment. "Oh? Unaccustomed? I see. Well, that's understandable. Totally understandable." He tilted his head at the being next to him. "Robbo. Customize him."

A pasty white man with patches of graying facial hair and a monk's tonsure, Robbo strode to Thanos, looked him up and down. Wearing a filthy robe with one pocket torn off, he was two heads shorter than Thanos and weighed possibly half as much. Just when Thanos was thinking how amusing was the idea of this little creature forcing him to kneel, a bright pain flared in the front of his skull, just behind his eyes. The world went a harsh and total white, dimmed, then flared again.

He gasped, rocked back on his heels, grabbed his head in his hands. Everything in him fought against moaning aloud, but it happened anyway; he heard himself groan like a whipped child.

The collar...Pain transmission along his vagus nerve. It was unlike anything he'd ever endured before.

"Strong cuss!" His Lordship commented.

The pain shot through him again, and this time Thanos screamed unselfconsciously and dropped to his knees.

"Better!" His Lordship declared. "Now, was that so bad?"

As Robbo stepped back, Thanos rubbed his temples, kneading away the pain. Tears dripped down his cheeks, wrenched from him.

"Ouch," said His Lordship, pursing his lips. "Psychic spike. Hurts, I'm told. Feels sort of like an ice-cream headache, dialed up to a hundred."

He stood from his makeshift throne and cleared his throat, a juicy, phlegmatic endeavor that concluded with him hawking and spitting a wad of gray sputum. A smallish troll-like alien scuttled to his side and caught the spittle in his hands before it could hit the floor, then raced off through a door.

"Now then," His Lordship said, standing over Thanos, "are you becoming *accustomed* to kneeling? Is this working for you? Because it's a lot more convenient for me, let me tell you." His eyes flashed different colors again—blue to green, brown to black—and then back.

Thanos massaged away the last of the psychic spike and gazed up at His Lordship. From this vantage point, he had a delightful view up the man's nose, twin craggy, hairy caverns glistening with greenish snot. "If my presence is inconvenient for you," Thanos said, "I apologize. I could make your life easier by leaving."

His Lordship's eyebrows shot up, and he clapped his hands with mirth. "Leaving? Did you hear that?" He turned in a circle, holding out his arms as though to gather in his entire entourage. "He wants to *leave*!"

Giggles, chortles, peals of laughter from the crowd. Thanos clenched his jaw, sending ripples through his broad ridged chin.

"And where would you go?" His Lordship asked. "We're deep in the Raven's Sweep. Nearest system is the KelDim Sorrow, and even that's *parsecs* away, and no life-forms, nothing habitable. I guess I could just toss you out an airlock...." He frowned, looking down on Thanos. "Should I toss you out an airlock?"

The answer was easy, but Thanos didn't know how His Lordship would react. He might take a no as a challenge to his own authority and eject Thanos into space just to prove a point.

"That would be a subpar course of events for me," he said in as contrite a tone as he could muster through his frustration.

His Lordship threw back his head and blasted out a series of guffaws that coaxed similar laughter from the others in the room. Thanos noticed that Demla, to his left, was laughing, too, though the amusement didn't reach his eyes. Bluko had—somehow—gone to sleep.

"Subpar!" His Lordship howled. "I bet! I bet you...Say, what's your name, Subpar Course of Events?"

"Thanos."

"Thanos." His Lordship dragged it out, tasting the name on his tongue as it slipped through his lips. "And you must be from the planet of the purple people, eh?"

"No. Titan," Thanos pronounced.

"Can't be. No purple people on Titan. Some lovely shades of ecru, and a lass I knew once who was the most spectacular blue. Azure, even. No, no, more like *cerulean*. But no purple people."

"I am...an exception."

His Lordship grunted noncommittally and shrugged. "Whatever. Let me explain how your life works now, Thanos of Titan. You are aboard the vessel the *Golden Berth*, and like all aboard this ship, you are my chattel person. Now, I know what you're thinking: *Slavery is outlawed in most civilized regions of the galaxy!* And you're right. It is. But this is not slavery. It's...it's..." He paused, snapping his fingers. "Robbo! What's that phrase, the one I keep forgetting?"

"Indentured servitude, my lord."

"Yes!" His Lordship tapped his fists together, and his blue eye went a bright orange for a few seconds. "Indentured servitude! That's it. Thank you. And how much have we spent on Thanos here, Robbo?"

"Eight thousand two hundred seventy-four yargblats, my lord. And sixteen twillum. For retrieval, medical care, food."

The monetary units were nothing Thanos had ever encountered before.

"Eight thousand!" His Lordship clutched his chest as though suffering a bout of angina. "So much money for so little reward! So much money, and all I get is *lip!*"

He lashed out with his staff at that moment, catching Thanos on the right side of his face. His Lordship was tall but scrawny. Thanos read the room and pretended that the blow rocked him to one side.

Breathing hard from his exertion, His Lordship drank in the hooting applause of those in the assemblage. Demla clapped weakly, an apologetic look on his face. Bluko stirred long enough to crow.

Thanos resisted the urge to rise up and put his hands around His Lordship's neck and squeeze until the man's head snapped off. Other than the synth he'd "killed," he had, as far as he could remember, never once in his life raised a hand in violence, but His Lordship was sorely testing that trend after only a few minutes.

Although...There had been the one time. When he'd thought of striking his father...

Is this my fate, then? To turn from a creature of thought and reason into a creature of base instinct and violence?

"We spent all this money on you!" His Lordship was saying, now pacing and gesticulating wildly. "The exo-ship extraction! The medical attention! The clothes you're wearing! All of it, from me, due to my largesse and my kindness!

All I ask in return is that you be polite and that. You. Pay. Me. Back!"

He punctuated those last words with repeated blows to Thanos's head and shoulders with the staff. They weren't terribly powerful, but Thanos feigned injury and collapsed to the floor.

The collar. If not for the collar… "I apologize for my spiritedness," Thanos said through gritted teeth. He had no desire to fawn over this absurd simpleton, but for now the best strategy was to play along. He looked at Robbo, the one with the control for the collar.

If I could only…

His Lordship held up a finger to call time-out, then bent over, gasping and wheezing from his exertion. A thick stream of snot and phlegm lurched from between his lips and hung there, too heavy to retract, but too viscous to break off.

"A little help!" he called.

That same troll-like creature scampered over with a soiled handkerchief and collected the snot, tugging it from His Lordship's mouth. It took more effort than Thanos would have thought.

His Lordship wiped his mouth with the hem of his cloak. "Where was I? Oh yes—pay me back! It's pretty basic. I do you a good turn, you repay me in kind. You will join the rest of this ship in my army, and when we get to where we're going, you'll kill a whole bunch of people for me, and then we're even. Got it?" He didn't wait for an answer. "Great! Glad we had this chat. Since you're feeling better, we'll get you out of the medical bay and doing something useful. Bye!"

The audience was over.

CHAPTER XIII

HE WAS ASSIGNED DANK, CRAMPED QUARTERS WITH CHA Rhaigor. The room was so small that Thanos's head bumped the ceiling when he stood fully erect, and if he strained slightly, he could touch two opposing walls at both ends of the room at the same time.

Cha eyed Thanos's bulk and sighed. "You can have the lower bunk."

The room carried a floral scent that Thanos could not identify, which made sense, given that he'd never left Titan before and Cha had never been to Titan. Cha hailed from the Sirius system. There were a dozen worlds orbiting that star, and Cha called them all home. His people were peripatetic, roaming the universe in search of students for their distinct flavor of pacifistic philosophy. He was a skilled medic doing his best to survive and help as many as he could under conditions that could most charitably be described as *deplorable*. Thanos could not help comparing him to the only other true friend he'd ever had, Sintaa. They could not have been more different. Cha was contemplative and quiet where Sintaa had been gregarious and boisterous. Sintaa had a big, ready smile, while Cha tended more toward a pleased and subtle grin. And of course, Sintaa had never left the Eternal City, while Cha had spent most of his life on the edge of the galaxy, preaching his philosophies to the barbaric unenlightened.

Thanos could hear the calm sureness in Cha's voice whenever he spoke about his practices—the discipline and peace he wished on all those he met. He quickly learned that Cha meditated at every chance and would expound his philosophies at any opportunity.

"You see, Thanos," Cha said calmly that first evening as they lay in their bunks, "the universe itself can best be imagined as a garden. If we care for the garden, it grows and thrives, and even those areas that are not tended to do better, for they neighbor well-tended plots. The more peace we spread, the more the universe itself responds with peace."

Thanos thought of the word *spread* and gardens and manure. It seemed apt.

And of course the universe was nothing like a garden. The universe was—as best physics could tell—a recurring cyclical spasm of matter and energy that expanded and collapsed on a timescale unfathomable by mortal comprehension. There was no point trying to explain this to Cha.

"There is a rhythm and harmony to the universe," Cha went on. "When they are in tune, life goes well for all beings and there is peace. The reverse is also true, commutatively: when we bring peace, the universe itself is in harmony. The more peace we bring, the more the universe itself provides peace. Don't you just wonder at the splendor of the universe we've been given?"

"I wonder only if this particular sermon might end so I can sleep," Thanos grumbled, then pulled his pillow over his head and tried to sink into the dark of sleep. It took a long time.

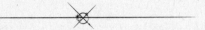

He dreamed.
Of her.
She told him...
He could not remember.

CHAPTER XIV

HE WAS ASSIGNED THE MOST MENIAL OF TASKS—SCRUBBING clean the reinforced pulsoglass that made up the *Golden Berth*'s four thousand one hundred and twelve portholes into the inky, empty blackness of outer space.

He knew how many there were because he counted them as he cleaned them. By the time he got to the last one, the crew of motley aliens and castaways had already dirtied them again, and so he started over.

Roaming round and round the ship's circumference. No beginning. No end. An ignominious fate for Thanos, son of A'Lars, son of Sui-San, putative Savior of Titan. A mind that once developed a perfect, painless, and fair method of killing was now put to the task of wiping windows clean of greenish alien slime that had hardened into a stubbly, pebbly shell.

Sometimes, he needed a chisel. The first two broke.

The one benefit to his task was that it took him all over the ship. Along the way, he met many of his fellow "indentured servants" who had never left their section of the ship. There was an entire family working the galley who were descended from the ship's original cooks and stewards—they'd never ventured farther than the general mess hall. ("My grandfather once brought a meal to His Lordship in his personal quarters," one of the cooks confided in Thanos. "Came back unable to speak. Later, we realized that was because His Lordship had removed his tongue.")

The entire ship was a sealed system, both literally (in the sense that it was spaceworthy) and figuratively (in the sense that pretty much nothing and no one entered or left).

They had their own society here. Their own currency. Their own culture, a hodgepodge of ten thousand different eras and worlds.

Thanos took advantage of his meanderings around the ship. So long as he did his job, no one bothered him. In fact, some of his fellow servants even seemed happy to see him. In short order, he was surprised to find that he felt more welcome and at home on the *Golden Berth* than he had in his entire life on Titan.

In spite of himself, Thanos found himself adapting to the rhythms and tides of life aboard the *Golden Berth*. He began to feel comfortable there, accepted by its low-class buffoons in a way the elites of Titan had never even considered. Much to his surprise, he began to relax, and even his attitude began to take on their loose and decompressed miens. If not for the danger still looming over Titan and the oppressive presence of His Lordship, he might have even begun to enjoy his time on board.

Still, as welcomed as he felt, this motley collection of ragged servants and slightly less ragged sycophants could never measure up to the memory of Titan and its people. He knew that he needed to get off the ship. And then find a way to the Kree Empire, where he could marshal forces to save Titan. It was imperative that he rescue his people from their own blindness and ego, that he force them to see the error of their ways and listen to him.

He needed a plan. He needed a way out.

The first order of business in any plan would have to be removing the shock collar he wore. He tried brute strength to start, gripping the collar tightly and applying all his muscle to it. It had clicked around his throat in two pieces, but nothing he did separated them even a millimeter.

Next, he purloined a medical laser when Cha was distracted in the medical bay. But the laser, designed to cut flesh and bone, had no impact on the metal collar, not even when he modified it to run off a stronger power source.

He was unaccustomed to failure. He'd never really had to plan beyond his initial impulses, letting his intellect guide the way to success. Now he was up against the limits imposed on him by circumstance, and it galled him.

He considered storming the control room, turning the ship around, setting a course for Hala, for Titan, for *anywhere*, really.

But there were loyalists to contend with. And besides, Thanos had no idea how to pilot a ship like the *Golden Berth*.

Lastly, he considered outright escape. Every day, while cleaning, he scoured the ship for signs of life pods or other vessels. For equipment he could use.

Nothing. No ejectables. None of the space suits fit him, and they were all of dubious integrity, in any event.

His Lordship was a dullard and a crank, but he was ineluctably in charge. There was nothing Thanos could do in his current predicament. He knew he had no choice but to play along for the time being.

For the time being.

If there is nothing I can do in my current predicament, then I will have to change the predicament, he realized. *And this will call for drastic measures.*

Night and day had only abstract meanings on a wheelship, but the crew did attempt to simulate them. Unfortunately, given the panoply of worlds from which the crew hailed, no one could agree on exactly how long a night or a day was supposed to be. So sometimes the days would be twenty-four hours long, bisected into day and night. Other times, a night would last thirty hours or more, or a day would go on for a week, or there would be three hours of darkness, followed by sixteen hours of middling, murky dawn, followed by a gray twilight of ten or more hours. It was maddening, until eventually Thanos learned to ignore light and dark altogether.

He was sleeping during an actual period of darkness during his fifth week aboard the *Golden Berth* when something woke him from a deep, dreamless sleep. He lay there in his bunk for a moment, listening, hearing only silence.

But there was something wrong about the silence. Something lurked within it.

An opportunity, perhaps.

"What's happened?" he asked aloud, not expecting an answer.

"The engines have stopped," Cha told him, already awake and sitting upright. "We're adrift."

The silence. He thought of the silencuriums on Titan, but that led him to painful memories of Gwinth and Sintaa, so he shoved his attention back to the present. He'd become as accustomed to the thrum of the engines as to the chill of the metal collar he wore. And now the sound was gone.

There was no atmosphere in space and, thus, no friction to slow and stop the *Golden Berth*. Inertia would keep the wheel turning, though eventually internal pressure would slow it down and gravity would become a memory.

But more important: Without its engines running, there was no way for the ship to accelerate when necessary or to maneuver. It would simply continue at its present course and speed until something got in the way. Like a planet.

Or a star.

Without engines, they'd be unable to resist the gravitational pull of most celestial objects. They would crash. And die.

"I have no intention of dying," Thanos rumbled, swinging his legs out of bed.

"Who said anything about dying?" Cha sat on the upper

bunk, legs crossed, arms extended, palms up. His eyes were closed. He was meditating. "The universe did not put us on this ship and fling us into the void so we could die."

"That sounds like exactly why the universe would put us on this ship and fling us into the void," Thanos pointed out, pulling on his clothes. "You believing your fate is larger than a silent meaningless death does not mean physics will stop working to kill you."

"You don't need to believe in the universe's plans for you, Thanos. The flowers grow regardless."

"A comfort to a man trapped in a rusting hulk of a ship with no way to maneuver," Thanos said, and wrestled open the ancient, malfunctioning door. He managed to slam it shut behind him before Cha Rhaigor could spew out more nonsense. In his time on the *Golden Berth*, Thanos had almost unconsciously come to like Cha; his confidence in the idea of an almost irrationally benign universe, on the other hand, rankled. Most of what Cha attributed to fate or general goodness flew in the face of the logic, reason, and science upon which Thanos had built his life. A regrettable flaw in an otherwise good companion.

He stomped through the corridors. He found the engine room, where Demla stood, scratching his head, peering at a flickering, static-filled readout. The ship was so old that all its controls were two-dimensional—screens and touch pads. No interactive holograms.

Demla was a minor engineering flunky who monitored the engines and was authorized to do no more than bellow for help if anything went wrong. With him was Googa, the chief engineer. As best Thanos could tell, Googa'd gotten the job because he happened to be nearby when the last chief engineer died. His Lordship made do with the resources at hand.

Speaking of His Lordship: He was there as well, standing imperiously in his velvet cloak, bare-chested and wearing a pair of unflatteringly tight underpants. As always, Robbo stood right next to him, ready to use the collar remote to brain-freeze anyone who looked at His Lordship with even the slightest disrespect.

"I don't want a primer on engine physics," His Lordship was saying to a cowering Googa, one eye throbbing through a rainbow of colors. "I just want you to start the engines again. We have hundreds of light-years to go, and it's going to take more than the three centuries I've allotted if we don't have engines. My plan requires meticulous timing. If we're off by a few decades, I have to start all over again."

Googa bobbed his head. "I understand, my lord. But we've run dry. As best I can tell, we're too far from any stars for our solar sails to pick up sunlight."

"Then find some stars!" His Lordship railed. "We're in *space*! It's *filled* with stars!"

"But we're in the Raven's Sweep, my lord! There *are* no stars here."

"'at's why's called the Raven's Sweep," Demla added helpfully.

"No kidding!" screamed Bluko.

"Shut that thing up," His Lordship growled, pointing to Bluko, "or I'll have it shape-shifted into a turd and flushed."

"Flush this—" Bluko began, cut off when Demla slapped a hand over his beak.

"I know why it's called the Raven's Sweep," His Lordship went on. "But there have to be stars *somewhere*. I can see them out the damned portholes!"

"Those stars are too distant for our solar sails to capture any of their energy, my lord." Googa paused. "Please don't kill me."

"Why would I kill you?" His Lordship asked. "You're the only one who understands the engines. Don't be an idiot. You're indispensable." He turned to Robbo. "I'm going back to sleep. If this imbecile doesn't have the engines running in, say, two hours, give him a headache that'll make him piss his pants and wish he had died in the womb."

"Got it," Robbo said as Googa whimpered.

His Lordship turned to leave and did a double take at the sight of Thanos lurking in the doorway. "What are *you* doing here?" he demanded.

Thanos ignored him and directed a question over his shoulder at Googa. "Is the hydrogen scoop functional?" Most vessels that could achieve anything close to the speed of light possessed a hydrogen scoop, designed to gather stray hydrogen atoms from the space before the ship. Space wasn't a perfect vacuum, and at near lightspeed, even an atom could be catastrophic in a collision.

"Com-completely func-functional," the engineer stuttered, flicking a terrified side-eye at His Lordship. "Uh, my lord...?"

His Lordship stroked the loose wattle of flesh hanging from his jawline. "Do you have any other questions, Thanos, or are you just here to banter about hydrogen scoops?"

"I have some thoughts on our predicament," Thanos allowed. "May I?" He gestured to the control board.

Googa swallowed hard and looked over at His Lordship, who nodded. Thanos squeezed his bulk behind the control board.

He studied it for a moment and found himself gesturing in midair for controls that weren't there. After a moment's confusion, he instead tried tapping directly on the screen before him. That worked.

"Huzzah!" His Lordship chortled. "Victory!"

Thanos ignored the jibe and the nervous laughter of the others. He quickly scanned the region, just on the off chance that Googa was an idiot who'd missed something.

Turned out Googa was *not* an idiot, at least not in this matter. There were, in fact, no stars within range. No sane or competent ship's captain would have ordered a trek through the Raven's Sweep without first being certain of having sufficient fuel to get through. His Lordship, obviously, was neither sane nor competent.

Still, His Lordship's fate was inextricably intertwined with Thanos's—for now—so he had no choice but to figure out how to get out of this predicament. Either that or spend the rest of his life drifting aimlessly through the Raven's Sweep.

As he became more comfortable with the machinery at his fingertips, he found it easier to formulate a plan. The *Golden Berth* was ancient and decrepit, but it had enough usable, functioning tech that he began to perceive the outlines of a way forward.

"There are no stars..." he began.

"I salute you, Admiral Obvious!" His Lordship crowed, and then nearly collapsed in a fit of coughing and expectorating. Demla, Googa, and Robbo all rushed to his side.

"No stars," Thanos continued, repressing his glee at the savage wheezing that had cut off His Lordship's mockery, "but there *is* an energy source nearby. A magnetar."

A magnetar was a hyper-dense neutron star that emitted no light but did emit strong magnetic fields. There was one four light-days from their present position. Magnetars did not last long—only about ten thousand years—so they were incredibly lucky that this one was active.

"We can modify the hydrogen scoop," he told them, "to collect gamma radiation. It's a simple enough procedure." The hydrogen scoop not only gathered up stray hydrogen atoms; it also directed them to the ship's internal fusion reactor, where they could be mashed together to create energy.

Googa left His Lordship's side and joined Thanos at the control board. "Well, yeah, but that magnetar isn't emitting any gamma radiation."

"It will," Thanos said. "We can use our defensive shields to create an overlapping series of magnetic pulses that will—"

"Mimic the magnetar's interior magnetic fields!" Googa exclaimed, his excitement growing. He hip-checked Thanos to shove him away from the controls, but Thanos was three times Googa's size and didn't budge.

"The result will be a starquake on the surface of the magnetar, which will throw off massive amounts of gamma radiation. We can capture it and use it to power the ship. But we'll need to have our timing down precisely—the starquake could last as little as ten milliseconds."

Googa pretended to double-check Thanos's math, nodding very seriously and grunting portentously as he skimmed through the numbers on the screen before him. When he was finished, he looked up at His Lordship eagerly.

Meanwhile, His Lordship had managed to recapture his breath and was wiping his lips on the back of his hand. "All I heard," he said, "was *Tech tech the tech to make the tech anti-tech and blah blah blah one one zero one one zero zero zero one.*" He flapped a hand at them. "Don't bore me with petty details. Can you make it work?"

"Yes!" Googa said immediately and enthusiastically.

"Yes," Thanos said a moment later.

"Good." Both eyes turned solid pink for a few seconds, the first time Thanos had seen them match. His Lordship chucked Robbo under the chin. "Kill Googa and bring me Thanos when he's done."

Googa's eyes widened. "My lord! I have served you *urrrrrrk!*" His speech devolved into a long, strung-out syllable as Robbo stepped close to him. Thanos watched dispassionately as Googa clutched his head and sank to his knees, then collapsed altogether at Robbo's feet.

A moment later, Googa's eyes exploded, spraying vitreous humor and blood on the floor.

"S'pose I gotta clean that up," Demla grumbled under his breath.

Thanos watched as Googa's body twitched far longer than he would have thought possible or necessary. Eventually, it stilled.

Robbo sniffed loudly and cracked his fingers. "What are you looking at?" he sneered at Thanos. "Get those engines powered up or expect the same."

He turned on one heel and left. Demla looked over at Thanos and whistled long and low, his eyes wide with disbelief.

A moment later, Bluko whistled, too. Thanos sighed.

CHAPTER XV

——⌒——

WHEN THE DOOR TO HIS LORDSHIP'S PERSONAL DINING
hall slid open, Thanos beheld a long, scarred table with only
one chair at the far end. His Lordship sat there, attended to
by a woman Thanos had never seen before—silvery skin,
pale-yellow hair, a kerchief tied around the lower half of
her face. Robbo shoved past Thanos and took up a position
at His Lordship's right.

"Thanos!" His Lordship boomed with exhilaration. "You
marvelous lavender bastard! I heard the engines start up ten
minutes ago. Have a seat," His Lordship invited, gesturing.

Thanos looked around. There were no other chairs.

"Oh, for Eternity's sake!" His Lordship fumed. "Someone get the man a damned chair! You just made me look
like an idiot!"

Robbo and the woman exchanged a meaningful glance,
then another, and another, clearly each telling the other *You
go!* Finally, the woman exited through another door and
returned a moment later with a fragile-looking chair, which
she brought to Thanos's end of the table and placed there
without so much as a glance in his direction.

"Have a seat!" His Lordship said again, with the exact

same expression and intonation, as if the previous invitation had never happened.

Thanos gingerly perched on the chair. It creaked and complained at his weight.

"Bring us some food," His Lordship commanded, then did a double take when he saw that the woman had already begun serving him.

"Damnit! Wait until I give the command before you start! There's no *point* to the command if you're already doing it!"

"My apologies, my lord," she murmured, bowing her head.

His Lordship shook his head. "You just can't breed good help anymore," he complained. "Five, six generations of them on this ship, and I think they're starting to get inbred. Some of these species aren't biologically compatible with each other—to say nothing of anatomically compatible—so you start the incest train, and that never ends well. Oh well." He shrugged and sampled something from his plate. "Bungling idiots make useful cannon fodder. We're going to need a lot of cannon fodder where we're going."

Thanos wasn't sure if he was supposed to ask a question at this point. The woman had just put a plate before him. The food upon it was gristly and swam in a malodorous gravy that jiggled on its own. Still, it was the most appetizing meal he'd seen since boarding the *Golden Berth*.

"Do you know why I had Googa killed?" His Lordship asked.

"No."

"Because he was useless to me. *You* found the solution, and you were able to execute it. I had no more need for him. I have to run a lean ship, Thanos. Resources are scarce."

The food on Thanos's plate, while vile, was easily equal to five times his typical daily ration. Yes, scarce. Intentionally so. But this was not the time to debate economics with His Lordship.

"Couldn't you have spoken to Googa?" Thanos asked. "Expressed your displeasure in another way and given him a chance at something else?"

"Conversation is all well and good, Thanos, but sometimes only brute force will suffice. I sense you understand this."

No, Thanos did not. His own plan for killing people had been humane and compassionate. He'd developed an alpha wave emitter that would quietly shut down a victim's conscious thought, then disrupt the autonomic nervous system. A quiet, peaceful, painless death. It would have been his own.

It still could be. If he could only return to Titan.

"I am a man in exile, Thanos of Titan," His Lordship was saying as gravy dripped from his lips and slid down his wattles. "You get that?"

"More than you'd think."

"Ha! Ha! Well then, I was exiled from the planet Kilyan about three, four hundred years ago. I lost count at some point."

"Your people must be long-lived."

"I hope so," His Lordship said. "I hope the bastards who kicked me off the planet are still alive when we get there."

"You're going home?" This much Thanos could understand and empathize with.

His Lordship nodded and explained: The plan was simple. He'd liberated the *Golden Berth* from its previous owners a hundred years ago, out by the galactic rim. The ship had been new then, and he'd decided to use it to return to Kilyan, kill those who'd deposed him, and retake the planet.

But Kilyan was far, far away. And he knew that he would be dramatically outnumbered.

"I wasn't terribly popular as a ruler," he admitted.

"I find that hard to believe," Thanos said, careful to keep the mildest trace of irony out of his voice.

"And yet it's true! They didn't appreciate me, Thanos. I let them keep *half* the grain they grew, *half* the livestock they tended! And for my generosity, I was booted off the planet and cast halfway across the universe."

"How did you survive?" Thanos stirred the food on his plate and then, reluctantly, dug in. *Better than usual* was still wretched.

His Lordship waved off the inquiry and kept talking. Once he was back in space and headed home, he realized that he would need an army. Unable to pay one, he decided to fall back on the time-tested method of simply conscripting those he needed. It was working well for him so far.

"So, you provide food and shelter," Thanos began.

"And transportation!" His Lordship admonished. "And a *cause*! Don't forget that, Thanos! A *cause*! I give meaning to the lives of these poor benighted wretches." He belched and drained his goblet. "Present company excepted. You're not a wretch. There's something almost noble about you, Thanos.

"When we get to Kilyan, my army will conquer the planet. And then you'll all have the honor of serving me in my palace. Which is quite nice."

"I see. So, the indentured servitude does not end with the army's victory?"

His Lordship sighed wearily. "Don't be dim, Thanos. Of course not! I'm going to need protection from the people we've defeated. A lot of them will die, but not all. I have to leave *some* alive to rule over, right? Think! Use that misshapen purple thing on your shoulders for something other than supporting that ridiculously huge chin."

"Yes."

"You'll like Kilyan," His Lordship said airily. "The gnat season only lasts a few months, and when the monsoons hit, the sky goes a lovely shade of black for days on end.

"I want you to be part of my inner circle," he went on. "Like Robbo and Kebbi here." He jerked a thumb at the woman by way of introduction. "Run the ship's engines. Keep us going in the right direction. And you'll have a pretty good life when we get to Kilyan."

Thanos said nothing.

"Don't be an idiot," His Lordship said, raising a goblet.

"There's no better offer for a million kilometers in any direction. What do you say?"

What choice did Thanos have? With a grim smile, he raised his goblet as well. "Proud to serve," he said, and drank.

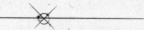

That was his last night in his shared quarters with Cha. The next day, he would be moved to a new chamber, closer to His Lordship.

"Do you think he'll bother telling me his real name?" Thanos mused, lying on the bottom bunk.

From above, Cha responded. "That *is* his real name. Had it changed legally a while back. First name: His; last name: Lordship."

Thanos groaned.

"When you think about it," Cha commented, "it's really not *that* bad." He rolled onto his side and poked his head over the edge of the upper bunk. "Since you're leaving in the morning and I won't see you again—"

"You'll see me. There's nowhere to go."

"—I wanted to ask you one question. May I?"

"You saved my life. You're entitled."

"Titan's a nice place, I hear. Why would you leave?"

With a sigh, Thanos turned away from Cha. "It was not entirely my decision."

"Not entirely?"

"Not at all," he admitted.

Cha whistled lowly. "What did you *do*? To get kicked off Titan?"

Thanos thought for a long time, but in the end, the simplest explanation was also the truest: "I tried to save the world."

This did not faze Cha in the least. "Ah. I see."

"Do you?"

"History is replete with tales of the emissaries of good sense and virtue who were disbelieved in their time, much to the woe of the unbelievers. You will find your just due, my friend. Good things come to those with patience. Flowers grow with time, not immediate gratification."

With a grumble, Thanos spat out, "Spare me. This optimistic, mystical nonsense is an egregious flaw in an otherwise perfectly acceptable friend. Why do you bombard me with this claptrap?"

Cha did not answer for a long time, so Thanos rolled over to face out again. Cha's face peeked out from above, his expression deadly serious.

"Because I believe you, more than perhaps anyone I've ever met, need it," Cha said quietly. "When we came upon you, you were ten seconds away from death."

"Coincidence."

"I have been on this ship for thirteen years. Not once has His Lordship deigned to send a rescue crew to a ship adrift. He usually either has it blasted out of space or avoids it. But he saved you."

"A mere glitch of compassion."

"No, Thanos. Some whisper of goodness spoke to His Lordship and stayed his finger on the trigger. You came on a path to us when you were aimed elsewhere. Perhaps your exile was meant to put this all in motion."

"There is no meaning to it," Thanos said with finality. "The only plan is the plan we are forced to create."

Cha retreated from the edge of the bed, and Thanos heard him settling into the cross-legged position for his evening orisons.

"The glorious thing, Thanos," his voice floated down after a moment, "is this: I know in my heart that your presence here is for a reason. You disbelieve it with equal ferocity, clinging to your rationality and your logic. But no matter how fiercely you believe it, you can never prove me wrong."

Thanos opened his mouth to speak but realized, to his dismay, that he had no rejoinder.

CHAPTER XVI

AND THAT NIGHT, HE DREAMED. THE DREAM OF HIS COMA.
It came to him again.

He dreamed *her*. She came to him. She touched him. She
told him what to do.

Remember when you wake, she told him. *Remember what
I have told you.*

I will, he promised, but even in the dream, he knew that
he had made this promise before and broken it. He feared
that once more he would awaken and forget, that he would
fail at so rudimentary a chore.

This time he did not. This time he awoke with her words
still resonant, still alive. This time was different.

In the morning (what passed for morning aboard the
Golden Berth, in any event), Thanos awoke and lay in his
bunk, blinking up at the bunk above him. He heard, saw,
and felt Cha move above him, vaulting down from his berth
to land on the floor. Still, Thanos lay still.

Cha stretched, yawned, and turned on the water in the little rusty sink they shared. The rust had eaten a hole through,
so they had an old helmet underneath, turned upside down,
to catch the drainage. Cha performed his morning ablutions,
then turned to address Thanos.

"You look awful," Cha said. "Breathe deeply. Find your center."

Thanos gave him a withering glare.

"What are you still doing here?" Cha asked. "I thought you'd be gone and in your new quarters before I even awoke."

"I had a dream," Thanos said slowly, reluctantly. "A recurring dream."

"Such dreams illuminate the underlying structure of the serendipity of the universe," Cha said with great seriousness.

"Stop it."

"No, truly. When you have a dream more than once, that is the universe speaking to you. It's a serious thing, Thanos." Cha crossed his arms over his chest and leaned back against the sink, a perilous feat, given the sink's lack of structural integrity. "Tell me about it."

With a sigh and some effort, Thanos drew his knees up to his chest and rested his forehead against them. The dream... The damned dream...

He was a creature of reason and science, not of intuition and superstition. He knew that dreams were nothing more than the brain's garbage disposal, a way for images, thoughts, and ideas that had gathered in the subconscious mind to be purged. They were nonsense and they were useless, and yet this one... This one seemed different.

"I first had it aboard my ship, when I was in my coma. I dreamed of... someone I once knew."

"Who?"

Thanos ground his teeth. "A woman. Nothing more matters. In the dream, she's dead, yet she speaks to me."

Cha raised an eyebrow.

"She whispered to me. She told me something."

Now Cha stood away from the sink, coming close, kneeling down by Thanos's bunk. "What? What did she tell you?"

And Thanos lied: "She told me to save everyone."

The lie was close enough to the truth. He yearned to return home, to see her again, to make things right.

But he was trapped. And no matter how much he plotted or planned, the collar and the rickety ship and the vacuum that waited outside to kill him stood implacably in his way. For the first time in his life, he could not think his way out of a problem.

"Save everyone," Cha mused. "A noble goal."

And an impossible one, Thanos did not add.

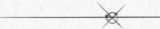

On the first day of his second new life, Thanos passed Demla and Bluko in the corridor on his way to the engine room. Demla offered a jaunty "G'mornin'!" and Bluko cackled madly. Thanos resisted the urge to pulp the shift-blot between his hands. Today, it had taken on the appearance of a throbbing globule of pus, with the mouth of a dog and the ears of a wombat.

"Engines at full," Demla reported. "Off t' break m' fast!"

"Breakfast!" Bluko howled, and Thanos ground his teeth together.

In the engine room, he checked power levels, assessed the state of the fusion reactor, and commenced routine maintenance. All the equipment—every last bit of it, including the maintenance drones—was on its last legs. The entire propulsion system needed a complete overhaul, but there were no resources to perform such drastic upkeep. As best Thanos could tell, the ship's engines had another five years in them. And that was under the most optimistic scenario.

He was beginning to think that Googa had lucked out.

Speaking of Googa—there was a wet stain still glimmering on the underside of the control board. Thanos wiped it off with a resigned sigh. He'd have preferred His Lordship *not* killed Googa, but since Googa was dead, there was no point being sentimental about it. Once someone was dead, what more could one do? His Lordship put it best—Googa had no longer been useful.

He had lied to Cha about his dream. Partly because he was still uncertain about what it meant, but mostly because he had no desire to hear Cha excavate his subconscious for any inane pseudo-significance.

And because far beyond saving everyone, right now he couldn't even conceive of a way to save himself. He would die on this ship, perhaps today, perhaps five years hence, but either way, he would die here, without a way home, without a way to save the people of Titan.

And because...

And because to think of *her*, to see *her*...elicited a very special sort of pain, the sort that was almost indistinguishable from pleasure.

When Robbo came to the engine room to check on Thanos's progress his first day, Thanos took the opportunity to attempt to gain some information about His Lordship's homeworld and the trip there. He had little data to go on, and more data was always good. The more information in his possession, the better he could plan. Were there star charts to show the best route to Kilyan? Was there a map of the local jump gates? Most interstellar travel was performed through jump gates or naturally occurring wormholes. Faster-than-light engines were expensive, fragile, and difficult to maintain. The *Golden Berth's* sublight engines were far more common, though Googa had done poorly at keeping them healthy and running. He'd been chief engineer because his father had been before him, not because of any skill in the area. Thanos suspected—more like, hoped—that he could find a quicker way to Kilyan. The planet didn't sound like much of an improvement over the ship, but it had the benefit of an atmosphere...and not blowing up.

At the mention of star charts, Robbo only chuckled ruefully and shook his head.

"There are charts, but they won't help you."

"Why not?"

Robbo looked around suspiciously. There were other minor functionaries in the engine room, but they were busy scuttling around, patching the ever-rupturing pipes and ductwork.

"Never mind. Forget I said anything." The majordomo wiped a bead of sweat from his upper lip.

"I have a job to do," Thanos pressed him. "I would prefer to do it well."

"We got something here called 'Need to Know,'" Robbo said. "And you don't."

Thanos furrowed his brow. Robbo knew something. More, he *wanted* tell Thanos. It was so obvious. People with secrets longed to reveal them—they only needed justification.

"I am the engineer now. I have to perform the tasks His Lordship wishes me to perform. If you know something that can help..." He trailed off, giving Robbo the opportunity to jump in and spill his guts.

Which is exactly what Robbo was dying to do.

"You're in His Lordship's inner circle now, so I suppose I can tell you..."

"Of course," Thanos encouraged.

"There is no Kilyan." Robbo said it with a combination of relief and sudden shock in himself.

It took Thanos a moment of confused blinking to process

this statement. Even then, all his mighty intellect could produce only a whispered and stunned "What?"

"I mean," Robbo said hurriedly, "there's a *planet*, all right. We passed it about ten years ago. Whole surface was wiped out. Neutron bombs. Buildings still standing, but everything living was dead and gone. Place was so radioactive that if you so much as sneezed in its direction, you'd start losing hair." Robbo patted his own balding pate somewhat nervously.

For the first time in his life, Thanos said the words "I don't understand."

"There isn't much to understand."

"What are we *doing*, then? Where are we going?"

A shrug. "I don't know, honestly. He's searching for something. He won't tell me what. But it has something to do with the Asgardians and some kind of power. He says he can resurrect the planet. He just needs to get his hands on 'it.'"

"It." Thanos realized he was gripping the control board so intensely that the rickety thing threatened to break off in his hands.

"Yeah. 'It.'"

"And whatever *it* is, the Asgardians have it."

"That's what His Lordship says."

"I see." Thanos detected no trace of ire or disappointment in Robbo. He was, apparently, happy to jaunt around the universe in a death trap of a wheelship, serving up psychic spikes as needed, all in the name of an insane infinity quest on the part of a lunatic. He was either as mad as His Lordship or a true believer. Or he wanted this mysterious source of power for himself. Regardless, there was no point to further discussion with Robbo.

"Thank you for the information," Thanos said.

"Just keep the ship going and point it in the direction His Lordship gives you," Robbo said as he headed for the door, "and everything will be fine."

CHAPTER XVII

SEVERAL DAYS LATER, THE INEVITABLE HAPPENED—ONE OF the wheelship's spokes, struck by a micrometeorite, buckled. Its dented, damaged, debris-pocked structure finally lost the last bits of its integrity. Even in the engine room, on the opposite side of the ship, Thanos felt the reverberations as the alloy hull twisted and pried itself loose from its moorings. The entire *Golden Berth* shook and trembled in space.

By the time Thanos arrived on the scene, most of the spoke had twisted away from its connection point with the wheel itself. A series of overlapping emergency shields held the vacuum at bay, but they wouldn't last long. Like everything else on the ship, they were rickety and well past their functional dates.

A cluster of crew members clotted the corridor to the tear site. Thanos used his size and status to bull his way through. Cha Rhaigor was already there, on his knees beside a bleeding Vorm, who couldn't stop thrashing.

"Stay still!" Cha commanded. "I'm trying to give you an injection!"

But the young Vorm was in too much pain to cooperate. Caught at the juncture of the spoke and the wheel when the tear happened, he'd been gashed across the abdomen by flying metal. Bruises formed up and down his flank, and blood gushed from his stomach.

Thanos stepped over to Cha's side and, without a word, leaned down and knocked the Vorm unconscious.

"Thanos!" Cha admonished.

"It was just a light tap," Thanos said.

"You *punched* him!"

"Now you can give him the injection," Thanos pointed out.

"You could have been gentler," Cha grumbled, easing the needle into the Vorm's arm. "Now I'll have to treat him for a concussion, too."

"Better than preparing him for a coffin." Thanos peered around. There were terrified crew members huddled just this side of the tear, as well as gawkers and onlookers. Just a few paces away from where he stood, the spoke twisted and dipped, sharp metal shards protruding from every angle. He could see more wounded crew members bouncing around down in the dark confines of the spoke.

The ship's artificial gravity had gone wonky down there, the tube waffled and flapped out of sync with the rest of the *Golden Berth*. The wounded were being smacked off the hull and ricocheted into and off one another.

"Clear this area!" Thanos ordered, gesturing to the crowd. No one moved.

"Move your asses!" he bellowed at the top of his lungs.

The crowd dissipated quickly, leaving only him, Cha, and the wounded.

"Those fields won't hold for long," Thanos said grimly. "We need a team to abseil into the spoke and get the wounded out. If we work from both ends, we can go faster."

Just then, a small black-and-white screen set into a nearby wall flickered to staticky life. His Lordship's image yawned into the camera.

"How's it going over there?" he asked.

"We have multiple casualties both within and without the spoke," Thanos told him. "But I have a rescue plan that I can execute. I'll need two teams of four each, medical assistance on both ends of the spoke."

He broke off—one of the fields crackled and spat, sparking out of existence with a flash of blue light. There was a strong, sucking wind for a moment, and then an overlapping field powered up to compensate. Still, he could see black space through the tear in the hull, and the whine of the fields told him that they wouldn't last long with the additional strain on their projectors.

"We can rescue them all," Thanos said, "if we act quickly."

His Lordship shook his head. "And risk the fields failing in the meantime, sucking half the ship's atmosphere out into the void? No. Not a chance. Activate the emergency cutoff."

Thanos shot a quizzical look at Cha, who had just finished stitching the Vorm's abdomen with a spool of old heat thread. "The spokes can be jettisoned," Cha said quietly, rocking back on his heels and staring at his bloody hands as though they were disconnected from his body.

"Jettisoned?" Thanos glanced up and around. Sure enough, he spied explosive bolts at the intersection of the spoke and the wheel, as well as a covered slit. He figured there was the same setup at the other end of the spoke. The bolts would disconnect the spoke, and the slit would no doubt open to slam down a blast door to keep the atmosphere in the ship.

"That won't be necessary," he told His Lordship. "We can rescue them."

Without waiting for a response, he stripped off his tunic and ripped it into strips, which he wrapped around his hands for protection. The null gravity in the spoke would make maneuvering difficult but would also make it easier to move the wounded.

"What are you going to do?" Cha asked.

Thanos backed up several paces. "Run. Jump." His momentum would carry him through the weightless area. He would grab as many as he could. Fling them to the other end if necessary.

"That's insane."

His Lordship chimed in. "Hey, Thanos! It's the switch on your left. Just hit it and we're done here. We can't risk the entire ship for a couple of crew members."

"There. Are. Ten," Thanos said through gritted teeth. "At least."

"A couple. Ten. Compared to the hundreds on board? Think!"

Thanos brushed aside the command. He took a deep breath and started to run—

—and the blast door came down so suddenly that it almost crushed him. He pulled up short at the last possible instant and managed to twist so he hit the door with his shoulder, not his face.

At the same time, a cry went up from Cha Rhaigor. Thanos whirled around, his shoulder throbbing, and saw that the blast door had come down squarely on the Vorm's head. The skull had been thoroughly smashed to pulp from the bridge of the nose up. A fan of blood and brain matter sprayed up the lower portion of the blast door.

"Oh!" His Lordship exclaimed. "That *was* the remote switch! Great."

The screen fuzzed back to black before Thanos could do or say anything.

Cha shook. With rage. With anguish. With shock. Thanos had never been good at reading people; he couldn't tell. But he knew that this called for a gesture of friendship and comfort.

The most he was capable of was to lay one hand on Cha's shoulder.

That was all it took. Tears erupted from Cha, and he collapsed against Thanos, clutching his hand as though it were a lifeline.

"He would have made it," Cha wept. "He would have been fine."

Thanos stared numbly at the blast door. Having been tucked away inside the ship all these years, protected and unexposed, it was in good shape—sturdy and pristine except for the remains of the Vorm's skull cavity on the lower third.

And he saw. He understood.

He couldn't just plot to escape the ship. For the sake of every living thing aboard the *Golden Berth*, His Lordship had to die.

CHAPTER XVIII

THANOS MADE A POINT OF SEEKING OUT KEBBI LATER THAT day. She had seemed, at that first dinner, to tolerate His Lordship, in contrast to Robbo's sycophancy. Perhaps he could learn more from her.

She again wore a kerchief over the lower half of her face, making her expressions inscrutable. But when he asked to speak with her privately, her eyebrows rose in a significance that he could not ignore.

They huddled in a small outlet berth for one of the escape pods that the ship no longer boasted. All of them had been used, Thanos learned, a hundred years ago, when the original crew ran like hell from the madness of His Lordship.

"So, you hate His Lordship and want to mutiny," Kebbi said matter-of-factly before Thanos could speak.

Thanos balked. He hemmed and hawed for a moment.

"Don't play coy, Thanos of Titan," she told him. "You're new here. All the newbies want to overthrow His Lordship and get the hell off this deathtrap as soon as possible. You haven't been here long enough to have your spirit crushed or your mind enfeebled by Robbo. So of course you want to team up with me, bump off the old man, and take the ship somewhere sane and sensible."

Thanos had planned on slowly and subtly feeling out Kebbi, eventually revealing his plans only if and when he decided she felt similarly and could be trusted.

So much for that idea.

"Is there a way to remove the collars?" he asked quickly. "Once they're off, we can overwhelm His Lordship and take control of the ship."

She blinked rapidly, and her eyes danced back and forth. "Why do you want the collar off?"

"The psychic spikes. Unless you know a way to get the control device from Robbo?"

Kebbi shook her head. "Oh my. Oh, you don't get it, do you? You think...The collars have nothing to do with the psychic spike. That's *Robbo* himself. It's his power. He's a psychic projector. The collars are just an identifier. An affectation of His Lordship's, really. They remind him of home."

With fingers gone numb, Thanos probed at the collar around his neck. All this time, he'd thought the collar was a weapon. But it was nothing more than an ornament.

Robbo was the true problem, then.

"Why is he so loyal?" Thanos asked. "He's trapped here like the rest of us."

"Some people lead," she said with a shrug. "Some people want to *be* led. He feels like it makes him a part of something bigger."

"That's insane."

"I never said it wasn't."

Thanos grimaced. "We outnumber Robbo. He can't possibly project psychic spikes into everyone at once. Why—"

"Why haven't we overwhelmed him, killed him, killed His Lordship, and taken control of the ship?" Kebbi asked.

The question was more straightforward and brutal than Thanos would have preferred, but it was honest. "Yes."

She shook her head. "It would be pointless. We have to keep His Lordship alive."

"Why?"

"Have you ever heard of a sympathy circuit?"

He confessed that he had not. "But I am not overly familiar with space travel."

"It's pretty simple," Kebbi said. "The ship is quantum-paired to His Lordship's heart. If his heart stops beating, the ship's engines overcycle, blowing up the ship and killing everyone on board." She thought for a moment. "Well, a few might survive, I guess, but explosive decompression'll kill them right afterward, so there's not much point living through the blast, right? If you think the spoke's breaking was bad...imagine that happening to the entire ship."

Thanos rocked back on his heels. His Lordship's health was poor—on a daily basis, the man coughed up enough phlegm and sputum to fill a tankard—and those he'd enslaved seemed overly concerned with keeping their captor alive and hale. Thanos thought of how everyone perched on every cough and sneeze from His Lordship's leaking, crusty orifices. The creatures who collected his sputum. For medical tests, no doubt.

Now he knew why. His Lordship's death meant the death of everyone aboard the *Golden Berth*.

"There is no way out," she told him. "This ship is the universe's most perfect prison, a rattling, broken-down suicide pact made solid, wandering the galaxy until either he dies—at which point we *all* die—or the ship falls apart."

"At which point we all die," Thanos supplied.

"Yep. All we can do is stretch out our days and hope for a miracle." She tugged down her kerchief for the first time, and he saw that the lower half of her face was a massive reptilian maw, the jaw low-hinged, her teeth a double row of more than a hundred needles, and her tongue forked.

"Got any miracles on you, Thanos of Titan?" she asked. "If not, don't bother."

He lay awake all that night. Partly because he had to absorb the new information he'd gleaned from Kebbi, but mostly because he feared another repetition of the dream.

Tossing and turning, he jumbled the facts together in his mind. His Lordship's health. The sympathy circuit. The psychic spike and the collars and the dead planet Kilyan, which made him think of Titan and its inevitable fate, which he would do anything to forestall...

And the power. *It*, whatever *it* was. His Lordship seemed to believe it was real, but His Lordship was insane.

Still, even the insane could be right. Sometimes.

He closed his eyes. He saw his mother in her psychosylum, screaming that he was death! Death! Death!

And this time, when he dreamed, he saw *her* again, only she was rotting before his eyes. Her cheeks were sunken and sallow, her flesh drying.

Gwinth! he called in the dream. *Gwinth!*

But she only spoke to him the same words she always said, and then collapsed into a heap of bones and desiccated flesh at his feet.

CHAPTER XIX

HE AWOKE TO A NEW PLAN.

To his pleasant surprise, the plan filled him with hope. He turned it over in his mind as he lay in bed, measuring probabilities, compensating for variables. The plan, he concluded happily, would work.

It would require cunning and caution. It would require his talent for technology. It would require assistance.

Most important, it would require violence. Perhaps even a great deal of it.

His body was capable of violence, he knew. Sometimes— as when he'd towered over A'Lars during their furious argument—he'd felt as though his body were a separate thing, a being of its own, with its own wants and desires. And sometimes what it wanted and desired was to put its hands around a throat. And squeeze.

So, yes, his body could commit violence, but could his soul? His mind? His heart?

He was willing to kill half of Titan and himself in order to save it. Killing a few of the aliens aboard the *Golden Berth* to save the rest—and himself—was just as reasonable and even more defensible.

He sought out Cha in the medical bay. Of all the people on the *Golden Berth*, Thanos trusted only Cha Rhaigor.

Cha was happy to see Thanos, but Thanos had no time for pleasantries. "Can we speak privately?" he asked.

Glancing around, Cha shrugged. "We're alone."

"Is this area monitored?"

Cha laughed. "Paranoia? On you? A poor fashion choice, my friend."

"This from the man who walks around shirtless," Thanos reproved. "Are we being monitored?"

"Of course not. His Lordship doesn't have enough trusted advisers to monitor the whole ship. Fear and self-interest keep everyone in line."

"Not for long," Thanos said, and then told Cha what he'd learned—that Kilyan was a fool's errand, that the ship had five years left at the most, and that His Lordship had no plan B.

Cha took the news as well as could be expected. He gasped for breath long enough that Thanos thought he would need to resuscitate his friend.

"Kilyan is a wasteland?" Cha trembled as he said it, felt around him for support. He slumped onto a bed. "We passed it a *decade* ago?"

"You wouldn't have wanted to live there anyway," Thanos said gruffly. It was the only comfort he could offer.

"It would have been better than this!" Cha shouted.

"Better than this damned ship, which smells eternally like refuse and flatulence because we can't vent safely! Better than eating the same ten meals galley staff can conjure out of whatever the food replicator regurgitates!"

Cha growled and rose up, tipping the bed over. He reached for a tray of medical instruments and hurled them against the wall. For a good three minutes, he exercised his rage on the instruments and gadgets around him. Thanos watched passively, understanding all too well that Cha's anger was like a forest fire that could not be extinguished but could only burn itself out.

"Breathe deeply," Thanos suggested drolly, a part of him enjoying the sight of Cha's placid shell finally cracking a bit. "Find your center."

When Cha punched a wall and broke his hand, his anger cooled to yelps of pain. Thanos put an arm around his friend's shoulder and guided him to the section of the medical bay that had not seen Cha's wrath. There, he wrapped Cha's broken hand in an old healie as he spoke quietly and calmly.

"When I was fixing the engines the other day, I noticed something on our long-range sensors. An old Kalami Gate about two light-years out. If we shift our course, we could hit the gate and jump free of the Raven's Sweep. Back to civilized space."

The *Golden Berth* did not have a faster-than-light engine... anymore. Its warp core had burned out decades ago. Using the ship's sublight engines to approach lightspeed would be dangerous but necessary if they were to get to the gate in anything like reasonable time.

Cha shook his head. "Most of the Kalami Gates aren't functional any longer. Besides, His Lordship would never allow it."

"I don't care what His Lordship wants. I'm talking about getting us to a place where we can free the people on this ship."

"Even if the gate works, who knows where in the infinite universe we'll end up?"

Thanos snorted. "First, it would have to be better than here. By definition. Second, the universe is not infinite. The universe is *expanding*, Cha. That's not a belief—it's a demonstrable fact. Therefore, it cannot be infinite, because it has boundaries."

Cha shrugged. "If the universe is expanding, what is it expanding into? What is beyond those boundaries?"

"We don't have time for me to tutor you in astrophysics and celestial mechanics," Thanos insisted. "We have more important things to discuss."

"A lot of the more well-cared-for crew are loyal to His Lordship. And you can't kill him because of the sympathy circuit. We have no choice. We have to keep His Lordship alive as long as possible and hopefully find a place to evacuate to before the ship falls apart—or he does."

"Even odds as to which will happen first," Thanos told

him. "But you need to trust me: I can kill His Lordship *and* keep the ship going. And I have a way to deal with Robbo as well. Are you with me? You're the only one I trust on this ship. I need someone at my side. And you are instrumental to my plan, if you can handle a little bloodshed."

Cha didn't even take a moment to consider, staring down at his broken hand swathed in the sweaty, half-chilled healie that had lost most of its gel. "He's been lying to us all along. Yes, of course I'll help." When he looked up at Thanos, his eyes shone with renewed hope and vigor. "This is why you were sent here, Thanos. I can't abide killing, but if it means liberating all of the souls on this ship…I believe that would be for the greater good."

"How convenient," Thanos rumbled. "I'm glad everything works out for you."

"Your hardness will be your undoing, Thanos."

"I'm fine with that." Thanos said brusquely. "All the well-wishing and inarticulate hope in the universe could not have found an easier way. But I'm glad to have you on my side. I have a plan. And we will need Demla's help."

Cha gabbled in shock before finding his voice. "Demla? Thanos, Demla is a fine, upstanding person, and a kind-hearted soul, but he is as the universe found him: dumber than a petrified turd. What can he possibly offer us?"

Thanos grinned for the first time since his exile. It felt good. "You'd be surprised."

He scrounged material from the engine room and some circuitry from the medical bay, scavenged from the implements Cha had conveniently broken.

His new quarters were no more spacious or well-appointed than his old, but they were his alone. Still, he couldn't risk working there. He was bunked near Robbo and His Lordship, and they had an annoying tendency to drop in and see him when he wasn't in the engine room. His Lordship constantly asked about power consumption and occasionally gave new coordinates to aim for, though the coordinates never seemed to follow any sort of pattern. As best Thanos could tell, if His Lordship was looking for something in the possession of the Asgardians, he was doing it by pawing blindly through mountains of dinosaur waste, hoping to find an undigested fern leaf.

Robbo stopped by erratically, unpredictably. Thanos realized early on that His Lordship's majordomo and primary weapon did not entirely trust him. Perhaps some of Thanos's enmity had leaked psychically to Robbo. Or perhaps he regretted telling Thanos His Lordship's secret. Whatever the reason, Thanos sensed that time was running out. He had to act quickly.

So he spent as much time as he could in his old quarters with Cha, building the first element of his plan.

"It's a hat," Cha said warily, watching as Thanos used medical adhesive to graft two pieces of dented, curved metal. Cha's hand had healed from its break, but he still tended to flex it randomly, as now, expecting pain every time. "How does a hat get us to mutiny?"

"It's not a hat," Thanos told him. "It's a helmet."

Fashioned of medical-grade steel and pieces of finer alloys scavenged from the ramshackle engines, the helmet contained meticulously soldered circuitry within its dome. It had taken Thanos two weeks to gather the materials and another week to assemble them. Each day—each hour—that passed, he feared discovery and the psychic spike that had exploded Googa's eyes. He also feared the ship splitting in two. And His Lordship casually, indiscriminately, deciding to kill off his new engine chief for no sane reason.

He had a great many fears, and not many options.

"A helmet, then," Cha said doubtfully. "How does a helmet move along your mysterious plan?"

Thanos sat back and admired his handiwork. He had used tools ancient or broken, and in some cases both, but still managed to cobble together the first piece of the puzzle that would oust His Lordship for good.

"I've noticed that Robbo has to be close to use his power. Within arm's reach."

"Yes. So?"

"That means it's transmitted on a short-distance wavelength. I've calculated how many could be generated by organic brain matter." He held the helmet aloft. It was blue with a gold stripe bisecting it. Above the eyes, it flared into two golden horns. "And this helmet blocks all of them."

"And the purpose of the horns?" Cha asked.

Thanos grunted. "They are there to intimidate those who might stand in my way."

"I'm sure that will work," Cha said approvingly. "As though the mere sight of you were not intimidating enough."

Thanos feigned a chuckle.

"So, Robbo cannot hurt you," Cha went on. "But you still can't hurt His Lordship. I've thought it through—even if you try to sedate him so that his heart keeps beating, his health is so poor that he probably wouldn't survive the process."

"He'll sleep," Thanos promised. "Permanently. That's where Demla comes in."

"I still don't understand how...."

Thanos told him. Cha's jaw dropped. And stayed that way for a very long time.

Demla had the night shift in the engine room, so he was waiting there when Thanos arrived in the morning. What passed for morning, at least. It had been only three hours since the ship's lights had gone out, and now the lighting savored more of crepuscule than of dawn, but it was close enough.

When Thanos entered, Demla immediately launched

into a litany of everything that had gone wrong overnight, what he had done to fix it, and what could not be fixed. Thanos pretended to care, and then, when Demla was finished, took him by the elbow and guided him to a spot near the fusion reactor's intake system. The noise there made being overheard unlikely.

"I need something from you," Thanos began.

"Anythin', boss!" Demla said with great verve. "Whatever ya need!"

"Boss! Need!" Bluko called out. "You betchum!"

If necessary, Thanos was prepared to threaten Demla. Unbeknownst to Cha of course, Thanos was even prepared to kill Demla, though he hoped such a path would not need to be embarked upon. His goal was to save as many of the poor souls trapped on the *Golden Berth* as possible, not slaughter them in the process of rescuing them.

He said nothing to Demla, merely looked significantly at his shoulder. Demla stared ahead blankly, not getting it.

Eventually, though, he realized. His face fell, and he pouted. "Aw, c'mon, boss! For real?"

"Boss real!" Bluko chattered. "Boss real!"

"I'm afraid so," Thanos said as gently as he could manage. "And it'll have to be right now."

Demla's shoulders slumped. "Yeah, yeah, all right."

"Yeah, all—" Bluko started, and then stopped when Thanos's hands closed over him.

CHAPTER XX

WEARING HIS HELMET, THANOS STRODE THE CORRIDORS OF the *Golden Berth*. Behind him was Cha Rhaigor, who carried a bulky chillwrap and dragged a jerry-rigged floating stretcher. No one stopped them or questioned them along the way; no one would question the ship's medical officer carrying medical equipment, and no one would dare raise a finger or an eyebrow or a voice to one of His Lordship's inner circle.

At the door to His Lordship's quarters, Thanos paused. He did not so much as look back at Cha or remind him, even with a word, of what he was to do next. Instead, Thanos simply went inside as though this were any other day and he were about to have the evening meal with His Lordship.

His Lordship was already at the table. Robbo and Kebbi flanked him, as usual. For a moment, Thanos wondered if Kebbi had some sort of power as well. That, he realized, was the one potential glitch in his plan, the one thing he'd not prepared for.

But he was ready. Cha was ready. Most important of all, Bluko was ready. He had to move now.

"Thanos!" His Lordship drew out the word: *Thaaanos!* "Thanos! What a pleasant surprise. And what an interesting choice of headgear. I never imagined you to be a helmet sort of guy. Anyway, I thought you were retuning the warp core. If we could get that back up and running...we'd be out of this Raven's Sweep in no time flat!"

"I regret to inform you that the warp core will have to wait," Thanos said. "I need something from you."

His Lordship shrugged and tucked into his meal. Robbo turned slightly toward Thanos, his brow wrinkling. *Did* he have powers beyond the psychic spike? Was he picking up on Thanos's intentions?

Thanos licked his lips. Kebbi's eyes widened just a tiny bit. She knew.

"What can I do for you?" asked His Lordship, oblivious, eating.

Thanos spoke the words he'd prepared and practiced: "I'm going to give you one opportunity to do what is right. I need you to step down from your position and hand authority over this ship and all aboard to me."

No one spoke. The air filled with a loud slurping sound as His Lordship sucked up something that appeared to be an obese variety of spaghetti covered in an oily brown gravy. The viscous goop spattered in all directions as the noodle vanished between His Lordship's lips; sauce dotted his chin, his wattles, the tablecloth, even the arm of Kebbi's tunic.

"A dead man says what?" His Lordship asked calmly, and Robbo came around the table, eyes alight with malice. When

Robbo came within range, Thanos staggered, bumped against the table, slapped both hands to his head, and bent over, keening.

"Spike him good!" His Lordship shouted, food spraying.

And then, when Robbo was within arm's reach, Thanos stopped pretending; he lashed out with one hand, grabbing the majordomo around the throat.

"What the ever-loving hell!" His Lordship cried out, his eyes alternating between red and a sickly chartreuse.

Robbo grabbed Thanos's wrist and tried to pry the Titan's hand away even while grimacing and focusing his eyes on Thanos's head. Clearly, Robbo was using every last bit of his psychic power and couldn't believe it wasn't working. Even with the shielding and nullifying circuitry in his helmet, Thanos felt the beginning of a headache in the back of his skull. He would have to end this quickly.

He applied his other hand to Robbo's throat. The major-domo made a sound like *Urrrr-uck!* and then his eyes rolled back in his head.

Thanos kept squeezing. He'd never killed anyone with his bare hands before, and he wanted to be absolutely certain. Under the pressure of both his hands, Robbo's throat col-lapsed. His spine crumbled. His head lolled on his shoulders, defenseless and uncontrolled like a baby's.

Releasing his grip, Thanos let Robbo's body drop to the floor. It made an undistinguished and generic thud. Very anticlimactic.

Clearing his throat, Thanos returned his attention to the other end of the table. His Lordship had scrambled behind Kebbi and cowered there now, pointing and screaming, "Kill him! Kill him! Do it now!"

Kebbi stood very still. Then, with a slow movement, she pulled down her kerchief, revealing again that distorted, distended reptilian maw. As Thanos watched, she opened it wider than would have been possible on any other humanoid. That forked tongue flicked out, and behind it he beheld something else—a longish, fleshy tube with a moist opening.

"Use your poison spray!" His Lordship howled. "Do it now!"

Kebbi spoke. "You need him alive, don't you?"

"Are you kidding me?" His Lordship swore. "I want him dead *now*!"

But she hadn't been speaking to His Lordship.

"I need him alive," Thanos concurred.

With a curt nod, Kebbi closed her mouth and pulled her kerchief back into place. Then, without so much as a look at her master, she stepped away from His Lordship and the table and strode past Thanos and out into the corridor.

It was just the two of them now. His Lordship scuttled behind his chair, as though that would provide protection from Thanos's wrath. With three long strides, Thanos closed the distance between them.

"I'll give you anything you want!" His Lordship screamed. "Anything! What *do* you want? I'll give it to you!"

"I want this," Thanos said, and closed his hands around His Lordship's throat.

Eyes gone flat white and now bugging out, His Lordship choked out words. "Can't...we...talk about...this?"

"Conversation is all well and good," Thanos said, remembering, grinning, "but sometimes only brute force will suffice."

"You're...killing...everyone...on...board..."

"You just let *me* worry about that," Thanos said, and squeezed harder.

He was careful not to kill, only to render unconscious. Just as His Lordship swooned into a dead faint in his arms, Thanos heard the door slide open. Cha and Demla rushed in with the chillwrap and floating stretcher.

"Get away from him!" Cha shouted. "I don't have much time!"

Thanos did as he was told, stepping aside so Demla and Cha could wrestle His Lordship's body onto the stretcher. Then they hustled him out of the dining room and vanished into the corridor.

Thanos considered following them. But, no. Either they would succeed or they would not. If they did not, his presence wouldn't matter; the *Golden Berth* would explode into a billion fragments, as it so obviously wished to do, and Thanos would be flung out into the cruel vacuum of space. But if they succeeded...

Ah, if they succeeded!

He took His Lordship's seat at the table. The food, still repellent, was at least marginally more palatable than the swill eaten by the rest of those aboard the ship. Thanos dug in, trying not to taste it.

A little while later, the door slid open and Kebbi entered. She sat at the opposite end of the table.

"So, are we to call you His Lordship now?"

"Thanos will do. Assuming we're all still alive."

"You have a plan," she said neutrally.

"I do. There is no guarantee it will work, but I do have one."

"And if it does work?" she asked, leaning her elbows on the table. "If you become master of this ship? You're still stuck with balky engines, a nigh-useless, unmotivated crew, and a hull that will fall apart if someone belches in the wrong direction."

"I'll try to keep everyone's intestinal distress under control," he said wryly. "Tell me: Why did you step aside?"

"Death was in the room no matter what. If you killed His Lordship, I would die, but then again, I'll die someday anyway." She took Thanos's goblet and drained it, managing to lift her kerchief in such a way that her mouth was still concealed.

"My parents were descendants of some of His Lordship's first conscripts. Never been off the ship in their lives," she told him. "They were emotionally compatible, but not anatomically. They made me in a test tube using some old, stale genetech."

"You are unique in the universe," he said, and thought he detected a smile—large, cavernous—beneath the kerchief.

"As are you." She saluted him with the goblet. "I suspect that—"

Just then, the door slid open again. Demla and Cha entered. Cha wore medical scrubs spattered in still-wet blood and a surgical mask that covered the bottom half of his face, but nothing could conceal the glee in his eyes.

"It worked!" he exclaimed.

Thanos's heart surprised him by skipping a beat. Some part of him had thought that this plan would not work, no matter how well thought through. But then Demla approached him and, with something like reverence, handed him…a thing.

A pulsating, gelatinous bulb roughly the size of both of Thanos's fists, the color of a bruise, with the consistency of worn rubber. It gently throbbed in his hands, reliably *lub-dubbing* along.

"Poor ol' Bluko," Demla sniffed.

By rote, everyone waited, anticipating the usual echo from Bluko. But Bluko wouldn't be responding anytime soon.

In Thanos's hands, he held His Lordship's heart, expertly removed from his chest by Cha's able hands. And then— before it could miss a beat—slipped into Bluko, the shift-blot who had been coaxed to take the form of a sac that would envelop the heart and keep it beating.

As far as the *Golden Berth*'s sympathy circuit was concerned, His Lordship's heart was just fine. It was beating. And it would continue beating until Thanos no longer needed the ship.

He grinned and held the heart aloft. "Step one," he said, and Cha, Demla, and Kebbi nodded along with him.

He was still young, not yet in his physical prime, and he was master of all he surveyed.

CHAPTER XXI

WHAT HE SURVEYED WAS, IN TRUTH, NOT MUCH TO BEHOLD. Kebbi's assessment of the ship and the crew were spot-on.

The announcement that His Lordship was dead and that Robbo's psychic spikes were no longer a threat went a long way toward assuaging the crew's fears and misgivings. They'd been under His Lordship's rule for so long that they didn't know how else to live, so Thanos left their conditions—as horrendous as they were—the same. For now. He fully intended to liberate every last one of them, but right now he needed them all to keep up their tasks. It was no good to win the ship only to have it fall apart.

Thanos rechristened the ship *Sanctuary*, just as he'd done with *Exile I*. Until he returned to his rightful home, all others would merely be temporary refuges.

"What now?" Kebbi asked. It was a day later, and Thanos had spent that time spreading the news, answering questions, dealing with various concerns that His Lordship had ignored, some of them literally for generations.

"Now," Thanos told her, "we see what His Lordship knew that he wasn't willing to share."

"Ah, the artifact." She said it sardonically.

"Do you think it doesn't exist?"

She shrugged. "I'm sure the Asgardians have possession of a great many artifacts. I've heard they are long-lived, damned near immortal. Worshipped as gods on some backwater planets and in the occasional shadow dimension. But an artifact that could fix a dead world?" She shook her head. "I think His Lordship was mad."

Thanos chuckled. "They called me mad, too, Kebbi. And yet here I am."

"Yes. Lord of a star-bound junk heap that will collapse around your ears should you breathe too hard."

He fixed her with a gaze. "Did you speak so impertinently to His Lordship?"

"No. But he could have had Robbo drive a psychic spike through me at any moment."

Stroking the ridges that adorned his jaw, Thanos considered this. "Can I trust you?"

"A question that has only ever been answered one way," she responded, "by liars and truth sayers alike."

"Then the answer is yes."

She laughed. "The answer is *yes*. The truth is *it depends*. You don't have Robbo to protect you, but your madness seems more compatible with mine than His Lordship's. You can trust me as long as I can trust you, Thanos."

He nodded. "I accept that."

Together, they searched His Lordship's personal quarters. It was a noisome, gag-inducing task. The quarters had not been cleaned in years, if not decades. Dust hung thick in the air. Soiled clothing, dirty linens, and rotting food intermingled into a fetid odor that defied description. It was practically its own life-form, a smell that took on sentience and followed them throughout the room. Thanos envied Kebbi her kerchief.

They found old holotapes from Kilyan, various sorts of interspecies pornography, half-written edicts and treatises that inevitably rambled off into declarations of war on His Lordship's long-dead enemies. They found dishes and glasses, goblets and flatware. They found ChIPs loaded with out-of-date star charts, delineating the presence of jump gates that had been decommissioned decades ago.

But on one ChIP, Thanos found a file tagged IMPORTANT and named *POWER*. He opened it on His Lordship's personal portable reader. The image on the screen, flat and two-dimensional, was difficult to manipulate and decode, but eventually he figured it out. It was a star map. The jump gate data were out of date, but the stars and systems themselves were still relevant.

The end point of the map was labeled ASGARD.

"Even if you could get to Asgard..." Cha said.

"I can," Thanos told him.

He, Cha, and Kebbi were in what had been His Lordship's dining room and now was Thanos's. The food was... passable. With the death of His Lordship, Thanos and his team had undertaken a survey of the ship's resources. They had discovered that the food replicators had been dialed all the way down to SUBSISTENCE, a way of preserving their stores and guaranteeing longevity.

Now that Thanos had already ordered the ship aimed at the Kalami Gate he'd discovered before his mutiny, they knew that soon enough they'd be back in the civilized galaxy. Within a day, they'd be at the gate, and assuming the ship survived the stresses of gate travel, they would arrive on the other side soon after. So Thanos had ordered the food quality dialed up significantly.

"Even *if* you could get there," Cha went on stubbornly, "and there's no guarantee of that because His Lordship certainly couldn't—"

"His Lordship wasn't even following his own charts," Thanos said. "He was merely stumbling around the Sweep."

"You're going to trust a lunatic's maps?" Cha asked wryly.

"Just because he was insane and incompetent doesn't mean he was wrong."

Cha chuckled and shook his head. "You'd have to fight your way through beings who think of themselves as *gods* to get what you're looking for. And then, even assuming you survived all of that, you'd need to get back *out* without being stopped, all while hauling whatever this artifact or weapon is."

"I'm surprised you're so impressed with the puissance of these 'gods,'" Thanos mocked. "Do you truly admire those who've been instilled with such violence?"

"I may dislike violence," Cha sniffed, scratching behind one pointed ear, "but I understand it and respect it."

"In any event," Kebbi put in, "the artifact itself is quite small, according to His Lordship's notes. Smuggling it out isn't the problem. The problems are all lined up before that."

Thanos shrugged. "If this artifact is as powerful as His Lordship thought it was—if it can truly rewrite the laws of nature—then it will be well guarded. I'll need inside information."

They sat in companionable silence for a while, eating. Then Cha spoke up.

"We," he said.

Thanos paused, his fork halfway to his mouth. "Sorry?"

"We. Just now you, you said, 'I'll need inside information.' But that's wrong. *We'll* need inside information."

"It's my intention to set you free once we go through the gate," Thanos told him. "You owe me nothing. I am not your owner. You are not indentured to me."

"You liberated us," Cha said. "I won't turn away from that."

"You're a damned fool," Thanos said, pleased. "A damned, damned fool."

"Then I suppose I am, too," said Kebbi. "Because I'm coming."

"No," Thanos said, shaking his head. "You have no part in this. You should return to your life."

"What life?" she asked with a short, unhappy laugh. "I

was born on this ship, and from my earliest days, I knew I'd die here, too. You saved me from His Lordship. You gave me the chance to live a life beyond this hull. The least I can do is help you out."

"If you do, that new lease on life you're so happy about may be considerably shorter than you'd like," he told her.

She shrugged. "At least I'll die outside."

As epitaphs went, Thanos thought, there were worse.

CHAPTER XXII

THEY HIT THE KALAMI GATE WITH THE FORCE OF A PEBBLE tossed against the tide. *Sanctuary* juddered and shook; her hull panels groaned. On Deck Five in the Hydroponics Arc, a panel split off, whisking ten souls out into the kaleidoscopic blur that was gate-space. Emergency doors slammed shut—eventually—and there was no further loss of life.

Thanos reminded himself that those deaths were the consequence of saving so many more. His Lordship had been right about something at least: Sometimes only brutality would suffice.

The ship's lights flashed and flickered all through gate-space. No one knew where they'd end up. Kalami Gates had been built millennia ago by the now-extinct Kalami, who had come to the Milky Way and attempted to exert an imperial will over half the galaxy. They'd been routed and crushed by a combination of the Kree, the Nova Corps, and a loose alliance of other races who had put aside their own bickering just long enough to boot the interlopers back out of the galaxy.

The Kalamis' gate technology was fussy and imprecise, but cheap and durable. Until better, more accurate tech came along, many worlds continued to use the left-behind Kalami Gates.

Over the centuries, gates had been decommissioned, torn down, or just plain abandoned. This one still functioned, but there was no way to know where it would spit them out. But anything had to be better than the Raven's Sweep.

They emerged, according to the navigation computers, near Willit's Star, a system on the outskirts of Xandarian space. Xandar, home of the Nova Corps. Of all the societies expanding throughout the galaxy, the Xandarians were one of the most open, accepting, and trustworthy. Cheers echoed so loudly down the corridors of *Sanctuary* that Thanos feared the ship might split apart from the din.

"How fortunate," Thanos said under his breath, scarcely believing their luck. Then again, the Kalami had fled from the might of the Nova Corps, so it made sense that there was a gate in the sector. The Kalami had used it to escape; Thanos was escaping, too, in the opposite direction.

"Fortune had nothing to do with it," Cha said somewhat smugly. And since he did not go further and invoke a ridiculous metaphor involving flowers—merely let the whiff of it linger in the air—Thanos allowed him his moment of satisfaction.

Sanctuary's command center bore all the hallmarks of His Lordship's lackadaisical discipline, but it was still the central node for the ship's functions. Thanos had directed his crew to clean and repair the bridge as much as possible during their trek to the Kalami Gate, but it still reeked of phlegm and body odor, now overlaid with the sharp scent of disinfectant.

By the time they had closed to within three AUs of Willit's Star, they were intercepted.

"Attention, unmarked vessel!" a voice blared over the most common hailing frequency. "This is Denarian Daakon Ro of the Nova Corps. State your affiliation!"

Kebbi, sitting in the second-in-command's chair, activated the ship's short-range sensors, and soon a large screen lit up with the image of a Xandarian Star Blaster. Thanos breathed out a sigh of relief he'd been holding since...forever.

"We are *Sanctuary*," Thanos announced, "and we seek refuge."

"Oh great," muttered Daakon Ro. "More refugees."

"Your comms are still active," Thanos said in an overly polite timbre.

"I know," Ro said. "Who or what are you fleeing from?"

"It's something of a long story," Thanos said. "Literally hundreds of years long."

"I should have taken early retirement," Ro grumbled. "Why didn't I listen to my husband?"

"Comms still open," Thanos reproved gently.

"And I still know that!" Ro shouted. "Power down your shields. I'm boarding you."

Thanos shrugged and glanced over at Kebbi, who mouthed, *What shields?*

Shortly thereafter, Daakon Ro was escorted to the bridge by Cha and Demla. The Xandarian was tall, well fed, well poised in a crisp, pristine Nova Corps uniform. His expression said that he was offended by everything inside *Sanctuary*. Thanos could hardly blame him.

"Holy hell, what in the three suns are *you*?" Ro spluttered when he first laid eyes on Thanos.

"I am Thanos of Titan." Thanos stood up from his command chair, well aware that this move made him even more intimidating. His presence purposefully filled the bridge that he commanded. "Welcome to *Sanctuary*."

Ro stared, his eyes bugging. "Titan? Are you sure?"

"Absolutely."

"I have never seen anything like you in my life. And I've seen quite a bit."

"We need your help, Denarian Ro." As quickly as he could, Thanos sketched out the history of *Sanctuary* and its crew, with Kebbi and Cha chiming in on occasion. (Demla, blessedly, remained silent the whole time.)

"This ship is a deathtrap," Ro complained. "And you've got me on it!"

"We've detected an outpost of yours on a planet orbiting Willit's Star. If you could just direct us to a landing pad," Thanos said with equanimity, "then you could leave—"

"It's not that simple. There are forms to fill out. There's a whole bureaucracy to—"

Thanos nodded once, sharply, and gestured to Demla, who approached him and handed him the pulsating glob of fleshy material that was Bluko.

"Denarian Ro," Thanos said, holding out Bluko as though

offering a gift, "right now, we all breathe on the sufferance of a shift-blot's patience and attention span. Perhaps you could speed the bureaucracy along?"

Ro pulled away from Bluko as though offered a meal of living maggots and dragon guts. "I'll…see what I can do."

The Xandarians wouldn't let *Sanctuary* land on their precious outpost without thoroughly examining the ship, but they quickly put together a refugee camp outside the colony's main administrative building and began ferrying His Lordship's victims down to the surface. Thanos remained on board until everyone was evacuated, then spent two more days on the ship with an annoyed Nova Corps tech named Lurian Op, figuring out how to disable the ship's sympathy circuit. It would have gone faster if not for Op's constant whining about *ancient technology* and *caveman systems*.

Still, they managed to get the job done. Thanos took a solitary shuttle to the surface of the imaginatively named Nova Colony Seven, where he joined the rest of *Sanctuary*'s crew in the hastily assembled refugee camp. It was the first time the crew of *Sanctuary* had breathed fresh air, stood on solid ground, or felt the heat of sunlight in a long time. For some—those born on the ship, who'd never been off the damn thing in their lives—it was a whole new world, quite literally.

The camp was a collection of phase-tents in a flat field.

In the distance, the skyline of the colony's main commercial center glowed with light and life. Thanos felt a tug toward it. Even on a basic outpost like this, Nova-controlled space was civilization. It was science and architecture. He could imagine civilized people discussing matters of import, matters of art and culture. No one would be obsessed with mere survival or keeping an old man alive long enough to figure out how to kill him. The city was the surest sign that he was once again moving in the right direction; it reminded him of home.

Then again, at this point anything that was *not* a spaceship would have reminded him of home.

It had rained earlier in the day, so Thanos's first footsteps on a planet since being exiled sank into mud. He trudged through the slop until he found Demla, crouched under one of the tents, staring up at the sky as though he expected fire to crash down.

"Water!" he croaked when he saw Thanos. "'ere's *water* comes down from up top!"

"It's called rain," Thanos told him. "You'll get used to it."

"Just ain't natural!" Demla complained.

Thanos held out his hand. "Here."

Demla's eyes widened and he forgot all about the impossibility of water falling from thin air as he beheld Bluko, still throbbing and encasing His Lordship's heart. "Bluko!" he cried, reaching out.

"Thank you for letting us borrow him," Thanos said.

Bluko chose that moment to shape-shift, flowing into a greenish feline form as he snaked up Demla's arm to perch on his shoulder. His Lordship's heart plopped into the mud.

"Well," Thanos said. "That's that."

He ground the heart deep into the mud with his foot.

CHAPTER XXIII

THE CAMP, HE DECIDED, WAS NOT MUCH BETTER THAN THE ship. It had the benefit of atmosphere and the distant hope of the Xandarian colony, but otherwise the refugees seemed just as beleaguered and downtrodden as they had been under His Lordship's rule. As Thanos walked the muddy, slushy alleys between the hastily erected tents and pavilions, he found himself thinking of the refugees as *his people*.

They're not, he reminded himself. *My people are on Titan. My people are in danger.*

His people. Sintaa. His mother. Gwinth, who still haunted his dreams, never speaking any but the same words. With each dream, she was more and more corroded, her flesh wilting, her hair dropping out in clumps. And yet he recognized her each time, knew her anew.

He had to get back. He had to save them.

A fight broke out in one of the tents. Thanos heard the cry as a crowd gathered around. Fifteen, twenty, maybe more, standing in the rain, stomping their feet in the mud and cheering as two of their crew mates battered each other with clenched fists.

He parted the crowd, shouldering his way through, and

grabbed the two combatants by their necks, hauling them apart.

"Stop it," he said. "Now."

"But he—" one began.

"I don't care," Thanos said. "You have a new beginning here. A new chance. Don't launch into it with idiocy." He shoved them away from each other.

He roamed the camp. Arguments and fistfights abounded. On *Sanctuary* and even on the *Golden Berth*, everyone had had a place, and everyone had known that place. Now the order was upended. No one knew where they belonged. Suddenly people had territory to defend, even if it was just the few square meters of somewhat dry turf under a phase-tent. They had belongings now, even though they were nothing more exotic than the refugee aid kits distributed by the Xandar government.

Give people who've had nothing something—*anything*—he realized, and they will fight to the death to protect it.

The fights and squabbles were bad enough. The suicides were worse.

It was an epidemic. The dead cut across all caste, species, and gender lines. Thanos found the grieving friends and families in every corner of the camp. There were as many reasons as there were deaths.

The gravity was too strong. The gravity wasn't strong enough. The air tasted strange. The food wasn't processed enough.

At the core, though, all the reasons came down to one: fear.

Thanos had rescued them from the only home and the only life most of them knew. Even the conscripts had become institutionalized, relying on His Lordship and the familiar confines of the ship to define and constrain their reality. Let loose in the world, *on* a world, they were at odds with themselves. They didn't know how to be free.

Standing in the rain, he reminded himself, over and over: *These are not my people. This is not my responsibility. I need to go home.*

Later, after the rain passed, Daakon Ro found Thanos. It wasn't hard to locate him—he was taller than everyone else in the camp by at least a deci.

"You need to register," Ro told him, glaring down at his boots, which were caked with mud. "There are forms for you to fill out."

"The bureaucracy hungers," Thanos said.

"It's *ravenous*," Ro said bitterly, trying to scrape clean one boot with the heel of the other. "I can't believe they put *me* in charge of this camp. I should have taken early retirement."

"You should have listened to your husband," Thanos said amiably.

"Damn right I should have!" He gave up the attempt with his boots and led Thanos to one of the larger tents, which served as a command center for the refugee effort. The phase-tent shifted its color and level of tangibility as they entered, allowing in more light and air.

Daakon Ro grumbled as he paged through a hologram generated by the tablet in his hands. "Thanos of Titan, right? Captain of the ship."

Thanos hesitated. Did he want his name recorded somewhere in a Xandarian database?

"Use my birth name," he said. "Sintaa Falar."

Ro arched an eyebrow. "Thanos is, what, a nickname?"

Thanos shrugged with indifference. "What else do you need? I'm in a hurry."

Ro chuckled. "Places to go? Didn't figure you'd be so eager to get back into space after limping here in that thing." He gestured vaguely to the sky, where *Sanctuary* sat in orbit, empty.

"Is there any news of Titan?" It had been a long, long time—it felt like eons—since his exile. Thanos feared the worst.

Ro paused for a moment, perplexed. "News? No. Nothing I've heard, at least. Titan isn't really a big news-making sort of place."

Thanos sighed in relief. If there was nothing to report, then the planet was still intact. There was still time to save what he could of his home.

"Now," Ro said, returning his attention to the holograms. "How long have you owned the ship in question?"

Thanos groaned and launched into his explanation again. Ro nodded along with him impatiently, then finally interrupted. "Look, I don't care how you got the ship or who you got it from. Right now, that rust heap is taking up space in orbit. I've got the Astronomy Council complaining that it's obscuring their mega-telescope's view of Venus or some such nonsense."

"How is this my problem?" Thanos asked.

Ro explained: *Sanctuary* had been stolen so long ago that all the statutes of limitation on the crime had expired...as had the original owners. Thanos was, for all intents and purposes, the owner of the ship. It was his responsibility.

So Thanos sold the ship for salvage and put the money into a smallish dart-yacht, the only thing he could afford. It was fast and maneuverable, with no offensive capabilities and only a token shield unit. Still, it would have to do.

He christened it *Sanctuary*, of course.

To his surprise, before he could take off, Cha appeared at the gangplank, wearing a loose-fitting pair of pants, an open-throated shirt, and gray boots that came up to his knees. His friend had spent several nights in the refugee camp, which was a far sight more comfortable and lavish than the accommodations aboard the old *Golden Berth*. He was fresh-faced and relaxed.

"Where are we going?" Cha asked without preamble.

"I won't hold you to what you said on the ship. Are you sure you want to do this?" Thanos asked. "You could stay here and—"

"And what?" Cha asked.

"And have a life," Thanos proposed.

Cha grinned. "You're going to *save* lives, Thanos. That's what I've spent my whole life doing."

Thanos grunted. He'd never told Cha exactly *how* he planned to save those lives. That was a debate he did not look forward to having.

Still, he believed that at some point, his rationality and data would overcome Cha's mysticism and pacifism. Thanos opened his mouth to respond, but another voice interrupted before he could begin.

"Got room for one more?"

It was Kebbi, standing at the foot of the ramp that led into *Sanctuary*, hands on her hips. She wore a robe made of a royal-blue silk and had a new red kerchief knotted across her lower face. Like Cha and Thanos himself, her neck was now bare of His Lordship's collar, thanks to a Xandarian technician.

"You're *free*, Kebbi. Go and—"

"Settle down?" Kebbi asked with sarcasm. "Enjoy the fruits of my labor?"

"Well, yes."

She laughed. It was a big, booming sound that belied her small size. "I was conceived and born on the *Golden Berth*. I don't know how to live on a planet." She looked around. "Honestly, can't even say I like it. Food's better, but...I'm a spacer, Thanos. I live for the vacuum."

"You're both mad," Thanos said. "But you are welcome aboard *Sanctuary*."

Re-entering the star-speckled blackness of space so soon after escaping near death on His Lordship's vessel put Thanos ill at ease. He wanted little to do with space travel; he wanted only to return to Titan, to save his people from their own blindness. And he would happily die in the process if that was still necessary.

If. Maybe it wasn't. Maybe there *was* another way. Maybe the Asgardian artifact would make such sacrifice moot. Maybe he would not even need to kill half of Titan after all.

"I asked around the refugee camp," Kebbi said, slipping into the copilot's chair, "and talked to some of the Nova Corps personnel." She looked around the confines of the ship. Cha was muttering and clanking around in the main cabin, sorting through the dart-yacht's limited medical equipment, so she raised her voice enough that he could hear, too. "There is an Asgardian outpost near Alfheim in the western arm. You said we need inside information...."

Thanos grinned and brought up the navigation computer. A reliable, recognizable hologram projected itself along his field of vision. He sighed with relief and joy and began plotting his course.

Sanctuary had no warp engine—it was a dart-yacht, designed for joyrides and party cruises around local moons.

But it was sturdy and could withstand gate travel. There was an artificial wormhole near Xandar that would take them to within a few light-years of Alfheim. Then it would be a long, slow trek to the outpost itself.

Which was good. He would need that time to formulate a plan beyond *Get information out of the Asgardians somehow.*

"Thank you," he told Kebbi. "You are more help than I've earned."

"Well," she said hesitantly, "there's a reason for that."

He put the coordinates into the ship's purpose-built intelligence. *Sanctuary* would pilot them to the wormhole on its own.

"Oh?" he asked, and turned to her, all other words dissolving. Something in the way she gazed at him...Her eyes...so expressive and so limpid. He briefly saw a vision of Gwinth, and it rattled him in a way he'd not felt since first awakening on the *Golden Berth*, helpless on the shores of turbulent destiny.

She locked eyes with him, then looked away. "I wasn't completely honest with you before. I have another reason for coming along. It's just that...I love you, Thanos. We're both unique, both without equal. I've loved you since I met you, since you came to His Lordship's dining room. Deeply. With my whole being."

Thunderstruck, Thanos could think of nothing to say. When he finally opened his mouth to tell Kebbi that he had no time for such things, she burst out laughing.

"I was kidding, you lilac moron! *Deeply. With my whole being.* You believed that nonsense?"

"Of course not," he said quickly.

"'Of course not,'" she said in a dead-on mimicry of his own stentorian voice. And then she chuckled much longer than was necessary.

CHAPTER XXIV

SANCTUARY DROPPED INTO THE WORMHOLE NEAR WILLIT'S Star at an angle of forty-six degrees to the ecliptic. Angles were of critical importance when traveling through wormholes—you'd be spit out somewhere else in the galaxy depending entirely on how you'd entered the wormhole in the first place. Off by a degree and who knew where you'd end up?

Forty-six degrees spat them out the other side, near Alfheim, where they nearly collided with a meteor. Only quick thinking and *Sanctuary*'s built-in debris-avoidance systems saved them.

"And the universe protects us," Cha said brightly.

"My reflexes protect us," Thanos retorted.

With the dart-yacht's poky engines, they had two months' travel before they would get to the Asgardian outpost. Its purpose, according to a non-updated copy of the *Galactic Index* preloaded into *Sanctuary*'s computers, was to act as a way station for Asgardians who bothered to leave the shining capital of the gods and descend to the baser realms of—

"Blah blah blah," said Kebbi, rubbing her eyes and leaning away from the hologram of the *Index*. "It's like a checkpoint for them. They pass through on their way to our realm, pass through on the way home after having screwed around with the mortals for their own amusement. Not many of them must come and go, given the size of this place. It's on a small moon at the edge of the solar system."

"Granted, it's been a few years since I was dragooned into His Lordship's service, but I can't remember the last time I heard about an Asgardian around this part of the galaxy," Cha commented. "They prefer Asgard, drinking and partying and occasionally going off to kill Frost Giants and Fire Giants." He raised his eyebrows significantly at Thanos. "And you're going to beard them in their den?"

Frowning, Thanos rotated some of the images and text in the hologram. "Not for nothing are the Asgardians considered gods by many. In any event, brute force will not suffice in this instance."

"Pity," said Kebbi. "Turns out you're good at it."

He grunted, remembering his hands closing around Robbo's throat, his hands on His Lordship. "I take neither pride nor pleasure in that. Still, artifice and guile will serve us in better stead than raw physical strength in this case.

"We need to sneak up on this Asgardian outpost. Get inside without their knowing."

"This ship doesn't have a cloaking device," Cha said. "I looked while I was organizing the medical supplies. Speaking of which: There aren't many. Mostly first aid and hangover remedies, and a cryococoon for serious cases."

"They'll see us coming thousands of kilometers away,"

Kebbi said with frustration. "If there were more meteors like the one we nearly hit, we could use that as cover...."

"If there were more meteors," Thanos pointed out, "we'd have hit one by now. No, you're right—we can't conceal our approach."

"Then we're dead," Cha said matter-of-factly. "Asgardians don't mess around. They tend to be 'hit you with a hammer and splatter your brains first, ask questions never' sorts."

Thanos pondered. "If we cannot conceal ourselves... then we must use our visibility as an asset, not a liability."

"How?" Kebbi asked.

"I'm not sure yet," he admitted. "But we have sufficient time before we're in range of their sensors. We'll think of something. If I learned one thing under His Lordship, it's that even though he seemed to be in complete control, with good planning, we were able to overcome insurmountable odds. We can do it again."

"If it is meant to be, it will happen," Cha said solemnly.

"No," Thanos said. "As always, we will have to do the dirty work on our own."

Sanctuary hovered into sensor range of the Asgardian facility, then drifted out, then blasted back in, skewing starboard, its maneuvering rockets firing awry.

At the helm, Cha Rhaigor slapped his hand on the broadcast controls and shouted, "Attention! Attention! All ships and satellites within two light-minutes of Alfheim! This is *Sanctuary*, en route from Willit's Star, with a medical emergency! Repeat, a medical emergency. Please respond!"

They didn't expect a response, and they didn't want one. To be sure none would be forthcoming, they kicked the engines into overdrive and blasted the ship right at the moon and the outpost. Before anyone in the outpost had time to assemble and transmit a response, they had already executed a rocky, clumsy landing outside the Asgardian edifice.

It was the only structure on the moon. Not hard to find.

The building seemed more carved than constructed, its facade a seamless gold that glowed in the light of the distant sun. Domes perched along the roofline, connected by sleek piping. Two enormous I beams lined the roof and peaked over the doorway, which was etched with the image of two ravens flanking an eight-legged stallion.

Over the frieze were the words HAIL KING ODIN AND HIS WISDOM, BATTLE-BIRTHED!

Cha was already in his space suit. He thumb-activated the environment shield over his face and dashed down the ramp from *Sanctuary* onto the moon's surface, towing an antigrav cocoon behind him. Not far from the door to the outpost, an atmospheric shield kicked in. He felt the tickle of breathable air even through his suit as he broached the perimeter of the field.

The door burst open. The man who emerged had bright-red hair and wore segmented steel leggings that shone with a high polish, black studded boots, and a royal-blue tunic that lengthened into a skirt. Large brass buttons—almost too perfectly round—studded the center of the tunic, and two massive steely epaulets held in place a voluminous cloak made of a burnished red fabric that rippled as though in its own wind. His muscled arms were bare save for wristbands of tough hide.

He held an enormous battle-ax in one hand, its shaft wrapped in brown leather strips, its blade gleaming and bright. He wore his beard long and knotted.

"Ho, traveler! Halt in the name of Odin!"

"We have a medical emergency!" Cha cried. "She's dying!"

The Asgardian crossed his arms over his chest. "I am forbidden by Great Odin himself to let none but the sons and daughters of the Aesir and Vanir pass."

Cha tapped a button on the cocoon. It slid open with a nearly inaudible hiss. Within, Kebbi lay perfectly still. Lights flickered around her.

"She developed hibernation thrush when we were in transit," Cha said, panicked. "You have to let me use your medical facilities!"

The Asgardian came closer and peered into the cocoon. The lower half of Kebbi's face was exposed in all its misshapen, horrific glory.

"Odin's Eye!" he exclaimed. "What *happened* to her?"

"We can't all be as pretty as you," Kebbi said, and let her jaw drop. The Asgardian had enough time to blink, and then

Kebbi's throat flexed and a toxic mist belched forth. Coughing and wheezing, the Asgardian stumbled backward, hands up. Too late, though. He'd gotten a lungful of the toxin, and it was choking him from the inside.

Cha recoiled at the sight; the Asgardian dropped to his knees, clutching at his own throat. Trembling, Cha stepped aside, helpless as Thanos emerged from the ship, hands clasped behind his back.

"Excellent," he said. "It will get easier," he assured Cha.

With Kebbi's help, he bound the Asgardian's wrists behind his back using stout cabling from *Sanctuary*'s repair stores. Together, they dragged him inside. Cha lingered outside for a while, then eventually joined them, saying nothing.

The Asgardian was still coughing. Tears streamed from his tightly shut eyes, running into his beard, dampening it to a blackish red. Thanos stood over him. "I assume from the lack of hue and cry that you are the sole emissary of this outpost."

The Asgardian spat up something red and thick. "You're mad," he choked out. "This is the royal territory of Odin of Asgard. He will—"

"Yes, yes, I know. I've been called mad before. It hasn't stopped me. I don't think it's as effective an attack as people think."

"Thanos…" It was Cha, speaking from behind him. "Are you sure about this?"

"Yes. Now ..." Thanos crouched down before the Asgardian. "I'm given to understand that your people fancy yourselves gods. What might you be the god of?"

"Something bloody and violent, I assume," Cha said.

The Asgardian slitted his eyes open. They were red, raw, and weeping. "I am Vathlauss," he rasped, his voice like metal shavings. "I will say no more than that."

"God of Murdering Helpless Innocents, no doubt," Cha snarled.

"God of Falling for Subterfuge," Kebbi suggested.

"Enough!" Thanos barked. "It matters not. I care only for the artifact."

Vathlauss coughed; some thin, bloody sputum dribbled down his chin. He shook his head and drew in a shuddering breath that twisted his face into an expression of great pain.

"I'd've thought Asgardians to be made of sterner stuff," Thanos said. "Perhaps our information acquisition will not be as difficult as we'd originally surmised."

"I'll tell you nothing," Vathlauss swore, coughing again.

"You'll tell us everything," Thanos promised.

He'd never tortured anyone before, but the basic concept was rather simple: inflict pain until the subject reveals the information you seek. Torture was not actually the best tool to use for information extraction. The more intense the pain, the more likely that the subject would say anything to make it stop. Still, it was the only option they had to make the Asgardian talk. They would have to be very careful.

"We seek an artifact of great power, one that your king holds on Asgard. We need to know where he keeps such things and how to get there."

Vathlauss nodded, thinking. "You begin by stuffing your head up your own arse..." he said.

Thanos grunted. "Cha, you may want to leave the room."

"Why?"

Thanos regarded his friend with the closest thing to tenderness in his emotional repertoire. "What I am about to do may offend your delicate sensibilities."

"Hey!" Kebbi complained. "Why aren't you worried about *my* delicate sensibilities?"

"I was not aware you had any," Thanos said. He opened the first-aid kit and selected a pair of scissors. "I suppose we'll start with this." He opened the tiny blades and held them up close to Vathlauss's left eye. "Unless, of course, you'd simply like to tell us what we need to know?"

"Take mine eye," Vathlauss said, holding his head erect. "I will be honored to resemble my liege and lord, Odin."

"Fine, then," Thanos said, and called his bluff.

Hours later, Vathlauss had told Thanos what he needed to know. Or at least as much as he could. He was missing one eye and several teeth, along with a finger on his left hand. The finger had come off early on, and Vathlauss had laughed. "I suffered far worse during the five hundred and twenty-seventh war with the Frost Giants!" he exclaimed, then guffawed until Thanos shoved the finger into the empty socket where his left eye had been.

Now Thanos sat on the floor across from Vathlauss, who had passed out from the pain. Thanos's clothes were stained with the Asgardian's blood, which ran as red and as heavy as that of any mortal Thanos had ever encountered. His gloved hands in particular were thick with it, and some part of him thought that this was wrong. He was not a doctor, not a sterile seeker of healing. The blood should touch his flesh. He owed that much to Vathlauss, who had endured quite exquisite pain at Thanos's hands. Pain so exquisite that both Cha and Kebbi had excused themselves under the guise of exploring the outpost for supplies.

And yet Thanos had remained. Had remained and had tortured this little godling for as long as it took. He'd felt nothing the whole time. No shame. No guilt. No nausea or revulsion. He was simply doing what needed to be done if he was to save the people of Titan.

He peeled off his bloodstained gloves, stiff and tacky, then dragged a finger through the blood. To feel it on his flesh. It was sticky and only partly dry. He rolled it between his thumb and forefinger until it dyed his fingers black.

Every drop shed saves millions more, he thought. *Every drop shed is another life preserved.*

He rose slowly, stiffly. According to Vathlauss, a ship came through this part of the galaxy once a fortnight—an

Asgardian ship bound for Asgard itself. Called the *Blood Edda*, it had permission to cross what he called the Bifrost, which was apparently some sort of special Asgardian wormhole technology that led specifically in and out of the kingdom.

"Odin's vault is in the castle," Vathlauss had said, choking on his own blood, pausing to catch his breath. "You can't miss it. It's the tallest damned thing in the kingdom. Once you're aboard the *Blood Edda*, you can bypass the Bifrost and go straight to the palace.

"What you seek must be the Aether," Vathlauss had continued. "The Infinity Stone."

"Infinity Stone." Thanos rolled the words over in his mind, feeling the heft of them, their psychic gravity. He'd never heard of such a thing before, but something in the way Vathlauss spoke the words, with an almost hesitant, reverent breath, told him volumes. The Infinity Stone. It existed. The artifact His Lordship had sought was not a flicker of madness in a dying man's diseased head. It was real.

He said it again, musing: "Infinity Stone."

"Yes. Bor, father of Odin, took it from the Dark Elves millennia past."

"And you believe Odin still has it."

"No one knows where it is. But the vault..."

And then Vathlauss had passed out.

Now, though, he stirred and coughed up something too solid to be mere blood, interrupting Thanos's deep thoughts.

He glared at Thanos with his remaining eye. "You'll die there, Titan. You'll die in the glory that is Asgard."

"Which is more than I can say for you," Thanos told him, and leaned over, reaching out for the Asgardian's throat.

God or not, he died just the same.

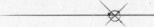

They had six days before the *Blood Edda* was due to arrive at the outpost. They spent the time exploring the building and planning.

The outpost boasted a magnificently stocked larder, the likes of which Thanos had never seen before. Entire sides of beef, salted and preserved. Kegs of sweet mead. Hardtack biscuits and honey-dipped cakes. They ate until they were sick, then threw up and ate again simply because it was worth it. Thanos had not eaten so well since Titan.

"It's going to get bloody," Thanos warned them as they lolled in a post-meal torpor.

"Going to?" Cha asked. "What do you call what you did to poor Vathlauss?"

"'Poor Vathlauss' would have killed us in an eye blink, given the opportunity," Thanos told him. Kebbi nodded in solidarity. "Your pacifism is noted and counterproductive. Especially since we may need to kill more of these Asgardians."

"You confidence is charming and perhaps unearned," Kebbi pointed out.

Thanos shrugged diffidently. "I told you both you were mad to join me."

"I stand by you," Kebbi said.

"As do I," Cha said after a moment.

Thanos blinked in surprise. "Really? I'd've thought the blood of an Asgardian would have changed your mind by now."

Cha considered for long moments, pinching the tips of his pointed ears, as he often did when lost in thought. "The Asgardians are a martial people, prone to bloodlust and bloodshed. I will not weep for their losses."

"I enjoy your special brand of hypocrisy," Thanos said with admiration. "Come. Let's take inventory."

In addition to its larder, the outpost also featured an impressive armory, considering it was crewed by a single staffer. Food and weapons—the cornerstones of Asgardian life.

There were axes and swords alongside more exotic fare: a recoilless pulse stave, a brace of grip-tight plasma knuckles, a lightning bow, and even something that looked like a cross between a rifle and a radar dish. When Thanos pointed it at a target and pulled the trigger, it issued forth a blast of invisible, pulsating sound waves that rattled his teeth and made his eyes bleed.

"Sonic screamer!" Cha shouted when it was over and they were all temporarily deaf. "Never seen one before!"

"Effective!" Thanos screamed back.

"I hate you both!" Kebbi yelled, blotting blood from the shell of her left ear. "Read the instructions next time!"

They made a tally of their available weapons, checked every entrance to the outpost, barricaded all but the front door. They wanted to give subterfuge a chance, but Thanos had a feeling that they would not get so lucky a second time.

"We have to be ready to fight our way aboard," he warned them. "We were fortunate to wound the God of Keeping et cetera early on—"

"You're welcome," Kebbi interjected.

"—but we can't assume we'll be so lucky the second time. It may come down to combat."

"Well, that's good," Cha remarked. "Because we have a Titan who's only been in a couple of fights, a medico who's never seen war, and a woman who grew up on a wheelship and has never been in a direct fight. Going up against a crew renowned across the galaxy for its bloodlust and fighting prowess. So how can it go wrong?"

"We trick them," Thanos said. "But we fight if we must, and we board the *Blood Edda*, commandeering it and making it our own."

Kebbi interrupted again. "Are we naming this one *Sanctuary*, too?"

Thanos said nothing. He'd been considering it. "Its name is not important. What matters is that we will be able to use it to traverse the Bifrost and enter Asgard."

"This is where the plan falls apart," Cha said.

"You're wrong," Thanos told him. "The plan does not fall apart at this point, because once we're in Asgard, there *is* no plan. Ergo, it can't fall apart."

"That doesn't comfort me," Kebbi said, to an agreeing nod from Cha.

"Without explicit information on Asgard, there's no point in making a plan," Thanos told them. It was simple. If need be, he would crash the *Blood Edda* into the palace and take advantage of the confusion to find Odin's vault. In the ensuing chaos, he would make his way back out. Not the best plan, he admitted, but the only one at his disposal. Let anarchy and surprise substitute for the weapons and army he did not have. "We cross the Bifrost and figure out the rest later."

He sounded more confident than he felt. Fortunately, the others couldn't tell the difference.

CHAPTER XXV

THE *BLOOD EDDA* CROSSED THROUGH THE WORMHOLE AT Alfheim exactly six days after Thanos and his crew arrived at the outpost. The Asgardians were nothing if not punctual.

Its arrival set off a series of automatic systems at the outpost. Security codes were transferred, cryptographic keys engaged at the quantum level, and the outpost machinery granted permission for the *Blood Edda* to land.

The ship hove into view on the moon's horizon. It looked like a great metallic bird, its wings frozen in place and frosted with gleaming steel.

It settled into the moon's dust a few meters from the outpost. After a moment, a ramp lowered and extended into the environment shield. Three figures strode down the ramp. Each wore skintight, flexible metal carapaces in a variety of colors—royal blue, deep crimson, solar yellow. They carried swords and photonic rifles and walked with the easy confidence of warriors who have seen blood and battle and lived not only to tell the tale but to live it again and again.

The three Asgardians entered the outpost and stopped in the entry hall. The place was utterly silent.

They shared a skeptical look between them. Then their leader cupped his hands around his mouth and called out:

"Ho, Vathlauss! Brother, battle-tested! Come greet your war-friends Snorri, Brusi, and Hromund! Wash our throats with mead and ale!"

The call echoed down the empty halls. Without so much as a coordinating glance, sensing something direly wrong, all three warriors drew their weapons at the same time.

Suddenly, the lights in the entry went out. The only light came from the hallway up ahead, and that was partially blotted out by a massive, hulking figure who strode closer into view.

"I'm afraid we've drunk all the mead," Thanos said.

"I will give you one chance…" Thanos began, but never finished his sentence.

"Hwat!" said the leader, Snorri.

"SEE, BROTHERS, MONSTER LARGE OF
    PURPLE FLESH AND COMBAT DIGHTED!
I LONG TO FLEX MY MUSCLES, TO HEAR
    THE SONG OF BLOOD AND BATTLE!
AND AVENGE OUR BROTHER'S SOUL,
    BRAVE-WORN, COURAGE-RIDDLED!"

With a cry, the three Asgardians launched themselves at Thanos, who stepped back a pace in order to have room to bring his sonic screamer to bear. He was wearing earplugs. The Asgardians weren't.

Still, they pressed on through the rippling, vibrating waves of sound that slammed into them. Snorri's nose spurted blood, which matted in his heavy mustache. Brusi growled and pawed at his left ear, which was gushing blood, but never stopped moving forward.

And Hromund let loose a bloodcurdling berserker war cry so loud that it momentarily overcame the pulses from the sonic screamer as he charged forward, swinging his sword.

Thanos's eyes widened at the sight of the battle-crazed Asgardian bearing down on him. He'd thought no one could resist the brain-scrambling frequencies of the sonic screamer, but here was, apparently, the God of Doing Things You Thought Were Impossible, just a meter or two away from cutting off the hands that held the weapon.

From her perch above the doorway, Kebbi dropped down to the floor between Thanos and Hromund, opened her mouth, and blasted out a cloud of venom. Thanos caught just a whiff of it, and it made his eyes water, but so great and all-consuming was Hromund's rage that he tucked his head down and rushed through the cloud. By the time he got to Thanos, he was bleeding from both eyes and both ears, with snot and blood gushing from his nose as well, but he didn't care. He swung his sword in a wide, blind arc, narrowly missing Kebbi but landing a solid blow on the sonic screamer.

Vibrations ran up Thanos's arms, jittering his shoulders, shaking the screamer right out of his hands. It landed, dented and spitting sparks, at his feet, no longer functional.

"For Vathlauss!" Hromund screamed.

"For Asgard!" Snorri cried.

"For Odin!" Brusi bellowed.

Thanos lashed out with a fist, catching Hromund under his jaw. It wasn't the most powerful punch Thanos had ever thrown, but it connected. That was all that mattered—he was wearing the plasma knuckles, which sent a burst of explosive energy coursing through Hromund's face. As Thanos watched, the Asgardian's chin split in two clear up to his mouth.

"Ooo assurd!" Hromund exclaimed, and—to Thanos's shock and great respect—kept fighting. His sword glanced off Thanos's armored gauntlet but left a long, deep scar there.

"We can't beat them!" Kebbi cried as she ducked a sword swing from Brusi. Even rattled by the sonic screamer and weakened by her toxin, the Asgardians were fierce warriors.

"We don't have to beat them," Thanos reminded her. "Cha! Change of plans! Do it now!"

In his earbud, Cha's voice came to him. "Now? But you and Kebbi are within the—"

"Now, damnit! *Now!*"

Thanos sidestepped Snorri's sword, then shoved the bloody Asgardian back a few paces. With a swift movement, he grabbed Kebbi by the elbow and dragged her through the door with him. As he watched, the Asgardians—again without so much as a coordinating glance at one another—dropped their swords and unslung their rifles. Thanos and Kebbi were dead in their sights at point-blank range.

"Damn!" Kebbi exclaimed.

Two things happened simultaneously.

First, Thanos slammed his fist into the control for the inner door. It slid shut just as the first energy blasts from the Asgardian rifles struck it.

Second, the outer doors swung open...and the Asgardians opened their mouths in silent screams as the vacuum of space sucked the air and heat from the entryway. They never got to fire a second volley of shots from their rifles as they were plucked from their spots and sucked out the door by the sudden outrush of air. Tossed by inertia high above the lunar surface, they shot hundreds of meters away before the moon's weak gravity dragged them back down to the ground. By then they were already long dead.

Inside, Cha screamed over the communicator. "Did it work? Are you alive? Did it work?"

Thanos tapped his earbud. "You should have more faith in me, Cha."

Kebbi sighed in relief and slumped against the wall. "I told you we should have just shut off the environment field before they arrived."

"Their sensors would have detected the lack of atmosphere, and they wouldn't have left the ship. We had to do it this way." He looked down at his left arm. Hromund's sword had done more than leave a cut in his gauntlet; he saw now that it had cut through the gauntlet and sliced open his forearm to the bone. The whiteness of the bone shocked him.

"Cha, we need medical attention." He used his good hand to bring up a hologram of the *Blood Edda*. "And then we're going out there."

Less than half an hour later, they re-established the environment field and went out to the ship. To Thanos's great surprise, Cha slung a rifle over his shoulder when he joined them.

"Bringing the *fist* in *pacifist*, I see," he commented. "I thought it would take longer for you to see the utility of violence."

Cha curled his upper lip. "I told you—I don't mourn for the Asgardians."

The ramp to the ship was still down and within range of the field, so they simply ambled from the entryway to the ramp, then up the ramp and into the tight confines of the *Blood Edda*.

Where they beheld a woman in a space suit, wielding a battle-ax, who cried out, "Vengeance! By Odin's empty socket!" and swung the ax in a broad arc.

It cut Thanos, in the lead, across his chest, and he watched his own blood jet out of him. He had just enough time to take a breath before the ax swung back again. Barely evading its deadly, blood-smeared gleam, he leaped to one side, colliding with Cha, who slammed into the bulkhead of the ship.

The Asgardian—surely the Goddess of Surprise Attacks, he thought in a moment of vertiginous, mordant sarcasm—seemed no more tired for her swinging of the massive ax. She lashed out again, this time striking Thanos squarely in the meat of his right shoulder. Blood and fire exploded in him. The ax was buried in his flesh and muscle; he could feel it, cold and slimy and burning all at once.

Beneath him, Cha struggled to unsling the rifle he'd brought with him, but Thanos's bulk made it difficult. Kebbi spat out a stream of intense, concentrated venom, but the Asgardian's space suit made her impervious to the poison.

"Blood-destiny!" she cried. "Vengeance-work!" The ax was stuck in Thanos, caught on a bone perhaps, and as she tugged and pulled at it, his entire body flared with impossible pain. It felt as though someone were trying to pull out his innards through his armpit.

Cha managed to wriggle one arm out from under Thanos. At the same time, Kebbi fell back a few steps and drew a pistol she'd purloined from the outpost's armory. When she pulled the trigger, nothing happened...

At first.

An instant later, the Asgardian threw back her head and howled, caught in the throes of a burst of electricity that set her neurons on fire. She danced like a marionette under the control of a toddler, her limbs jangling and flailing.

Most important of all, she let go of the damned ax.

Thanos groaned and rolled onto his back, giving Cha the freedom to aim his rifle. He took a shot at the Asgardian and missed, the plasma bolt erupting instead on a bank of equipment nearby. The equipment exploded into a gout of fire.

"*Pyro-danger!*" the ship's artificial intelligence cried out. "*Pyro-danger!*"

Thanos bellowed in pain as he moved even farther to give Cha a better angle. The ax, still stuck in him, bit deeper into his flesh with every motion, no matter how small.

Cha fired again. Kebbi did at the same time. The Asgardian was caught in the cross fire, and she screamed, her space suit now in flames from the heat of the blasts. The ship's voice became more panicked, and suddenly vents opened and there was a loud hiss of an invisible gas.

And the ramp, Thanos noticed through pain-blurred eyes, was closing. The ship's protocol was to protect itself and its cargo. It would seal the exit and flood itself with nitrogen gas to extinguish the fire.

Thanos could survive on pure nitrogen for a time; Titan's atmosphere was thick with the stuff. He didn't know about Cha or Kebbi...or the Asgardian, for that matter.

With all his strength and with a cry of pain, Thanos forced himself to his feet. The air stank of flame and blood, charred meat and ozone. He could barely see through the haze of smoke.

With an effort that surpassed everything he believed about his own limits, Thanos reached behind himself and took the handle of the ax in his free hand. Screaming into the smoke, he wrenched the blade free. A moment of singular bliss and no pain was immediately consumed by a successive moment of torment that refused to go away. His body felt as on fire metaphorically as the Asgardian was literally.

Barely able to stand, he clutched the ax as blood streamed from his shoulder, running down his arm, slickening the handle. As he watched, the Asgardian's flames died and then snuffed entirely. The nitrogen had done its job. The fire was out, and the ship was re-oxygenating.

She stood tall and proud still, her space suit now a melted second skin. He could not imagine the sheer agony she must be feeling, and yet the only spark in her eyes was one of anger and revenge.

"By ... Freya's beauty," she said, her voice low and halting as she took shallow breaths, "I'll ... have your ... *balls* ... for this."

Cha struggled to his feet next to Thanos. Kebbi came up to his side. They outnumbered her three to one, and yet they were the ones frightened and unsure. The Asgardian slapped her hands together, and the plasma knuckles she wore on each hand sparked to life, sheathing her fists in a bleakly yellow coruscating light.

"Stand down," Thanos told her, his voice shaking. He fought to steady himself, but it was all for naught. He was grievously wounded and couldn't pretend otherwise. "You're hurt. You can't win."

"You're hurt, too," she said. "I've sung my battle-song on the frozen wastelands of Jotunheim. I've breathed hotter fires on the lava shores of Muspelheim. I fear no man, god, or beast. I am Yrsa, daughter of Jorund and Gorm." Her lips curled into a cruel, knowing smile. "You are mortal dung to be scraped off my boot. Yield and your deaths will be honorable."

Before Thanos could respond, Kebbi swore a vile curse and threw herself at Yrsa, who batted her away with a plasma-powered fist. Kebbi reeled off to one side and collided with a series of switches and buttons.

"Damage threshold exceeded," the ship reported. *"Prepare for emergency evacuation."*

In an instant, the ship's thrusters engaged. Thanos was tossed back against the bulkhead from the momentum of the sudden takeoff. Yrsa jerked to one side but grabbed a nearby handhold and kept her feet under her. Cha crumpled to the floor, and Kebbi went stumbling across the chamber to collapse into a chair.

The force of the impact against the wall sent a blistering red shockwave of agony through Thanos, starting at the site of his injury and radiating outward. He dropped the ax and swooned with pain.

Through lidded eyes, he watched as Yrsa strode over to Cha, her fists alight with power. Her stance was wobbly, her movement stiff from the melted space suit, but she was confident and vigorous as she raised a fist.

But before she could bring that powered blow down upon Cha's unprotected skull, Kebbi pounced on her from behind, wrapping her arms around Yrsa's throat, keening at the top of her lungs. She bit down on the Asgardian's head with that wide maw, her needlelike teeth ripping away the space suit and the flesh beneath it. Specks of blood spattered against the wall.

Thanos fought through the pain. He felt around blindly for the ax; his fingers found it and needed two tries to close around its handle. With a growl, he rose to his feet and staggered to where Yrsa was thrashing about the cabin, twisting and turning and trying to land a punch on Kebbi, who clung tightly and kept tearing away hunks of skin and material with her teeth.

Cha got to his feet, bracing himself against the wall. "Be careful!" he cried. "Don't hit Kebbi!"

In that moment, though, all Thanos cared about was killing the Asgardian witch who stood between him and the end of this madness. He hefted the ax over his head, bellowed with the pain that burst from his shoulder, then brought it down. Hard.

And missed.

At the last moment, Yrsa clumsily danced to one side,

still swatting at Kebbi. Thanos's ax crashed into a control panel, spraying steel and wiring in every direction. A panel exploded off and spun wildly through the air, smacking into Cha and knocking him out cold.

"Damage assessment: mortal!" the ship announced. *"Executing retreat protocol!"*

"Don't you dare!" Yrsa cried out, finally finding the leverage she needed to flip Kebbi off her. Kebbi landed on her back, and Yrsa stomped once on her head, then kicked her in the face. Kebbi slid across the floor, perfectly still. "Keep us here!" Yrsa yelled to the ship.

"Override," the system said. *"Retreating."*

With a speed that impressed and terrified, Yrsa ran to Thanos's side and kneed him in the gut, then spun him around and punched him in the gash she'd axed into him. He roared in pain and struck her with his fist, sending her sprawling back across the cabin.

"I'll say this for Asgard," Thanos hissed, "they breed their women strong."

Yrsa responded with a string of invective so vulgar that Thanos had never even heard a third of the words before.

"This ship is retreating to Asgard," Thanos said, laughing through his pain. Blood welled up between his lips, and he spat a mouthful. "Which is precisely where we want to go. You've failed."

"You slew my boon companions," she snarled. "There is no force in the universe that can keep me from killing you."

"Your boon companions were weak," Thanos told her. Darkness had begun to creep in around the edges of his sight. Kebbi was dead. Cha was unconscious. "We are strong. Like you. Join us. We're going to save lives."

"By killing people?"

"Yes. Precisely."

She let loose a mighty yawp and leaped at him. Thanos fell back, knowing that he had no defense—

And Kebbi collided with Yrsa, crashing the two of them into the control panel again. The ship lurched in space. A klaxon rang out, and a new voice warned, *"Off course! Off course!"*

Kebbi's face was a mash of blood and hanging scales. She could barely move her mouth, but she managed to hook her lower teeth into the skin of Yrsa's jaw...and dragged up, raking furrows into the Asgardian's face, shredding the skin of her cheek to reveal the inside of her mouth. Her tongue flapped madly as she keened and howled like a gutted wolf.

Kebbi dragged herself off the Asgardian and over to Thanos, who sank to the floor and cradled her in his arms. Her left eye hung loose from its orbit, and her skull was caved in on one side.

"Thank you," he whispered.

"Told you before..." she slurred. "Meant it before. When said loved you. Meant it."

"You did?"

"No, you naïve, clueless...!" she remonstrated, and died in his arms.

Thanos gritted his teeth. He let Kebbi slip from his arms and, bracing himself against the wall, forced himself to stand. Across the cabin, Yrsa held one hand over her ravaged, bleeding face; with the other she ran fingers over the ship's controls. Competing voices called out:

"Override!"

"Controls locked out!"

"Götterdämmerung protocol!"

And over and over.

He made himself walk to her. He stumbled at the last moment and collided with her, knocking them both to the floor.

"You damned fool!" she said, blood spraying in every direction from her mouth and through her cheek. "We're not—"

"You killed my boon companion," Thanos told her, groaning with pain. The blackness was almost entirely across his field of vision now, but he could still see her, could see the sudden terror in her eyes. "There is no force in the universe that can keep me from killing you."

She pummeled him with both fists until the power in her plasma knuckles went dead. Thanos didn't budge. He lay atop her, holding her down, and he took her head between his massive hands and he closed his useless eyes and squeezed and asked fate or the universe or whatever powers there might be for just this one favor.

The *Blood Edda* tumbled through space, its engines misfiring, its guidance system damaged by the conflict that had raged within. Its protocols demanded that it gain entrance to the Bifrost and return to Asgard, but those protocols had been countermanded by its commander, who had, in her confusion and pain, entered conflicting orders into the control system. Safeguards had been damaged or deactivated in the fight, and now the *Blood Edda* was firing its thrusters in competing directions, trying desperately to comply with all its orders, no matter how mutually exclusive.

It approached the wormhole near Alfheim, tried to course-correct away. Couldn't.

The *Blood Edda* hit the wormhole at a sharp angle and vanished.

Thanos woke to red lights flashing and the voice of the ship's computer screaming warnings, alarms, alerts. He could barely move.

"Thanos! Thanos!"

It was Cha. He'd awakened and was strapped into an emergency crash-couch. "Get up!" Cha screamed. "You have to get up and get to a—"

Cha's words were swallowed by a burst of sound and light

the likes of which Thanos had never heard or seen before. Without proper calculations or protections, they'd hit the wormhole. The *Blood Edda* was now in gate-space, hurtling through the universe with no direction, no course, no safety measures engaged.

Thanos, blissfully, passed out again.

CHAPTER XXVI

HE DREAMED.

He dreamed of *her*.

Gwinth reached out to him. Her skin sloughed off her hand like a rotting glove.

Not yet, she said. *Not yet.*

He opened his eyes. Smoke purled before him. He felt fire nearby.

He could breathe. Barely. Racked by a spasm of coughing from the fumes, his body protested with great agony. The ax. He was damned near cut to pieces.

The smoke parted for a moment, and he saw something loom over him. Standing on two legs, its skin was gray, with a hard shell covering that was blackish green and shiny.

It reached out for him with hands that had too many thumbs, and he sank into the black again.

The next time he awoke, it was for good. He lay in a cocoon of some viscous substance, a white, sticky webbing that wound around his upper body. It smelled slightly of sulfur and bitumen. When he tried to raise a hand, he found that he was bound up in the stuff and couldn't move. He fought against it, and a few strands broke.

"Whoa! Whoa! Don't!" a familiar voice called. Thanos craned his head to the left and saw Cha limping toward him, a similar web wound around his left leg like a cast. "Don't do that!"

"Cha..." Thanos's voice was weak, his throat raw and unslaked. "What's happened to us?"

Cha approached the edge of Thanos's cocoon. It was suspended from the ceiling of what appeared to be a dank cavern that smelled of rot and old food. It swayed slightly when Thanos moved.

"This is a healing mesh," Cha explained. "You've been cocooned for medical reasons. They're healing you."

"Where is Kebbi?" Thanos demanded, though he knew the answer.

"Dead. The Asgardian, too."

Thanos could not spare the energy to sigh. He'd hoped that in the smoke and confusion and pain of the battle with Yrsa, his assessment of Kebbi's injuries had been off.

"I was in a crash-couch," Cha went on, "so I survived the impact. You..."

"I am not yet ready to die. I am—"

"You are alive by great fortune, Thanos. Even you must see that now."

"Luck applied unequally cannot be truly great," he said,

thinking. "If the universe were the fair and equitable place you like to imagine it is, Kebbi would still be alive. And I would not be this misshapen wretch you see before you, and you would not be tethered to me, made to suffer."

"I suffered before I met you. Kidnapped by His Lordship. Taken from everything I knew. You are a blessing, not a curse, Thanos. And I am grateful they saw fit to save you from the wreckage of the ship."

"Who are *they*?" Thanos asked.

Cha hesitated a moment. "They are called the Chitauri."

MIND

Conquer yourself first; the world will follow.

CHAPTER XXVII

IT TOOK MONTHS IN THE HEALING COCOON BEFORE THANOS could support himself again, much less walk. A year and then some passed before he stood on his own two feet and emerged from what he had initially thought to be a cavern.

It was not a cavern. It was a creature, a living monstrosity unlike any he'd ever seen or even heard of. His hosts called it a Leviathan. Like them, it was part insect, part reptile, and part machine. Thanos had never encountered their like before, and he was both disgusted and astonished by them in equal measure.

He had been suspended in the healing cocoon within the mouth of the Leviathan, recovering and slowly piecing himself back together. Now the teeth of the great creature parted, and he and Cha stepped out into the sun for the first time.

The sun was disappointing, to say the least.

A hard black disk in the sky, throwing off precious little light and heat. He understood suddenly why the Chitauri had merged their flesh with machines—insects and reptiles could not survive in such cold conditions, but by melding technology to their biology, they could compensate for their evolutionary weaknesses.

Cha had explained something of the Chitauri to him as the long weeks became longer months in his cocoon. They were a caste-based society, with different social ranks for different assigned tasks. There was a domestic caste, which attended to the mundane tasks of reproduction and the tending of the hearth, while the science caste sought ways to improve the Chitauri biology and technology, securing through artificial means what nature had not deigned to give them.

And there was a warrior caste, he learned, but that caste had accomplished little.

"They share a hive mind," Cha explained. He'd been ingratiating himself into the Chitauri's good graces and learning about their culture while Thanos convalesced. "So there's no superior thinker, no one who can develop tactics and strategy from the perspective of an outsider. They don't know how to create. They have no art."

Thanos stood atop a bluff that overlooked the Chitauri central city, his hands clasped behind his back, Cha at his side. He had hiked up here as a way of testing himself, to see how much of him had survived the battle of the *Blood Edda* and the ensuing crash on the Chitauri homeworld.

He was winded. He was weak. He was no good to anyone. Not now.

"They need someone to guide them," Thanos said, pursing his lips.

"What are you thinking?" Cha asked.

"I am thinking that only an egotist or a fool does not

learn from failure. The egotist blames others, and the fool is not wise enough to assign blame at all." He sat down and stared off into the distance.

Cha sat next to him. The black sun dipped below the horizon, throwing its wavering purple light into the mountains. "You blame yourself for Kebbi's death."

"I blame myself for much. If I learn from it, it will not be so bad. I've had a year to do nothing more than think. It's been . . . instructive."

"And what have you learned?"

Thanos considered. "My goal is grand. But perhaps it makes sense to accomplish it through intermediaries. Rather than exposing myself to harm. Perhaps if I'd warned Titan of its impending calamity through someone else, someone who did not wear this purple and distorted face, my people would have listened. And maybe if we had sent someone ahead to the outpost, Kebbi would still be alive."

"You can't know that."

"No. But look out there and understand, Cha." He gestured out to the city. It was a conglomerate of Leviathans, all arranged around a central vessel called a mothership. It was orderly and distinct, like bees in a hive or ants in a hill. The Chitauri moved with precision, each one a part of a larger whole.

"There is a perfect army here, if only someone could harness it. No need to risk myself or you."

Cha nodded slowly. "There's someone you should meet," he said.

"Are you proposing to help me build an army?" Thanos was mildly amused by Cha's sudden turn away from pacifism. "Did the battle with the Asgardian awaken your own Sirian brand of bloodlust?"

"Hardly," Cha sniffed. "Quite the opposite. But you're trying to save lives on Titan. I believe in that cause. If an army is what it takes to make your people listen, then let's have an army. Violence as a bulwark against greater violence may be ethical after all."

"You're an insufferable optimist," Thanos told him.

"As are you, my friend."

"No. I'm a pragmatist."

Cha shrugged. "In this case, they are one and the same."

Together they entered a small Leviathan through its open mouth. Thanos had not yet become accustomed to the spongy surface of the beast's tongue beneath his feet, and suspected he never would. The mouth was humid and dark, lit by a bioluminescent spittle that ran down the "walls."

Toward the top of the gullet, they found a protuberance of cartilage that had the rough shape of a table, with a figure sitting behind it. As they approached, the figure stood.

Like all Chitauri, the creature looked to be a hybrid of insect and reptile, with the steely mechanics of a cyborg added for good measure. It opened its mouth and hissed neutrally, as though merely proving it could. Something about its demeanor, though, struck Thanos as different from the other Chitauri he'd met. They had been bent to tasks, rarely meeting his eyes or pausing to speak to him. This one, though...

"What is it?" Thanos murmured to Cha.

"Not *it*," Cha whispered back. *"He."*

"Welcome, Thanos of Titan," the Chitauri hissed. "I am called the Other."

"The Other," Thanos mused. "As opposed to what?"

The Other raised his hands, flexing the two opposable thumbs on each one. The Chitauri's only significant natural evolutionary advantage. Their enhanced manual dexterity just barely made up for the bad luck of being born cold-blooded on a frigid world.

"There is no *what*," the Other said. "I am simply Other. Apart. Distinct." He hissed the *s* in *distinct* as though angry at it.

"He's a mutation," Cha said, "though they don't have that word. He isn't part of the hive mind."

Thanos raised an eyebrow. "A deviant. A genetic misfit. Like me. Unique."

The Other inclined his head in agreement. "As you say."

"Then I will say that it is a pleasure to meet you." Thanos extended his hand.

The Other stared at it until Cha prompted him with "We've practiced this, remember?"

The double thumbs wrapped strangely around Thanos's hand, but it was a good first handshake on this new planet.

"I owe you a debt of gratitude," Thanos said, "for saving my life and the life of my companion. I regret that we have nothing to offer except our thanks."

"You have more than that," the Other said. Without warning, he touched Thanos's temple. Thanos resisted the urge to pull away.

"You have your brain," the Other told him. "And we wish to use it."

Thanos shot an alarmed glance at Cha, who shook his head minutely. *It's not what you think*, that shake communicated. *It's okay.*

"I am fond of my brain where it is," Thanos said. "It serves me well there."

The Other bowed ever so slightly. "My apologies. I am still unaccustomed to your tongue, and my meaning was not clear. You may keep your brain, Thanos. We wish you to use it on our behalf."

"What for?" Thanos mused. "From what I've seen, your society runs well. Your people are fed, clothed, and safe. What more do you need?"

"Chitauri wish to conquer," the Other said without inflection, as though discussing the weather. "Chitauri wish to leave this world and find other, warmer climes. We have weapons and skills. We have technology and power. But no leader. The warrior caste cannot adapt to combat situations because all decisions must go through the hive mind first. Too slow. The hive mind is a yoke."

"So you need someone at the reins of the cart," Thanos said, stroking his jaw. "Why not you? You have independent thought."

The Other shook his head slowly. "I lack the experience. I can communicate directly with the hive mind, influence it, guide it. I can issue commands, but I do not know what those commands should be." He paused here and tapped his four thumbs together in a complicated gesture. "You, Thanos, are a warrior. You have bested an Asgardian. You can lead us."

Cha nodded to Thanos. "You said you wanted an army."

Thanos touched his chin, feeling the ridges that fate and cruelty and genetics had put there. "Yes. Yes, I did."

He made a pact with the Other that very day: He would bring the Chitauri to a new world, one more palatable to them, and in return they would be his soldiers, his intermediaries as he sought to save Titan.

"But these goals need not be consecutive," Thanos told him. "We can achieve them mutually. We can work on them at the same time."

The Other nodded. "Yes. This is sensible and acceptable. It will save time and bring us each our desires that much quicker."

"Then we have an accord," said Thanos.

It was mutual exploitation, and both parties were fine with it. The Chitauri would gain a new homeworld, and

Thanos would gain an army that could impose his will on Titan. Each time the universe handed him a setback, he found a way to turn it around and reorient himself toward his ultimate goal. His flexibility was as important as his pre-planning. He hadn't been able to reach Hala. The Asgardians had bested him. Fine. No single plan was his only plan. His mind was fecund. He could adapt.

The trip through the wormhole at Alfheim had been impromptu. With the *Blood Edda* totaled on impact, Thanos had no way to determine at what angle they'd entered the wormhole or how long they'd traveled within it. The unique black sun in the Chitauri world's sky made it difficult to reckon the precise placement of stars.

He spent the better part of another year on the Chitauri homeworld figuring out how to get back to Titan. During this time, he also inventoried the Chitauri's supplies and weapons, as well as their fighting abilities. The Leviathans were capable of interstellar flight, it turned out—great, ghastly beasts that could live in the airless vacuum of space, bearing Chitauri safe within them.

Too, the Chitauri possessed a rudimentary teleportation technology. Thanos had never seen anything quite like it— it seemed to open mini-wormholes in space-time, creating portals that could transport a being from one spot to another without bothering to cross the distance between.

He spent a great deal of time experimenting with this technology. Many Chitauri died during his clinical trials, and many more lined up to participate. With so many corpses at his disposal, he also began a series of investigations into Chitauri anatomy and biology, scrutinizing them down to their bizarre, tripartite genetic structure. His father had taught him the elements of genetic manipulation, and soon Thanos was breeding a hardier warrior caste. The Chitauri were grateful. Once again, science delivered to them what nature could not.

His experience on the *Blood Edda* haunted him. On the *Golden Berth*, his intellect and size had been sufficient to win the day, but against a prepared, capable fighter, he'd been useless. With the Chitauri as sparring partners, he trained in a multitude of armed and unarmed fighting techniques. Many more Chitauri died as his skills improved. They didn't seem to mind. They were a fertile, fecund species who shared a mind; individuals were fungible.

With his training came an appreciation for the capacity and capabilities of his body. He'd spent his life despising his physical form, retreating into intellect and reason. His had been a life of the mind.

But now he could hurl a spear a hundred meters and strike his target dead-on. He could fend off four trained Chitauri warriors, his body's speed and resistance to harm a marvel to him. He learned how to anticipate his opponents' moves and counter them, his body and mind—for the first time in his life—working in concert. His bulk, his broad shoulders, his height... These were *advantages*. And he couldn't believe he'd ever allowed himself to think otherwise.

In time, he came to enjoy the training. The thrust and parry, the feint and dodge. He was becoming a fighter *and* a thinker. A warrior-intellect.

He felt joyously unstoppable.

Still, he knew he'd missed his opportunity to invade Asgard and claim the artifact, the thing Vathlauss had called the Aether, or the Infinity Stone. It was possible he didn't need it, though. He could adapt to the new reality of his situation. No Asgardian weapon, true, but his original plan might still suffice. If he could return to Titan with an army, that would be persuasive.

Cha was at his side the whole time as he sparred and planned and recuperated, reminding Thanos to rest, exhorting him to take care of himself. "What good is it to return to Titan as a conquering hero and savior if you die yourself?"

Thanos didn't bother explaining to Cha that dying on and for Titan had always been part of the plan.

"I'm surprised you've agreed to this accord at all, Cha. What does your particular brand of listless pacifism say about armies? Soldiers? Cannon fodder?"

"They're only barely alive," Cha said. "I've been among them much longer than you have. They don't think the way we do. They don't have independent, individual souls."

Thanos couldn't help remembering Robbo and what Kebbi had said about him. *Some people lead. Some people want to* be *led.* "Is that all that matters?" he asked Cha. "Soul, not mind?"

"If any one of them dies," Cha pointed out, "there are a thousand others in the hive mind who have the same thoughts and memories and impulses. I don't question their minds. But if thoughts are communally shared, where is individual liberty? Where is the individual's ability to discern between right and wrong?"

They argued such issues long into the inky-black Chitauri nights, huddled in the maw of a Leviathan, warmed by its body heat. In time, Thanos grew used to the fetid odor of the beast.

He spent hours poring over charts and plans, applying the same intellect that had led to his discovery of the flaw at Titan's core to the problem of returning to his home. Within a few months, they'd established contact with some nearby trading routes. Shortly after that, they were able to contact Xandar and Hala, opening channels of communication that made it possible to begin plotting a star chart that would take them from the Chitauri homeworld to Titan.

And one night, Thanos was awakened from a deep sleep by Cha, who stood over him, trembling ever so slightly, his lips turned down and his eyes moist.

"What's wrong?" Thanos asked.

"We finally re-established a line of communication across the arc tangent of the galaxy," Cha said. "I got a message through to Titan. Or so I thought."

Thanos sat up. He knew. Deep in his heart, deep in his gut, he knew. But he made Cha say it anyway.

"It's happened," Cha told him. "I'm so sorry, Thanos. It's happened."

He retreated to the hills over the Chitauri city. He wanted to be alone in his grief. None of them could understand. The Chitauri literally had no words in their language to describe the death of a loved one, since everyone's thoughts were shared anyway. A dead Chitauri's experiences lived on in all other Chitauri. And Cha...

He lay out on a field of hardy grass, staring up into the night sky. The Chitauri homeworld had three visible moons, two of which he could see tonight. From perturbations in the tides, Thanos had calculated that there had to be a fourth moon as well, this one locked into orbit with one of the other three such that it couldn't be seen.

The sky was black and cold. His breath fogged the air. One moon glimmered redly, while the other shone a bright white. It made him think of His Lordship's mismatched eyes.

But only for a moment. Because then his thoughts returned, inevitably, to Titan.

Titan, which had broadcast a signal into the universe, warning any and all travelers to stay away. A signal that had been amplified and retransmitted through the galaxy, eventually picked up by Cha.

Calamity had arrived. As he'd known it would. As he'd promised.

Until the very instant that Cha told him, Thanos had held out the tiniest hope, borne on a shard of self-doubt, that he'd been wrong all along. That he'd miscalculated and Titan would thrive.

Instead, he'd been proven right in short order.

Sintaa and Gwinth. The only people in the entire universe other than Cha who Thanos could call *friends*. It was possible that they were already dead. They had forsaken him at a crucial moment, yes, but he'd forgiven them almost effortlessly. They were scared. Fear spurred poor judgment. He hoped they still lived, even though he knew the odds were long. His dreams of Gwinth continued her decay—he held a foolish notion that since she was not completely rotted away in his dreams, that maybe she was still alive, waiting for him to rescue her.

He told no one of this thought. It was his and it was pathetic, and he concealed it greedily.

Then there was his mother.... How safe was *she*, locked away in that storehouse for mad Titans? Was that the best place for her, attended to by synths, who would most likely survive the initial wave of chaos? Or was being in the psychosylum like being handcuffed to a block as the water rose around you?

And his father...

He refused to think of his father at all.

He could not recall the last time he'd wept. As a child, certainly. He would not cry now.

He wished, however, that he could.

It took several more months to outfit a Leviathan to survive passage through the unstable wormhole. And then Thanos and Cha bid the Other farewell.

"When next we meet, Thanos," the Other said, "the Chitauri will have a mighty army, ready for our mutual benefit."

"Thanos looks forward to leading such an army," Cha said smoothly. Thanos himself was too busy making the final calculations for travel through the wormhole. Too busy shunting memories of Titan to a place in his mind where they could not distract him.

His deal with the Other, the plans they'd made together . . . They didn't matter anymore. He wanted only to get off this damned frigid planet. Back to Titan. Surely, there were survivors. Surely, not *everyone* had been killed. . . .

He no longer needed an army. He needed a miracle.

Got any miracles on you, Thanos of Titan? Kebbi had asked him once. *If not, don't bother.*

He had no miracles in his possession, but he had to do something anyway. He had to try.

They lifted off from the Chitauri homeworld at midnight, passing through the dark atmosphere and into the darker reaches of space. It was the first time Thanos had seen the planet from above; he had been unconscious and near-dead when they'd arrived on the exploding remains of the *Blood*

Edda. The entire globe looked like a grimy black pearl, coruscating dirty light refractions from the useless sun.

"What's our plan?" Cha asked quietly, so as not to be overheard. The Leviathans weren't intelligent, but they were connected to the hive mind, and Thanos hadn't yet figured out how great a distance the hive mind could project over.

"We enter the wormhole at a thirty-two-degree angle against the plane of the elliptic," Thanos told Cha, showing him a quickly rendered hologram of their flight path. He had had to install special controls that bonded with the Leviathan's cortex in order to be certain the beast could maintain the proper approach angle. "That should take us back to civilized space. Where, hopefully, we can sell this monstrosity for enough money to rent a space ark with medical facilities."

The garbled message from Titan that Cha had received was actually a repeating warning from a beacon placed in orbit around the planet:

"ATTENTION, LOCAL TRAVELERS: Avoid landing on Titan. REPEAT: Avoid landing on Titan. Environmental Hazard and pandemic. Set course for Ceti Prime instead."

"An environmental disaster brought on by overcrowding," Thanos said. "Just as one of the outcomes my models predicted. And the resulting deaths must have overwhelmed the mortuary and funereal systems. There would have been bodies in the streets for days, more than likely leading to an outbreak of antibiotic-resistant pathogens. A global pandemic."

He buried his face in his hands. "I warned them, Cha. I warned all of them, and they didn't listen!"

Cha rested a hand on Thanos's shoulder. "I know, my friend. The universe sought to speak through you, and they ignored its wise counsel."

"Enough!" Thanos growled, slapping Cha's hand away. "I see no balance in children dead in the streets! I see no harmony in innocents choking to death on poison air!"

Cha backed away slowly. "Of course. I'm sorry."

He left, leaving Thanos, grief-stricken, to retreat deeper into the gullet of the Leviathan.

They entered the wormhole at precisely thirty-two degrees. The Leviathan shook and twisted and roared, but the additional plating they'd grafted to its outer carapace sufficed, and it survived the trip.

They wound up in Kree space. Thanos smiled grimly at the irony. At the onset of his exile, he'd intended to go to Kree space, marshal his forces, and return to Titan. Now he was doing precisely that, though far too late.

Fortune smiled upon them, and on one of the Kree rimworlds, they found a trader who was fascinated by the Leviathan's intermingling of insect, reptilian, and mechanical parts. They walked away with enough money to rent a medium-size cargo ship and install dozens of auto-medical bays. Cha spent the better part of a week fine-tuning the bays to respond to Titanian physiologies while Thanos retrofitted the ship's loading shuttles to serve as ambulances from the surface to the ship.

He was going home. He was going home at last. The thought, the reality, the *truth*, struck him at odd, random times. Particularly when he was trying his best to concentrate on the task at hand, it would assail him from nowhere, and he would be forced to step away from his work for a moment, to bask in it, to process it, to let the intermingled joy and grief wash over him.

He could not hope that Gwinth or Sintaa had survived. The odds were long against them. But he would take whomever he could. He would load them into his shuttlecraft and bring them to the cargo ship-*cum*-hospital, which he had already—appropriately—renamed *Sanctuary*. Once aboard, he and Cha would succor those who could be saved and ease the pain of those who could not. They would give comfort to the dying and life to the rest.

And then...

And then they would find a new world. A ship full of refugees was rarely welcome in most parts of the galaxy, but Thanos would find a place. A new world. A final sanctuary for the survivors of Titan.

They blasted off from the Kree rimworld more than a year and a half after the initial message from the Titan beacon had reached them on the Chitauri homeworld. In Kree space, they no longer had to rely on the haphazard and dangerous placement of wormholes. There were transport gates in every system, sometimes more than one. With the last of their monetary reserves from the sale of the Leviathan, they paid the gate toll to Titan and received an automated warning:

"*TRAVELERS: Be aware that the Titan system is currently under voluntary quarantine. You travel there at your own risk.*"

Hovering just above the gate, Thanos looked over at Cha, who had joined him in *Sanctuary*'s cockpit. "Your last chance to abandon the Mad Titan's quest," Thanos told him.

"They need us," Cha said simply.

Thanos engaged the forward thrusters and guided them into the gate and to his home.

CHAPTER XXVIII

FOR THE FIRST TIME IN YEARS, THANOS BEHELD THE orange-swaddled orb that was Titan. From a distance of thousands of kilometers, the planet looked exactly the same as it had when he'd left, with no indication as to the havoc that lurked beneath the haze.

Warning buoys drifted in descending orbits around the globe, sounding their alarms as he guided *Sanctuary* closer and closer.

"WARNING! You are nearing a quarantined planet! Proceed at your own risk!"

Which was precisely what he planned to do.

At sub-lightspeed, it seemed to take forever to find a reasonable parking orbit. He'd expected to pick up signals from survivors by this point, but the local comms channel was silent and dead.

He established an orbit as close to the planet's atmosphere as possible. He wanted minimal distance for the shuttlecraft to travel.

Sanctuary was a cargo ship. She had not been designed to land on planets, to suffer the stresses of gravity. For that, they had the shuttlecraft, which were built to ferry pallets of cargo from ship to surface and back but had been modified by Thanos to serve as a combination of ambulance and clinic. Thanks to the automated piloting systems, he estimated they could rescue four thousand Titans at a time from the surface of the planet to *Sanctuary*.

They waited. Thanos assumed that survivors would have clustered in the Eternal City, but he didn't want to send his shuttlecraft there without being certain. There was a chance—however small—that people had fled the clotted and disease-wracked city streets for the open foothills of the cryovolcanoes.

"There's a signal," Cha said suddenly, pointing to a holographic readout. "It's weak, but it's not background noise. It's definitely a signal. From here."

Thanos's eyes widened. "The center of the Eternal City," he rumbled. "The MentorPlex."

"The what?"

It was forever ago that he and Sintaa had stared up at the floating androids as they assembled the MentorPlex, casting A'Lars's will into reality.

"Never mind," Thanos said. "It makes perfect sense that survivors would gather there." He stood abruptly from his command chair, barking orders over his shoulder as he left the cockpit. "Send the shuttlecraft to that location. I'll take the command module down myself."

"You're going down?" Cha leaped up and followed him. "Thanos, you don't know what it's like down there! The surface...the disease..."

"I'll be in an environment suit."

They marched through the corridor of the ship, toward the command module drop point. "That might not be enough," Cha argued. "You don't know exactly what sort of pathogen you're dealing with. You can't risk yourself like that."

Thanos paused at the door to the command module. "They've been terrified and lost for years," he told Cha. "If we just send down a fleet of shuttles and a message to get on board, they won't listen. They need someone down there to tell them it's safe."

"You could die," Cha warned him.

The concern was touching, if misplaced. Thanos offered a tight, humorless grin. "I haven't yet."

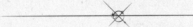

He thumbed open the door. Beyond lay a large chamber, in the center of which was a small, sleek vessel. The command module. From here the captain of *Sanctuary* could run all the ship's functions while outside the ship itself. Cargo vessels frequently turned off life support to conserve energy during the laborious process of loading and unloading, so the command module was where the captain would supervise that procedure while the ship was crewed by robots and artificial intelligences.

He rummaged in a nearby locker for his environment suit. The standard suits that came with *Sanctuary* had been too small for him, so he'd taken two apart and welded them back together. He tugged experimentally at the seams; they held.

"At least take this," Cha said with exasperation.

Thanos turned to his friend. From another locker, Cha had unearthed a medium-length pole with a flaring, curved spike at the end.

"Where did you get that?" Thanos asked.

"I liberated it and some other gear before we sold the Leviathan. Take it."

Thanos stared doubtfully at the Chitauri battle-staff that Cha held out to him. "I don't need a weapon. These are my people."

"They've been ravaged by disease and disaster," Cha protested. "They're not the people you left behind. And may I remind you that they were never quite fond of you to begin with?"

Thanos bristled at the comment—not from its harshness but rather from its truth. Time had a way of whitewashing memory. The acrimony of Titan had faded in his mind, become a background to the greater need of his people. In his thoughts, his own love for them had become turned around and twisted into reciprocal love for him. He thought rarely of his father or of the looks of shock and disgust that had been the backdrop to his childhood. Instead, subconsciously, he permitted himself mostly memories of Sintaa, of Gwinth, even of the synths who had cared for his mother.

His mother. He thought of her, and not of her madness.

"Titans are proud but not stupid," he told Cha. "They know now I was right. They'll welcome me with open arms."

"I'm worried about exactly what kind of arms those might be," Cha replied. "Live up to your people's reputation: Don't be stupid. Take the damned staff, Thanos. Just in case."

With a resigned sigh, he accepted the weapon and collapsed it to its carry-form. "I'm only doing this because the irony of a pacifist insisting I be armed amuses me," Thanos told him.

"I didn't give it to you as a pacifist," Cha replied. "I did it as your friend."

Thanos piloted the command module through the thick soup of Titan's atmosphere, trying not to think of his last voyage of this kind. He'd been going in the opposite direction in the vessel known—temporarily—as *Exile I*. He'd been certain that his people were doomed, and now he had proof that he was right.

When he broke through the cloud cover, he beheld devastation.

Even kilometers above the Eternal City, he could make out the outline of the City perimeter. Just barely. It had been encroached upon by a massive flow of cryomagma from the ridge of cryovolcanoes. Orange dust swam everywhere— consolidated organonitrates from the cryo-eruptions. The cryomagma would have exploded to the surface, swamped the City, and then almost immediately frozen solid. Those struck by its initial blast would have been flash frozen in an instant.

The sudden drop in temperature would have caused the City's weather-modulation systems to overcompensate. The cryomagma would have melted and then refrozen....The City would have gone into a panic.

Worse yet, he noticed new foothills on the west side of the City. Plate tectonics in action. With the cryomagma moving from under the crust to the surface, the delicate subterranean balance had been disrupted. The geologic plates beneath the City had shifted, with the western plate rising up to create a whole new topography...and probably wiping out half the City in one fell swoop.

Thanos gritted his teeth and kept an eye on the hologram that was locked onto the signal Cha had received in orbit. It was stronger now, under the cloud cover, and it was definitely emanating from the MentorPlex.

I'm truly going home.

He found a clearing ten kilometers from the MentorPlex, in what had been a shopping bazaar. The stalls and kiosks were abandoned, many of them folded away, leaving him enough room to set down the command module.

His environment sensors told him that the air outside was breathable but contained high levels of carcinogens and at least four unknown pathogens. He slipped into his environment suit and tested it for leaks. It was sound.

When the entry portal to the module opened, a dull wind picked up as the air pressure between the module and the outside obeyed the laws of physics and balanced. Orange dust swirled into the command module and lay in thin sheets on the control board. He stood in the doorway and hesitated, gazing out at the utterly empty bazaar. In his experience, no part of the City had ever been so barren. It almost didn't seem like Titan at all.

After a moment, he turned back and tucked the collapsed Chitauri staff into a holster at his side, then stepped down onto the surface of the planet Titan for the first time in years.

All around him, eddies in the air spun cyclones of dust. The air was cold, almost as cold as on the Chitauri homeworld, despite the brighter, warmer sun.

He looked around, half expecting to see someone approach him, half expecting bodies stacked ten deep. But there was nothing. The bazaar had been abandoned.

"Cha," he said into his comms, "I've arrived on the surface."

Static responded to him. Too much pollution in the atmosphere. He couldn't broadcast with the low-powered personal comms unit. He would be cut off from Cha for the duration.

Consulting his handheld scanner, he confirmed that the signal was coming from the MentorPlex. It towered over the rest of the City, its upper stories swathed in dust and clouds.

The tower was bent slightly, leaning off-kilter, no longer perpendicular to the ground. The same groundquakes that had razed the western side of the City had wreaked havoc on A'Lars's grand accomplishment as well.

Thanos double-checked the oxygen-nitrogen mix in his air tanks, then began walking home.

It was slow going in the confining environment suit, and as he got closer, the streets and walkways became clogged with debris, trash, and then bodies.

The first body he saw was a young girl, no older than eight or ten. She lay in perfect repose, as though she'd become tired and decided to take a nap here on the walkway. Thanos knelt by her. She seemed so peaceful that he could not believe she was actually dead, but when he touched her, she did not move, and her flesh had the yielding, slippery feel of a corpse. She had died here, and the cold and the aridity had preserved her thus. It was worse than finding her rotting or skeletal. She was a parody of life and of death at the same time.

"Sleep well, child," he murmured, and continued on his way.

He thought of Gwinth, the Gwinth of his dreams. She was rotting away. Not at all like these eerily preserved cadavers. The dream did not match reality. Maybe that meant she still lived....

He chided himself for superstition. For giving into mysticism and magical thinking. Dreams were nothing more than dreams. She was alive or she was not, and the difference had nothing to do with the random neurons firing in his brain at night.

By the time he arrived at the MentorPlex, he had become inured to the sight of bodies. He'd stopped counting at a hundred, finding it pointless. He had proposed killing half of Titan, and now so many more were dead. He'd been right beyond his wildest imaginings.

How many had survived? A few thousand in the Mentor-Plex, he surmised, and twice that number in shelters along the edge of the City.... Perhaps as much as ten percent of the population of Titan in the best-case scenario.

He could have saved *half* of them. If only they had listened.

Within half a kilometer of the MentorPlex, the roads were so clotted with bodies and refuse that he drew his staff and locked it into its full fighting length to use as a walking stick as he maneuvered over and around piles. He no longer paused to mourn the dead. There were too many. The smell overwhelmed the air recirculators in his environment suit and soon the stench of dead and desiccated bodies filled his helmet. He increased the antibiotic and antiviral mix of chemicals in his breathing air to compensate.

The MentorPlex's lean was more egregious the closer he got. He began to wonder how the building managed to keep from toppling over, so steep was its angle. A'Lars's architectural and material-sciences genius was evident in the mere standing of the tower.

The main entrance was jammed shut by fallen steel and

rubble. It took Thanos an hour to navigate the treacherous, cumbered circumference of the tower to the emergency portal along the eastern side. The door's controls worked, but a short circuit somewhere had disconnected them from the door itself. Every time he pushed the button, he was greeted with a success trill and a flash of green light, but the door would slide open only an inch before shutting again.

So he wedged the Chitauri staff in the inch-wide gap when it appeared, and leaned into it with all his weight. Chitauri metal and his raw strength won out, and the door ground open even farther, then stuck there. Just enough room for Thanos to squeeze in.

He was in the lobby of the MentorPlex, where tenants and visitors would pass through on their way to the lifts. The lights were out. An emergency protocol, no doubt. Power had to be conserved for life support in the necessary areas of the MentorPlex. Splashy, abstract photonic art had decorated the walls, but without power the place was just a small, dark chamber with a floor covered in a scrim of orange dust. According to his portable scanner, the signal was coming from below the surface. In addition to five hundred stories above the ground, the MentorPlex also extended fifty stories below. A perfect place to wait out the environmental disasters and keep quarantined from the plague.

His environment suit had a built-in headlamp, which he now activated. The orange dust swirled around him in eddies conjured by his footsteps. There were no bodies here.

He'd passed through this lobby more times than he could readily recall. It had been a place of life, cramped with comers and goers. Now it was empty and hollow.

The antigravity lifts were offline, of course, since there was no power. He broke down the door to one with the help of the Chitauri staff and gazed into the black abyss of the empty lift shaft. The scanner confirmed that the signal emanated from down there.

A fifty-story climb. Or drop, if he slipped.

Back outside, he rummaged through the wreckage and scrap piled around the building, until he found several lengths of stout cable, which he fused with blasts from the battle-staff. Dragging it inside, he tied the new single cable around an outcropping of bent steel. He tested it with all his strength.

Before he could change his mind, he tossed the free end of the cable down the shaft and began his descent.

After ten stories, his arms and shoulder complained. After thirty, they burned with the effort of hauling his own considerable body weight. The only way he could mark his progress was by twisting to aim his headlamp down occasionally to make sure there was nothing impeding his progress. As best he could tell, it was one endless black well all the way down.

He reached the bottom with inches of cable left to spare, his shoulders afire, his fingers numb and sweat-slick in his gloves. The scanner told him that the air was free of pathogens and safe to breathe, so he removed the helmet of his suit and wiped perspiration from his face with the back of his hand.

He was in the ink-black bottom of an elevator shaft that stretched from his position to nearly a kilometer in the sky. Wind whispered above him. Echoes and creaks sounded all around. The entire MentorPlex seemed as though it could collapse in on him at any moment.

All the more reason not to dally. The door to the lift was to his right—he bashed and slammed his way through it, aware that the sound of his approach was probably sending thrills of fear into the survivors. Still, there was no way to be gentle.

When he entered the corridor, a series of lights flickered to life, dimly illuminating an old maintenance access hall-way. Power had been conserved for the last meters leading to the survivors.

He walked down the corridor, lights coming to life ahead of him and fading behind. It was a short trip to a large, stout door. Too thick and sturdy for him to blast or bash through. With a slightly trembling hand, he reached out to touch its surface. It was cold and clammy.

Beyond this door lay the remains of his people. They could have been trapped within for years. He hoped their better natures had won out, but he prepared himself for a tableau of blood and horror. Being cooped up for so long, with the weight of the calamity upon them, could do horrible things to the psyches of even the kindest and best-adjusted people.

He rapped at the door, the sound blunt and muted. Just when he thought nothing would happen, a small hatch opened in the ceiling. A globe drifted down and bathed him in a green light. A body scanner.

The door slid open as though it had been installed and freshly oiled the day before. Thanos steeled himself and stepped inside.

The door slid shut behind him, simultaneous with overhead lights sparking and flaring to life.

He'd expected a hovel, an overcrowded room gone to filth from the presence of scores of Titans crammed into the only safe location and forced to subsist there.

Instead, the room was bright and clean. Obsessively clean, really—he spied not even a mote of dust. It measured perhaps ten meters to a side, the walls polished and gleaming steel, the floor and ceiling cast in a burnished alloy that reflected and held the light. It was a box, and it was empty except for a long oblong crate at the far end.

Thanos double-checked his scanner. The signal was strongest here. It was coming from *right here*. But there was no one—

The oblong crate hissed and the lid opened. A figure within sat up, then stood. Thanos fumbled with his scanner, lost the battle, and dropped it with a resounding clatter and clang.

It was his father.

It was A'Lars.

He had survived.

His jaw dropped as he beheld his father, surely the last person he expected to see. "Father!" Thanos exclaimed, then berated himself for saying something so obvious and pointless. For all he'd accomplished since his exile, he reverted to a child in the presence of his father. Foolish.

As he watched, his father climbed smoothly and gracefully out of the crate, then stood erect and, gazing directly at Thanos, began to speak.

"Welcome. I am A'Lars, architect of the Eternal City of Titan. You are speaking to a synthetically intelligent version of myself. I, tragically, died in the environmental collapse that killed the population of Titan."

"Wait." Thanos stepped forward. "Repeat that."

The synth that wore his father's face tilted its head and smiled somewhat indulgently. "I am equipped with a variety of personality inventories depending upon my conversation partner. Please hold still for bioscan."

Closer to his father than he'd been in years, yet farther away than ever, Thanos stood motionless as the synth scanned him. When the scan was done, its facial expression softened just slightly.

"Thanos," it said. "My son."

"Father. What's happened? Where are the survivors?"

The synth smiled sadly. "There are no survivors. The

environmental disasters combined with a global pandemic to form an extinction-level event. Every living thing on Titan is no more."

It delivered the news in an approximation of a gentle tone, which somehow infuriated Thanos all the more. His father had never used such a tone with him, and yet he had programmed his synth to speak to him thusly, should the synth encounter him. And since A'Lars had bothered programming the synth to recognize Thanos, that meant...

"You knew I'd come," Thanos whispered. "You banished me from my home, but you knew I'd come. You were relying on me to save you, despite yourself."

"My son." The synth opened its arms for an embrace, still smiling that sad smile. "My faith in you has been rewarded. You have returned to us. We are saved."

"Saved?" The synth's biotechnical circuitry must have corrupted over the years, in spite of the clean room in which it "lived." "There's no one to save. Everyone died."

He realized that he'd clenched his fists and his jaw, that angry white flecks of spittle had gathered on his lips and in the grooves of his chin.

"My son," A'Lars said from the synthetic realm of almost-life, with a sympathy and a kindness he'd never expressed while alive. "There *is* a way. Let me show you."

And he smiled. Not a sad smile. A bright one, a joyous one, and it twisted his face into something unrecognizable, something that had never existed in life.

"You let them all die!" Thanos stepped back. "I told you it was coming, and you ignored me! No, you did *worse* than ignore me. If you'd ignored me, I could have forgiven you. Because at least then you would have the excuse of not hearing my warning. But you *listened* to me. You heard everything I had to say. And you *still* banished me!"

"Thanos, that is all in the past. There is a path to the future, for you and for Titan. Please. Hear me out. Our people are dead, but they may yet still live."

Shaking his head, Thanos felt the room press around him. He was keenly aware that he was fifty stories beneath the surface, fifty stories away from open space and air, no matter how befouled. Fifty stories under a tower that listed dangerously and could collapse in on him at any moment. He'd never been claustrophobic before, but now the walls seemed closer, the ceiling lower.

"You're mad," he said, his voice trembling in a combination of fury and fear.

"No, Thanos. Behold! The Gene Library!" With that, a small hatch in the floor at Thanos's feet opened and an orb the size of a head drifted up, hovering in position between them.

"Gene Library?"

"My greatest invention," said not-A'Lars. "Long after your exile, I found myself reexamining your data and predictions. I arrived at similar conclusions, with variances well within a statistical regularity. Once I realized that your predicted environmental collapse could actually occur, I took it upon myself to collect DNA from certain Titans, the very best of us. These samples have been preserved here, in perfect cryostasis, waiting for rescue. With them, you can clone our people back into existence, Thanos. Titan will live again!"

Staring at the Gene Library and its smooth, unlined surface, Thanos found himself—quite to his surprise—performing calculations. DNA samples could be small. The globe was only half a meter in diameter, but that could contain *hundreds of thousands* of samples, properly and conservatively stored.

Including...His mother? Sintaa? Gwinth? Dare he believe it?

No. He knew his father. A'Lars preserved "the very best" of Titan. Sintaa and Gwinth would not have met his elitist standards. Nor would poor, mad, flawed Sui-San.

Thanos reached out and touched the cold, perfect exterior of the Gene Library. It was functional and beautiful, a true testament to his father's craftsmanship and dedication to detail.

Dedication to detail. Yes. To all details except the ones that mattered.

"You took nothing upon yourself," he said quietly.

"I'm afraid I didn't hear you," A'Lars said calmly.

Thanos's upper lip curled. He pulled his hand away from the Gene Library.

"I said, you took *nothing* upon yourself! You're a synthetic person. A *thing*. You think you're A'Lars, but you're just his ghost. You're what he *thinks* he was, rattling around in the confines of your artificial skull."

"You're upset," the synth said soothingly. "This is understandable. You've endured serious trauma. I can offer you a mood-stabilizer, if you like. Then you are to take the Gene Library with you. Return to a place of safety, and use it to resurrect Titan."

"Couldn't resist investing your simulacrum with your penchant for giving orders, eh, Father?" Thanos said sardonically. "Still telling me what to do from beyond the grave."

The synth clucked its tongue in a way A'Lars never had, though perhaps he thought he had. "Thanos. Think things through and you'll agree that my way is best."

"Fight me!" Thanos shouted. "Tell me I'm wrong and you're right! Then maybe I'll believe you're A'Lars and do your bidding!"

The synth smiled somewhat indulgently. "I'm not programmed for conflict with you, Thanos."

Somehow, that spiked his rage higher, fueled his anger. *Not programmed.* Not programmed *for conflict with you, Thanos?*

With a roar, Thanos unsheathed the Chitauri battlestaff at his side. It snapped to its full length instantly, and he swung it in a wide arc, bringing its electrified blade into contact with the synth's neck. For an instant, the synth's expression was one of such horror and shock that Thanos thought it was truly his father brought back to life, that he'd made a terrible mistake.

But the blade continued, severing the head, and Thanos saw not actual blood, but rather what he knew to be the viscous biofuel that coursed through the artificial veins of a synth. The head bounced once on the floor, then lay there. The synth's body remained standing, poised, as though rudely interrupted mid-thought.

For some reason, that odd, headless preternatural calm enraged him further. He raised the staff and brought it down again, this time cleaving the synth's torso in two down to the end of the sternum.

"*This* is conflict!" he shouted. "*This* is conflict with Thanos!"

When he wrenched the staff's blade free, it skidded off to one side, striking the floating Gene Library, which shot away from him and spanged off a wall. It hovered a little lower in the air now, dented on one side. As he stalked over to it, Thanos detected the hissing sound of escaping gases. The liquid nitrogen with which A'Lars had preserved the DNA samples was turning to gas and escaping.

"Good!" Thanos crowed. "Good! You deserve it!"

He raised the staff over his head and brought it down on the Gene Library. Sparks shot out at the impact, and the globe smacked into the floor, then bobbled back up into the air, spinning on its equator. Another crack had appeared in it.

"Good!" he cried again. "You deserve to die! You all deserve to die!"

With each word, he smashed the staff against the globe again. It ricocheted off a wall, shook wildly, spun away, drifted in the air, hanging there, unable to maintain its normal height.

He hit it again.

"You should have *listened* to me!"

Smack!

"Why didn't you *listen* to me?!"

Smack! The globe pinged off the floor, bounced, rolled. It couldn't hover any longer.

"You could have *lived*! I could have *saved* you!" he bellowed, throwing aside the staff, kicking the globe across the room, where it cracked against another wall. He scooped it up and found purchase in one of the cracks.

He ripped open the Gene Library. Liquid nitrogen containers spilled everywhere, freezing the floor and sending up a cold mist. A splash of it landed on his bare skin, freezing it instantly, but he barely felt it.

Slender tubes fit into precise little grooves on plates within. Thanos started breaking them open, first one at a time, delighting in it, then by the fistful when one at a time was too slow.

He was there for a long time, killing Titan all over again, as the synth that pretended to be A'Lars slowly sank to its knees, then tipped over and performed its own simulation of dying.

"You could have been alive," Thanos whispered when he was finished. "Half of you could have survived."

Tears streamed down his face and hissed in the pools of liquid nitrogen.

"I brought no miracles, Kebbi. Why did I even bother trying?"

CHAPTER XXIX

WHEN HE DOCKED WITH *SANCTUARY* MANY HOURS LATER, Thanos had regained his composure. The time in the survival room beneath Titan seemed to have taken place long, long ago. As though it had happened in history and he had heard about it from someone who'd read the story.

They were gone. All gone. The Mad Titan was the only Titan to survive. He was the last son of a dead world.

Cha raced eagerly to the command module once atmosphere was restored to the docking chamber. "The shuttles are all ready. I'm just waiting for your word."

Thanos regarded Cha with pity. Cha would never understand. Cha never *could* understand. Cha believed that there was a purpose to all things, including suffering. But Thanos knew the truth: There was no purpose. There was no plan. There was only luck and bleak coincidence.

And stupidity. And arrogance.

"There are no survivors," Thanos told him.

"But the beacon—"

"Automated system. No one is left alive." He brushed past Cha and made for the airlock that led back into *Sanctuary*.

"But, Thanos…!" Cha called after him. "What do we do? What do we do now? Thanos? Thanos!"

SOUL

We are the sum total of our decisions, not of our beliefs.

CHAPTER XXX

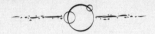

DEPRESSION OFTEN YIELDED LASSITUDE AND LACK OF hunger. In Thanos's case, it was the opposite.

He returned from the surface of Titan and within a day, found himself absolutely ravenous. Cha brought him great steaming trays of food from the ship's replicators, seemingly more than any one being could consume without becoming ill. Thanos downed it all and asked for more.

He set up a makeshift gym in one of the ship's cavernous cargo bays and exercised as though sweat and exertion could resurrect the dead. Between enormous meals, he pushed his body to its limits and beyond.

Sanctuary remained in a parking orbit around Titan for weeks, then months, as Thanos ate and trained through his grief and rage. Cha spoke little, for there was no point in speaking. Thanos did not respond.

Except once. One time. When Cha ventured to tell him that Thanos did not need to let the death of Titan define him, that his life could still be meaningful and—

Thanos had turned to Cha with murder gleaming in his eyes. "Enough."

One word. Two syllables. They sufficed. Cha spoke no more.

The rental period on the ship expired. Cha fielded hails from the owner, stalling and hoping that Thanos would come to his senses sooner rather than later. He contemplated piloting the ship back to occupied space on his own. But what good would that do? To have them both arrested and thrown into debtors' prison somewhere along the Galactic Edge?

Cha believed in Thanos because Cha believed in his own place in the universe. That it was not random or haphazard. And if Cha's place in the universe was by Thanos's side, then Thanos's mission must be good and right.

But what now? What now, with the mission forever null and void? Could this be the end? Did his path and Thanos's path end in defeat?

Or—as Cha suspected but could not voice to his friend— did the universe have a grander plan? The destruction of Titan was a setback that would lead to a greater victory.

The hails from *Sanctuary*'s owner were becoming more frequent and more incensed. Cha didn't even bother opening the channel anymore when a hail came through. Having abuse heaped upon him by an irate Kree would not help Thanos, and it obviously wasn't helpful to Cha, either.

At last, Thanos deigned to leave his makeshift gym/ quarters. He came to the bridge, where Cha was listlessly watching Titan spin below, an orange-encircled tomb for an entire race. He couldn't imagine the horror.

"Cha," Thanos said, the first time in months he'd spoken Cha's name.

"Yes?"

"Flush the starboard cargo bay into space. Then let's put in a course."

Cha blinked. Thanos had been living in the starboard cargo bay for months now. "Flush...?"

Thanos shrugged and took a seat in the navigator's chair. "It disgusts me. There's nothing in there I need. Purge it."

Cha shrugged and keyed in the command. An airlock opened on the starboard side of the ship, and everything within—all of Thanos's discarded food, sweaty clothing, and improvised exercise equipment—was sucked out into the vacuum of space.

"Where exactly are we setting a course to?" Cha asked. Thanos was sitting in the navigator's chair, but he'd not moved to enter in coordinates, so Cha summoned a star chart hologram at his seat.

"We're returning to the Chitauri homeworld."

"The owner of this ship is—"

"I am the owner of this ship," Thanos said. "If the previous owner wishes to contradict me, he can discuss it with my army of Chitauri."

"So...we're thieves?"

Thanos turned to Cha, but without heat or anger. His expression was mild. "I have need of the ship. I have a greater cause than transporting fruits or machine parts."

"Oh? Transporting an army?"

"No, Cha. We are transporting two things you care about quite a bit: hope. And salvation."

On the Chitauri homeworld, they picked up two squadrons of armed and armored Chitauri warriors, as well as the Other. Then, Thanos had Cha lay in a course for the planet Fenilop XI, a world three light-hours from the jump gate at Ceti Beta.

"Why this world?" Cha asked.

"I've been studying it," Thanos revealed. "It has similar environmental and population dynamics as Titan. We're going to save them from themselves, Cha. You were right: The end of Titan is not the end of my quest. And I was right, too—we must kill half to save the rest. This time, I won't fail. This time, we have proof, the evidence of Titan's fall. We will succeed."

Bearing in mind his failure at the Asgardian outpost, Thanos this time chose to remain aboard *Sanctuary*, sending the Other as his emissary to the king of Fenilop XI.

King was actually a misnomer. The ruling monarch was elected, not selected by accident of birth, and served for a term of thirty local years. For that term, though, he or she was supreme ruler, aided by a legislative body, but not bound to it. Unlike the wretched democracy of Titan, this form of government made things simple: Convince one person and you've made your will into law.

They rigged the Other with a microphone and transmitter so they could monitor the negotiations from aboard the ship.

The Fenilops were tall. Almost obscenely tall—two and a half meters on average. They were slender, with a pliable, almost breakable appearance, and grayish-silver skin that sparkled in any available light. The Other had never looked more like an insect than when he approached the court of His Majesty Loruph I.

"Your Majesty," the Other said, as he'd been coached, "I am humbled and honored to speak to you on behalf of my lord, Thanos."

"I've not heard of *Thanos*," said the king. "What world does he call home?"

"He calls no world home, Your Majesty. He is a nomad, world-less. He has lost his people and his planet to the same plagues that lurk in your own paradise. Have you heard of Titan?"

An adviser leaned in to whisper in the king's ear, but His Majesty flicked him away. "I have. A most wretched and sorrowful happenstance. Thanos hails from Titan?"

"He is the last of their kind, Your Majesty. And his tragedy has charged him with a mission: to prevent Titan's fate from befalling other worlds."

On *Sanctuary*, Thanos listened, holding his breath. He and Cha exchanged a hopeful glance.

"You speak true," the king said, sighing. "My own science

advisers have warned me that we are in grave danger of complete environmental collapse. For all my power and authority, I am helpless to stop it. I can do many things, but I cannot compel my people to stop reproducing." He leaned back in his throne. "Your lord, Thanos, he has a solution?"

"He does. I will let him explain it to you."

With that, the Other activated a holographic receiver built into his armor, which projected an image of Thanos from *Sanctuary* into the throne room. They had scaled up the hologram so Thanos's eyes were on level with the king's.

Thanos decided that a bow would not make him seem weak, and was, in fact, the polite thing to do. He bowed to the king of Fenilop XI.

"Your Majesty and your courtiers, I bid you good morrow from my ship in orbit above your planet. Forgive me if I elide the niceties of our first meeting—there are urgent issues to discuss."

"Go on," the king told him, gesturing.

"Years ago, I proposed a solution to Titan's inevitable demise, one that was rejected by the people, to their eventual dismay and destruction. I hope and believe that you will not do the same."

"I would hear of your solution, Lord Thanos."

It was the first time someone had called him *Lord Thanos.* He was inordinately pleased, and paused for a moment to absorb the pleasure before continuing.

"The solution is simple, ruthless, and incontrovertible,"

Thanos said. "You must eliminate fifty percent of your population, and you must do so immediately."

Aboard *Sanctuary*, Thanos stared into the hologram projector. The throne room had gone silent. Was there a problem with the audio transmitters? He wished they'd had time to outfit the Other with visual sensors as well as aural. They could see him, but Thanos could only hear them.

After a protracted silence, the king spoke. "Forgive me, Lord Thanos. I am unfamiliar with Titan humor. Was I supposed to laugh?"

Thanos seethed but fought to keep his ire from showing on his face, projected so much larger down on the surface. "This is no joke. I proposed the same solution to Titan, and they rejected it. You know the results of that rejection. Where half could have been spared, now *all* are dead. You can avoid this fate. My euthanasia technology is painless and can be altered quite easily to conform to your species' biology."

More silence.

"Every moment you delay, Your Majesty," Thanos said with heat, "is one moment closer to an extinction-level event for your planet."

"And how am I to convince my people that this is the correct course of action? I am their monarch, but I will not put people to death who have no wish to die."

An easy question. Good. "You submit yourself as the first volunteer," Thanos said. "Lead by example."

The next sound Thanos heard from below was a dry

chuckle. "His Majesty has left the room, Thanos of Titan," said a new voice. "I am Viceroy Londro. While some may appreciate your humor, I'm afraid His Majesty does not. If you have a serious proposal for us, I am willing to listen."

"You've heard my proposal!" Thanos's rage sneaked up on him, pounced, and sank its claws into his shoulders. He could not see the throne room, but he could see devastated Titan, orange with dust, wrecked and ramshackle. He could smell the bodies. "I warn you—if you do not take drastic action, your streets will clot with bodies. Your monuments will fall. You will be less than dust, a dead world with no savior, no memento, no story to tell. You will—"

"My lord." It was the Other, speaking calmly. "I've been escorted out of the palace. They're not listening."

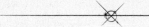

Cha entered the bridge of the ship with the Other, who had just returned safely to *Sanctuary*. Thanos sat alone, slumped in the captain's chair, staring out at the curve of Fenilop XI through the window before him. The planet was a banded beauty, rainbows of soil and water making it a chromatic wonder turning slowly before them.

"They will all die," Thanos said quietly.

Cha put a hand on Thanos's shoulder. "There are other worlds in danger, Thanos. We'll find them. We'll refine our message. We'll save them."

"Yes. We will. But first, we must conclude our business

here on Fenilop XI." He rose from his chair and pointed to the Other. "Have your troops mustered and ready for combat within the hour. We will target the capital city and its defense forces first, then the outlying military bases."

The Other bobbed his head and left the bridge. Cha stared slack-jawed at Thanos.

"Close your mouth, Cha. The sight of your gaping maw is unappealing."

"What are you doing? Why are you attacking them?"

"They're all going to die anyway, Cha. We saw the results on Titan, did we not?" Thanos settled back down into his seat. "Hastening their demise may save some of the planet's resources, making it available for settlement by a wiser species at some point in the future. Besides, this way I am sparing them all the slow death of disease and geologic upheaval, granting them instead a swift, merciful death." He arched an eyebrow. "Do you not approve?"

"I...They..." Cha cast about for words. "They are innocent! What was it you said back at Titan? 'I see no balance in children dead in the streets!'"

"Exactly. That is their fate, if we do not act. Speak not of *innocence*, Cha. This is the path. It is not about innocence or guilt—it is about life and death. One begets the other. As I said—these people are already doomed. The science of it is irrefutable." He paused a moment. "If a weed chokes a flower, you kill the weed so that the flower may live. Do you not?"

Cha stammered. "I—I suppose so...."

"In the garden of the universe, we have much weeding to do. If you'd rather not, then"—he strummed his fingers on the arm of the chair—"there are shuttlecraft at your disposal."

Cha's mouth opened and closed, opened and closed. At last, he offered a small shrug. "I believe in our path, Thanos."

"Good. According to my scans, the Fenilops don't have long-range super-atmospheric weaponry, so we should be safe here. But just in case, lay in an emergency retreat course."

Cha went to the navigation pod and did just that. Meanwhile, the Other was preparing his troops.

CHAPTER XXXI

THE CONQUEST OF FENILOP XI CAME SWIFTLY. THE KING AND his advisers thought Thanos to be a madman with no resources and no recourse to their rejection. They were shocked when the Chitauri ships rained lightning and fire from the sky.

They'd never seen anything like a Chitauri army. No one had. Moving in perfect lockstep, with hive-mind coordinated precision, the Chitauri soldiers captured the capital city in no time. The nearby military bases were crushed by a brace of Leviathans.

Thanos's orders were simple, so simple that even the lack-brained Chitauri could follow them: Kill every living thing you see. There was no need for the grand strategies of war, for the thrust and counterthrust, the capture of key territories and the holding of hostages for negotiations. No one would be suing for peace.

This was slaughter, plain and simple. Kinder, Thanos knew, than leaving these people to the capricious mercies of their own planet's chaotic revenge.

The war was one-sided. With the element of surprise and the willingness to discard the usual stratagems and rules of war in favor of utter ruthlessness, Thanos had an early advantage that he pressed and pressed and pressed. The Chitauri's teleportation technology made them impossible to counter.

Still, as combat dragged into its third week, he watched from the sky above and told Cha, "We need more Chitauri. More Leviathans. More weapons."

Cha, who had not slept much since the beginning of the war, looked up from his monitoring station, where he was in communication with the Other to direct troops where they were needed. "More? My projections indicate that we'll have their entire military either destroyed or under our control within another day. Then it's just a mop-up operation to kill the survivors. By the time any reinforcements would arrive, we'd be done."

Thanos permitted himself a smile at Cha's expense. "Oh, your naïveté amuses me, Cha. I speak not of our current conflict but of our next one."

It took a moment for the remark to penetrate the layers of sleepiness that had accreted around Cha's brain. He said, "Next one?" in the tone of a complete dullard.

But Cha wasn't a complete dullard. Thanos took pity on him. "You've done good work, Cha. Get some sleep. The Chitauri know what to do, and I can relay my own commands to the Other, if need be."

"Next one?" Cha said again, rising and heading to the door. "Next one?"

Yes, Thanos thought. *The next one.*

Chitauri scavenger teams pillaged Fenilop XI for usable resources and matériel. It was just pragmatic. There was no one left alive on the planet to use any of it, so Thanos might as well take it.

He was grateful that he had a cargo ship at his disposal. Most of the Chitauri soldiers remained in the Leviathans, which now floated side by side with *Sanctuary*, leaving the cargo space free for the raw ore, food stocks, and technology ferried up from the planet.

They made a stop at the Chitauri homeworld to replace dead soldiers and ramp up their numbers. Then, without hesitation, they set out for the next planet Thanos had identified as being in danger of Titan's fate.

CHAPTER XXXII

THIS TIME HE CHOSE NOT TO SPEAK TO THE RULERS OF THE planet. Denegar was a balkanized world, made up of more than thirty different territories, ruled by sixteen different forms of government. There was no global ruling body to appeal to, and going to each territory would take too much time and amount to nothing, in any event. Even if he could convince the leaders of most of the territories, any holdouts would mean no consensus. A waste of his time.

Instead, he gambled on the tactic that had backfired on Titan but could work here: He projected a hologram of himself worldwide, explaining the situation and his solution. On Titan, his people's predisposition to distrust him had made this gambit a failure, but here, on Denegar, no one knew him, and no one had any reason to distrust him.

He projected the hologram live, speaking in calm, measured tones. Cha encouraged him to smile frequently. "People trust those who smile."

He was both pleased and surprised that Cha was still with him. He'd expected that the killing of Fenilop would have chased away the Sirian for good. But days after they broke orbit over the planet, Cha had emerged from his chambers and a lengthy meditation.

"We have the same end goal, you and I, Thanos. We both seek peace, equilibrium, balance. I am willing to explore your means to this end."

Thanos could not and would not let it show, but he was glad to have Cha with him, even as he badgered Thanos to smile.

"Is that more received wisdom from the universe?"

"No, Thanos. It's just part of life."

Thanos had reluctantly agreed. He punctuated his entreaty with smiles, with gentle gestures.

He implored them. He importuned them. He had charts and graphs that bolstered his argument, proving that...

"...within three generations, Denegar's natural resources will have been exploited beyond a tipping point. Your water will be so contaminated that it will be unfilterable by current technology. A rare influenza variant currently percolating on your easternmost equatorial continent will evolve to spread via airborne vectors. And your atmosphere will be so polluted that global climate change will cause radical swings in local weather patterns. You will suffer tremendous hurricanes for which you are unprepared, as well as rising ocean levels that will swamp your coastal habitats.

"You may think: *Who is this man, and why should we heed him?* I am Thanos of Titan, and I have issued this warning twice before, on two different planets. They are both now dead worlds, with not a single breathing soul on either. One of them is my own home, Titan, a planet of surpassing beauty, technology, and generosity. Yet my people did not heed my warning, and now that world is as dead as the vacuum of space.

"And so, people of Denegar, I implore you: Mind my words. My solution seems radical and heartless, I know, but trust me: It. Will. Work. You will sacrifice greatly, yes, but you will also *benefit* greatly.

"I have spoken directly to the people rather than to your ruling class so that you might all know the truth and, in your numbers, find the wisdom that is often lacking in leaders.

"This comms channel will remain open. I await your reply."

He switched off the outgoing audio and looked at Cha.

"Well?" he said.

Cha slid his hand over the control surface, generating a hologram of the surface of Denegar. *Sanctuary* was a smallish dot in orbit. As they watched, lines rose up from Denegar, heading for the ship.

"Super-atmospheric fusion warheads launched," Cha said with a sigh.

"Evasive maneuvers!" Thanos barked. "And unleash the Chitauri!"

The Battle of Denegar was both shorter and far bloodier than the Battle of Fenilop XI. The Denegarese had multiple militaries and did not hesitate to use them. In retrospect, Thanos thought the length of his oratory gave them time to prepare and launch an attack. He had assumed a level of rationality and intelligence on the part of the Denegarese.

He would not suffer such presumptions in the future.

Fortunately, his Chitauri were more than up to the task. Bolstered by reinforcements from the homeworld and now seasoned by one battle (the experience of which was instantly inculcated in the entire warrior clan, thanks to the hive mind), the Chitauri ranged over Denegar like a swarm of maggots on a corpse. The planet wasn't dead, but it soon would be.

Thanos watched from the safety of *Sanctuary*, which Cha had moved to a higher parking orbit, beyond the range of the super-atmospheric missiles. He stood at the fore of the bridge, hands clasped behind his back, watching the planet grind its slow turn beneath him, imagining that he could see individual explosions below.

"They could have lived, Cha," he said through clenched teeth. "Half of them could have lived! Thrived! Gone on to gestate new generations! Damn it, Cha, why don't they want to live!" He thumped his fist against the panel of hardened crystal that formed the window. "Why?"

"We cannot know the path of the universe," Cha told him. "We can only walk it."

"I will continue on this path," Thanos seethed, his breath fogging the window, "until the path is no longer necessary.

Send scavenger units to the surface with our shuttlecraft to strip the planet of everything we need."

Cha nodded and turned on his heel.

"Oh, and Cha . . . ?"

"Yes?"

"I'm tired of flitting around space in this glorified cargo pallet. See if there are any intact warships we can appropriate."

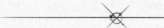

By the time they attempted to persuade a third planet, Vishalaya, word had spread. The Mad Titan Thanos, *Warlord Thanos*, had come. They were met at the edge of the solar system by jump-ships and dreadnoughts. Thanos had hoped that the slaughters on Fenilop and Denegar would have served as warnings to future worlds, omens that they should heed his advice.

If the military vessels gathering on his long-range sensors were any indication . . . apparently not.

The new *Sanctuary* was a military jump-ship that had never gotten off the ground during the Battle of Denegar. Sitting in its command chair, Thanos finally felt as though he had the means to execute his will.

"Attention, *Sanctuary*," a voice crackled over an open hailing frequency. "This is the RSS *Executrix*, of Her Majesty Cath'Ar's navy. Turn back or be fired upon."

Thanos sighed. The Other sat to his left, Cha to his right. Thanos waved at the air as though something stank.

"Kill them," he said, "and then we'll see if *Her Majesty Cath'Ar* is willing to discuss the horrors her people will soon face."

Thanos watched on a holo as his Leviathans swung around from the sides of *Sanctuary* and plowed into the RSS *Executrix*. Since they were primarily living tissue, the Leviathans didn't show up on most conventional sensors. They were perhaps the most perfect stealth weapon in space warfare.

In short order, they disabled the *Executrix* and ripped open its hull. Bodies spilled out into space. Other ships had begun a rescue run, but *Sanctuary*'s photon guns held them off until the Leviathans could engage.

"It's too easy," Thanos murmured.

"Perhaps the ease of your victory here will compel this queen Cath'Ar to parlay with you," Cha said. "Take you seriously."

"Your optimism is welcome in this instance, but unwarranted, I fear. Anyone who greets us with a show of force is not going to listen to our proposal with an open mind. Prepare our forces for a planet-wide death sweep." Thanos heaved himself out of his chair. "I will be in my quarters. Alert me if this queen calls, begging for mercy."

The queen did indeed call, and she did indeed beg for mercy. Thanos explained what mercy was: Fifty percent of her people dead. Including her.

"You must be mad," she said via hologram to Thanos, who studied her with the bored listlessness of a snake at noon. Her species was bipedal, with a distinctive whorl pattern of raised flesh just beneath the hairline, descending to just above the eyes. It was hypnotic to watch.

"I hope your arithmetic skills are superior to your military acumen, Your Majesty. Half your population is better than none."

"We are not weaklings, as on Fenilop. Or disorganized, like the Denegarese. You will not slaughter us all, Warlord Thanos."

He leaned forward. That whorl...It seemed almost to move on its own. "I have no wish to slaughter you all, Your Majesty. But I cannot bear the thought of your world continuing to suffer under such benighted idiocy. Surrender now and offer up half your people. It's simple math."

"Try us," she said, and disconnected the comms.

Thanos left his quarters and strode down the corridor to the bridge. Within were the Other and Cha.

"You were listening in?" he asked.

"Of course," said Cha.

"Launch the assault."

"As you command," said the Other.

In a parking orbit around the planet Vishalaya, Thanos stared at the endless stream of shuttlecraft soaring from the planet's surface to his cargo ship, now rechristened *Mercy*. Restocking the Chitauri army was taking longer than the conquest and depopulating of the planet itself had.

In the reflection from the window, he caught a glimpse of Cha approaching him.

"Three planets, Cha. *Three*. In how long? How long since we left Titan?"

Cha spoke after a moment, confirming Thanos's math. "Nearly a year."

"Three worlds in a year. At this pace..." He shook his head. "Too slow. We need to find a way to identify these worlds and speak to them en masse. And we need to be more persuasive."

"Yes. The endless slaughter is...enervating."

"Enervating?" Thanos asked.

"Such killing..." Cha shrugged. "No matter how necessary it may be, such killing weighs heavily on your soul, no doubt. It does on mine."

Thanos laughed a hearty, honest laugh. "Weighs heavily on my soul? No, Cha. Once, perhaps, I saw killing as a necessity, the better of two options. It was pragmatic and expedient." He paused, considering. "It still is those things, of course. But, Cha, I've come to the conclusion that"—he leaned forward, both hands flat against the window—"killing is an absolute, universal *good*. Killing clears the chaff from the wheat. Killing subtracts that which would multiply into danger. Killing obviates crisis. Focusing on the killing is the wrong perspective, in any event. We're not looking to kill half of them; we're trying to *save* half of them."

"If killing is a universal good," Cha said, speaking slowly, anticipating an interruption. When none came, he went on. "All things serve their own purpose. There *is* a purpose to all this death. We have merely yet to see it." He put a hand on Thanos's shoulder. Patted him there. "We are guided by the universe itself, by its ineffable quest for harmony. We will continue on the proper path."

Thanos was amazed. "After all this time, after everything you've done and witnessed...You actually still believe there is a path to universal peace. Unreal."

"Deep down, Thanos...so do you. Why else do you keep me around, if not to remind you of what you believe?"

Thanos grunted, curled his upper lip. Then, without a word, he stalked away from the bridge.

CHAPTER XXXIII

THANOS KNEW THAT HIS CAUSE WAS JUST AND HIS PATH righteous, but he also understood that most intellects were neither refined nor enlightened enough to comprehend it. He resigned himself to a life of misapprehension, of unnecessary conflict in the face of brute and savage denial of plain, obvious facts.

And so it was a pleasant surprise to him that—as his infamy spread—there were those who not only agreed with him, but also sought him out as he sacked their worlds. A pittance among the billions dead, yes, but the idea that even one person out of a planet's entire population might heed his warning was a greater number than experience had taught him to expect.

He took them on, of course, and with the genetic largesse of his experiments on the Chitauri, he modified and empowered them, making them his vanguard into the universe.

In turn, they adored him like a father. They gave themselves new names, rechristening themselves in his honor. They were Ebony Maw and Corvus Glaive, Proxima Midnight and Cull Obsidian, names dredged from the grimmest pits of fever dreams and black omens. He set them loose upon the universe in his name, preaching his dire warnings, seeking out new worlds and new places to conquer.

They called themselves his children. But they were not. They were his tools, his weapons. Sent out into the void in pairs or as a group, they heralded his eventual coming, guided his forces on the ground, ruthlessly enforced his will.

They also inspired him.

"We have been too thorough," Thanos told Cha one day as they sped between systems. His underlings were already ahead of them, on a world called Zehoberei, one ripe for Thanos's brand of global modification. "If there is even one person on a planet who believes in our cause, that life is worth saving and exploiting."

"So...no more wholesale slaughter?" Cha asked a little too eagerly.

"We have enough plunder from our conquests to fuel our cause for another century. Perhaps we should try balance on a worldly scale."

Cha raised an eyebrow. "Mercy? From Thanos?"

"A *different* mercy," Thanos chided him. "Imbalance still exists. The mercy of the grave has sufficed until now, but going forward we will be more thoughtful in our purges. It has been safer to eliminate entire populations so no one would remain to seek us out in the name of revenge. But now...Now we will try something different. We will enact the Titan protocol, eliminating half of each world. And as those worlds recover, they will stand as examples to others that our way works."

Cha considered this. "We'll also want to be sure to eliminate any and all military capacity," he pointed out. "Otherwise, we'll have to watch our backs more so than usual."

Thanos grinned with sheer pleasure. "Pragmatism from the idealist. I'll convert you yet, Cha."

From this angle, the small planet Zehoberei hung in space, a brilliant green-blue jewel on the black velvet backdrop of a starless nebula. They had entered the Silicon Star System, with its twelve planets, only one of which was habitable.

Zehoberei. Home to three billion sentient souls. All of whom were guaranteed to die in a few short generations, unless Thanos was obeyed.

He was not.

And so he attacked.

He watched the assault from the bridge of his ship, as he'd done so many times before. From up here, it was merely a light show—occasional bursts of yellow and orange from the surface of the planet. Nuclear fire rippled along coastlines, spilling like lava from the shore.

He skimmed his battle plans and saw that nothing needed to be adjusted. The Zehoberei had made no moves or countermoves that he had not already anticipated. The conclusion was foregone. He realized, to his surprise, that in the midst of war, he was...bored.

"When did genocide become rote?" he asked Cha.

Beside him, Cha looked up from the small holoplate that

streamed data direct from the Chitauri Leviathans. "Are you having misgivings, Thanos?"

"And if I were?"

Cha clucked his tongue and waggled the tips of his pointed ears, something he only did when deep in thought. "Wholesale slaughter is an egregious evil," he said at last. "But not when in service to a greater good. Still, there are many paths to victory. You can always choose another one."

Thanos snorted. "Victory itself is meaningless to me. I only want to help."

Cha's lips quirked into a concerned mien. "I know where this is headed. You know I don't like it when you join the Chitauri in battle. It's dangerous."

"More dangerous is allowing a distance between myself and our battles. It may grow and mutate into distance between myself and my cause. I need these experiences, Cha. I need to see the devastation for myself. As I did on Titan. To rededicate myself. To remind myself what we're fighting for."

Consulting the holoplate, Cha nodded to himself. "Well, there's an area on the western continent that's been swept clean. You could—"

"No. As always, I need to see the suffering." He knew that witnessing only the antiseptic aftermath of the Chitauri's cleansing of the world meant nothing. It was like observing the end result of a surgery. You learn nothing from the stitches and the scar. Only by watching the surgeon's hands in the blood and the viscera could you come to comprehend the mechanics of medicine.

"It means nothing if I do not live it," he told Cha. He thought back to the days before the massacre aboard the *Blood Edda*. How he had used his own hands to torture and kill Vathlauss. The feel of the Asgardian's blood, tacky and slick at the same time, between his culpable fingers.

"Not a chance," Cha said resolutely. "You've done it before, and every time it was too big a chance to take. We just can't risk it."

Thanos turned to his friend and curled his lip in a parody of amusement. "I was not asking permission, Cha."

"It's too risky," Cha insisted, swallowing hard, but standing his ground. "We can't take the chance of something happening to you."

"We," Thanos said in his deepest and most intimidating tone, "do not make the decisions on this ship."

Defiant, Cha pulled back his shoulders and thrust out his chest. He and Thanos glared at each other for long moments.

Cha swallowed hard. "Thanos, please! Think about what you're proposing! What you're risking!"

"I am prepared. I've trained with the Chitauri for a long time. I have my battle armor, which they forged for me to my exacting specifications. No harm will come to me, my friend."

In the end, Cha surrendered. As Thanos had known he

would from the beginning. That was, in fact, why he valued Cha so much as a friend—Cha pushed back. But never too much.

On the surface of Zehoberei, Thanos strode through the remains of a village on what had been one of the northern continents. It was summer in this particular spherical cap of Zehoberei and the heat bore down on him, mitigated by only the passing shadows cast by great plumes of smoke from nearby, where his Chitauri warriors had set off a plethora of bombs.

The village was in ruins, its buildings and infrastructure reduced to rubble under the unrelenting assault of the Leviathans and Chitauri weaponry. Overhead, his soldiers zipped through the sky on their war-skiffs, while on the ground, infantry surrounded him, a hilariously ineffective protective shield since Thanos towered over the Chitauri by half a meter, resplendent in his blue-and-gold battle armor.

Bodies—burned, bloodied—littered what was left of a street. A brace of Chitauri dragged the corpses out of the way as Thanos and his retinue passed. Along both sides of the road, his troops stood at attention. In the distance was a massive arch, beautiful and resplendent in its design. He was pleased it had survived the war. Beauty had its place in the universe and should always be left unsullied when possible.

The smell of blood was in the air. Along with burned flesh. And terror, which had its own peculiar odor, the stench of overactive adrenal glands.

The Zehoberei people were green-skinned, tall, and lean. Their bodies stacked as well and as easily as any others.

Behind a planked barricade, a woman huddled in fear with a child. Her daughter, he could tell. As the Chitauri encircled them, something amazing happened, something that instilled in Thanos a gratitude that he'd witnessed it:

The girl—acting on an instinct Thanos had never beheld before—moved and interposed herself between her mother and the Chitauri.

In that moment of shock and amazement, Thanos almost missed the opportunity to act. At the last possible instant, he ordered the Chitauri to stand down temporarily.

A child. Sacrificing herself for her mother. It was supposed to be the other way around. Thanos's contempt for the mother was rivaled only by his astonishment in the girl.

There was something about her. . . . He could not tell. He had no words for it, and this alone almost paralyzed him. She said nothing, merely gazed up at him without fear, without reproach.

"What is your name?" he asked, holding out his hand.

"Gamora," she said.

And—marvel of marvels—she took his hand.

He could not remember the last time he'd felt the touch

of another's flesh without violent intent. A warmth suffused him.

And he realized: Her mother was about to die. The Chitauri advanced, and Ebony Maw was chattering away in the background. (Maw, so appropriately named, as he never did learn when to shut his mouth.) The Chitauri were like a computer program—they would execute their mission without fail or thought unless deterred.

Thanos swept along Gamora and brought her to the archway, away from the violence about to be perpetrated upon her mother. Still, the girl craned her neck, twisting and turning for a glimpse of her parent.

Even though Gamora's mother was useless and contemptible, Thanos could not let the girl suffer the sight of her death. To distract her, he reached into a compartment on his armor and withdrew a jetted doubledirk, a small, boxy handle from which sprang two short blades. Proxima Midnight had found it on some primitive world she'd been exploring and had brought it to him as a gift. It was nearly useless in any sort of real combat, but he carried it with him. As a reminder.

Not of Midnight's generosity. But of something else.

"Look," he told Gamora, popping out both blades. "Perfectly balanced, as all things should be." He held it out to her on one finger, the weapon poised and stable.

She turned to watch him and the blade, her eyes widening at the sight of it. He took her small hand and balanced the doubledirk on her finger. It wobbled for a moment, but steadied.

"See?" he told her. "You have it already."

She smiled, pleased with herself.

In the background, the Chitauri murdered her mother, but Gamora didn't notice.

CHAPTER XXXIV

ABOARD *SANCTUARY*, THANOS GAZED AT A HOLOGRAM OF Gamora as she slept in a secure room not far from his own. Cha burst in without signaling, as he often did, an affront that usually annoyed Thanos at the very least. But not today. Today, he cared only for the girl, still asleep, and what would come next.

"What are you doing?" Cha demanded. "Genocide isn't enough—you're a . . . a kidnapper now?"

"You climb the rungs on the ladder of sin in an odd order, Cha Rhaigor." Thanos did not look up from the hologram. He wanted to observe the moment she awoke.

"There is killing people as quickly and cleanly as possible, and then there is abducting them and . . . and—What *are* your plans?"

Thanos sighed. Cha had a tendency to forget to whom he spoke. Their long friendship accorded him a measure of respect and a tolerance for overstepping his boundaries. And Thanos was genuinely grateful for the endless hours of work Cha had dedicated to the cause of saving lives. But he was tiring of Cha's liberties. So long as he spoke so in private, that was one thing. If he dared to challenge Thanos before the Other . . .

Or the girl . . .

"She ignored every survival instinct in her body," Thanos said, his voice reverent, his eyes still locked on her tiny, slumbering form. "The mother cowered when she should have fought, leaving her daughter to act as a living shield. And against all odds, against every possible shred of logic and reason, Gamora did exactly that. Even when faced with an army and a clearly superior opponent. You can't invent that, Cha. You can't manufacture that kind of . . . heart."

"Will you turn and look at me, at least?" Cha asked.

"No. I'm watching my . . . my child."

Cha stepped around Thanos. He didn't dare interfere with the hologram, but he stood just to its left, hovering at the edge of Thanos's vision. "She's not your child, Thanos. She had parents."

"She's an orphan. I'm adopting her. It's quite simple."

"May I ask why?" Cha asked, exasperated.

Thanos sighed. He didn't feel like explaining himself—to Cha or to anyone else.

He had an army. A disciplined, lethal, obedient army. At his word, he could lay siege to entire worlds, obliterate armies, massacre whole species into extinction.

But it was always at *his* order. He had to be the one in command. Of everything. At all times. The Chitauri could hardly think for themselves. They couldn't plot or plan or strategize. And Cha, while capable, was no tactical thinker.

He kept the ships running and the supply lines stocked and humming, but he couldn't prosecute a war. He had no stomach for the necessary brutality of it and no mind for the planning of it. Even Ebony Maw and the others fell victim to their own sycophancy and awe; they could not plan on a global scale.

But this girl... This raw, untapped potential... Oh, the things he could teach her to do!

"Do you really want to be a father?" Cha asked gently.

"I cannot live forever. If I die with my great work undone—and the odds are that I will—then someone needs to carry on in my name."

"Why her? There are the others, like Ebony Maw...."

"They came to me late in life. She is still a child. I can mold her, recast her in my image. We laid waste to Zehoberei. We took the only thing from that planet worth taking. She is the very best of them, and that should be preserved. We will raise her. Teach her to lead our armies. We have the finest army in the galaxy, perhaps the universe. We will make her its head."

"The Chitauri don't know *how* to teach!" Cha protested. "They have a hive mind! They learn instantly from one another, so they've never had to develop any method for education."

"Then I will teach her myself." He grinned. "Look, Cha; she's awake."

They sat across from each other at a table in Thanos's personal chambers. He'd had the table brought in and set up by two Chitauri, since he usually ate his meals on the bridge, in the commander's chair. It felt strange to sit at a table, to have another person sitting across from him.

Her fear and uncertainty came off her in waves.

He let her eat. She was ravenous, and devoured everything put before her.

"Are you going to kill me?" she asked eventually.

"No!" He was surprised to hear the horror in his voice; until that very moment, he hadn't realized how invested he was in her. "I *saved* your life. I have no intention of ending it."

She considered this for long, silent moments, until finally saying, "You *spared* my life. There's a difference."

He grinned. Such mental dexterity in one so young... He'd chosen her wisely.

"I'm pleased that you're so well-spoken. It betokens an orderly mind. You're mature and intelligent beyond your years."

"Why did you do it?" Gamora asked. "Did they really have to die?"

He nodded sadly. "I wish it were not so. I truly do. But the universe is out of balance, my dear Gamora. Were it not so, I would be happy on some backwater world in a forgettable

SOUL

part of the galaxy. Doing something simple and durable. Perhaps farming. But I have a greater responsibility, one I cannot shirk."

Her eyes darted back and forth as she digested what he'd said. "What do you mean?"

"Where there is imbalance, I bring balance," he told her. "Where there are worlds and people in distress, I bring relief and mercy." He paused for just a moment. "I won't lie to you, child. This means I kill a great many people. I don't want to do this. I take no pleasure in it. But it must be done."

"Why does it have to be you?"

He allowed himself a moment to enjoy her. Just a moment. She'd smoothly skipped over the issue of *what* he did, accepting its necessity. She was a miracle.

"Because I am the only one who can."

"What about me?"

"I want to offer you an opportunity. To join with me. To become my right hand. Your species has a set of interesting and helpful physical characteristics. Your epidermis is more durable than a typical bipedal mammal's, shielding you from some levels of physical harm. Your muscle tissues are denser than usual as well, which accounts for the strength you exhibit even at such a young age. This makes you a perfect candidate to stand at my side. To learn the ways of war, of death, of necessary brutality. To be the extension of my arm throughout the galaxy as I do what others are too stupid or too cowardly to do."

309

"And what's that?"

"Save the future. Through reason, preferably. But with blood and fire, if need be."

"You want me to be a soldier?"

His eyes widened. "No!" he exclaimed. "No, no! I want you to be ... my heir. You will be by my side. You will reshape worlds with me. It will be a magnificent life, child."

"I have a question," she said somewhat timorously.

"Of course."

"What's your name?" she asked.

He hesitated only a moment. "Call me Father."

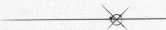

She was smart and mature for her age, but still, it would take a long time for them to bond, for her to learn to trust.

That was okay. They had a long time. The distances between planetary systems were great, and even at lightspeed, it could take weeks or months to traverse those distances.

He began her training in earnest immediately, clearing out space on his cargo vessel *Mercy* to act as a rifle range, sparring ring, and gymnasium. She had natural talent and the advantages of youth and evolution on her side, but he was pitiless in his training. He set Chitauri on her in practice sessions, using actual battle-staves and ordered to kill her.

"It's too dangerous," Cha cautioned him the first time.

"She'll survive or she won't," Thanos said with a stoic tone he did not completely feel. "If she does, she'll improve. If not, she was never meant to stand at my side."

In her first scrimmage, locked in a room and told to escape, she killed two full-grown Chitauri and injured a third. Bruised and burned by a battle-staff, she stumbled to the door, figured out how to operate the keypad, and opened it. The injured Chitauri made a last attempt to stop her; she trapped it in the door and slammed it on her way out, bashing the Chitauri's head into paste as she collapsed in the outer corridor.

"See?" Thanos told Cha, pleased.

"Luck," Cha sniffed.

"If so, it will wear out soon enough and we'll be done."

Her luck held long enough for her skill to catch up. As they traveled from world to world, slaughtering populations, Thanos continued training Gamora. She grew strong, powerful, confident.

After each session, he personally attended to her wounds with a gentleness that surprised him. He'd thought his capacity for tenderness to have been exhausted years ago. Gamora made him want to take care of her.

"I know this seems cruel," he told her more than once. "I know *I* seem cruel. But everything I do, I do for you, for your generation and your progeny, and their progeny and so on. These actions will kill despair and enliven hope."

"I believe you, Father," she replied.

Thanos could not prevent a broad smile from creasing his face.

"Why are you smiling?" she asked, flexing her arm. She'd been cut almost to the bone in her left forearm during a fight with one of the Chitauri's best warriors. She was almost ten years old, and her body was scarred like that of a grizzled veteran.

"There are few pleasures in my life. One of them is hearing you call me Father."

She took his hand in hers. Her hand was larger now than it had been that first day on Zehoberei, when she'd barely been able to clutch his finger. He squeezed, felt the heat of her flesh, the thrum of her blood. His daughter.

His *daughter*.

"She will grow to hate you," Cha warned later, when they were alone. "You slew her family. Right now, she is enamored of you. Your power enthralls her. Your generosity dazzles her. But as she grows more and more powerful, she *will* begin to wonder why she should suffer you to live."

"In her own way, she loves me," Thanos replied. "She strives to better herself, to better prepare to be my right hand."

"Keep an eye on your right hand," Cha said mordantly. "It may slit your throat."

Thanos grunted in something like assent. If the time

came that Gamora truly believed she could kill him, then that would mean only that she was truly ready and worthy to stand by his side. Fighting endless hordes of Chitauri and weaklings on the planets they razed, though, had taken her as far as it could. It was time for more.

"I think she needs a sibling," he told Cha.

Thanos put out the word to Ebony Maw and his ilk that he needed another child, one preferably close to Gamora's age. His studies indicated that this would provide optimal opportunities for bonding.

Maw and the others paraded before him a plethora of children scavenged from the smoking ruins of a multitude of worlds. Proxima Midnight, though, turned up a girl with disconcertingly purple-tinged blue skin, not the same as Thanos's own, but close enough that he wondered what his life might have been like had he been born on her world, not his.

At first, he dismissed her. Her quaking form offered no challenge to Gamora, who desperately needed a sparring partner more ambitious than the endless parade of Chitauri she had taken to killing almost casually during her training sessions.

But that skin... He could not look away from her. She was small, hairless, with no pupils, and the shade of her skin was so close to purple that he thought she could almost be ... his.

He crouched by her and took her chin between his thumb and forefinger, tilting her face up so they gazed into each other's eyes.

"Welcome to *Sanctuary*, my dear," he told her.

CHAPTER XXXV

THE GIRLS—GAMORA AND THE NEW ONE, NEBULA—GOT along as well as could be expected. For a time, this pleased Thanos, to witness the sisterly bonds forming between them, their common experiences forging a potent and lasting welded seam of affection.

This lasted for the first month or so, at which point he realized that if the two of them thought of each other as allies, they would inevitably mount a united offense against him. Utterly counter to the point to having them in the first place. He needed them loyal to *him*, not to each other.

And so he began testing them against each other, manipulating them into each other's orbits, forcing them into conflict, as often as Thanos could come up with a new test. To his pleasure, they each failed, no matter how hard they tried. They were almost evenly matched, with Gamora more often than not having the upper hand. She could best Nebula but never land the killing blow.

It was the best possible training for both of them.

"And will you be adopting more war orphans?" Cha asked with some asperity as Thanos watched them spar. "Should I retrofit *Sanctuary* to serve as an orphanage in addition to a capital ship?"

Thanos grunted.

"I'm serious, Thanos. When you took Gamora on, I understood. You happened upon her; you were struck. Coincidences often pave the way to finding our place in the order of the universe. And yet…"

Thanos cut off his friend with a single raised hand.

"Two of them will be enough for now," he conceded. "Look at them fight. As though born to the pits of hell."

"Yes, you've conjured quite a pair of demons, Thanos."

Thanos clucked his tongue. "No, no. Not demons, Cha. My daughters. They will always be by my side."

"They would just as soon rip out your heart as shield it," Cha warned.

"That will change in time."

"I wish I could be as certain as you are, old friend. As it stands, I think you're just whetting the blade that will eventually open your jugular."

With a deep chuckle, Thanos turned away from the window into the training room. "Trust me, Cha. I've thought this through. The best brainwashing allows the subject a modicum of independent thought. I allow Gamora and Nebula to hate me because it makes them think they still have choices and free will. But they are too accustomed to this life now. They've ingested my philosophy and accepted my dominance, whether they realize it or not. They are my children, and while children may hate their parents, they rarely raise a hand to them."

"Rarely," Cha said drily.

And Thanos thought, unbidden, shockingly, of A'Lars for the first time in...in...

For the first time since that day, fifty stories beneath the surface of Titan. For the first time since he'd hacked the synth's head off and smashed the hope of Titan under his boot.

He had killed the synth that wore his father's face and spoke in his father's voice, but he knew that he never could have done that to his true father. No matter how much he loathed A'Lars, no matter how much he despised the man for condemning Gwinth and Sintaa and Sui-San and millions of others to unnecessary death, he could not have killed him. The proof lay in the simple fact that he hadn't. That when presented with his father's recalcitrance, he hadn't simply killed him and moved on with his plans, unfettered. He had been younger then, yes, and not yet inculcated by war in the ways of violence. But even in his youth, he'd known what death was. How expedient it could be. Still, he'd not killed A'Lars.

"I will be—" He paused, captivated by the sight inside the training room. Gamora had broken Nebula's battle-staff, along with her left leg. But Nebula had managed to climb onto a stack of crates, just out of Gamora's reach. Every time Gamora thrust her staff at Nebula, Nebula pulled back just enough to evade the blow. They were stalemated.

This is how it went, constantly. Gamora bested Nebula,

who managed to find a way to keep from being thoroughly defeated. She never lost, but she never came close to winning, either.

"Do we still have the leftover biofusers from the last round of Chitauri upgrades?" Thanos asked.

Cha blinked. "Well, yes. But we don't need—"

"Come with me." Thanos thumbed open the door and stepped inside. Nebula saw him first, and there was a palpable sense of relief from her. He disliked that she saw him as her savior, rather than relying on herself.

Gamora sensed his presence a moment later. She turned and collapsed her battle-staff, standing at attention. "Thanos," she said stiffly.

"Relax, my daughter."

He held out a hand to help the injured Nebula down from the safety of her perch. She took the hand and limped her way down, finally leaning into him when she had the floor under her feet.

"What happened, my child? How did she beat you?"

"I didn't see her—"

"Ah," said Thanos, and jammed his thumb into Nebula's left eye.

"Thanos!" Cha erupted, and sped to Nebula's side. She had dropped to her knees, keening in pain, her hands clapped to the empty socket, which bled profusely.

Without shifting his attention from the motionless Gamora, Thanos spoke. "She said she could not see. We'll biofuse an enhanced eye into her. Perhaps that will help, going forward. Take her to the medical bay for the procedure, Cha."

He did not move or even glance away from Gamora as Cha escorted Nebula, limping on her broken leg, one hand over her socket, from the training room. A spotty thread of blood trailed her.

Gamora's expression had not changed in the slightest during the entire exchange. He stared at her in the growing silence as she pointedly did not look back, anchoring her gaze instead off into the middle distance over his shoulder, as though he were not even present.

"Do you think me cruel?" he asked at last.

There was a great hesitation as she thought, and then finally she met his eyes with her own and said, "Yes."

Thanos smiled. He had decided during the hesitation that had she said *no* or failed to look him in the eye, he would have killed her.

"I'm so very proud of you," he told her. Words he'd never spoken or heard before.

After she adjusted to her new eye, Nebula did better in her next match against Gamora. She still didn't win, though.

"See how she does with new knees," Thanos instructed Cha.

CHAPTER XXXVI

IN HIS PERSONAL CHAMBERS, THANOS SAT AT AN INTERFACE desk, preparing plans for his next assault. His army no longer used gates to travel, unless they chanced upon one of the old Kalami Gates. Security around most gates made it difficult for someone as notorious as Thanos to use them. So they relied on super-lightspeed for most of their travel. Even so, the great distances between systems meant long stretches aspace, with plenty of time for thinking and strategizing.

For each world he tried to persuade, Thanos tailored his message intricately. And, at the same time, prepared for war. Because, well...

Cha signaled before coming in this time. Thanos did not look up as the door slid open. Cha was silent for too long, hovering over Thanos's shoulder.

"Speak, my friend."

A long pause. Then: "Is it fulfilling, Thanos?"

"Is what fulfilling?"

"The girls. What you do with them."

"Being a father to these girls?" He cogitated on the question for a long moment, then took another. "Yes. It is."

"Perhaps it's time to reconsider what we're doing, then."

Thanos looked up from his interface desk. Cha had long

ago become part of the background of the ship, one more piece in the puzzle he assembled on a regular basis in an attempt to understand and guide the universe. Now, though, looking at his old friend, Thanos thought he could see the entirety of their history together, written in the fine lines and crenellations on his face. They had been at war—at wars, really—for years now.

War had only made Thanos stronger and more certain of his path. As for Cha...Thanos could see now the weakness that roiled in his friend, the fractures in his beliefs and their relationship that had grown over time with each billion slaughtered.

"You think I would settle down, Cha? Settle for the pleasures of parenthood, when there is a universe out there in desperate need of the sort of help only *I* can provide?"

"Well, I—"

"I will not be derelict in my duty. I will not surrender my mission, my cause. I take pleasure in my children because they are my finest tools, the expression of my abilities and my knowledge and my destiny. Without the mission, we are purposeless and nomadic, Cha. Put the thought out of your head. Be strong."

Cha opened his mouth to speak, but just then an alarm klaxon rang. They stared at each other. The klaxons *never* rang.

Thanos leaped up from his desk, and together they dashed to the bridge, where the Other sat in the command chair, hissing to himself. At Thanos's entrance, he stood and gestured at the main screen.

"Surrounded, Lord Thanos," he grumbled in his slow, overenunciated voice. "Fifteen of them. Nova Corps Star Blasters."

"Should have expected this day to come," Thanos muttered. "But we're nowhere near Xandarian space."

"I guess they decided to take the initiative," Cha told him. "Prepare the Leviathans?"

"Yes. And open a comms channel to the lead Xandarian ship. I'll stall."

A moment later, the main screen flickered and flared to life. A hologram distended from it, forming into a long-forgotten, but immediately familiar, face.

"Daakon Ro," Thanos said, almost pleased. "You never took that early retirement. Your husband must be devastated."

Ro's face had changed not much in the intervening years, save for some wrinkles around his eyes and perhaps a slight lengthening of his forehead. He grimaced. "My husband passed three years ago, Thanos."

"You have my sincere condolences."

"Somehow I believe you."

"I rarely lie."

"No, but you've managed to kill a whole hell of a lot of people since the last time I saw you. Body count is something like half a trillion."

Thanos shrugged. "I haven't been keeping track. I've not

touched Xandar—your world is in wondrous balance. And the last time I checked, Denarian Ro, none of my incursions have been into any Xandarian territory. The Nova Corps has no jurisdiction over me."

Ro shook his head. "The other systems and territories are terrified of you. They've requested our help under the terms of the Treaty of Mazar. And don't ask: It was signed something like ten thousand years ago, but it's still enforceable."

"And so you're here to kill me."

"To arrest you, if possible. Come quietly." Ro paused, licked his lips. "I heard about Titan. What happened there. Pretty horrible. But you can't bring those people back by killing your way across the universe."

"I'm not trying to bring them back." Thanos caught a gesture from Cha out of the corner of his eye. The Leviathans were in place. "I'm trying to save lives."

"If you don't mind my saying so, you sure have a funny way of showing it."

"Ro, you were kind to me at a time in my life when I needed kindness. In acknowledgment of that, I'm going to give you thirty seconds to reverse your course and go back to Xandar."

Ro smirked. "One: I'm afraid I can't do that. Two: I have fifteen Nova Corps ships with solar guns aimed at your shield pods and engine core."

"Twenty seconds," Thanos said.

"How's this for acknowledging kindness?" Ro said. "I'll actually let you get to zero before I blow you out of space."

"Ten seconds," Thanos said, and at the same time signaled Cha to attack.

In anticipation of the day when some foolish world or desperate system or ignorant space pirate would attempt to blast him out of existence, Thanos had taken the precaution of having ten Leviathans trail the rest of his fleet at a distance of roughly one light-minute. They were spread out far enough that to normal sensors they simply appeared to be asteroidal space debris.

During his conversation with Daakon Ro, those ten living ships had closed the light-minute distance to the Nova Corps Star Blasters. With ten seconds left on Thanos's countdown, they attacked.

On-screen, Daakon Ro's hologram gasped and turned. Over the audio of the comms channel, Thanos heard panicked cries and shouts of alarm.

"What the hell!" Ro exclaimed, looking around. "Thanos! What the hell!"

The Leviathans did not so much assail the ships as they *swarmed* on them. They insinuated themselves into the Nova Corps's attack formation so swiftly that the ships couldn't fire without potentially hitting their own vessels. Lightning blasts sizzled from the Leviathans' blast ports, and the great beasts twitched their muscled lengths as they coursed through the ships' assault pattern. The vacuum-hardened outer carapaces of the Leviathans plowed through the alloy hulls of the ships, ripping them open to the empty death of space.

Daakon Ro's hologram fuzzed, sparked, then collapsed into dead static.

The assault took only a few minutes. When it was over, one Leviathan was dead, two were wounded, and all fifteen Star Blasters were obliterated. Debris, bodies, and globules of blood drifted in the zero-gravity tomb of deep space.

"I rarely lie," Thanos said to the empty screen. "But *rarely* does not mean *never.*"

Thanos leaned back in his chair and steepled his fingers before him. "As I was saying, Cha: I will not surrender. I will not give up. Life needs me on its side."

Cha clucked his tongue and gestured outside the main pulsoglass portal. An exploded Xandarian corpse drifted by, caught by the microgravity generated by *Sanctuary*'s mass. The body would orbit the ship like a broken, bloody moon until they increased speed to the point that friction would burn it to ash.

"Yes. Life needs you," Cha said without a trace of sarcasm.

"Your point is taken." Thanos heaved himself out of his chair. "Perhaps there is another way. Only a fool or a zealot clings to his original plan and does not seek new methods of attaining his goal."

"I'm pleased you distinguish between fools and zealots," Cha said happily.

"A mistake I won't make again," Thanos said as he left the bridge.

Retreating to his quarters, Thanos spent days in deep study. With Cha distracting his daughters, he allowed himself to sink deep into the data at his disposal. His chambers came to resemble the silencurium of his memory—there was no sound save for the occasional whisper of his own breath or the infrequent hard thump of his heart when he realized something anew.

He downloaded statistics and data from satellites orbiting distant worlds in far-off solar systems. He pored over information gleaned from obscure tracts and hidden caches of knowledge. He calculated and he massaged his intelligence and he applied his considerable brain to the question of *how many worlds* needed to be saved. And how best to save them?

The results were chilling. They made him so despondent that he did not leave his quarters for another week, simply lay in his bed and stared straight ahead at nothing. At absolutely nothing.

It was no longer a matter of saving individual planets, he realized. He'd been too nearsighted and too shortsighted to comprehend the sheer enormity of the problem ahead of him. The planets were in danger, yes, but the planets existed as parts of the universe.

And the universe itself was in danger of succumbing to the same fate as Titan.

The universe was vast, but not infinite. There was a finite number of habitable worlds and thus a finite supply of resources to support life. The number was enormous, yes—almost unimaginably so.

But it *was* a number. It was finite and limited, and therefore...

According to his new calculations, and based on his models—now tried on the ashes of hundreds of worlds—within the next one hundred billion years, the universe would run out of the resources to support life.

When he'd first calculated that number, he had laughed with relief. One hundred billion years was an unimaginably ridiculous length of time. It was almost an obscenity.

And yet...

And yet time was inexorable. One year or one hundred billion of them: The day *would* come. And did not the people of one hundred billion years hence deserve their lives as much as those living in the present? Who was he—who was anyone—to claim that a life lived *right now* was more valuable or worthy or deserving than one lived one hundred million millennia from now?

By that time in the future, there would be multiples of *sextillions* of living sentients in the universe. A staggeringly large number.

And every single one of them would be doomed.

Why should a child in the future suffer, starve, and die in horror just so a child today could live in comfort?

He could continue to travel the cosmos and try to fix planets and civilizations one by one, but...

"It's a big damned universe out there," he whispered to himself.

And that night, the dream came to him again, for the first time in years.

Remember what I have told you, Gwinth said. She was almost completely bare of flesh at this point, her body a loose-jointed skeleton hanging with gobbets of leftover skin and scraps of muscle that did not know how to let go. Her jaw clicked as she spoke.

And he remembered when he awoke. He always remembered now. Ever since he'd lied to Cha.

She said, *Save everyone.* That's what he'd told Cha all those years ago on the *Golden Berth*, when he lived under the yoke of His Lordship.

But that was not all. That was only half of what she'd told him. Quite literally.

You cannot save everyone, she'd said.

It made so much sense now. His algorithm, applied not to a planet but to the universe as a whole. To save the universe for the people of the future, he needed to kill half of it. He needed to kill half the universe.

He laughed at the thought. Laughed for a long, long time.

"Thank you," he whispered. "Thank you, Gwinth, for leading me down the right path once again."

He summoned Cha, his warrior-daughters, and the Other to the bridge. They were the only beings in his army capable of independent planning, and while his intellect outweighed theirs—combined—in every possible measure, he did feel that there was value in other perspectives, no matter how wrong.

Cha sat at the navigation pod, his chair twisted around to face Thanos in the commander's chair. The Other stood ramrod straight nearby, and his daughters…

The girls were girls no longer, verging on womanhood. Insolent and filled with hate and anger, they were so focused on their loathing for him that they did not realize how he'd made them his perfect weapons. Soon would be the time to unleash them with his armies, to watch them kill in his name as they deluded themselves into thinking that they were just biding their time, looking for his weakness.

He had no weakness. They would kill for him again and again, hating him, and do his loving work.

Nebula lounged in the weapons pod, her back against one chair arm, her legs draped over the other. Gamora perched atop a console nearby. They sparred and they bickered, but they also stayed close to each other, as though subject to some unspoken but understood détente that they enforced so long as it was to their mutual advantage.

"You've heard the problem," Thanos told them. "We've been taking the plodding course of going from planet to planet, identifying those with environmental issues like Titan's. But the universe as a whole is endangered. The problem before was merely staggering in its scope. Now it is nearly impossible to conceive. I welcome your suggestions for a solution."

"Gee, Dad," said Nebula, "why don't we just build a bomb big enough to kill half the universe? Do it in one shot."

"That's stupid," Gamora grumbled.

"At least I'm contributing," Nebula said, her remaining organic eye flashing with anger.

"Contributing something stupid is worse than just keeping your mouth shut in the first place."

Nebula spun in her chair, a blur of motion so fast that even Thanos had trouble keeping up with her movement. But before she could do anything else, Gamora was at Nebula's throat with a blade.

"Not now," Thanos said reprovingly.

Gamora snarled and jerked the blade away. Nebula sidled away, a hand to her throat. Her cybernetic eye spasmed open and closed, a sign that she was losing control. Thanos gave her his sternest glare and she settled down.

"A bomb big enough to kill half the universe," Thanos said once the room had calmed, "is an attractive notion, but imprecise and impractical. It's not as though I can snap my fingers and make it so. But something must be done.

Inevitable death is a sad enough fate for an individual or a world; for an entire reality? Unforgivable."

Cha folded his arms over his chest and *hmmph*ed. "You cannot expect to understand the machinations of fate."

"How convenient for fate," Thanos remarked.

"It was always a crazy idea," Nebula said sulkily. "Now it's just a bigger crazy idea. Running around the universe, killing off people in order to save them . . . Insane."

"Sanity is a matter of perspective, determined by social norms," Thanos told her. As he spoke, he watched Gamora, not Nebula. Gamora's expression, as always, revealed nothing of what she was thinking. He found her stoicism impressive and unnerving. "I am not bound by social norms. My sanity is not at issue."

"Says you," Nebula snarked.

"Indeed." Thanos opened his hands wide. "I am still amenable to suggestions."

No one spoke.

"Have we come this far only to meet a terminal pause?" he asked the room.

"Come this far?" Gamora said with the slightest hint of a smile at the corners of her lips. In their teen years, both his daughters had developed a mild rebellious streak. Gamora spoke less often, but with more bite. "How far have we come? A billion inhabited worlds in the universe, with billions of souls on each one. And you've killed less than a trillion in total so far." She clapped slowly, mockingly. "Well done, mighty Thanos, Warlord Thanos. Truly, the stars do quake at your footsteps."

"Say the word," Nebula urged, "and I'll cut her tongue out."

"And give me a robotic one, like yours?" Gamora asked sweetly. Nebula leaped up from her chair and launched herself at her sister, who sidestepped at the last possible instant and rabbit-punched Nebula in the side. Nebula gasped in pain and flew over the control console, crashing into the bulkhead. Gamora smoothly vaulted over the console, her knife already drawn.

"Gamora! Nebula!" Thanos barked, his voice cut off somewhat by the sound of Nebula's strangled gasp for breath as Gamora landed on her solar plexus. "We do not have time for this!"

Shielded from Thanos's view by the console, they scuffled there for a few moments, grunting and cursing. Finally, Thanos rose from his seat, leaned over the console, and hauled them to their feet, where, despite his massive hands on their shoulders, they continued to swing and swipe at each other.

"You vex me," he informed them, squeezing so tightly that bones in Gamora's shoulder ground together painfully. Nebula's new artificial shoulder complex whined electronically. "Vex me no further."

He shoved them to the floor.

"Sure, Dad," Nebula said darkly.

"As you say," Gamora said with an indifferent toss of her hair.

He waited until they had taken seats again—once again damnably close together; these two could not stand to be together, could not abide being apart—and then returned to his own seat.

"A problem of enormous size does not always require a solution of equal size," he said. "Sometimes finesse, critical thinking, and planning may suffice where brute force cannot."

"Like the way we overcame the three Asgardian warriors near Alfheim," Cha offered.

The mention of the Asgardians made Thanos think, surprisingly, of Kebbi. He'd not thought about her in years, and he was stunned to find that the memory of her was both clear and painful, as though its clarity sharpened its edges, making it difficult to turn the remembrance over in his mind. She had been the first sacrificed in the name of his mission, the first to have the trust she'd put in him repaid with her own blood.

He did not mourn her passing. But he mourned the loss of her presence. They were not the same, though the distinction was probably too fine, too nuanced for others.

"The Asgardians..." he murmured. "Their artifact."

Cha shook his head. "Thanos. That was *years* ago. I'm sure the Asgardians have redoubled security on their... what was it called? Their bespoke gate technology?"

"Bifrost," Thanos said absently.

"Right." Cha stared at Thanos, tilting his head this way,

then that. "Thanos? Are you actually considering this? Again? Do you remember what happened last time?"

Thanos closed his eyes and—for a moment—was back on board the *Blood Edda*. Smoke purled from control panels. Kebbi was dying in his arms even as his own blood fled his body with fierce rapidity.

In his life, he had conquered many worlds, brought many species to extinction. In the past several years, he had gone from one war to another. Yet those moments with Cha and Kebbi on the *Blood Edda* were the closest he had ever come to death.

"I remember exquisitely," he told Cha, opening his eyes. Across the bridge, his daughters scrutinized him, as though they'd finally found the weakness they'd sought all these years. He filed it away for later. "I remember coming very, very close to victory, at a time when we were younger, less puissant, and without resources."

"You want to mount an assault on Asgard?" Cha asked, his voice high-pitched and terrified. "Are you serious? All to seek out something that may not even exist? His Lordship was not exactly..."

"Sane?"

"I was going to say *a reliable source of information*. But yours works just as well."

"The Asgardian we first encountered," Thanos mused aloud. "Vathlauss."

"The one you tortured," Cha said, managing to keep a tone of judgment out of his voice.

"Yes, him. *He* certainly seemed to believe that Odin was hiding something. Something monumentally powerful."

Cha threw his hands up in the air. "This is madness. I've gone along with much since we met, Thanos, but invading the home of Odin himself? In pursuit of something that may or may not even exist?"

"Aether," Thanos murmured. "He called it Aether. The Infinity Stone."

Cha had opened his mouth to argue further, but at the words *Infinity Stone*, he froze. After a moment, he managed to say, "Is *that* what he told you? He said Odin had an Infinity Stone? You never told me that before."

Thanos shrugged. "It no longer seemed to matter. We had no way to return to Asgard. But..." Something occurred to him. "*An* Infinity Stone? There's more than one?"

"I don't..." Cha scratched at his head in bemusement. "I don't know. You hear things. Rumors. Space lore. Especially out on the Rim, where I was doing my work before His Lordship abducted me and pressed me into service. People tell all kinds of stories. But, still—it would be crazy to try to take an army to Asgard on the mere word of a dying man."

"I agree. *That* would be madness. We first need to ascertain whether the artifact exists. And then what it is and what it does. And *then*, if it is worthwhile, we will raze Asgard to find it."

Cha shook his head. "How exactly do you propose to learn all of this? Are we going to find and torture more Asgardians and hope this time it works out?"

"Lorespeaker."

It was the first time the Other had spoken since the meeting had been convened.

"Excuse me?" Thanos said.

At the same moment, Cha groaned loudly and said, "Oh no!"

"Lorespeaker," the Other said again, very precisely. "Lorespeaker will know. He knows everything."

"Don't be an idiot!" Cha howled, pointing at the Other.

Thanos nodded minutely to Gamora, who came up behind Cha and put a strong hand on Cha's shoulder. The Sirian calmed down almost immediately.

"What is a Lorespeaker?" Thanos asked.

"Not what. Who," the Other explained. "The Lorespeaker knows everything worth knowing. All the stories. The Lorespeaker hears all and knows all. Every legend. Every myth. Every tale."

"Why have I never heard of this Lorespeaker before?"

Cha fumed in his seat, arms folded over his chest. "Because it's a fairy tale, Thanos."

When the Chitauri shrugged—which wasn't often—their carapaces clacked against their cybernetic implants. It was an oddly hollow sound, and the Other made it now. "It is a big universe, Lord Thanos. No one knows all of it. Except the Lorespeaker."

Thanos held up a hand to forestall Cha's indignant interruption.

Cha spoke through clenched teeth, eager to leap up from his chair but mindful of Gamora standing behind him. "The Lorespeaker is a charlatan. He knows as much fiction as fact and spews them in equal quantities." He turned his attention to Thanos. "Don't listen to this...bug. The Lorespeaker will lead you down a path that ends in a black hole, then push you in."

Thanos considered this. "What harm can there be in at least consulting with this Lorespeaker? If he speaks truth, so be it. If not, we are no worse off than before."

"The Lorespeaker lives within the KelDim Sorrow," Cha said, his voice swamped with pleading. "It's madness to go there."

"The KelDim Sorrow?" Thanos frowned. "That sounds familiar." He held up a hand to keep anyone from speaking as he sorted through his memory, seeking that term. He had a nearly perfect recollection, but with so many memories crammed in, it could be difficult to locate just the right one.

And then it hit him. His Lordship. The first time Thanos had met him, kneeling quite against his will, as Robbo stood over him...

And where would you go? His Lordship had asked. *We're deep in the Raven's Sweep. Nearest system is the KelDim Sorrow.*

"His Lordship," Thanos murmured. "He knew of the KelDim Sorrow."

Even that's parsecs *away,* His Lordship had continued, *and no life-forms, nothing habitable.*

And it suddenly made sense. Thanos ground his teeth together and damned himself for being a blind fool, an incompetent dullard who could not see properly the path laid out for him.

His Lordship had sought the Asgardian artifact. And had steered the *Golden Berth* right into the Raven's Sweep, which abutted the KelDim Sorrow. It wasn't madness or stupidity.

"It was a *plan,*" Thanos said aloud.

"What was a plan, Dad?" Nebula asked.

He opened his eyes and fixed his gaze on Cha. "His Lordship wasn't randomly flitting about the Raven's Sweep. He was seeking the KelDim Sorrow and the Lorespeaker, wasn't he? To confirm what he thought he knew about the Asgardian artifact."

Cha did not flinch or turn away from Thanos's glare. "I don't know. Maybe. I wasn't privy to His Lordship's plans. You were in the inner circle, not I."

"Gods of hell," Nebula swore. "Listening to old people talk about the past is the most boring thing *ever.*"

For once, her sister agreed. "Someone get to a *point,*" Gamora said with an emphatic nod. "Any point."

Thanos gestured with a finger in the direction of the door. "You're both dismissed. You, too," he said to the Other. "Cha and I will speak alone."

Once they were the only ones on the bridge, Cha slammed an open palm on the table. "Come on, Thanos. It's me. Cha. The others don't know you like I do. They didn't watch you hauled comatose and near death from your first ship. They didn't watch you cleaning the portholes on the *Golden Berth*."

"No, they didn't." Thanos stood, pulling himself to his full, intimidating height. "They fear me. And respect me. Do you? Or do you think I'm still that helpless pup His Lordship pulled from a dying spaceship? Or the broken fool you tended to after the *Blood Edda*?"

Cha groaned and scrubbed at his face with both hands. "Thanos, I'm trying to save you from yourself. We both almost died in the Raven's Sweep. It's parsecs in every direction of starless *nothing*. You found a magnetar, and we got lucky when you found the old Kalami Gate. You can't think we'll get lucky again like that."

"We have a different ship. Different engines. We'll plan for the Raven's Sweep."

"Once you get through the Sweep," Cha told him, "your problems have only begun. The KelDim Sorrow is an entire solar system that was wiped out millennia ago. And not wiped out in the sense that *you* do, where you leave biomes and lesser species intact. These are total scorched globes. Not a bird. Not a butterfly. Not a *blade of grass* lives on those worlds, Thanos. Fifteen planets like that, all of them orbiting the remains of a star that died long ago." He leaned over the table, his eyes wide, his voice deep with pain and omens. "There's no light. No heat. Nothing at all. Only a rumor that somehow this blasphemous creature called the Lorespeaker lives on one of those dead worlds, muttering to himself the stories only he cares about and only he knows."

Thanos contemplated this for a full minute. An eternity for one with his intellect.

"Nothing you've said," he told Cha, "frightens me. Not in the least."

"It's madness!" Cha leaped up from his seat. "You're talking about plunging the ship and your crew into a years-long trek through the most blighted corner of the galaxy, all for a reward that may not even exist!"

"Do you have a better suggestion?" Thanos demanded. "We are at an impasse. We cannot continue on our current course."

"So you'll take a blind leap into the universe instead? Congratulations, Thanos," Cha said bitterly. "It took years, but you've become His Lordship."

With that, Cha stalked out of the room, leaving Thanos alone on the bridge. Cha's words echoed far longer than he would have thought possible.

You've become His Lordship.

Thanos turned to behold himself in the reflective surface of the ship's pulsoglass. He saw, with eyes unencumbered by ego or prejudice, confidence. Strength. Robustness.

His Lordship had been a weak, puling, unscrupulous

wretch who loitered at death's door and was willing to drag others with him over the threshold.

I am not His Lordship. I am Thanos of Titan. I am the savior who will bring balance to the universe.

And I will let no one stop me.

Later, Cha came to Thanos in his personal quarters, where Thanos sat at his interface desk, plotting a new course.

"The Other tells me that you've ordered most of the fleet back to the Chitauri homeworld," Cha said without preamble.

Not turning away from his work, Thanos responded. "Yes. It's long past time for them to begin settling their new homeworld. They have more than lived up to our end of the bargain."

"So. You're resolved, then. To seek out the Lorespeaker."

"To learn the truth about the Infinity Stone. Or Stones, as the case may be. Yes."

"There could well be other sources of inform—"

"I will not traipse around the universe, picking up bits and pieces of lore and truth from a thousand sources when I can quite likely get it all in one fell swoop."

"Then I can go no further, Thanos. I've allowed you to seduce me into your quest and your madness, but here I will not yield! This new plan of yours is insanity atop insanity. You must stop. Here. Now. You must turn back."

Thanos tilted his head, pondering. "You don't want me to

stop because it's madness. You want me to stop because you know I can do it."

"I know no such thing."

As they spoke, Thanos stared at his hands, his fingers manipulating the holographic star charts that would lead them to the Raven's Sweep. Once there, they would find no stars to guide them. They would have to maintain a precise and perfectly balanced course through the Sweep if they were to come out on the other side in the KelDim Sorrow. Back to the Raven's Sweep, the place that had almost killed him. He had no fear of it, but caution and fear were not the same.

"Don't worry. I'm being very careful, Cha. I've learned the lessons of His Lordship's failures."

"Have you? Or have you just modified them to suit your needs?"

Thanos spun in his chair. For a moment, it was as though he were seeing Cha for the first time, opening his eyes in the medical bay on the *Golden Berth*, beholding that too-orange skin, those ears. That ridiculous kilt he used to wear.

And for some reason, this made him think of Sintaa, whom he'd not spared a thought for in years, not since he'd returned from the blasted and dead surface of Titan. Sintaa, who had been his friend, who had tried so hard to make Thanos part of something bigger.

Now Thanos *was* something bigger. His quest was more important than his own life, or the life of anyone else. It was the most important thing in the universe.

How fortunate, he realized, that Titan died. That his people had not heeded his warning. If they had, he would have committed suicide long ago, and never would have lived to bring balance to the universe.

He could not entertain Cha's notions of destiny and pre-determined fate, but he could acknowledge and celebrate simple luck.

"This is my task, Cha. I will complete it. It's as simple as that."

"There's nothing simple about what you propose. Killing half the universe. It's madness."

"You didn't seem to have a problem when we were doing it one planet at a time."

Cha worried his lower lip and started pacing. "It happened so gradually . . . and it made sense. At first, the idea that you could save a world here and there . . . A worthy goal, to be sure. But now . . ."

Thanos sat silently for a moment, regarding his oldest friend. He knew exactly where this was headed, and it was long past time, he realized. "Your pacing is unnerving me. Let's walk instead." He stood and bade Cha follow him into the corridor.

Together, they walked down empty halls. With most of the Chitauri outfitting the Leviathans for a return to their home-world, *Sanctuary* was nearly empty, save for Thanos and Cha, the Other, and the pair of demons he called his daughters.

"I've been thinking about this a lot, Thanos," Cha told

him as they walked. "I'm trying to put myself in your shoes. I know your dream means much to you. *Save everyone.* A noble goal. But you've gone too far."

"You put too much stock in my dream, Cha," Thanos said, with a hand clapped on his friend's shoulder. He'd always known that someday he would have to tell Cha the truth of his dream. It was only fair. Thanos was many things, but rarely a liar, as Daakon Ro knew too well.

"I did not tell you the whole truth of my dream, Cha," he said, stopping in the middle of the corridor. An airlock hatch was nearby, and Thanos leaned against it. "She did not tell me to *save everyone.* That was only half her message."

Perplexed, Cha tilted his head to the side. "What was the other half?"

"She said to me, *You cannot save everyone.*"

Cha mouthed the words once, then again, then a third time. His eyes widened with each iteration.

"It...wasn't a directive..." he said slowly. "It was... a statement of fact. And yet you continued anyway. Even though you knew that you couldn't actually save everyone."

"Yes. Because," Thanos said gently, "that is our only path forward. To defy death and allow for life."

"Defy death?" Cha laughed once, sharp and bitter. "You damned hypocrite! You don't *defy* death—you *enable* it! You've delivered billions to death!" He held his head in his hands. "You...How did I not see it before? How did I not know?"

"Because you were blinded, as so many are, by your

preconceptions and your rigid adherence to your own way of seeing the universe. You sought a massive change in the balance of the universe, a tilt toward peace. And you were so desperate for it that you threw away your own beliefs to follow the one who seemed to offer it. But peace is just a by-product of balance, Cha. And balance requires sacrifice."

"No!" Cha moaned, crumpling against the wall. "When I first met you, you killed in desperation, to save Titan. Now you kill because you *couldn't* save Titan. Your destiny was always slaughter."

Thanos drew in a deep breath. "Don't presume to tell me what I can and cannot do, Cha. I could have saved Titan, had that been my desire."

Cha goggled at him. "Are you mad? What are you talking about? They're all dead. They were dead when we got there."

And so Thanos told him what he had discovered, fifty stories below the surface of Titan, in the clean room at the root of the MentorPlex. He told him of the synth that had worn his father's face and spoken with his father's voice, and he told him of the Gene Library and what he'd done to it.

Cha's eyes could widen no farther. They trembled and shook as tears leaked out of them.

"You're not a savior," he said, his voice rising as he went on. "You're just a killer. You enjoy it. You sow death like no other, but at your core, you're a coward, Thanos! A coward! You hide behind this ship, behind the Other and the Chitauri, and now behind those girls!" Cha grabbed Thanos by the arm, pleading with him. "Listen to me. It's not too late. You can't continue on this path! You must repent and find a peaceful—"

Thanos reached out and took Cha's head between his hands. With a single, simple twist, he snapped Cha's neck.

Cha's expression went slack, dull. Thanos had known it would come to this someday, that Cha's heartfelt belief in the innate goodness of the universe would inevitably overwhelm friendship, loyalty, and common sense. It was not the first sacrifice Thanos had made on his quest. He hoped it would be the last.

"I had no choice," Thanos whispered. "I think perhaps you understand."

Then he cycled open the airlock, shoved Cha's body inside, and re-cycled. The inner door closed; the outer door opened; Cha's body ejected into the unforgiving, frigid blackness of space.

He took a moment to himself, staring at the blank surface of the closed airlock.

He'd done the only thing possible.

He'd done the *right* thing.

Yes. The right thing.

On the bridge, Thanos informed the Other that "Cha Rhaigor is no longer part of our mission."

The Other merely nodded.

POWER

True strength neither needs nor makes excuses.

CHAPTER XXXVII

WHEN *SANCTUARY* ENTERED THE RAVEN'S SWEEP, IT BORE only Thanos and his children. The Other had joined the rest of the Chitauri to prepare for their exodus to a new homeworld. Any of the planets Thanos had ravaged would be suitable and far superior to their current home; they had their pick.

He planned the trip through the Sweep carefully. At super-lightspeed, it would take less than a year to traverse the Raven's Sweep. But that was the mistake His Lordship had made, thinking that speed was all that mattered, that he could bullet through the Raven's Sweep and come out on the other side.

He'd been wrong.

The great distance involved meant that super-lightspeed travel would drain the engines of their power, leaving the ship stranded—like the *Golden Berth*—without a way to refuel.

Thanos would not allow his plans to turn on lucking into another magnetar.

He plotted a slow, methodical course through the Raven's Sweep, one that would take close to two years but would leave him with enough power in his engines to return.

He spent his time training Nebula and Gamora, watching their mutual hatred grow even as, paradoxically, they bonded closer and closer. Their emotions had become twisted parodies of love, hate, and devotion. They yearned to kill Thanos, to kill each other, perhaps even to kill themselves, and yet their desire to prove their own superiority overrode those urges. They couldn't kill him, because they craved his approval. They couldn't kill each other, because they needed someone to dominate. And they couldn't kill themselves, because that would obviate everything else they wanted and needed and thirsted for.

They were the perfect assassins.

As he learned one night when he opened his eyes from sleep, only to find Gamora standing over him. In her hands, she held a Chitauri battle-staff, one that—he could tell at a glance—had been upgraded considerably, if sloppily. Attached to it was a pulsometric lightning flange, powered by a slender fusion bottle that she'd grafted onto the haft. The whole thing crackled silently with pitiless power. A stealth weapon and a devastating power armament at the same time.

He was proud.

"Do it," he told her.

She hesitated. Then, with something like sadness in her eyes, she thumbed off the pulsometrics and turned to leave.

In the morning, he punished her for not following through. And from then on, he made certain to double-lock the door to his quarters when he slept. Yes, the thorny, twisted confines of their emotions acted as a sort of shield, but no shield could hold forever.

Training his daughters did not occupy all his time. He returned to his studies, specifically to genetic engineering, picking up where he'd left off on the Chitauri homeworld. The Chitauri were good soldiers, but he had begun to think they could be improved upon. Using samples of their DNA, his own DNA, and some genetic samples from the worlds he'd vanquished, he began to work on what he thought of as his Outriders—fiercely loyal, bred only for combat. He planned to breed thousands of them, millions if possible, to be his vanguard throughout the galaxy. Eventually, they would replace the Chitauri, who were capable but also limited by their hive mind. Thanos wanted soldiers he could preprogram from birth.

One day, hard at work at his biochemical forge, he sensed a presence behind him and turned quickly. In his own way, he loved the girls, but he did not entirely trust them.

It was Gamora, weaponless, standing a safe and respectable distance from him, her hands twined together anxiously.

"What do you need?" he asked her, annoyed at the interruption.

"Why did you kill Cha Rhaigor?" Gamora asked him.

Thanos sucked in a breath. "Honestly, I never realized you made much note of him."

"He was the only other adult on the ship. You didn't think we'd notice when he was gone?"

True. He nodded, conceding her point. "What makes you think I killed him?"

She snorted the sort of derision only a child in the throes of adolescence can muster. "No escape pods were jettisoned. There are no jump-ships missing from the launch bay."

"Ah."

"Nebula and I looked through the whole ship. Even in the engine room. We didn't find anything. So we figured you killed him and threw the body out an airlock."

Her tone was calm, almost nonchalant, but her lower lip trembled ever so slightly when she spoke.

"You and Nebula worked together?" he asked.

"Don't change the subject." Her quivering lip stiffened. "The Chitauri ignored us. The Other barely tolerated us. Cha was actually *nice* to us. We liked him. Why did you kill him?"

He thought carefully before answering. Not because he planned to lie to her, but because he wanted to tell her the absolute truth to the best of his understanding. There was little cause for lies between father and daughters, in this or any other matter.

"He challenged me," he told her.

"He always challenged you," Gamora said with a tilt of her chin. She would someday be devastatingly beautiful, a trait that would make her task even easier. Few were perspicacious enough to perceive death behind a scrim of comeliness. "Why now?"

With a great sigh, Thanos stood and clasped his hands behind his back, turning away from her to look out at the starless expanse of the Raven's Sweep. "We are at a critical juncture in our mission. I need absolute obedience."

"Nebula and I don't always obey you. When will you kill us?"

He twisted just enough to peer back at her. There was no fear or concern in her expression. She masked her emotions well. "Cha was a friend. You are my children. There's a difference. Children are supposed to be willful and disobedient on occasion."

An image of his father came to him for the first time in many years. Not of the synth that pretended to be him, but of A'Lars himself. Thanos had never asked him, in tones as blunt as Gamora's, *Why do you continue to tolerate me? Why do you suffer my existence? Why haven't you locked me away next to Mother in a psychosylum?* But he was certain that the answer would have been roughly the same as the one he gave to Gamora.

"We're not really your daughters," she said, a note of sulking in her voice.

"You are my children in every way that matters."

CHAPTER XXXVIII

THE KELDIM SORROW WAS AS BLEAK AND AS BLIGHTED AS Cha had described. For a full day of travel, Thanos did not even realize that they'd exited the Raven's Sweep and entered the Sorrow, so black and desolate were the vistas outside *Sanctuary*'s pulsoglass portholes.

But then the ship's sensors detected a planet-size mass. The ship automatically compensated for the gravity well, shifting so as not to become trapped and collide with the dead world.

And dead it was. Thanos had murdered billions but had left the worlds as untouched as war possibly could. Years after his assaults, trees still grew; grass carpeted the prairies. Predators stalked their prey through verdant jungles and over rolling veldts. The whole complex farrago of life still bloomed and clashed on those worlds.

Here, the planets were utterly denuded, scoured clean of even microbes. They were rocks and sand, pillars of stone and frozen lakes of magma. Lifeless marbles scattered on the black felt of reality.

And at the center of them, the axis on which they all turned, a crumbling, dying star, more shadow than light, noticeable mainly by the sparks that occasionally spat from its core out into the cold reaches of space.

355

The KelDim Sorrow was as dead as anything could be. Thanos felt great sadness and great admiration in equal measure.

There were fifteen planets in the KelDim Sorrow and threescore moons of sufficient size to merit examination. Thanos called up a three-dimensional chart of the system, then plotted the most efficient course that would take *Sanctuary* to within scanning range of each planet and moon.

According to his calculations, he would need at most three weeks and six days to scan them all.

He got lucky. Halfway through the second week, his scanners detected something on a large moon orbiting the fourth planet from the distant, dying sun. It was a heat signature, consistent with life. And it was so small in comparison to the surrounding gloom and cold that he almost missed it.

A chill ran down his spine. What if he *had* missed it? What if he'd continued on his path, scanning every world, and had ended up finding—so he would believe—absolutely nothing? And then left the KelDim Sorrow without so much as a souvenir to mark his arrival, left without any of the information he so desperately needed?

But, he reminded himself, that had not happened. He'd spied the heat signature and now had *Sanctuary* in a geosynchronous orbit above the spot.

Cha would have said, *When the universe is in harmony,*

all things wind up in their proper place, Thanos. Of course you found it.

He reminded himself that Cha had been a superstitious fool and that it was for the better that he was dead.

The girls joined him at the ship end of the shuttle drop portal. *Sanctuary*'s shuttles had an old-fashioned propulsion system that needed the assistance of a drop portal, like a pebble blown or sucked through a straw. The shuttlecraft would engage engines, and then the far end of the drop portal would open, and the change in pressure would suck the shuttle out into the vacuum of space.

Thanos donned an environment suit, trying not to think of the last time he'd done so. Before his trip to the surface of Titan. He'd had to jerry-rig a suit by stitching together two normal-size ones. Now he had a bespoke environment suit crafted for him by the Chitauri, with his own special modifications.

"What's to stop us from taking the ship and leaving you here?" Nebula asked saucily.

"Two things," Thanos intoned, ticking them off on his right hand. "First: You haven't the proper training to maintain the power balance in the engines, so you'd run out of power before you could get back to civilized space. Second: Without me as a counterweight around, at this point in your training you'd kill each other before you broke orbit."

They exchanged knowing glances. Gamora said nothing. Nebula snorted in a way that meant she'd been bested but couldn't admit it. "Might be worth it," she said.

With a detached shrug, he turned to enter the shuttlecraft, then paused, as though remembering a long-buried memory, and turned back to them.

"Oh, and one more reason," he said. "There's a modified sympathy circuit on this ship. If it travels more than a light-year from me, it will explode, killing everyone on board."

"Checkmate," Gamora said. Despite herself, she was grinning.

Thanos climbed into the shuttle and disengaged from *Sanctuary*. The last thing he saw was Nebula, scowling at him from the ship end of the drop portal. And then the space end opened, and with a lurch, he was yanked unceremoniously out into space, with only the thin alloy skin of the shuttle between him and vacuum.

The shuttle fell more than flew to the surface of the moon. Its engines were relatively weak and were best for maneuvering. The moon was large, its gravitational pull strong—the shuttle careered toward it as though eager for a union.

Thanos landed close to the structure he'd observed from orbit. It was a low building, no more than a story or two, assuming the inhabitant was roughly humanoid and standard-size. The structure seemed small, but he had no idea how big the occupant was.

There was no appreciable atmosphere outside the shuttle. He locked down his environment suit and stepped outside, wary. Even with a genteel name like the Lorespeaker, there was no guarantee that Thanos would not be greeted with violence. Most beings who chose to live in such abject isolation protected their privacy with great jealousy and zeal.

All around him, there was a sudden flash of light and a *whoosh*ing sound. He recognized it as an environment field snapping into place. According to his suit's readout, the area around him was now habitable.

Mindful of how he'd slain three Asgardians by shutting off such a field at just the right moment, he decided to keep his suit on and active. He started walking toward the building, whose entrance was shrouded in darkness.

As he neared, a figure emerged from that darkness, walking with slow, steady steps toward him. It wore a cloak patterned in red and gray, with a hood over its head. A belted sash drew in the waist, and supple gray boots came to its knees, kicking up dust as it strode closer. It carried something that was either a short staff or a long scepter. Perhaps a meter in length, curved. Its top quarter was wrapped in frayed strips of hide.

Thanos stopped in his tracks and decided to allow the figure to advance no closer than two meters. Any closer and he would need to attack.

As though it could read his mind, the figure stopped at precisely two meters distant. After a slight pause, it peeled back the hood, and Thanos beheld a face like an upside-down triangle with rounded corners, a fringe of bluish hair above the ears, and a thin, pointed beard of the same bluish hue.

Thanos had expected someone old and wizened, a wrinkled and broken-down ancient. The Lorespeaker, as best he could tell, appeared to be not much older than Thanos himself.

Shorter, though. He grinned up at Thanos and spoke with a voice freighted with age and contemplation:

"Welcome! I can tell by your expression that you were expecting someone a little older."

"Are you the Lorespeaker?" Maybe this was an assistant, a majordomo...

"I am. You wonder about my age, I'm sure. I'm much older than I appear. My people are exceptionally long-lived."

"And who might those people be?"

The Lorespeaker shrugged indifferently. "The others like me. Answer me this: Do you truly want to continue to stand outside? There's little to see...." He swept an arm out to encompass the gray rocks and flat sand plains.

Thanos conceded that this was so. He followed the Lorespeaker into the building.

Inside, the place was cluttered with old, old technology. It took Thanos a while to identify some of the pieces and their purposes: a stove, a flat-screen entertainment/information appliance, a freezer. Thanos wondered exactly how long the Lorespeaker had been here.

"There's a persistent environment in here," the Lorespeaker told him. "You can take off that suit."

The Lorespeaker seemed to be breathing fine, and the suit's screen confirmed that the building had an atmosphere. Thanos peeled off the head covering of his environment suit and took a breath of slightly stale air.

As though just remembering to do so, the Lorespeaker smiled. "May I offer you some tea?"

The building made Thanos feel claustrophobic. The walls were too close, the ceiling too low. He agreed to the tea and tried to find a place to sit.

"Sit anywhere," the Lorespeaker told him as he set down his scepter on a counter and began rummaging through a cabinet. "I have a tea that I only open for guests. It's been quite a while; let me find it."

Thanos found a sofa that seemed sturdy enough and wide enough to accommodate his frame. The entire place was meticulously clean, with shelves of orderly ranks of old data-disks, big, flimsy early-generation ChIPs, and a stack of things that—to his surprise—turned out to be actual bound-paper publications. He had only seen such things in a museum.

Unless the Lorespeaker had access to some sort of galaxy-spanning teleportation technology, there was no way to replenish his stores. Where did his food come from, without replication technology...and no way to grow it? What did he do for new entertainment, for diversion, for information acquisition?

Thanos began to feel unsettled. Something was wrong

here. Something was very wrong. He couldn't quite put his finger on it....

"Ah! Got it!" The Lorespeaker held up a smallish tin, crowing. "I knew it was in here! Let me just put the kettle on...."

As Thanos watched, the Lorespeaker activated the stove. A glowing red ring appeared there, and he placed a bulbous vessel atop it. "A nice cuppa," the Lorespeaker said. "Just the thing for a chilly night, eh?" His expression brightened. "That's my attempt at a joke, Thanos. It's been a long time since I told one. Did I do it wrong?"

Thanos blinked. "How do you know my name?"

The Lorespeaker plucked up his scepter and settled into a chair across from Thanos. "My blessing and my curse is a sort of...cosmic awareness. It has its limits, though. To a distance of roughly three parsecs, I am aware of almost every occurrence and happening."

Thanos arched an eyebrow. It was as significant an expression of disbelief as he was willing to display.

The Lorespeaker chuckled. "I understand if you don't believe me. Allow me to prove it. In orbit above this planet is the ship you came here in. There are two young women aboard. One is a Zehoberei—"

Thanos arched his other eyebrow, this time in surprise. "I know where they're from."

"I have a significant storehouse of Zehoberei myth and history in my head. It would be a pleasure to—" He broke off for a moment and stared into the middle distance. Just when Thanos had decided to say something, the Lorespeaker shivered out of his reverie. "It would be a pleasure to share those with her."

"This is what you do?" Thanos asked. "You remember histories?"

"Not histories—stories. Myths. Legends. *Lore*, Thanos. Some of it true, some of it false, some of it truer for being invented."

"Why here? Why so far from the people whose stories you tell?"

"In any sort of civilized system," the Lorespeaker explained, speaking slowly "there's too much input. A constant awareness and a constant stream of information. I'm capable of sorting it and ordering it—barely. I would forget to eat, to bathe, to sleep.... And when I *did* sleep, I would dream the dreams of billions of souls around me." He sighed. "It was untenable. I needed to go somewhere quiet."

"You needed to become a hermit."

"It's not that I rejected civilization. I just couldn't be around it. I'm more than happy to have visitors, if they can get here. The juxtaposition of the Sorrow to the Sweep was a perfect coincidence for me. Parsecs of silence in every direction. Absolute isolation." He grinned and acknowledged Thanos with a slight raise of his hand. "Though with the possibility of guests who are determined enough."

Thanos returned the salute. "Do you have many visitors?"

"Not often. A few years back, there was a ship lost out in the Sweep, right at the edge of my perception. I thought it might be headed this way, but it was not to be. I could tell you more, but I see by your expression that I've made my case. Tea?" The kettle, as he called it, was whistling, steam pouring from a vent at its top.

Thanos, who had never witnessed tea made in such a fashion, nodded. He watched as the Lorespeaker undertook a lengthy ritual. First, he placed dried leaves in a mesh. Then he poured the boiling water into a cup, over and through the mesh. When the cup was full, he dunked the mesh inside, then repeated the whole process with a second cup. It took forever.

"Now we let it steep." The Lorespeaker smiled at him and sat across from Thanos. He sighed contentedly and clapped his hands together. "What can I do for you?"

Eyeing the two steaming mugs, Thanos asked, "How long does it steep?"

"A few minutes. Is *that* what you came here to ask?"

"No," Thanos said drily.

"I didn't think so." The Lorespeaker leaned over the mugs and inhaled deeply. "Ah! Jazzberry and hibiscus! Smell that, Thanos! Isn't it delightful?"

With a resigned sigh, Thanos did as he was bade, leaning forward and drawing in a breath.

"It's delightful," he said. "May we speak?"

The Lorespeaker stared at him for a protracted period.

Just as Thanos was about to speak, the Lorespeaker shuddered and returned from whatever place his mind had gone to. "Of course we may speak. Was I preventing you from speaking? If so, I apologize. It's been so long since I've spoken with someone that I may have forgotten the protocols. Or maybe they've changed. How are people *talking* these days?"

Thanos regarded him quietly for a moment. "You're asking the wrong person."

"*Hmm.*" The Lorespeaker nodded gently, considering. "Well, let's see how this tastes." Picking up both mugs, he held one out to Thanos, who accepted it.

The tea was surprisingly sweet, with a buzzy sort of aftertaste.

"Good, yes?" The Lorespeaker seemed highly invested in the answer.

"Yes. Good." Thanos sipped some more. "Now, if we could move on to the purpose of my visit…"

"Of course. Perhaps I should explain first exactly how this all works." With the word *this*, the Lorespeaker pointed at his own head. "The peculiar neurology of my brain is such that once I know something, I cannot forget it…but all of my information is recalled in the form of stories. Bards and tale-tellers and oracles throughout the universe are not particularly fond of me, needless to say. Although I suppose my exile here has diminished their animus somewhat."

Thanos coughed impatiently. He had become unaccustomed to waiting for his turn to speak.

"Of course," the Lorespeaker said quickly, getting the hint. "My apologies. As I said, I don't get a lot of visitors. My small-talk skills are rusty at best."

"I never possessed them in the first place. Perhaps we should just skip ahead. I am seeking an artifact," Thanos told him. "One of great power. Rumored to be in the possession of the ruler of Asgard."

The Lorespeaker frowned, for the first time evincing an emotion that was not glee or satisfaction. His bluish whiskers trembled ever so slightly at the terminus of his downturned lips.

"Odin. You dabble with powers beyond your ken, Thanos. Very daring."

"I have cause to be daring. I seek the Infinity Stone."

The Lorespeaker shrugged. "Which one?"

An image of Cha Rhaigor flickered momentarily, like a sudden sharp bite at the back of Thanos's brain. "So there *is* more than one. I've heard Odin possesses one, called the Aether."

The Lorespeaker made a sound that Thanos thought was a giggle, but which quickly turned into a cough. "Your pardon," the Lorespeaker said, and drank some tea before continuing. "Odin has many artifacts in his possession. There are stories of dwarven metal and hammers that only gods may lift and a box that contains winter. Are you certain about the information you've received?"

"Truthfully? No. But I believe the Asgardians are hiding *something*." He explained—as briefly as possible—his time on the *Golden Berth* with His Lordship and the information he'd gleaned from plundering the dead man's data. For good measure, he also explained what he'd learned from Vathlauss.... And then, because the natural next question would be *Why didn't you follow up on that?* he recounted the assault on the base near Alfheim and the battle against Yrsa on board the *Blood Edda*.

At the Asgardian's name, the Lorespeaker perked up, his lips twitching into a grin. "Ah, Yrsa! I know that name. The Goddess of Combat in Close Quarters."

Suddenly the battle on the *Blood Edda* all those years ago made much more sense.

"In any event," Thanos said, clearing his throat, "I have ample reason to believe that Odin is in possession of this Aether."

The Lorespeaker's grin widened into a satisfied, delighted smile. "There is a story I could tell you.... Actually, more than one. One is about Odin and the Dark Elf Malekith. One is about the planet Earth. Another is about the planet Morag and the fate of that world."

"I'm not interested in stories, just information."

The Lorespeaker clucked his tongue and wagged a finger. "Tut-tut, Thanos! I've told you how my mind works. If I could simply produce information, I would. But I must tell you a *story*."

Folding his arms over his chest, Thanos leaned back in his chair. "Very well, then. Regale me."

The Lorespeaker's lips quirked into something like a grimace. Something about it set off all Thanos's internal alarms. He tensed; his fingers curled into his palms. But it was just a moment, a tic, perhaps. A misfiring neuron. As quickly as the expression appeared, it faded into the Lorespeaker's more serious and relaxed mien.

"Oh no. It's not that simple. You have to give me something first, Thanos. That is the price for my knowledge."

Thanos unclenched his fists and ran his hands down his flanks, proving the flatness of his garb. "I have nothing to give you. I came empty-handed."

The Lorespeaker shook his head. "Not something physical. I have no need for gifts. I want your *story*. I want a memory. Something true and deep. Don't try telling me what you ate for breakfast this morning. Although...honestly, I'd like to know. I can't help it. When you have a memory like mine, you thirst for knowledge."

"I ate an omelet of bloodeagle eggs with toast and blinkenberry jam," Thanos told him. "We have a well-stocked larder aboard my vessel, with food stores from a multitude of vanquished worlds at our disposal. I'd be happy to offer you—"

He broke off. The Lorespeaker wasn't listening. Instead, the man sat almost perfectly still, licking his lips, eyes closed. His eyes vibrated behind those lids, and Thanos imagined the biochemical processes at work, etching his prosaic breakfast into the permanent memory structures of the Lorespeaker's unfathomably complicated brain.

"Good. Great!" said the Lorespeaker, opening his eyes and smiling brightly. "Now, you need to give me some important memory of yours. Something significant. Make it a good one, Thanos, and I'll tell you everything you need to know about that thing old Bor took from the Dark Elves. Which, I can tell you, isn't even actually on Asgard anymore." He grinned slyly. "Interested?"

Thanos was desperately interested, but he had no idea what sort of memory might satisfy the Lorespeaker's curiosity. He clenched his fists and thumped his knees lightly. To come so close! All his answers resided in the skull just a few decis away from him, and if there were a way to rip them right out, he would.

"There's no rush," his host told him. "Not for me, at least. Take your time. Think about it."

Thanos gave brief consideration to kidnapping the Lorespeaker up to *Sanctuary*, where Nebula and Gamora could perform the dull necessities of torture that would pry the requisite information out of the man's living brain. But, he reasoned, a brain as powerful, as complex, and as unutterably alien as the Lorespeaker's could potentially be resistant to the usual torments and inducements. It was a risk he couldn't take.

CHAPTER XXXIX

WITHIN THE CONFINES OF HIS MIND, THANOS REVISITED HIS life, replaying the great battles, the wars. The decisions he'd made that had turned the tide of bloodshed to or against him. The triumphs, both close and foregone. None of them, he decided, would prove to be of exceptional interest to a being who had memorized the greatest wars and conflicts in the history of the known universe.

Was it possible he'd actually achieved nothing of note? That in pursuit of greatness, he'd stumbled into mediocrity? Was Thanos not a savior but rather just another warlord, traipsing around the galaxy, taking what he wanted, with no higher purpose?

The Lorespeaker gestured broadly with his scepter. "Have I stumped you, Thanos?"

Thanos grumbled noncommittally. The Lorespeaker asked him if he would like some food while he thought.

Thanos considered this. "Where do you get fresh food? There's no life in the KelDim Sorrow."

"I have a hydroponic garden under this building," the Lorespeaker explained. "I can show it to you, if you like...."

Thanos had more questions, he realized. They would

help him stall as he contemplated the Lorespeaker's demand for a story.

"How do you stay here," Thanos asked, "alone, isolated in this one building, and not go insane?"

"Oh, but I *do* go insane!" The Lorespeaker's tone was bright, unaffected, honest. "It happens every few years; I just lose my mind for a little while."

"And then..."

He offered Thanos a wide, radiant smile. "And then I find it again."

"How do you entertain yourself? How do you learn new things?"

The Lorespeaker tapped his temple. "You forget; I don't forget. I remember everything I have ever seen or heard or learned. I have a near-infinite array of information to pore over, to study. I am always looking for new connections and patterns. If I need entertainment, I need only recall any one of the nearly infinite stories I've been told." He gazed at Thanos, licking his lips. "Speaking of stories... Have you come up with one yet? I'm not trying to rush you, certainly not on my behalf. I'd be happy to have you stay as long as you like. But I sense you have a particular urgency."

"Yes. I have a task that must be completed in the next one hundred billion years."

The Lorespeaker did not chuckle or even smile at Thanos's

attempt at humor. He merely nodded very seriously. "Well then, we should get started."

He could stall no longer.

"I don't know what story to tell you," Thanos admitted. "My life seems suddenly exceptional and banal all at once. I've been an outcast my entire life. By birth and social fiat at first, by my own choices and actions later. I have subscribed to the highest possible standards, believed only in the noblest causes, sacrificed everything, all to arrive here. And now it seems pointless. My task is so enormous that I cannot encompass it, even in my own great intellect. It falls to me to save the universe from itself, and yet the universe seems to conspire against me."

When he was done, he half expected the Lorespeaker to laugh at him, to order him out of the domicile. Instead, the other simply gazed at him, hands clasped. "I see."

"Do you?"

"You believe you are charged to save the universe. That's a big job. Who gave it to you?"

"I gave it to myself. I saw what others could not. Did not. Would not."

"There's more. Something you're not telling me."

With a sigh, Thanos recounted his recurring dream.

"You cannot save everyone," the Lorespeaker murmured.

"But I can save some."

"Do you believe this dream is something more than merely a dream?"

Thanos barked laughter that filled the Lorespeaker's

home. "No. Don't be absurd. This is simply my own mind reflected back at me, telling me what I need to know in direct language."

"You began your life with the cards stacked against you," said the Lorespeaker. "You were a monstrosity, a deviant, in a world that appreciated conformity and order. You learned an important lesson: Those who stand out, who excel, are beaten down by those who can neither stand out nor excel, using whatever excuses they can."

"They were not all like that," Thanos said, thinking of Gwinth and what she'd said to him: *We're not our parents. We don't hate and fear just because something is different.*

And then he realized it: The memory he needed to give to the Lorespeaker. It was his and his alone, and it had nothing to do with war or death or blood. It was, he knew now, the moment that defined him, a moment of light and love.

"I kissed a woman," he said slowly. "A special woman."

The Lorespeaker perked up. "The Warlord has a heart after all. Go on."

It had been a long time ago. Several lifetimes, for all intents and purposes. At first, Thanos wasn't even sure he could remember the kiss with any sort of fidelity. He experienced a moment of horror when he realized he could not remember her face. It had been supplanted in his memory by the dream-Gwinth, the decaying revenant who'd haunted him since his exile.

But it was just a moment. It passed and he discovered that

as soon as he leaned hard on one tile of memory, other tiles surfaced around it. He remembered the walk through the cluttered, clotted streets of the Eternal City, surrounded by those who were now dead. Sintaa, also dead, tugging him, obstinate and reluctant, into the silencurium.

And the girl. The girl with the close-cropped hair, bright red. Her pale-yellow skin, sprayed with a freckling of light green. And her first, shy smile as she moved so he could sit with her.

He would never forget her face again. He would not allow himself to.

The drink he had drunk that night: green, bubbly, and too sweet, tasting of melon and elderberries and ethyl alcohol. He could taste it again on his tongue, even now, as though he'd just tippled it.

All of this, leading up to the kiss. The first kiss, when he'd come to understand his yearning for connection, his need to understand himself so he could hope to bond with others. That kiss, the first time he felt humane tenderness, a blending of people.

"I felt incomplete," he said to the Lorespeaker, "but with that kiss, I knew that if I pressed forward, if I became the person I needed to become, that I would capture the feeling I needed all along. That the kiss would then mean something. I knew it. I've been seeking it. If I can save the universe, then I will become the Thanos who was worthy of that kiss."

He still wore his battle armor, but he'd never felt so

vulnerable in his life. Not even when bleeding and dying on the end of Yrsa's war-ax.

There was more to tell, if need be. How he had then found the courage to go at last to his mother. The shame and disappointment of that meeting. He had it all in him and he could tell it all, no matter how much more vulnerable it would make him. It was worth it, if it led him to the power to save the universe.

The Lorespeaker smiled a genuine smile of childlike glee. "What a lovely little anecdote, Thanos. Thank you for that."

"Is it enough?" Thanos asked gruffly. He felt his limbs about him, his muscles twitching. He was not a lovesick, lovelorn, love*torn*, broken boy. He was a warlord. A conqueror. He had dredged up the memory and given it freely, but he would not let himself wallow in it. There were more important tasks ahead of him; the past could stay behind.

With a slow nod, the Lorespeaker said, "It will suffice."

"Then tell me of the artifact."

"It's not that simple...."

Thanos stood abruptly, pulling himself up to his full, intimidating height. He cracked his knuckles and hovered over the smaller man. "I am not one for games, Lorespeaker. Don't misinterpret my fond memory of a bygone age as weakness. I have murdered *worlds*. One more gallon of blood on my hands will not disturb me in the slightest."

The Lorespeaker chuckled, absolutely unworried, and stood up, tapping his scepter against Thanos's chest. "Thanos,

Thanos, Thanos! We're friends! No need for threats. I'm going to tell you everything you need to know. I just need to do it as a *story*, you see? It's right there in my name: Lorespeaker." He twirled his index finger around his ear. "That's how my brain works, remember? It's not a loose collection of facts and figures up here; it's an interconnected skein of characters and notions and plots."

"Just be quick about it," Thanos said.

"I will edit on the fly as judiciously as I can," the Lorespeaker promised. "We will call this story…oh, let's see… *The Parable of Morag*! Are you ready?"

With a grumpy twist of his lips, Thanos flopped back onto the sofa, which groaned loudly in complaint. "I suppose I have no choice."

"Great!" The Lorespeaker clapped his hands together and wrung them joyfully. "Let's begin!"

CHAPTER XL

The Parable of Morag

THE WORLD OF MORAG CIRCLED—STILL CIRCLES, actually—the binary eclipsing M31V in the western spiral arm of the Andromeda Galaxy. There are a trillion stars in the Andromeda Galaxy, and so trillions more worlds, yet this one has particular meaning for us and for our story.

Morag today is not dead in the sense that the Sorrow is dead. Life still thrives there, in the form of vegetation, rodents, and a particularly dangerous species of amphibious predators. But intelligent life was wiped out millennia ago, owing in part to Morag's own hubris.

For though Morag was a world of many technological wonders, the people of that flourishing civilization ignored the evidence of their science in favor of the evidence of their eyes. Told by data that their world was imperiled, they instead clung to the evidence before them, which told them that the weather was perhaps a bit colder this winter or hotter this summer, but surely nothing to worry about.

They learned soon enough how wrong they were. The drastic temperature fluctuations brought about by global climate change melted the polar ice caps, and the planet was entirely flooded. No one survived.

Except, as mentioned before, the Orloni rodents and the weird crocodile-like things that thrived in the water, and so on.

But before they died, the people of Morag built a great temple to hide and preserve their most powerful artifact: an Infinity Stone.

Yes, an Infinity Stone! The people of Morag had been entrusted—or perhaps *cursed*—with the possession of this, one of the most potent and powerful artifacts in the entirety of the known universe!

"If it's so powerful, why didn't they use it to save their world?"

"Hush! I'm getting there!"

The Stone was powerful, true . . . but that was *all* it was. Powerful. It was, in fact, the Power Stone itself. Legend tells that it was a purple bauble, which could enhance the bearer's physical abilities, imbuing him or her or they or it or eir or pers or vis or xyr with incredible power. The ability to manipulate energy! The strength to lift buildings! Power enough, when properly channeled, to obliterate entire worlds!

But not, sadly enough, power to *save*. Power to *protect*. The Power Stone could only be used for violence and destruction. In the face of encroaching global catastrophe, it was useless.

Yet the people of Morag knew that the Power Stone must be protected and preserved. They restrained its great power in an Orb, then built around the Orb an entire temple devoted to the housing and protection of the Stone.

Like the rest of the planet's civilization, the temple was consumed by the hungry, overfed waters of Morag. Yet, it is whispered that every three hundred years, the waters recede enough to make the temple accessible. And that perhaps someone very brave...

Or very foolish...

Or very both...

Might be able to enter the temple and possess, at last, the lost legacy of the people of Morag: the Infinity Stone of Power!

CHAPTER XLI

"I'VE NEVER HEARD OF SUCH A THING," THANOS SAID. "AND I don't see how it could be of use to me. I already possess the power to lay waste to worlds."

"Ah, but you must consider where the Stone *comes from*, Thanos!"

"And that is…?"

"Your wit is sharp, your mind strong, yet your education is lacking. Have you heard of the Celestials?"

"No."

The light of realization flashed in the Lorespeaker's eyes. He licked his lips and thrust a triumphant finger in the air and…

CHAPTER XLII

The Parable of the Universal Powers

IN THE WAKE OF THE UNIVERSE'S CREATION, THERE AROSE the Celestials! Beings enormous in power, in stature, and in influence. They are to us as gods to ants, more powerful than even the mighty Asgardians. Some say they were born in the heat of the Big Bang. Others that they came into being billions of years later, predating the rise of intelligence and civilization throughout the universe.

However they were born, they were the first of the great species to roam the stars. And they had the potential to wield the Infinity Stones.

The Stones were the remnants of a universe that preceded our own: six singularities that survived the Big Bang and were forged by unimaginable beings into concentrated ingots. Each one had a characteristic tied to a specific aspect of the universe as a whole: Time, Space, Reality, Mind, Soul, and of course Power.

As time passed and the young universe aged, the ingots came into the hands of beings of great powers, such as the Celestials and their kin. They were modified and tinkered with, until they were six great Stones, each one capable of imbuing its wielder with almost limitless power within its specific domain.

So powerful were the Stones that no one could control them entirely. And as time wore on, the Stones were lost, one by one, eventually passing into the realm of legend, then myth . . . and then outright forgotten. Today, few know what an Infinity Stone is, and even those who do don't necessarily believe they exist.

But they do, Thanos.

They do.

CHAPTER XLIII

DURING THE SECOND PARABLE—WHICH SEEMED TO BE more about the Stones than about the Celestials, but he said nothing on this score—Thanos had leaned forward, elbows on knees, his fingers steepled before his frowning visage. His brow furrowed with concentration.

It was, of course, ridiculous. Absurd. He dismissed the very idea of such things. They had no place in the rational universe as he understood it. They were a...

A moron's fable.

A bedtime story to recite to credulous children, who could believe such things existed in the cosmos.

But...

"Six Stones," he said slowly, as though contemplating the seriousness of it. "One each to control different aspects of the universe."

"Oh yes!" the Lorespeaker said excitedly. He gesticulated wildly with sudden passion. "The Space Stone, for example, is *blue*. That's the one I believe Odin has had in his possession, though I have been told an interesting tale of how he came to send it to a place called Earth. A sort of cosmic backwater, really. Nothing worth noting, except that there may very well be an Infinity Stone in the midst of all the monkey-men there.

"And then there's the Soul Stone. That one's orange, and I know for a fact where it is, and I will tell you the story now—"

"Don't bother."

The Lorespeaker's wounded expression almost—*almost*—induced Thanos to change his mind, but he remained resolute. He had no more time for fairy tales.

Still the Lorespeaker prattled on, now twirling his scepter like a baton. He had broken out in a sudden sweat along his brow and his words came almost too fast: "The Reality Stone was acquired by the Dark Elf Malekith during one of Svartalfheim's many wars with Asgard. And *those*, Thanos, are tales I shall regale you with shortly, for they are truly awesome. In any event, this is the Aether of which you spoke. Taken from the Dark Elves by Bor, father of Odin, who hid it far from any living being, for it was too powerful to entrust to anyone. So, no, I don't believe you would have found it, even if you'd been able to breach Asgard's defenses.

"The Time Stone was lost millennia ago but resurfaced in Kamar-Taj, in the possession of the Ancient One. Put a pin in that—*lots* of stories to tell there! And the *Mind* Stone... Well, you wouldn't *believe*—"

"I don't want to believe any of it," Thanos interrupted forcefully. "Rocks that predate the universe? That control the fundamental forces of reality?"

"Believe what you wish," the Lorespeaker snapped, miffed. "The universe does not care what you do or don't believe."

That was beginning to sound suspiciously like Cha's insistences. Thanos clenched his furrowed jaw.

"If these Stones exist, why are they not used more often?"

The Lorespeaker offered a short bark of laughter without a hint of mirth. Something had changed. Something in the air itself.

"They are *hidden*, Thanos," the Lorespeaker said, as though badgering a child, "because they are too powerful. And because the Celestials and the others, the ones whom the Celestials fear, keep close watch on the Stones from afar."

"This is complete madness."

The Lorespeaker smiled indulgently. "Of course. Rise, Lord Thanos."

Thanos stood. "Are you trying to prove a point?"

"Why not hop on one foot?"

Thanos grunted. "I am not here for your amusement."

"And yet you're amusing me."

Looking down, Thanos realized with sudden horror that he was, in fact, hopping up and down on one foot.

His eyes darted to the Lorespeaker. As Thanos watched, helplessly hopping up and down, the Lorespeaker slowly unwound the strips of hide from the top of his scepter, revealing an ornate top quarter that split into two tines, one longer than the other, both curved. Nestled between them was a shining blue stone of some sort, vaguely egg-shaped.

A stone...

He riffled through his memory. "I thought the *Space Stone* was blue." Thanos realized he no longer had control over his own limbs. He was still hopping up and down like a marionette wielded by a puppeteer with too few fingers.

"What?" the Lorespeaker asked absently, then glanced over at the Scepter as though seeing it for the first time and...giggled. It was a horrendous, haunting sound that chilled Thanos's blood. "Oh. No, no. This is merely a protective shell, to keep the full measure of its power from—" He broke off. "Stop hopping; it's annoying me now."

Thanos came to rest on both feet. He fought mightily to move his arms but could not. He was frozen in place.

"It's the Mind Stone, Thanos," the Lorespeaker intoned, leaning in, leering. "The *Mind Stone*."

Thanos's eyes were still under his control, and he shot a glance over at the Mind Stone, which glimmered in the light of the Lorespeaker's domicile. He couldn't imagine how such a thing could be possible, but he was living proof. The Infinity Stones were real.

"How?" he asked.

The Lorespeaker flapped his hands exasperatedly and began walking slowly around Thanos, occasionally touching an arm or his back. His demeanor had changed. No longer was he gentle and curious; even his amusement was disturbing and intense.

"Oh, the details would bore you. And I'm not sure of them anyway. I...acquired the Stone millennia ago. Before I could truly put it through its paces, my cousins ambushed me and trapped me on this godsforsaken speck of space dust. Imagine it, Thanos—trapped on this mud-ball with one of the most powerful artifacts in the history of the universe... and no one to use it on." He screamed quite suddenly, bellowing to the ceiling and to the dead sky beyond, then just as suddenly snapped back to fix his gaze on Thanos with a truly happy and satisfied grin. "Until *you*."

"Fine. You have me." Thanos's heart raced, but he worked to keep a tremble out of his voice. "Now what?"

The Lorespeaker ignored him, standing back and pointing at Thanos with the tip of the Scepter. "Your eyes...Do they always glow blue like that?"

"I...No."

"I'm still figuring out exactly how to use it," the Lorespeaker confessed. "You're my first test subject since my exile, so many years ago. Truly, I can't even say how it would work in the hands of another. For me, with my brain already configured the way it is, it allows me to control you. To read you. But you know that, don't you?"

Thanos felt compelled to answer every question, even the rhetorical ones. "Yes."

"What does it feel like, Thanos?" the Lorespeaker whispered, coming in close. "Does it feel like...spiders eating your brains from the inside? Does it feel like...a great, churning wheel in your skull, grinding your free will to powder? I really want to know."

It felt like both of those and, yet, at the same time, it felt like a vast ocean of peace in which he could wallow. His independence and individuality were being overwritten by the Lorespeaker and the Mind Stone; the psychic pain was tremendous. And yet, he also felt warm and comforted at the same time. It felt as though he—the essential core *he*— was being pulled from his own body and his own self, to be replaced with something else. And at the same time, he welcomed it.

The Lorespeaker leaned in closer, still whispering. "As I told you, Thanos: Sometimes I lose my mind. It's different every time. And this is what it looks like *this* time."

He stepped away and withdrew a long, wicked knife from the folds of his robe. "And now, the test!"

With a bloodcurdling blurt of laughter, he plunged the knife into Thanos's chest.

Everything in Thanos's mind and body screamed to move, to dodge, to flinch, to crumple, to cower, to lash out, to strike back. A thousand different responses roared through him, every single one of them nullified by the control of the Mind Stone. He could only stand there as the blade struck him, as it rammed through his clothes, cut through his flesh, his muscle...

Blunted against his rib cage. He actually heard the sound

of steel striking bone—*shhhuuunnnggggkk*—at the same moment that the vibration of it ran up his sternum, spread along his clavicle, and rattled his skull.

The Lorespeaker released the handle, leaving the knife embedded there. He shut his eyes and took a long, deep, shuddering breath. "Oh. Oh. Yes, yes. If you had even the slightest bit of free will left in you, you would have at least *tried* to avoid that. I think...I think if I pushed the Stone just the tiniest bit, you would lose all sense of yourself in an instant." He smiled. "But I must confess, Thanos: I like the idea of it taking time. I like the idea of you suffering as every last bit of you slips away."

"You're truly insane."

"That's what my cousins said," the Lorespeaker responded, dreamily, eyes still closed. He tittered at the memory. "Cousins. Cousins. Stupid, stupid cousins... Two of them teamed up to strand me in this forsaken place. They wanted the Stone for themselves, but didn't dare get close enough to take it. So, we stalemated...." He drifted off and sighed in discontent. "Well, enough about that. They thought I would die here. And I didn't. Haven't." He opened his eyes and grinned, baring his teeth, his voice gone creepily singsong. "Won't. Thanks to you, Thanos. My savior."

The nerves where the knife had struck Thanos had gone into shock at the moment of impact, but now were awake and screaming. He could only grit his teeth. He'd suffered worse—this pain was nothing compared with that visited upon him by Yrsa, for example—but the inability to move made it nearly unbearable. He was completely helpless for the first time in his life.

"I've had time to do nothing but plan," the Lorespeaker went on, "and now that you're here, I'll...Oh, is that knife bothering you? Take it out."

Unbidden by his own mind, Thanos's hand reached up and pulled out the knife. It dripped with his blood. A river ran down his chest and fell in fat droplets on the floor.

"I can't have you dead. Not yet. But you're a hardy sort, aren't you? Big and strong and tough and unapologetic about it. Good. True strength neither needs nor makes excuses. You're going to need to be strong. It's going to be a long, painful process by which I figure out how to transfer my consciousness into your body."

Thanos managed to keep his eyes from widening in shock. *What?*

The Lorespeaker smirked. "You have a remarkable poker face, but I can still read you. We have a two-way connection now. I know what you're thinking. I've known since you landed here. All that nonsense about 'cosmic awareness'? It was the Stone all along. It can do so many things!" He spun around and snapped the Scepter forward. A beam of energy shot forth and exploded against a wall.

"See? It's made me smarter. It lets me see into your mind. It lets me control you...I suspect it could also generate life itself, Thanos."

"It's driven you mad," Thanos said.

"Probably. But that's all right. Madness is no inhibitor to one with an Infinity Stone. I've always seen the world differently. A jumble of stories and myth, endlessly mashed together..." He shook his head, a troubled look on his face. "When you have so many narratives up here"—he tapped his forehead—"sometimes it's tough to keep them in order. I perceive the world differently than you do. Since I have all of the stories in my head at once, I can relive them in any order. We live in a prism, not a line."

Thanos realized that he had precisely one weapon at his disposal: his own voice. The Lorespeaker, probably in a desperation borne of his long, lonely exile, was allowing Thanos some modicum of thought. It wouldn't last. Thanos had to use it while he could. Stall. Distract. Until... until...

Something. Maybe. He'd been reduced to raw hope. Cha would have been both amused and pleased.

"You will not best me," Thanos promised him.

"Oh, but I already have! Because in my time here, I have mastered myself. Conquer yourself first; the world will follow, I always say."

"The universe is large and time is long," Thanos said. "And you are ill equipped for it, having been stuck here."

"The universe doesn't frighten me. The universe is not infinite. It merely pretends to be so." He reached out for the knife in Thanos's hand, thought better of it, and said, "Cut your face. Not too deep. Just enough to draw blood."

With no command from his mind, Thanos's hand rose. He watched it come closer and closer, the bloody knife glimmering. Then the point of the blade caught the flesh just under his right eye and dragged down, carving a shallow, weeping furrow along his cheek. He shuddered involuntarily. Then again, everything he was doing was involuntary.

"Now down your arm," the Lorespeaker ordered. "Again, not too deep. I want you alive."

Thanos drew the blade down his arm, parting his flesh along the sharp edge. A stitch of fire raced along the path. Then, at the Lorespeaker's command, he dragged the blade across his chest, bisecting the wound already there.

"Why torture me?" Thanos asked. "You can read my mind for anything you want to know."

"I'm just making certain that my control is absolute. As I said before, I haven't been able to test it. I spent many centuries looking for a way to leave this place and work my mischief on the universe. I always believed it was possible, but I never made any progress until I started *doing things*, Thanos. We are the sum total of our decisions, not of our beliefs. That is the truth. And truth is a mistress harsher than death. As the universe will learn when I walk it as you."

It took an effort, but Thanos managed a weak chuckle. Anything else would have required more control over his throat and gut than he currently possessed. "I think you'll be surprised by the sort of welcome you receive from others with my face. I'm a bit famous."

"Don't try to talk me out of this!" The Lorespeaker balled up a fist and punched Thanos in the nose.

Thanos's nose wasn't broken, but it felt out of joint. Blood ran in twin streams down the lower half of his face.

"*Do not* try to talk me out of this," the Lorespeaker growled, cradling his injured hand. "I've been planning this for"—he tilted his head back, lips moving as he counted—"well, for more centuries than I can count up to. Once I'm free of here, I'll use you to bring more and more people to me for the controlling... Soon enough, I will control entire populations. Entire worlds! And eventually..." The Lorespeaker's breath came faster and faster as he spoke more and more excitedly, his eyes dancing. "Eventually, I will *control* the universe, Thanos! I will be in every living, thinking being in all of creation!"

"That will take just about forever," Thanos said quietly. "Trust me—I've done the math."

He struggled with those words. The warm ocean around him was everywhere, and the wheel in his mind was spinning faster and faster. He was losing every last piece of who he was. In moments, he would cease to be. "I'm exceptionally long-lived," the Lorespeaker said mildly. "I don't mind taking forever." Then, with a chortle, he swung the Scepter in a wide arc, then brought it to his lips and kissed it. "I'll finally understand it all. The entire universe. I'll combine all its disparate chapters and forms into one grand story, where the only character is *me*."

Drowning in his own brain, his body alight with pain, Thanos reached out for something—anything—to cling to.

Sintaa's smile…No. Only pain and loss there.

His mother…She was gone, too. As was Gwinth. And Cha. And then…

His daughters…

"The pathway between us is so powerful right now…." The Lorespeaker inhaled deeply, as though captivated by the scent of a fragrant bouquet. "You're thinking about those girls up on your ship. Oh, Thanos! Thanos! Oh, the horrible things you've done to them. Do you truly believe that is love? Poor Nebula, more machine than person now. You don't deserve those girls. Or anything else, for that matter. And now you're thinking about the atomic structure of genes, trying to block me from learning more about your daughters. Worried about them, are you? Don't worry. When you take me up to your ship, 'Father,' I will take good care of them. They will be mine, too."

Thanos pressed his lips together and let out a low, grinding moan that caused the Lorespeaker to tilt his head to one side. "And now…you're…Are you really in *that* much pain, Thanos? Stars above, Titan—I'd've thought a powerful warlord such as yourself would be used to a little blood every now and again. I have to say I'm a bit disappointed."

"You should get used to disappointment for the little time you have left to live," Thanos managed to tell him, focusing mightily.

The Lorespeaker threw back his head and cackled. It was a giggly, depraved laugh, one that knew no boundaries or morality. "I applaud you, Thanos! Brave to the end! Tell me: Why are you so confident?"

Thanos enjoyed the fact that he could grin; his own blood—dried now—cracked as his lips peeled back from his teeth and turned up. "Because I managed to stop thinking about my daughters."

"What?" said the Lorespeaker, right before Nebula shot him in the back with a blast from a Chitauri battle-staff.

The Lorespeaker stumbled forward, barely able to keep his balance. He nearly collided with Thanos but caught himself right before he did so.

"It'll take more than that," Thanos ordered the girls over the Lorespeaker's shoulder.

The Lorespeaker opened his mouth. To order Thanos to kill the girls, no doubt. And Thanos could have and would have, had he been so commanded. But there was panic in the Lorespeaker's eyes, pain in his expression, and he stumbled over his words as they fought to spill out of his mouth.

Before he could manage a sentence, Gamora had cut off his head with a single, efficient stroke of her battle-staff. Thanos would have watched the head fly off its neck and bounce on the floor, but the explosive gout of blood that erupted in his face blinded him, so he missed enjoying that sight.

He heard the *splat-thud*, though, when the head hit the floor. That was nice.

A moment later, his limbs loosened and his body came back online. The controlling pathway between his body and the Lorespeaker had been severed as neatly as the Lorespeaker's head. Thanos wiped blood from his eyes and beheld his daughters before him, his pair of demons, his perfect assassins.

"Well done, girls," he rumbled.

"Thanks, Dad," Nebula said in that tone of voice that indicated she was too disaffected to care, but cared nonetheless.

"Especially you, Gamora."

Nebula's jaw dropped. "Why especially her?!"

"Because she actually killed him." Thanos pressed a hand to his chest wound, the worst of those inflicted on him. It was already clotting nicely. "We'll be leaving now. Get that and bring it with us." He gestured to the head, which had rolled into the kitchen and fetched up against the freezer.

Nebula and Gamora raced to grab it. Nebula just barely edged out her sister, pouncing on the head and holding it up by the hair.

"What about this thing?" Gamora asked, pointing to the Scepter. It had landed close to the Lorespeaker's body.

"Don't touch it," Thanos ordered. Gamora hesitated just an instant, then backed away.

Lips pursed in concentration, Thanos crouched by the Infinity Stone. The blue stone glimmered. He half expected a shock when he touched the Scepter, but he felt nothing more than smooth alloy. He picked it up in one hand.

It seemed so small. It seemed infinitely large.

"Um," said Nebula, still holding up the Lorespeaker's head. Blood dripped out of the severed neck. "Why are we taking this?"

"His brain was exceptional. I want to examine it to see if it can be of use. As for the rest of this place, we'll firebomb it from orbit." He strode to the door, then paused, turning to look back at them. "Why did you come for me?"

The girls exchanged a look that was subtle but unmistakably confused. "You weren't in touch," Gamora began slowly. "It was the longest we'd been without..." She trailed off helplessly.

His brainwashing, it seemed, was complete.

Nebula jumped in, sneering. "You always said that if we were concerned or worried, there's probably a reason. So..."

"Yes. I also taught you always to aim for the head. When we get back to *Sanctuary*, you'll be on restricted rations for a week, Nebula."

CHAPTER XLIV

ABOARD *SANCTUARY*, THANOS WATCHED AS TWO INFINITY-class orbit-to-surface missiles etched a slow, glowing arc down to the Lorespeaker's enclave. The rotation of the moon meant that the missiles disappeared over the curvature of the orb, vanishing from view.

An instant later, twin mushroom clouds blossomed from the other side of the moon, erupting up and out with such force that they were visible even from orbit. The moon shuddered, and an alarm klaxon went off on *Sanctuary*.

"Looks like we knocked that moon out of its orbit," Gamora said.

From a spot across the bridge, where she lounged against the bulkhead, both arms crossed over her chest, Nebula said in a bored tone, "Told you two missiles was overkill."

"What do we do now?" Gamora asked him.

Thanos had no ready answer. He watched the nuclear fire spilling into space as the moon juddered and twitched out of its orbit. It would most likely be caught up in the nearest planet's gravity well, possibly colliding with it and driving *that* celestial body out of its own orbit. A cascading effect, no doubt. He did the math in his head, calculating orbital velocities, elliptical orbits, apogees, and perigees. If his rough reckoning was right, the worlds of the KelDim Sorrow would end up either pulverized or spinning into the remains of the nearby sun.

Good enough.

"What do we do now?" he said to Gamora, repeating her hanging question in his own grave voice. "What I do best."

"Kill more people."

"No. I'm going to think."

He left them on the bridge, alone, and retreated to his quarters.

He spent most of the trip to civilized space—out of the KelDim Sorrow and back through the Raven's Sweep—in his quarters, thinking. Plotting. Planning. He placed the Scepter that bore the Mind Stone in a bracket on the wall and spent long hours staring at it, drinking it in. Its power throbbed and seemed to melt the air around it. He yearned for it and feared it in equal measure.

That was as it should be, he knew. Utilizing an item of such power should not be undertaken lightly.

The Infinity Stones weighed on his mind. He'd thought that a Stone could solve his problem, but his experience in the Mind Stone's thrall had taught that for all the Stones' power and despite their name, their power was still limited. As the people of Morag had learned, Power alone was not enough. It had to be applied appropriately.

The Mind Stone could make people agree with him, yes, but he would still need to travel from world to world. Perhaps if joined with the Space Stone, to shrink the distance between worlds... But he would still need to conquer each one.

The Time Stone, then. Roll back the years; save those who'd already been lost... but it would only work locally. And so on.

And then the solution occurred to him. It was so simple and so vastly complex at the same time that it wrenched from him the first genuine laughter he'd experienced in years.

Emerging from his quarters just as *Sanctuary* emerged from the Raven's Sweep, Thanos was met by a Nebula who looked leaner and angrier for her ration restriction. He allowed himself a slight grin of satisfaction. In addition to her food punishment, he'd also charged her with cleaning every pulsoglass opening along the hull of the ship. When she'd complained, he told her that this had been *his* very first duty in space, and that he expected her to excel at it.

The portholes gleamed.

"We've emerged from the Sweep one light-month from Mistifir," she told him. "Prime opportunity for us. They're on the brink of environmental collapse. They'll listen or we can take—"

"Maybe later," Thanos told her as they entered the bridge. Gamora, sitting in the command chair, leaped up.

"We're hunters now," he told them. "Seeking very specific prey."

"Who?" asked his favorite.

"Not *who*, my dear Gamora—*what*. The Infinity Stones."

The girls stared at each other, then turned to him. "Which one?"

"Not which one. We're going to get *all* of them. But no one must know that I am the one collecting them. The two of you will be my vanguard." He sighed in contentment and reached out to stroke their faces. "In a few short years, you will be the age I was when I was exiled from Titan. Unlike me, you will not have to founder and thrash about for purpose, for a cause. You are fortunate, my darlings, to be my daughters. We will gather our Stones, and no one will realize I have them until it's too late."

Gamora said nothing. Nebula elbowed her sister, but when she could not prod anything out of her, finally spoke up herself. "You want the two of us to traipse around the universe looking for a bunch of glowing *pebbles*? Do you have any idea how long that'll take?"

"I do. That's why you won't do it alone. You'll work through underlings, minions." He stroked his jaw, thinking. "We killed a platoon of the Xandarian Nova Corps. They will never look at us with anything but hate and death, but the Kree, for example, may be amenable. And there will be others."

He walked over to the foremost extreme of the bridge

and stared out at the speckling of stars. The Raven's Sweep was receding behind them. The past was receding behind them. Ahead lay the Stones and the future and all its glorious possibilities.

Time and Soul and Mind and Reality and Space and *Power.*

No single Stone would achieve his goal. But *all* of them ...

With such power, he could wrest planets from the sky.

And he heard a voice in his head. Cha's. Or maybe it was Sintaa's. Already, they were merging, his past rapidly fusing into a single block of memory that could not inhibit him.

Don't get too far ahead of yourself, the voice said. *Before you start pulling planets down, you have to find the other Stones. And* ...

He would need protection from such power, lest it destroy him. If Odin had possessed a Stone, then Odin was the answer. Thanos would return to the Chitauri homeworld and plunder the wreckage of the *Blood Edda* for a Norse metal strong enough to shield him from the Stones' power.

Space roared by. The stars blurred.

You cannot save everyone, she had told him in his dream. And with that, he banished her from his memory, purged her. He was no longer Thanos of Titan or Warlord Thanos.

He was simply Thanos. Savior of the Universe.

He clenched his fist, imagining a gauntlet there, and he smiled.

No, he could not save everyone. He could not even save
most of them.

But that was never the plan. He would save half. Exactly
half.

While Nebula sulked, Gamora approached him. She was
not bold enough to touch him, but she stood close by, her
reflection hovering near his own in the pulsoglass.

"What are you thinking?" she asked him.

After some hesitation, he answered her. "I am thinking of
the Asgardians."

"What about them?"

"They called themselves gods." He snorted a laugh. He
had faced down Asgardians when at a thousandth of his
current power and defeated them. With the Stones in his
hand...

Thanos curled his lips, peeling them back to reveal vul-
pine teeth and a deadly, knowing smile.

"I will show them what true power is. *I* will become a
god...."

TIME

We live in a prism, not a line.

CHAPTER XLV

TIME IS NOT ABSTRACT.

Time is a Stone.

"You're a coward, Thanos!" Cha tells me. *"A coward! You hide behind this ship, behind the Other and the Chitauri, and now behind those girls!"*

It is years later. Cha is dead. Titan is dead. Soon, half the universe will be dead. I am aboard Sanctuary. *The protective doors to my vault slide open and the Gauntlet glimmers there in half-light, not quite gold.*

I have seen this moment before. I have lived it. It is happening for the first time, the second time, the millionth time.

I reach for it. I reach for my truth, my destiny, my inevitability.

(Gamora, falling from the cliff. Cha, neck snapping in my hands. I am alone, alone in my past, my present, my future. As it was meant to be. As it must be.)

"Fine," I say. *"I'll do it myself."*

ACKNOWLEDGMENTS

"Fun" isn't something one considers when thanking people who helped out, but this does put a smile on my face.

First off: Thanks to Russ Busse, who signed me up for this insane gig, held my hand, and kept me from setting things on fire. Also many thanks to Alvina Ling, who has always had my back. I am especially grateful for my agent, Kathleen Anderson, who has shepherded my career to this point, and who said to me, "So, they want to talk to you about someone called *Thanos*. Do you know who that is?" Oh yes.

I have to thank everyone at Little, Brown who made this book possible, including Lindsay Walter-Greaney, Barbara Bakowski, and all the folks in Design and Production who made this book look so good. Big shout-out to the folks in Sales and Marketing, too—the book doesn't matter if you don't know about it, people!

Over at Disney Publishing, thanks to Stephanie Everett, Elana Cohen, Julia Vargas, and Chelsea Alon. And at Marvel Studios, thanks to Will Corona Pilgrim, Nick Fratto, Eleena Khamedoost, and Ariel Gonzalez.

I would be remiss if I didn't mention Jim Starlin, without whom there would be no Big Purple, no Snap, no Gauntlet.

Lastly, thanks to my friends and family who tolerated my disappearance into the MCU for wide swaths of time, especially my long-suffering wife, Morgan Baden. I promise, babe—you survived The Snap.